AN EARL,
THE GIRL, and
A TODDLER

Books by Vanessa Riley

A Duke, the Lady, and a Baby

An Earl, the Girl, and a Toddler

AN EARL,
THE GIRL, and
A TODDLER

Vanessa
Riley

ZEBRA BOOKS
Kensington Publishing Corp.
www.kensingtonbooks.com

ZEBRA BOOKS are published by

Kensington Publishing Corp.
119 West 40th Street
New York, NY 10018

First Zebra Trade Printing: May 2021

ISBN-13: 978-1-4201-5225-8
ISBN-10: 1-4201-5225-4

ISBN-13: 978-1-4201-5226-5 (ebook)
ISBN-10: 1-978-4201-5226-2 (ebook)

10 9 8 7 6 5 4 3 2 1

Printed in the United States of America

To Frank, Gerald, Marc, Chris, David, Jamil, Jimmy, the strongest men I know.
To my cousins and uncles and friends, peace be unto you, know I pray for you all.

AN EARL, THE GIRL, and A TODDLER

CHAPTER I

It was a universal truth that when the world was dark, it was time to rest.

A light shined in my eyes. The sleep I desperately sought on the lumpy cot was stolen again. The smell of sulfur, the horrible rotten egg smell came from a plaster preparation to someone two cots away. Twenty beds in this forsaken place.

"Ma'am, if you can't tell me your name, I'll have to remand you to custodial care."

This man and his minions had stripped me of my clothes like I was a *ragamuffin*. The ring, the band that left a light circle about my finger was ripped from my hand. I was lucky to have a chemise on my shaking limbs.

The fool pried at one eyelid and waved the candle again. "Who are you? Answer me."

How was I supposed to respond to such a rude request? I told him and everyone who'd listen: I didn't know. A hundred times I said this and sobbed until my throat was raw. A hundred and one utterances wouldn't make it different.

No one listened.

All was gone.

Nothing rattled in my head but the sharpest sense of loss.

My arm bent beneath me, under my bosom like a bad habit. I should be holding something close, something precious, something mine.

Gone.

I was angry and wanted to sleep.

The tall man tossed up his hands. "I give up. She's gone mute."

His footsteps echoed like I was trapped in a bottle. The hospital door opened. Light crept in, blinding me, hiding the shadowy faces, the men making decisions.

Didn't care anymore. *Ol' Jancros. The thieves.* The thieves took everything.

"Are you sure she's Jemina St. Maur?" the physician asked.

A mumbled voice answered him.

"She's in shock. We can't put her out, not like this."

"Doesn't matter. Bedlam." Those words were clear. The Ol' Jancros were set to send me away. The name didn't sound like home. Nothing did.

"That place is for the lunatics, sir. She's just come from a wreck. She's lost everything. She needs more time to grieve."

Footsteps. Footsteps echoed. Outside of this room, it all disappeared. I was left with people more hurt than me. Some died. I heard the gasps. That I remembered.

I needed to be gone.

Where? I was too angry to choose. A nap would make things clearer. If I could close my eyes, I could make it all go away.

The old man returned and shined that awful light one more time. "This is your last chance. Who are you? Defend yourself or you'll be sent to Bedlam. You don't want to go there. It will take a miracle to get out."

Raising up on my elbow, I stared him down, through his smudged spectacles and breath of rancid coffee. "I lost everything. Does it matter?"

The old prune frowned and wrote something on paper.

Turning away, I balled up into my ratty blanket. No more answering questions when no one would answer mine.

I'd lost everything, everyone who mattered. I'd rather be a lunatic than to live without 'em.

CHAPTER 2

October 18, 1812
Portsmouth, England

The blue and purple flowers of the ironwood tree he'd pinned to his waistcoat had flattened and almost lost their scent. P. Daniel Thackery stood on the docks, awaiting his turn. Dozens of people were ahead of him hoping to talk with an officer of the HMS *Belvidera*. He'd already lost four hours holding his place in the slow, snaking line.

Daniel traced the buds of the lignum vitae—as these flowers were called in Jamaica—from stem to stamens; he kept breathing, kept sampling the concentrated honeyed fragrance. It lulled the dull panic stirring in his chest.

Phoebe had to be alive.

Looking up in Portsmouth's cloud-filled sky, he wondered how much time he had before the rain fell upon the throngs of people coming for news of the lost ship, the *Minerva*.

More left the line.

Daniel took a few steps forward. He could clearly see the officer—a lieutenant, by the braiding on his onyx jacket—mouthing words that made the hearers weep. That wouldn't be him, sent away with nothing, no dreams, no proxy bride from Jamaica.

The salty breeze stole one of Daniel's petals. Like a purple feather, it fluttered, the air carrying it to the edge of the dock. It hung there, teetering.

Closing his eyes, he remembered the jig he'd done this morn preening in front of his dressing mirror. A pile of discarded waist-coats sat at his ankles—lavender, indigo, purple. He'd driven his valet ragged going in and out Daniel's legendary closet to bring him the different hues and different buttons—from brass to silver to pearl wanting to match the lignum vitae, Phoebe's favorite.

Vanity was a dangerous luxury for a wealthy man who'd built his fortune from careful investments. Yet, a man valuing a good tailor wanted to look perfect. It wasn't every day one met their wife.

All his plans couldn't be lost because of the sea.

Another couple wept and departed from the lieutenant.

Daniel looked away, down to his dusty boots. The gloss his man-of-all-work, Marc Anthon, put on them seemed wasteful now.

"The cursed sea did it!" An old man stormed away. He was right to blame it.

The sea ferried folks near and far. Yet, it had been forced to swallow the souls beaten by war, killed by piracy, or discarded by the slave trade.

Perhaps that's why the water revolted. Every so often it became violent like a drunk, punching at anything—innocent or guilty.

Why else would the *Minerva*, a peaceful ship porting innocent passengers go down?

"Phoebe Dunn is alive. She's alive."

He repeated this like a chant and clasped the flowers—a love token inspired from the letters they'd exchanged over a courtship of eighteen months. At times, she'd send two at a time. Daniel devoured each.

Dragging his feet with the forward movement of the crowd, he hoped to God when it was his turn, he'd receive a miracle.

He opened his greatcoat. He'd grown miserably warm witnessing a woman, fifteen or twenty people ahead, sob. Blinking, he couldn't look away, until he jabbed his palm with his dulled cravat pin. The prick hurt but drew no blood. *Bottle it all—all the disappointments, the despair, all the pain.*

That was his motto since age six. Sorrow changed nothing. It didn't repair his mother's heart, didn't bury a wayward father. It definitely didn't restore the *Minerva* to the harbor.

White sails should billow and flap, anchored to its strong mainmast. The ship couldn't be a smashed derelict hull left adrift until the HMS *Belvidera* floated by and picked up the pieces.

His new bride—the darling woman who'd won his cautious, hesitant heart—should walk down the gangplank with the surprise she said she'd bring tucked under her arm. She should be where the lieutenant stood, searching for Daniel, a man with wilted lignum vitae.

Her eyes—he'd discover if they were the deepest brown, the color of harvest wheat, or darker like the leather spines of his trusty law books.

Anything would be beautiful.

He merely needed to see her, alive.

Twelve people stood between him and answers.

A man lunged at the lieutenant. "Someone will pay," he said before sailors dragged him away.

Someone would pay. Daniel.

He always did, but this time, it was his fault.

Hadn't his desperation to be with Phoebe made him insist she come to England now during the island's wet season? The British were to impose a blockade. Once in place, the Royal Navy wouldn't allow any crossings. They did this to halt American aggressions in this War of 1812.

An old woman stumbled into Daniel.

He stooped and helped her up. Tears flooded her sunken cheeks. "My daughter, sir. My poor girl is lost."

He reached into his coat and handed her his handkerchief, one of his treasures with initials embroidered in silver thread.

She shook her head. "Thank you, but it's too fancy for me." She started to walk away but turned back. "There's two survivors, sir. Just two. Hope you're lucky. My daughter . . . she's at the bottom of the sea. I can't get to her."

Those bottled-up feelings of hopelessness he'd tried to suppress doubled, ripping at his heart, pressing upon his lungs. He took his lignum vitae and handed them to her. "It's not much, but maybe you can honor your daughter with these flowers."

Sobbing anew, the old woman took them and walked to the edge of the dock. Her head dipped in prayer. Then she cast his sentimental offering into the water.

Six people ahead, a burly man cussed worse than a sailor. "That was my only son."

He spit at the officer, then disappeared into the crowd.

The antics didn't bother Daniel, not as much as the old woman standing alone.

In court, when the judge hammered his dark judgments, the wailing of spectators in the gallery of the Old Bailey became riotous. Daniel was immune to the sound.

But not to the look of a woman in pain.

His hand stung. The pin this time drew blood.

Three in line.

Daniel wrapped his handkerchief about his palm. He fretted smearing the ink on the marriage license displaying his whole hideous name, Peregrine Daniel Thackery, and that of Phoebe Monroe Dunn.

Lord in heaven this can't be all he'll have of her. He couldn't be a widower, without memories of being married.

"Step forward," the lieutenant said.

Daniel's turn.

He braced like he waited for the jurymen's verdict.

The lieutenant, with his rumpled bicorne, a half-moon-shaped hat, stared at him with a frown hinting of disgust. "Who are you here for?"

"Phoebe Dunn." His voice warbled a little but boomed upon her surname.

"Unaccounted for, but—" The man harrumphed. "Well, with the boat coming from Jamaica, I reckon we found her."

"Reckon?"

"Well, she's not in the capacity to say."

Daniel's heart pounded a double rhythm—his Phoebe was alive, but hurt?

"Is she injured? Incapacitated? Mute?" Was that Phoebe's surprise, that he'd be the only one to ramble on about their days?

Didn't matter.

He wouldn't love her any less. Nothing could stop the true communion of souls.

The commander put his hands on Daniel, patting his shoulder. "Now calm down, boy. You wouldn't expect her to be able to answer."

Ignoring the condescension, Daniel stepped back. Frankly he was used to it, and demanding his earned respect as one of the king's barristers would change nothing. "Where is Phoebe Dunn?"

"I'll bring her to you. She has to belong to you. No one else colored has come."

Daniel buttoned his lips. Ends justified the means. He wasn't here for a fight but for Phoebe.

The lieutenant waved, and one of his reefers brought forward a bundle. The sailor shoved a beautiful Black baby into Daniel's arms. "Here's your Phoebe Dunn."

The child, a year or more old, latched on to his waistcoat, grabbing a pearl button.

He didn't know what to say. This wasn't his bride.

"Did anyone else survive?"

"Just a woman. She was taken away by her family. Very bad

shape." The lieutenant folded up his papers with all the passengers' names. "The gown the infant wore when we plucked her out of the sea was expensive. Should've known a fancy gent like you'd show."

Daniel was Phoebe's family here, but this baby wasn't his bride. "If I hadn't arrived, what would happen to her?"

"We'd give this baby to a dockworker or to one of your people working the brothels. The hospital and orphanages don't want the Black ones. Glad you arrived. Saved me work. Next."

Shaking, angry, cheated, Daniel left the line, but he held the little girl tightly to his chest. He couldn't hand her back, not to this lieutenant who'd be careless or evil with an infant.

His man, Mr. Anthon, his newest employee, jumped down from his carriage. "Sir, where's the missus?"

Daniel's throat closed as he shook his head. He couldn't say Phoebe was dead.

"Oh no, Mr. Thackery. They're not keeping her! They can't treat you like this. Let's—"

"Mr. Anthon, please. Normally I appreciate your outbursts. Not now. We must leave." Daniel hated chastising the spirited young fellow, but they needed to be away.

Daniel coughed; everything ached. "The door, Mr. Anthon."

The young man looked deflated but held it open. "Yes, sir. Where to?"

"To my aunt. I think she and her women should've returned from Bath. My aunt . . . she'll know what to do."

His footman peeked at the child who still clutched Daniel's buttons. "She's mighty attached, sir. Suppose your legal work never ends?"

Anthon's deep brown eyes narrowed; his dark hand clutched the mantle he proudly starched. "Let's hope, your aunt, Lady Shrewsbury, will solve this little one's problem. Nothing has changed for abandoned Blackamoors since you or I were young."

It hadn't.

Didn't Daniel see that every day in court? It was only when he personally aided others, much like his beloved aunt, did things change.

He shifted the babe in his arms and watched Anthon adjust the horse's reins.

The young man was a street urchin turned pickpocket who Daniel reformed. He had a feeling, with encouragement, this footman would become one of his most faithful servants.

It struck him, Mr. Anthon's wisdom, deep in his soul. Daniel had found a way to honor Phoebe.

"Head to Finchely instead. I think I know what to do."

"Very good, sir. We can send for Shrewsbury later."

Much later, after Daniel had everything done to protect Phoebe's surprise.

He settled into the carriage and looked at this sweet girl's eyes.

They were open and very brown like wheat.

"Phoebe loves you. I can tell. So I must love you too."

The little thing reached up and knocked his spectacles and clamped a hold of his nose, the wide, flat thing he used to sniff out baked treats.

Eighteen months courting Phoebe and no word of this girl.

How could she not talk about her daughter? How could she not tell him he'd be a stepfather?

The baby puckered and drooled but didn't cry. He took a small piece of bread from his picnic basket and put it to her tongue. The child gulped, but except for a swallow, she uttered no sound.

His wife, like all women, had her reasons for her secret. That felt better than thinking Phoebe couldn't trust him to love her and another man's child.

As an officer of the court, he'd investigate to see if there wasn't a brokenhearted family looking for this little one, but as the lieutenant said, no other Blackamoor showed. This child had to be Phoebe's girl.

Looking at the way the babe trusted him eased the pain tightening about his chest. He hadn't lost all. He still had something. He had hope.

"I like my surprise, Mrs. Thackery." His voice had become a wet throaty whisper. "I'll raise this child, our . . . Hope. Yes, Hope, to be wonderful."

With both fists clasping his buttons, the wee girl drifted to sleep in his arms.

CHAPTER 3

JEMINA ST. MAUR

Two years later, June 2, 1814
London, England

It was a universal truth that a widow in need of saving had lost the man and the means to be rescued. In my case, it was up to me to save me.

Miserable.

Miserable was such an ordinary word. It didn't convey enough feeling, not the highs and lows of the moment. I was miserable because my elbow throbbed. Banging it on the chimney of our last mission left a gash, very black and blue and bloody. Shouldn't I be better with all the practice the Widow's Grace's secret gambits afforded? I suspected I might've always had a problem with heights. I don't remember.

Miserable.

Miserable because the roasted pheasant served for dinner was dry. The bird on my Wedgwood plate deserved a better way to die. The lack of a decent sauce added to the cruelty. Our hostess, Lady Bodonel, should have more charity if she insisted on throwing weekly dinners, that I and her daughter-in-law, Patience, must attend. My dearest friend, the new Duchess of Repington, was in demand, but I mustn't let Her Grace suffer an overdone bird alone. Maybe I was a cook once. I don't recall.

Miserable.

My new fancy slippers were stiff and tight. I'd begged off from dancing all night, but the gossip about my being the heiress of the Season made everyone—well, almost everyone—try for my hand. Other than a legal paper with plenty of zeros, I didn't know why I had this twenty thousand pounds, or if it was deserved. I couldn't say.

Miserable because he looked at me, then turned away. Daniel Thackery, the only man not to ask for my hand, sat across the table chatting with Lady Shrewsbury, his aunt.

What was he telling her? What was his complaint this time?

The handsome man, always short in his speech unless offering corrections, stared at me again, or at the bandages wrapping my bruises. The doctor's stitches couldn't be hidden by my lacy tan sleeves.

Fumbling with his dancing gloves, white linen with cherry-red threads at the cuff, my barrister frowned again. Such a waste for his smooth lips. I'd draw them well, if I sketched people. Though I was good with charcoal and paper, I don't think I was an artist.

Thackery hated when anyone working with his aunt hurt themselves. And we weren't supposed to mention it to him. He wanted less and less to do with Lady Shrewsbury's operations. It made him fussy.

Yet, there were times, like now, on this third glance, when the all-knowing man didn't see I'd noticed him until too late. Caught, our gazes tangled like there was no one else in the room, in London, or on the earth. This look, it was as if we enjoyed a juicy secret that was only ours to share.

The tawdry tidbits would make us laugh. He'd offer a rare smile, one that showed the small gap in his teeth that made him look young and human and less jaded.

But we have no such secret. Miserable.

He turned away, and my thoughts scattered. I sipped from my glass of punch. Lady Bodonel's horrid dinner was crowded, but the regulars—politicians and peers and pretty women—had become more familiar to me.

"You don't have to eat any more, Jemina," Patience said. She was at my right in a wonderful gown of peach satin with a ripe orange banding of dyed silk beneath her bosom. "Pretend. Move things about. That's what His Grace does."

The duke escaped again, some military thing or Wellington thing or cannon thing. He always had a *thing* to stay as far from his mother as possible.

My dearest Patience suffered in his stead—the bad food, the bad guests who made sly jokes about her being foreign, and the bad music from showy fortune hunters like Lady Lavinia. The woman clad in gold, I'd heard she searched for husband number four.

Nothing wrong with a woman looking to secure her position, but I hated that she exhibited herself, wiggling on the pianoforte bench in a bodice that barely covered her off-key lungs. That shouldn't be necessary to gain a man's attention.

With a hand to her stomach, Patience slid her plate backward an inch. A server in silver dashed to the table and took it.

Her warm-brown heart-shaped face looked so relieved. She leaned toward me. "Lady Shrewsbury says at month's end she'll have the informant's whereabouts. We have time for your arm to mend."

"Good." I nodded. "The widow Cultony needs proof. Her trial for theft is weeks away."

A footman in a cranberry-red mantle came to Thackery with a note. The barrister dropped a glove as he took the paper. His large coal-black eyes loomed behind his spectacles. They blinked fast. He sprang up. "Lady Bodonel, thank you for having me. A pressing matter—"

"No. Sit, you should."

"No, ma'am, the Lord Mayor requests—"

The lithe blond woman blew a heavy, breathy noise that shifted the peacock feather dangling from her headpiece. "You've been elevated. You're an earl now. The new Lord Ashbrook.

When will you give up this work business and assume your place in society?"

The man bit his lip, bowed, and broke for the nearest exit.

Dinner guests fluttered their fans, but the talk was on Mr. Thackery, well the new Earl of Ashbrook.

Patience grasped my hand. "And here I thought His Grace's mother, the old girl, had become more liberal inviting him. Mr. Thackery is a peer. He'll be on everyone's guest list now. Poor man, Lady Shrewsbury says he's been a hermit since his wife died."

The pianoforte clanked. Lady Lavinia stretched her fingers and began another song, but her eyes were not on the keys. They were on the barrister's exit.

CHAPTER 4

DANIEL—OUTED BY THE GOSSIP

Trudging down the hall of Lady Bodonel's Mayfair home offered the feeling of walls closing in. Daniel reached for his cravat, as if he were being strangled.

What could the Lord Mayor want now? Had Daniel missed something in his aunt's dealings. Had one of her widows exposed the Widow's Grace organization? Did the clues lead back to him?

"Daniel, wait."

The light, imperious tone made him stop midway. Flicking his finger, he motioned to a servant. "Have my carriage brought."

The fellow nodded and trotted down the gold carpet.

Then Daniel turned to face his aunt. "Yes, Lady Shrewsbury."

She wrapped her arm about his, surely part affection, part coercion. The woman was a force of nature, like the powerful sea. "Nephew, you haven't replied to my missives."

"I'm busy in court. There are clients depending on me."

"Daniel, you know I need your assistance. My women—"

With a gentle tug, he freed his arm. "I can't do it anymore. The stakes are too high."

She crossed her arms about her impeccable silver gown with long sleeves, and he wondered if the silk hid wounds too.

"Now that you're an earl you wish to back away from the fight?"

He shook his head. "I have to go to the Lord Mayor. He's never happy with me. He'd speak out against my appointment if not for fear of the Prince Regent's disapproval."

"You have favor, Daniel. You need to use it. This is what we planned."

"What we planned? Or what you planned?"

"Yes, Daniel, I have plans for your life. I saw the promise in you early, and you've never disappointed me. You always do what is right. The Widow's Grace is right."

He cleaned his spectacles, trying to think of a way to reason with a woman who was like his mother. "It's not gone unnoticed that widows are winning more cases at the Court of Chancery. Or that my name is on too many documents for inmate release at Bedlam. It's been linked to suddenly appearing evidence against powerful families. Questions are being asked."

"They need to question the laws, Daniel. You're a peer; you can take it up in the House of Lords."

"I still sleep with one pillow since you told me the Black Duke of Florence was smothered by his cousin."

"Yes, but Alessandro de' Medici actually died from a stabbing."

That technicality was to make Daniel feel better? He took a breath. "I won't take my seat and become more of a target."

"You're being ridiculous, nephew."

"My horrid uncle rarely took his seat. Perhaps later, when Hope is older and all is more settled, I might, but not now. She needs to know I'll be home . . . on time."

Aunt's sherry eyes popped wide. "My niece? She's not doing well again?"

"Her nightmares are worse. She wasn't speaking for so long, and now that she is, she's screaming from her dreams. She wants me to make it better. I don't know how other than being at Finchely rocking her. That means I shouldn't be hauled off to Newgate."

"That won't happen. You're too clever. Daniel, you're a good father. She's secure. She'll be so proud of what you've done."

"Not if I'm disgraced. Not if every aspect of my life is scrutinized and destroyed."

"You sound as if you have something to hide. What is it, Daniel?"

He did have a secret to keep, but his dear aunt was too busy getting her operatives hurt to be of help. Daniel looked to the doors, hoping Mr. Anthon would come with his carriage.

"Nephew? What is it?"

"Lady Shrewsbury, you haven't time for my troubles. You need to spend your days finding replacements for your favorites, the Duchess of Repington and Mrs. St. Maur."

"Those women are very capable, but they haven't fulfilled the Widow's Grace promise. They must help other women, fivefold. They will serve a little longer."

"Oh, they are done. His Grace, the Duke of Repington will stop his wife once he learns of the risks she's taking. And Mrs. St. Maur, the gentle but loud woman, will be whisked away by a suitor before you get her killed climbing roofs."

"Killed? You're exaggerating."

"Mrs. St. Maur has a nasty gash on her arm." He took Lady Shrewsbury's hands in his. "We need to stop. We've done enough. You've done enough."

"We're making headway. Women are getting their rights back."

"Don't you understand?" He waited for a servant to walk past, then drew Lady Shrewsbury closer to a hall, one laden with Roman statues that looked like the awful ones the Duke of Repington had at Hamlin Hall.

"Aunt, if it's learned I've looked the other way, allowing widows to engage in burglary . . . all will be lost. My little Hope needs to know her father is coming home."

"You're in trouble, Daniel? Has someone made threats? Tell me."

He bit his lip and bottled up the rage swirling inside. "I can fight my battles. It's time to move forward. Let the duchess and Mrs. St. Maur and the others go on with their lives. You should too. Retire from your operations. A place in the country with me and Hope."

"It's my life's work, Daniel. Women need women to advocate."

"Well, I'm not a woman, just an overprotective, fretting nephew. I'm disqualified." He bent and kissed her cheek. "Think of tamping things down or—"

"Or what?"

She needed to see his concern, his unsaid fears; he looked straight into her eyes.

"Or end the Widow's Grace outright before someone dies or I have to choose between aiding you and coming home to Hope."

Not wanting to wait and give his aunt a chance to change his mind, he left, trudging his way down the hall of gaudy gilded mirrors and on to the portico. Then he stepped down to the circle drive, right into the path of the unusual, alluring Jemina St. Maur.

CHAPTER 5

JEMINA—UNEXPECTED WOMAN

I surely startled him. Mr. Thackery, now the Earl of Ashbrook, with eyes the color of the night sky, stood before me. They could be mirrors, older ones with the silvered back worn to show the pure glass.

"Mrs. St. Maur, what are you doing out here? Tell me you're not on a mission for my aunt."

With a shake of my head, I held out his glove. "You left so quickly. You dropped this, Mr. . . . . my lord."

He blinked away the small smile that bloomed. "Mrs. St. Maur, how did you make it out here? I was just in the hall."

"The Duchess of Repington and I have found many routes to escape Lady Bodonel."

He took the glove, fingered the soft lawn fabric before stuffing it into his pocket. "The Widow's Grace business makes you all magicians, vanishing and appearing."

"At least you don't call us witches."

"Never." He clasped my hand for a minute, then released it. "Some are cruel when they don't get their way."

Those secrets I knew he possessed sparkled in his eyes like a candle's flame. I was helpless in a way, wanting to be drawn to his light.

"It's very wrong." His tone wasn't baritone. It definitely wasn't pitchy or squeaky but something midrange, solid and dependable. "It's wrong to call women protecting themselves names. You're strong. You all are."

"The families who are against the widows curse us. They hate the information we find. Others hate our means."

That lip-biting thing happened underneath the glow of a torch. "Oh. You heard my words with Lady Shrewsbury."

"It's hypocritical, don't you think, to be selective in the means for outing truth?"

"Are you calling me a hypocrite? I'm concerned for your safety."

Raising my bandaged arm, I only let out a small yelp as I folded it about my middle, about the bodice of my simple gown. "Lord Ashbrook, it's lovely you're concerned. But you are a hypocrite."

His mouth opened. Then shut, then opened. "If I must be insulted, at least you did it in a gentle way, not with your loud indoor voice."

"Since it is you usually adding correction, how could I miss the opportunity to dish some pompous platitudes back? *Cack mowt kill cock.*" I covered my lips. I'd let one of those phrases from my dreams slip.

"Well, this cock's mouth won't kill me, ma'am." His head dipped. "You win with your Jamaican turn of phrase, Mrs. St. Maur. It's dark. Return inside and continue to enjoy Lady Bodonel." He touched my arm, then pulled back immediately like I was flame.

Couldn't be that, for he was fire. Beneath his structure and lectures burned a passion for justice and a desire to protect everyone in his sphere. I'd seen it. Once Patience and I snuck into the Old Bailey to watch the proceedings for a member of our fellowship. Ashbrook was very good in his defense.

"Don't give up so easily, sir. I might be convinced if you confess."

"Confess? That would mean I've done something wrong,

Mrs. St. Maur. Do you have something to accuse me other than this hypocrite business?"

There were secrets in his eyes boiling beneath his skin. If I could goad it out of him I would. Maybe I should try.

I stepped into his path. "You rescued me from Bedlam. I don't think I ever thanked you."

"No thanks. You shouldn't have been there. Never should've happened. Now, be a good girl and go—"

"You never said why you found me. Typically, a widow's blood family will come to Lady Shrewsbury. Did my family?"

"Happenstance. It was happenstance that I came."

"Happenstance with paperwork? What do you know of my family? Who are the St. Ma—"

"You are getting a bit loud now. Ma'am, my carriage will be here soon."

"You don't want me to talk of my family. This isn't the first time you've changed topics on me. Any time I get you alone to discuss my past, you distract me, tease me, anything but tell me the truth."

His hand slipped to my shoulder, then to my hurt arm, stepping so close that I could smell the bay of his cologne, a good Jamaican fragrance. That I did recall.

"Your life is before you, Mrs. St. Maur. You can be anyone you want. You don't need to remember anything."

"You make amnesia sound pleasing."

"There are many things I'd like to forget. Now go inside. I don't want the heiress of the Season accosted."

"I've forgotten everything but the condescension in a man's voice. I will go in when I wish, when I'm done interrogating you."

"Interrogating? Trying to match wits with me, Mrs. St. Maur?" He bowed his head and stepped around me. "Where's Mr. Anthon?"

"Do you run from battle so easily? What about me or my past makes you a coward?"

"This is no battle. We're allegedly on the same side." His back

Chapter 6

Daniel—The Family Business

Watching the impossible, adorable woman walk back to dinner set Daniel's pulse to race. Her hair, lush brown with highlights of his favorite red, he assumed fell to her small waist, maybe those thick hips. Her tresses were up and curled with wisps teasing her long neck, a neck that may have been swathed in jewels in the life she'd forgotten.

Jewels earned or more so stolen by the sugar trade should be forgotten.

"Daniel, no. Not her."

"*Not her* what, Aunt?"

"No to her or any of my widows."

He hadn't considered anything more, had he?

Of course not.

Not when her past could ruin everything he'd worked to protect. He cleaned his spectacles. "All this Widow's Grace business is too much. Now, the Lord Mayor summons at this hour."

"The lane is crowded, Daniel. It could take an hour or more. Have you thought about simply not going?"

Daniel wrenched at his neck, wondering how deflated and wrinkled his pristine cravat had become. "I must go. Any delay gives the Lord Mayor time to spin his own conspiracies. At nine o'clock tonight, I will explain away his latest suspicions and hope no runners show up at Finchely. Then no one is carted away because of the Widow's Grace."

"Well, it's not as if you've ever done anything wrong for yourself. You could be a priest."

He winced at who he'd become or forced himself to become. "I was daring and impulsive once."

"Never, Daniel. You've always been responsible."

This version of himself that Lady Shrewsbury praised sounded like the saddest romp. He made himself the best barrister and father he could be. No one would ever question a bachelor raising Hope away from the Dunns of Jamaica.

"It's time for a change, Aunt. Two years as a monk, a self-righteous and apparently hypocritical monk, has been too much. Would a little impulsiveness hurt my reputation? There's much to consider."

"Daniel, you're being ridiculous."

"No, this is food for thought. Perhaps, there's a brothel I could visit after the Lord Mayor's inquiry and still arrive at Finchely in time to have breakfast with my little Hope."

Saying the foolishness aloud made the tightness in his chest loosen. He did need to make changes.

His aunt hugged him. "You're a young man, Daniel, and a good father. Go home. Don't let anyone threaten you anymore."

"Very nice of you to say, but then you will create Widow's Grace tasks to fill my schedule. Of course, that will lead to another meeting with the Lord Mayor."

She pinched his ear. "Moving forward has nothing to do with the Widow's Grace. You're burning for companionship? Take a bride. It's been two years since Phoebe's death."

The headache he thought gone returned. His disparaging thoughts on marriage, derived from the plights of his aunt's women, made him want none of it.

With a kiss to Lady Shrewsbury's cheek, he returned to his closing argument. "End the Widow's Grace, Aunt, before someone gets hurt, before we lose everything. I'll give you to the end of the month to decide if you need my help to do it."

He left her with her head shaking, dismissing his wisdom, but the smartest person he knew had to come to the same conclusion. The Widow's Grace had become too dangerous. It needed to end.

CHAPTER 7

JEMINA—END OF JUNE, BACK TO WORK

The fog felt wet and smothering on this cool summer night. I hid in the shadows of the Lincoln's Inn, waiting for my friend to pry open the panes. We couldn't be discovered. The barristers working here would surely return us to Bedlam. It wasn't as if we'd be able to admit we were on a secret mission.

The taste of burnt spun sugar, sugar that had been scorched beyond creamy caramel to soot, lingered on my tongue even after leaving Lady Bodonel's latest party. The blackened substance served atop her dessert tasted so bitter my stomach ached. Yet, I'd rather be in her parlor smiling at that poison than having to shimmy up a knotted rope and flail on the side of the building. My arm had mostly recovered. It would be a shame to injure it all over again.

I tugged the rope. The javelin hook—or assegai, as Patience called it—felt secure. She'd flung and caught it in an upper branch of the oak tree leaning against the building.

Where was my friend? Why didn't she have that window opened?

I peered up into the thick canopy of leaves but couldn't see her. It never took Patience more than a few minutes to pry open any anything. Why did tonight have to be difficult?

"Patience?"

My voice was low. I made sure of it. I'd been told I was loud, but my barrister's opinion didn't matter . . . much.

"Almost in, Jemina. I'm slower than usual. That food, it sickened my stomach."

"You too? You think your mother-in-law did it intentionally?"

"Lady Bodonel? No. She's just a terrible hostess, but everyone comes since she's Busick's mother. My poor duke."

Hearing Patience's voice made the tension in my muscles uncoil. She was still safe, still with me.

"Hurry up, Your Grace."

Patience uttered no response, but she hated when I called her by her title. Maybe she'd found a way inside.

I gulped air and packed it in my chest as if it were my last. My prayer: let nothing go wrong.

I knew what it was like for things to go wrong. It felt like sinking in deep waters, like cold waves growing higher, lapping at my feet, then my knees, then nearly over my head—

"Come on up, Jemina. I'm inside. The rope's secure. The assegai's not moving."

My palms were slick with sweat. The last time, I slipped and nearly rolled off the roof, nearly broke my arm.

"Jemina, I won't let you fall. We take these risks for the Widow's Grace, for our sisters. For Mrs. Cultony, Jemina. You can do it. You always do."

If Mrs. Cultony was ever to regain custody of her children, she needed the notes the crown's barrister had compiled. Then she'd be able to dispute the false testimony of her late husband's family and expose their scheme to defraud her.

Focused on that poor woman, I lifted my foot against the tree trunk. "Hold the rope. I don't like it rocking."

"You can trust me, Jemina."

I could. Patience had proven this many times. It was myself I doubted.

With a firm grip, I started and wedged my buckled slippers

into the knot of the tree. The widow's prayer sat on my lips. "The holy habitation is the protector of widows, providing relief and favor. This is the widow's grace."

Saying it aloud was better than reciting *Jesus wept* or any other short scripture that stuck to my faulty memory. Suffering from amnesia these past two years made everything but the present unreliable.

"You're halfway, Jemina. Lady Shrewsbury was right. This office houses four desks, that's four barristers. The information for Mrs. Cultony has to be here."

Wham. A face full of leaves. The smell of oak and cut celery filled my nostrils. Climbing a few more feet, I saw Patience's smile, her heart-shaped face.

Then I slipped.

I braced to hit limbs and gain a mouth of dirt, but Patience grabbed my good arm and pulled me into the window.

Holding her tight, I refused to let go. That loud heart of mine roared. It might not be in my chest anymore.

"All is well. Look at me, Jemina. All is well."

My lungs sounded like whistles. "Thank you."

"I'm sorry, Jemina. A better friend would find an easier way into the building and not force you to face your fears."

"Not scared of all high places, just ones where we can't use stairs."

I squeezed her tight, like she'd awakened me from a nightmare. "You're the best. The sooner we retrieve Mrs. Cultony's custody papers, the sooner we can return to His Grace and enjoy hot tea on the ground."

"Oh, please don't let Busick discover we're . . . well, you know . . . we're ah . . . um at the Lincoln's Inn without an invitation."

Moonbeams boring through the fog highlighted Patience's tawny eyes. She knew this was a burglary even if all we took was paper.

From her pocket, she pulled out two candles and lit one for me, one for her.

I caressed the silky column. The scent of honey from the burning beeswax reminded me of innocence, but what was innocent about fire? We were guilty of doing wrong to make things right.

Patience shrugged. "We'll have to check all the desks for Widow Cultony's prosecuting barrister."

Four desks.

Two were cluttered with books and notes bound with scarlet ribbons.

Another was piled with papers falling into a chair.

The last, by a hazelnut-brown-colored sofa, drew me. Neat, orderly, it would be a fast search. The precision of the center pile alone, how it sat equidistant from the edges was mesmerizing. What type of man would take such care?

With my candle, I admired this barrister's clever hand, his humored questions of a witness's testimony in the margins.

The handwriting, it looked familiar.

This was Barrister Thackery's script. This was his desk.

My pulse exploded. He noticed everything. This felt worse than burglary, like a violation. My stomach soured as it had with the burnt caramel.

"Patience, why would Lady Shrewsbury have us enter an office where her nephew worked? Couldn't he get the paperwork?"

"Maybe she doesn't want him involved anymore. That's one less desk to search. He'd never take a case against a cheated widow."

She was right.

The man was honorable as much as he was ornery. "Let me put things back, so he'll find no fault."

I brushed at the stack, patting the edges, risking paper cuts. The pages wouldn't behave. They shifted and poked out.

Breathe. I'd have to take my time and lay the pages down.

One after the other, I organized them. Then I saw my surname, St. Maur. I looked again and read my whole name—Jemina Monroe St. Maur.

It felt strange looking at my name, the one I had to relearn these past two years. It held no life—no memories I could grasp.

"Jemina, did you find something?"

"My marriage contract, Jemina Monroe to wed Cecil St. Maur. What type of name is Cecil? Why not something with passion, like Caesar?"

Patience came and lifted the paper. "Jemina St. Maur. Could there be another Jemina St. Maur?"

"Perhaps, but not on Daniel Thackery's desk. The barrister who produced a widow's dower of twenty thousand pounds in a flourish of papers forgot to show me this one."

Stupid me for just accepting his help without asking questions. Stupid me for believing the man who rescued me from Bedlam was honorable. "Why would he not give this to me?"

"The document bore a seal from Jamaica. The West Indies. You *are* from the islands."

Snippets of that life—a bright feather touching my chin, bits of color, the warm sun—had to be true.

"Jemina?"

My lips didn't work. No syllables.

She held me and rubbed my back. "All will be well. Don't get stuck."

My thoughts settled. "Patience, I had a husband who had the decency to leave me money, and I haven't the decency to remember him."

"That's not your fault."

"A concuss of the skull, that's what the physicians said before offering me this name, Jemina St. Maur."

My insides sickened again. I almost remembered a place, but nothing of my husband.

"You're strong, Jemina." Patience had her hands on me, steadying me. "You kept my head when I thought all was lost. You stood up for me when I couldn't. Whatever this means . . . we'll figure it out."

"Daniel Thackery, the Earl of Ashbrook knows my secrets."

Frenzied, I turned back and tore through the pile, the pile that should've been so thick I wouldn't have seen the contract. "He knows. He knows about me."

Watching me, nodding, Patience sat behind his desk. "Then, let's flip through the man's drawer. Let's see what else he hides."

"He has my life, and he's chosen to keep it from me."

"Maybe he hasn't found a convenient way to share. You two are always arguing or ignoring each other."

Or he's quoting me poetry in the dark.

I resettled my gaze atop the desk and started a second pass through the stack. Soon I found a torn piece of paper from the *Cornwall Chronicle*, a register from Jamaica. "A list of names . . . a list of passengers who quit the colony."

I saw my name, full and complete again—Jemina Monroe St. Maur. The word *FOUND* was written next to it. Aside Cecil St. Maur's name was penned the word *LOST*.

This I knew.

"Well, this was Ashbrook's proof I was a widow. This is why the Widow's Grace took me on."

"I'm sorry, Jemina." My friend took the list. "The ship was called the *Minerva*. The countess can—"

"What? My 'problem' is solved. I'm freed from Bedlam. I have an inheritance. When we've helped our fifth widow, I'm done."

"Never. We're in this together. The duke will discover more. He'll be your champion. He loves discretion—and minding *my* business. I think almost all the servants are military or in league with him."

Patience was brave and independent yet so certain of her husband. I wondered if I loved a man named Cecil the same way.

The coldness inside me told me no, not a Cecil. I scoured the passenger list of the *Minerva*, looking for more St. Maurs—a sister, a brother, a child?

Nothing.

What if I saw my flesh and blood and felt nothing?

"We have a mission, Jemina. A widow to save."

"Tomorrow is for me." I returned to stacking the perfect column of papers. "Thackery's desk needs to look untouched, even if I want to set it on fire."

"He'd notice char."

Floorboards creaked. Someone stood in the hall.

Patience dashed out the window to the ropes and into the tree. There was no time to follow.

I blew out the candles, closed the window, and hid behind the sofa.

CHAPTER 8

DANIEL—BREAKING AND ENTERTAINING

Outside the door to his shared office in the Lincoln's Inn, his overly affectionate companion for the evening, Lady Lavinia Nell, stood behind Daniel with her arms draped about his chest like a fine tailcoat, an expensive one.

He patted away her hands and went into his coat pocket for a key. "This is my office, Lady Lavinia. You'll see it, then I'll return you to your carriage."

"Your mood is still fouled from that solicitor harassing you before the dinner."

"Mr. Mosey did work for my uncle. The man is a worm." Both men were.

Daniel dropped his key but snatched it up before Lavinia became more hands on. "Yes, Mosey took the shine off my evening. His Tonbridge firm represents those with unsavory holdings." Slavers, intercolonial transporters of people—unsavory, evil.

She brushed at Daniel's shoulder, fingering lines in his formal ebony tailcoat. "Let me polish you and make your eyes sparkle."

"Lavinia, go home. I'm not in the mood for amusement."

"You're in the mood for something, why else am I here?"

It would be bad form to say he needed a distraction, that he was bothered seeing Mrs. St. Maur's new suitor, Mr. Willingham, hovering about her.

"Open the door, Lord Ashbrook. I want to see where the scales of justice are made right."

"That would be the Old Bailey court. Not here. Stop by Tuesday. I have a trial where I'm the barrister for the Crown."

"Let me in again, Daniel." She snuggled closer almost pressing him into the knob. "Looks a little small."

He pried free, putting more space between them. "It's large enough."

"You seem nervous, sir. Brandy or a port will do you good. Or maybe we can do something to make you more relaxed?"

Daniel didn't drink, nothing more than a social sip to not upset his hostess or colleagues. "No, my dear. I am fretting. Trying a new nanny for my household. It's the first night in a long time I didn't put my little girl to bed."

"I've heard it's been a long time since you put a big one to bed too."

He dropped the key again. "Don't pay attention to gossip. You should know better."

Searching, he found the key near the woman's white silk slipper. Daniel forwent the offer of her long leg moving closer to his face and sprung up fast. "Lavinia, no. Down, my lady."

"I'm not your puppy, Daniel. But I do orders very well."

"Then maybe I could give you Max for a week. My pug is still a belligerent dog."

"That's not what I want."

He pressed the key into the lock. The door opened with a screech, and he lit the wall sconces. "See, nothing fancy. Go home. Your tour is complete."

Lady Lavinia wiggled inside. Her garnet-colored dress had a low plunging neckline. It screamed curvy and trouble, the kind of trouble he missed.

"Daniel, do you remember when you enjoyed my company?"

His thumb slid on the indentions of the brass key, some sharp, some worn with age. He'd been tempted by Lavinia, but that was fueled by jealousy.

"Daniel, you've gone quiet. You do remember us, how we were?"

Lady Lavinia was his first substantial affair of the heart, but a cub young in his law practice was not what the daughter of a marquess wanted. She had targets on the deeper pockets of peers.

He put away his key. "We're both older and wiser. And never without caution."

"You used to be such fun, scandalous fun, and now you're a peer. We should celebrate with champagne and cherries." She fingered his chest. "I heard your uncle fought to keep your elevation from happening. Did he die spitting?"

Yes. A full-throated vomit. "Just rumors. Go home."

"I've rarely seen you finish a glass of wine. The late Earl of Ashbrook loved his porter. Your father too."

Daniel moved to the rear of his desk, groaning. His father was a stew of all things, sad and disappointing. The man's lack of control was a reminder for alcoholic abstinence. "I don't need to overindulge to enjoy my evenings, Lavinia."

Sitting on his desk, she spun and lifted her slipper onto his chair arm. "I've watched you, Daniel, saw your rise in the courts. Though you are one of Prinny's favorites, you've worked twice as hard to become one of the Crown's top barristers."

This made him smile. The Prince Regent did claim favorites, Blackamoors of extreme talent like Bridgetower, the supreme violinist; Richmond, the prize pugilist; and Daniel, the Socratic mind. These were the prince's successes.

"I hear you're always working, my dear man. Such a waste to be so diligent and stifled and handsome." She stood beside him. Her thumbs skirted his cravat and dipped into his shirt. "You know what they say about all work and no play, Daniel, darling."

He kissed her hand and moved it to his chair. "I think that has implications for a man named Jack. I, on the other hand, possess a different name and different ethics. Work is my play."

Slipping from the desk, she crouched beside him and slid her hand again to his coat. He doubted she hunted for lint.

"Daniel Thackery, the new Lord Ashbrook. Such a nice ring to it."

"Lady Lavinia, please. You promised to leave after you saw my office. I have to be home soon for my daughter. I'm not interested in a social mistress."

"Have you thought of taking a social wife, Daniel? A woman with connections could be of use. I could even help with the dull stuff, parties and such."

He looked away and searched a drawer for his notes. One of Phoebe's might be there. "Tomorrow's trial will be exhausting."

"I'm sorry. I forgot your heavy devotion to a woman you never met. Oh my, Daniel. You're still in love with her?"

Perhaps.

How could he not be, reading her notes every night. Imagining the conversations, they would have about her . . . his daughter, Hope.

"Daniel, you look as if you've eaten a lemon."

He pushed out the smile he saved for impotent judges. "Some charity, Lavinia. I'm sure you cared for at least one of your three husbands."

"But I had each of my husbands. You have letters."

That cut a little too close. "Lavinia, please leave."

She rubbed at his shoulders, then set a whisper to his neck. "I'm teasing, Daniel. You're always so serious, so careful. When does Daniel ever play?"

It was scandalous to be in this office, his work office, with a woman known for such.

Daniel walked to the door and opened it. "Mrs. Dunn and I met a thousand times in letters. I remember every jot, every spirited word. I think you've amused yourself enough at my expense. Good night."

She sauntered over and slammed the door, then put her arms

about his waist. "Words. You love them, but from what I recall, you do your best work in silence."

"That was a young man. Now, I'm an old one with responsibilities."

"Barely thirty. You're in your prime." Her nails clawed at the tense muscles of his back. "The right wife can help."

"Watch the waistcoat. The threading is fragile."

"Then we should take it off."

"No, Lavinia. And no, I need no wife. And you have too much of a personality to be a mere mistress. It's best we stay friends."

"I want you, Daniel, and I want you to marry me."

Why was his aunt and now Lavinia trying to marry him off?

"Daniel, are you too good for dear old Lavinia? You're hunting for one of those young misses in white. Some virginal thing that wouldn't look twice at you because you weren't a gentleman of leisure."

He cocked his brow and stared. "If I were to need companionship, it would be an unassuming, scandal-free mistress, not a wife. Not again."

"You've changed, Daniel. Or shall you demand I say Lord Ashbrook? You've taken on airs since your elevation. I'm not good enough."

"You want to call me a nose-up barrister?"

Her lips pressed tightly together, but he dared her to mention the things he taught all his friends in the *ton* to forgo—his race, his father, and now his daughter. His other friends knew better.

Lavinia laughed; the notes vibrated against his tight chest. He relaxed and joined in. "Isn't there someone waiting for you at home, Lady Lavinia? A poodle, another husband, a riding instructor?"

She put her hands into his thick-curled hair, sculpted on the side and up top, and claimed his mouth.

Lavinia was good, irresistible and Daniel was losing this argument. He was lonely. Wasn't there something nice about a woman knowing what she wanted?

She worked off his coat, but the notion of how tawdry it was to be seduced in his office, the place he worked so hard to gain a seat pressed. He pried free and noticed additional legs for the sofa.

Two bore slippers.

"Daniel, what?"

Slippers with buckles.

Scandal. A witness.

"There's surprise evidence, Lavinia. We must say good evening, now."

"Daniel?"

"New information." He pointed her to the slippers; ones he'd seen earlier this evening dancing with Willingham. He walked Lady Lavinia to the door. "We'll continue this discussion later."

"Will we, ducky? Or will someone else be on your diary schedule? Feet have a tendency to multiply."

"My dear, I'll be in touch."

"You'd better, my Lord Ashbrook, you'd better."

She left.

A sigh steamed from his nostrils, clouding his lenses. He spied rope dangling from the window. This was a serious Widow's Grace operation, done at his office, at the Lincoln's Inn.

He plopped onto the edge of his desk and folded his arms.

"We're alone now, miss. You can make your presence known."

Jemina St. Maur sprang from hiding. Her shiny brass buckles gleamed on her yellow slippers. With hair spilling from her chignon, she stood inches in front of him, reared her arm and slapped him, hard.

"You're impossible, Daniel Thackery."

Nodding, he agreed to things being impossible, such as a weakness for freckles and the deep cupid bow of her lips.

"Why strike me? Jealousy over two consenting adults' private discussion doesn't become you."

"Not her. This." She waved a piece of paper at him.

Creased, yellowed by two years—he knew exactly what it was. His memory conjured up every name on the torn page of the *Cornwall Chronicle*, the list of passengers boarding the *Minerva*, including his Phoebe's.

"Well, Mr. Thackery?"

He should've burned the paper.

Everything was at risk, because he was a sentimental fool.

Still, he said nothing, just stared into Mrs. St. Maur's glorious, furious eyes.

CHAPTER 9

JEMINA—DEBATING A BARRISTER

I stood in the Lincoln's Inn, not caring that Ashbrook caught me in the midst of breaking into his office. Shame should be mine for that and slapping him.

My heart wouldn't slow. It beat loudly, and I waggled my finger in his face. "Just because you're an earl or a barrister doesn't make you immune to deception."

"It's an earl *and* a barrister. But you are correct. Sometimes I have to resort to tricks in court."

"How could you? How could you withhold knowledge of my being on the *Minerva*?"

He sighed but said nothing, merely rubbed his jaw.

"Lord Ashbrook, this is criminal."

Tweaking his jaw, he cleared his throat. "Can you tell me what crime has been committed? All I see is attempted burglary by a member of the Widow's Grace."

"Lying. That's a crime, sir."

"Technically, it's a commandment, not a legal crime, ma'am. Very unfortunate, if I had lied, but I haven't."

"You did; you had this paper—"

"Mrs. St. Maur, I've never denied having paper. There's plenty on my desk. Did you move my stack?"

"You are unfortunate." I leaned and knocked his pile, not enough to scatter it but it was definitely off center now.

His face went blank, but I had that secretive feeling sweep over me. This man knew more but wouldn't say.

"I wish I was you, Ashbrook, so I can be in on the joke. I want to be included."

"What? Why?"

"'Cause then I'd have something. Something special and private. Something that I knew and didn't have to doubt."

His mouth opened, then he showed a little peek at the gap in teeth. "You confound me. I expected you to be mad and to continue to be loud and lash out, but not this . . ."

"This what?"

"Can't explain it. It's not defeat or resignation. But it's something potent, and I hunger to see what you'll do next."

"Please don't try to charm me. My husband's whole name is on this paper."

Stretching, Ashbrook pushed out his legs, then looked at the floorboards. "Do you remember him?"

"No." My fists clenched; my chest trembled. "My amnesia is complete."

"Then a name on a list means nothing."

"Don't you think . . . think . . ." I started shaking, violently trembling; the next moment I was swept up in my barrister's arms.

And he whispered more sweet lyrics.

Elate with hope her race no longer mourns,
Each soul expands, each grateful bosom burns,
While in thine hand with pleasure we behold
The silken reins, and Freedom's charms unfold.

I didn't know what any of it meant, but I liked the sound of his voice in my ears, the scent of his sweet starch on his cravat and the strength of his arms pressing me to his chest. He held me until the thudding of my heart slowed.

"There, there." He put his palm under my chin and raised it. "If we're in agreement, we can discuss things reasonably. Are we on the same side for now?"

"Fine. Yes."

My voice sounded airy, but I clung to his embrace. I wasn't ready to let go. "A truce."

With a nod he moved several feet from hugging range. "Why are you here, breaking into my office?"

"I was sent for another barrister, the one working on Widow Cultony's charges. Her husband's family is claiming some type of fraud."

"My aunt didn't ask me." He tugged on his cravat. "I suppose that's progress. I told her . . . Well, it's progress."

Another secret. "You're frowning, my lord. Have you gained a conscience?"

"Not any more than what I had. Was Lady Lavinia in on this, she kept wanting me—"

"Yes, I overheard."

"No. She wanted me to go home. Never mind." He undid his mangled cravat. "Check the desk by the window. I heard my colleague discussing the upcoming Cultony trial."

The Duchess of Repington tapped on the window. "Can you let me in?"

Ashbrook stormed to the window. "The two of you? Of course." He threw open the panes and offered a hand to Patience, pulling her inside.

"Your Grace," he said, "does the duke know you're climbing trees, breaking into men's offices?"

"No, but if you tell him, tell him I did it in a dress."

She tugged at a ribbon about her waist and the skirting of a gown came down over her white breeches, which almost looked like stockings. "See, ladylike."

"Technicality, Your Grace." Daniel rubbed at his face, his jaw looking red.

My silver band, one his aunt had given to me and each of her widows, had made a mark.

"Sorry, my lord, but excuse me." I said with folded arms, tapping my buckled slipper. "You still haven't told me why you have this list with my name and my husband's name."

He tugged free Patience's rope and rolled it up. "Most widows who've been redeemed and handed a fortune do miraculous things like go on with their lives, not burglary. What is it you want from life?"

If I said my dearest wish, he'd laugh or he'd whisper he wished I had my dreams too. The man was good and annoying.

"What is your new goal?" he asked. "I hope you figure out what you want and seize the opportunity. A woman who knows what she wants is fierce, don't you think?"

"Why do you care? Tell me, *Lord Ashbrook*."

"The way you say my title, hot and tight, almost seething, it's like a sneer or obscenity on your lips."

"Ashbrook, Ashbrook, Ashbrook." I puckered, sputtered, then released all my breath.

The duchess smoothed wrinkles from her skirt. "What are you two arguing about this time?"

"My husband, Mr. St. Maur." I waved the paper. "His withholding information of Cecil St. Maur, Jemina St. Maur, and our demise."

"Technically, only his." He bent and picked up his coat. "It's the list of passengers for the *Minerva*. You are listed as found. My wife is listed as missing, but she died too."

I stilled and stared and wanted to cry. No wonder he looked at me so strangely. I lived, and the woman he loved died. "I'm sorry."

With a quick toss, he pitched his coat to the desk, then snatched the paper. "I prefer pseudo obscenity than pity. I discovered this list when I hoped that maybe my wife hadn't boarded the *Minerva* in Jamaica, but she did. She's a victim of the sea."

Suddenly cold, freezing, I wrapped my arms about myself.

He cleared his throat. "It's good to have the *Minerva* business out in the open. No more protecting you from it. The shipwreck binds us together."

The duchess sank to the sofa and studied the Cultony papers. "I don't recall a Thackery on the list. It's not fair to confuse my friend."

"It's there, Your Grace. Phoebe Dunn was my wife."

He said the name, and I closed my eyes, hoping for a glimmer of something. Maybe I had a memory to share of his wife, but I had none. My life except for the past two years remained blank.

"Mr.—Lord Ashbrook," the duchess said, "are you all right? You look a little ashen. I saw her hit you. Jemina does have a good punch."

"Fine. Quite fine, I assure you."

He wasn't fine. That was a lie. His voice was too low. His eyes had drifted to the left. The poor man still mourned his wife.

Ashbrook walked to the door and held it open. "If you two are done ransacking my colleague's things, we can end this reunion. Go home, Your Grace, to that adorable boy of yours. Little Lionel needs his mother and her dearest friend home safe."

The duchess headed for the door, but I kept trying to read his gaze.

"Ashbrook," she said, "come to dine with Repington next week. You and Jemina can practice more than a minute of civility. If you chose to forget we were here, I could have some coconut bread baked for you. Or one of the desserts your aunt says you are fond of."

"Bribing a servant of the court is inappropriate, Your Grace. But since you are a great baker, exceptions can be made. Good evening."

I circled to his desk and slid my marriage contract out of the stack. "I'll have this."

He took it from me. "No, this is my copy that needs to be with your inheritance documents in case questions are asked."

"But it's mine."

"Go to Jamaica and get another copy, ma'am." His clipped tone left no room for misunderstanding. He bowed to the duchess and pointed to the hall. When we crossed the threshold, he slammed the door.

Hackling, twisting up my gut. "Patience, he knows more. I can feel it."

I turned to head back into Ashbrook's office, but Patience clasped my hand. "Another time. Let's head to Sandlin Court before His Grace suspects we've been on a mission."

She was right, and I followed her down the steps. But I purposed to find out all Lord Ashbrook knew about me, even if I had to climb every tree to get to him.

CHAPTER 10

DANIEL—THE GENTLEMEN

Too much prep for trials, too many meetings with solicitors consumed Daniel's week, and indeed made him a very dull man. The hint from his friend Bridgetower about card play seemed as good an excuse as any for Finchely's resident hermit to entertain.

Moreover, the buzz and gossip among his pals would keep him from responding to the notes the duchess and Mrs. St. Maur kept sending.

They disturbed his desk, broke into his office. He wasn't in the wrong for avoiding them.

Still.

St. Maur's paper smelled a little like jasmine. The duchess's a mixture of lavender and coconuts.

With a shake of his head, he released thoughts of Mrs. St. Maur and his fear of her digging up rumors about the *Minerva*. The fellows, the friends who understood him, started arriving and taking spots about the dining table.

His sandy-colored pug, Maximillian snoozed at his side. The adorable thing barked as each man arrived, then flopped over in a drooling sleep.

Not exactly a watchdog, but Finchely was a house far from town, and there wasn't much to see.

Daniel ran his hand along the fine mahogany surface polished to the highest shine. The striping of zebra wood inlays reflected the candlelight and mirrored the back of his thick paper cards.

The table and room were particular favorites of Daniel's mother. The rare dinners she threw left all in amazement.

He was four, looking over the twisty stairs in the great hall, watching people arrive. The excitement was not all from her dishes or carefully planned menus. It was more so the curiosity that a London merchant's daughter with family ties to the Black Caribs of Dominica could excel at white soup, white linens, and vanilla conversations. He so wanted to come home to Phoebe and discuss their days over a sumptuous meal and candlelight, just the two of them, or three with Hope's addition.

The fellows gathering would fill the dining room with colorful talk, their take on mundane politics, movement on abolition, mistresses and marriage.

Not in that order, but the night wouldn't be complete without at least one *huzzah, you fool,* or a *what were ya thinkin'?*

Well, this was sort of a family dinner for brothers. Didn't quite honor his mother's notions, but he knew she'd understand.

"Your turn, sir," Mr. Anthon said as he took the place of the often late Bridgetower.

Mrs. Gallick came in with a new platter of sweet biscuits, these with currants and caraway seeds. "Love hearty eaters."

From the sideboard, the Scottish woman removed the platters emptied of lobster and pheasant and the dish bared of roasted plantains.

His friends were the picture of politeness, not once bemoaning his choice of lemonade to their lust for rum or brandy.

Once alone, John Beef—the grandson of the famed Jack Beef, the man-of-all-work extraordinaire to Magistrate Baker lowered his goblet, the stem making a *wop* sound. "It's odd that you'd now call us together. Don't mind me, I'll always find time for a good meal and to take your money, Barrister."

"I have no excuses, friends." Daniel snatched a roll and smothered it in raspberry jam. "At least, none that are good. It's been too long."

Beef offered a slight sneer of agreement under his carefully trimmed mustache. His calloused brown hands slammed a winning set of vingt-et-un. "I win, outcounted Prinny's brain."

"Luck is with you tonight, Beef." Daniel added to the man's tally of six in a row. "I know I haven't been a social butterfly in a while."

"A butterfly?" Mr. Gerard, the butler at Sandlin Court, the Repingtons' Town residence, laughed as he shuffled the deck. "More of a reclusive moth. I heard it's been nearly two years since you've been social."

Between work, Hope's struggles, and his aunt's gambits, he hadn't the energy to entertain. It took chaperoning the Duchess of Repington and the slap-happy Mrs. St. Maur in a caper to gaming hells to remind him of life beyond the courts and Finchely.

He swept up his new cards, a three of diamonds and two of spades, very far from a winning twenty-one. "My apologies. Fellowship is important, and if you keep your voices low, my little Hope will not disturb us until it's time to read a bedtime story at ten."

Grinning, Mr. Gerard held his cards close to his eyes. "That seems a might late for a child? Maybe those law books told you the wrong way to raise a babe."

The older gentleman wore his salt-and-pepper hair powdered. His sable skin held deep laugh lines about his mouth, suggesting he was given to humor. Yet, the tease pricked. Daniel constantly fought the feeling he was doing the fathering wrong.

Then Hope would call him Pa-Papa with her little stutter. It righted his world.

"Sorry, I'm late." At fifteen minutes past the appointed time, George Bridgetower slipped into the room and took his customary seat by the window.

Mr. Anthon bounced up, but Daniel waved him to another seat. "You've earned a place tonight. I'll spot you a few bits."

The smile on the young man's face spread to his brown eyes.

Bridgetower nodded, "Yes, stay. That way we get more of your employer's money when you both lose."

Mr. Gerard dealt him cards.

It was nice to see Bridgetower, a fellow Prinny prodigy, in good humor. The past few years had been a struggle. Between his mother's death and the falling-out with the legendary Beethoven, Bridgetower had a run of bad luck.

Elegant in his gray coat and pale green waistcoat, the violinist whistled as he studied his hand. The tune was probably an upcoming masterpiece in the making.

Sitting back, Daniel was struck by the unwanted commonality among the younger set—Anthon, Bridgetower, and himself—a lack of fathers. Daniel's died young, consumed by drink. Mr. Anthon's was felled by bullets in the Peninsula War, leaving his family to certain poverty. And Bridgetower—his tried to exploit the son's talents. The man made such a ruin of things the Prince Regent stepped in and returned the father to Prussia. The prince provided for the violinist's continued studies and even gave a stipend to support the fellow's poor mother.

"You have that look, Thackery. Pardon me, Lord Ashbrook," Bridgetower said. "You're caught in your memories?" He hummed a bit more. The rhythm was peaceful, luscious and rich. "Have you lost too many trials this month, or is it the anniversary of your wife's death?"

Mr. Anthon tossed him a cross look. "He does not lose trials."

Laughing, Daniel patted the young man's shoulder. "I do. I merely forget to say. Problems with the Lord Mayor but nothing I can't handle."

Beef downed his lemonade and smacked his lips. "Tart. I know you're partial to tea, but do you have anything more substantial to drink. A porter?"

Never. Not in Finchely again. "Alas, this is not an ale house, but one of my client's did send a delightful bottle of rum."

The man plunked his glass with his finger. The crystal made a harp's cry. "That's what I am talkin' about."

Ringing a bell, Daniel summoned the spirits, something he had prearranged with Mrs. Gallick. She entered carrying a tray of fine silver goblets and the rare bottle.

"Lord Ashbrook thought pink lemonade would become dull," she said.

The loyal woman seemed to watch Daniel pour healthy glasses of the amber for each man. His remained empty, then she filled his crystal with more lemonade.

Once Mrs. Gallick left, Beef held up his goblet. "Who shall we toast first? Our new earl or Bridgetower's new heiress?"

Schooling his face, Daniel made every muscle stone. His thoughts drifted to Mrs. St. Maur, the heiress he'd made the toast of London. The dower he'd crafted and used his legal expertise to *discover* along with carefully planted gossip with the chatty Lady Bodonel had served its purpose. Mrs. St. Maur was celebrated.

Instead of a quick courtship and marriage to a sensible peer, she'd become a target for everyone, the *ton*, merchants, everyone. With her beauty and hint of island lore and the rare times she slipped into Jamaican patois, she'd be heavily sought after. Men with a weakness for misses from the Caribbean like himself and the Barbadian-descended Bridgetower.

Yet, that was the cruel rub. Daniel found himself incredibly attracted to her, thinking of her too often, and alas jealous of the attention she garnered.

"Ladies first, gentlemen," he said, lifting his lemonade.

Bridgetower's wide flat nose flared in triumph, as if he'd finished another sonata. "Miss Mary Leech-Leak is amazing, but her father may have aspirations for more than a genius."

Mr. Gerard shook his head. "She's lucky to get you. The woman is regarded by most as mistress material."

Squinting, Daniel tilted his head. "That's not a nice thing to say."

"It's not my opinion. I hear she's quite nice, but having worked for Lady Bodonel for many years, the viscountess is a source for gossip. She says Miss Leach-Leek is mistress material 'cause of her parents, the one Leech, the other Leak not marrying."

Daniel could see the violinist seething. "That's disrespectful. And anyone can be a mistress despite their upbringing."

"Do you remember what a mistress is, Ashbrook?" Beef shuffled the deck three times. "Gossip says you're a squeaky-clean hermit."

A year of living on the streets made Daniel value things like water and clean clothes and neatness. "I do like soap, Beef. You should try it more often. And I am sure if there was a Mrs. Beef you'd be dedicated solely to her."

"Then there shouldn't be one for a long time," Beef said, then tapped his chest. "John Beef is dedicated to the chase."

Mr. Gerard hammered the table. "Huzzah. Vingt-et-un!" He scooped up his winnings, then dealt again. "As I was saying, gentlemen, Mr. Leak, the father, is rich from the cotton fields but too rich to find time to marry the lass's mother."

"None of this matters." Bridgetower's fingers curled into a fist. "Miss Mary is divine. Say no more of this rubbish."

"It matters, young man. It will always matter until abolition takes hold." The sour look on Mr. Gerard's face told the silent story that pervaded the Blackamoor community, one of coercion or dark promises of freedom for trapped colored women in the colonies.

The butler took a napkin and wiped at his mouth as if it held vomit. "Origins aside, the *ton* doesn't want an illegitimate bride unless they're very desperate for income. Those concubine wife arrangements from the West Indies are too much for the earl's church folks."

"You mean the churchgoers who sow oats, procreate, then fret the mixing of bloodlines." Mr. Anthon's words held bitterness. "Holy hypocrites."

Daniel understood this problem firsthand. His uncle, the late earl, tried everything but murder to keep him from being the rightful heir. He hoisted his glass again. "Miss Mary Leach-Leak is lovely with a beautiful face, a glowing olive complexion, one that might've turned my head if—"

"If you hadn't decided to mourn forever and become a monk?" Bridgetower clinked his glass with Daniel's, then spread his winning cards on the table. "Vingt-et-un, my lord!"

Laughs filled the room. Daniel chuckled but cringed inside. It was best two years ago to be a monk, to mourn harder and longer and produce ample testimony and witnesses of what a good father he was in case questions about Hope's guardianship or the *Minerva* ever arose.

He'd done a good job. No one would ever think of sending the child to grandparents who never asked anything about her.

Rubbing at his brow, he examined his cards, stewing over why he was still a monk.

A tug on his leg explained all.

At his boot was little Hope, smiling big with freckles on her bronze nose. "Pa-Papa read?"

She'd crawled to him, not walked. That meant she'd gotten down those slick stairs. Readying to offer a light admonishment, he scooped her up.

She clung to his neck as if he'd disappear. That took the steam out of any fuss. It always did.

"Gentlemen, you know my Hope, the little lady of the house." He shuffled her into the crook of his arm, her favorite position. "Now, princess, we have another hour before story time. Papa is playing with his friends. Right, men?"

"Oh, yes." They all said, while grinning at how this little thing could have him wrapped about her pinkie.

"Pa-Papa, story. You said it was for sleepy. I sleepy now."

Her speech was slow but catching up, and her small patience reminded him of a certain duchess.

Mr. Anthon oversold his deal with a draw of a queen that blasted him past twenty-one. "Can you still play, sir?"

That was the question of the day.

Bridgetower looked at him, then hummed the tune he had as he entered. " 'He's my rock, my defense. I shall not be moved, in the trembles, by the waves. My rock.' "

Miracles of miracles, his hardened, drinking friends sang too. Anthon's falsetto blended with Mr. Gerard's baritone and Bridgetower's words. " 'He's my rock, my defense. My rock. Oh, my rock. My rock.' "

Cynical Beef smirked, downed another glass of rum, and made eyes at Hope. "You'll have a handful, Ashbrook, when she's older."

His little angel smiled like she understood, but the unfinished hymn had her yawning. She pressed against his chest and clutched his buttons.

When Mrs. Gallick stepped into the room, all went silent but Daniel. " 'I shall not be moved in the trembles, the waves. My rock.' "

His housekeeper had seen him too many times gentling this angel to sleep.

His friends mustn't want their reputations softened. This, Daniel mused, wiped Hope's mouth with his handkerchief, then handed the drooling child to his housekeeper.

Humming Bridgetower's song, Mrs. Gallick tiptoed out the door.

"Gentlemen, I think you've helped me past my ten o'clock curfew."

"Good." Beef said, "I want more of that earl money, since I'm not looking to ensnare an heiress, yet. I'm having too good of a time with my ladybirds. Consider joining the fray."

"Oh, he will." Mr. Gerard scooped up the deck and shuffled.

"Ashbrook hasn't decided on what he wants, old or new money." The butler stared at him with wizened eyes of ash and gold.

Old money meant Lady Lavinia had been chattering about Daniel.

New money was an odd phrase. Were there rumors about him and Mrs. St. Maur?

A rumbling laugh came from the hall. Bill Richmond, Prinny's favorite pugilist stood at the door. His hulking shadow, with arms thick like a blacksmith's, the ebony man cut a dashing figure. Pity he was seldom late unless he ran into trouble. "What did I miss?"

"Not sure," Daniel said. "A seat is always here for you. All is well?"

The big bruising man sat, adjusting his elegant emerald coat underneath him. "Yes. Had a few errands."

A collective breath released. No trouble was good.

Card play continued, but Mr. Gerard kept smiling at Daniel.

He might've seen him gentling another girl, a big one with amnesia. Everything would be better if Mrs. St. Maur went on with her life and put to sleep those ideas of digging into the past. Her delicate hands could ruin everyone's future.

Chapter 11

Jemina—Restless and Questioning

Midnight.

Tossing about in my bed, I turned from the window and tried again to find a comfortable spot on the mattress. I hugged my pillows and wondered if I'd always preferred the left side. Had I always needed to be near a window to sleep?

Did I curl into Cecil's chest when storms gathered?

Had he said he loved me in those last moments of the *Minerva*?

Did I, could I have offered the same to him?

I hated I saw nothing when I closed my eyes. No husband, no lousy boat, just the shadow of something missing. My only comfort if one could think it a comfort was that my nightmares of rushing water, consuming water was true.

One answer out of a hundred questions.

Two weeks passed since our burglary and being caught by my barrister. I still couldn't understand why he'd keep this from me.

A soft rap sounded on my door, and I welcomed the distraction. "Come in."

Patience leaned inside. "I wanted to check on you. I know you haven't been sleeping."

"Still the same. Restless."

A silvery robe flowed about Patience as she floated inside. Her bare feet made little sound as she came to my window and leaned against my white table, the place where I drew.

"Lady Shrewsbury sent a note. The information we found looks good. She hopes it's enough to save Widow Cultony."

My shoulders shrugged as I climbed out of the bed. "I hope so. I don't think we can break into the Lincoln's Inn again. Could we?"

Patience clasped my hand. "No, Jemina."

"There has to be more. Ashbrook has secrets about me. He has to have more information on Cecil St. Maur. I owe my husband something, but all I'm thinking of is the earl."

"Oh." She turned to my sketches or the dull whitewashed wall. "Keep confessing to what I already suspected."

"I'm hating how comforting his embrace was and that I remember every one of his hugs, the way he smelled, the starch of his cravat. It tickles my nose. I hear the sound of his voice whispering poetry."

"Oh, oh." Her face claimed the biggest smile, something cheeky and *uzimmie*. She saw me, understood my fretful mind.

"Shameful, I'm sorry." I leaned against the windowsill. "I suppose two years is more than enough for proper mourning."

She looked up with her lips drawn in a line, no *I thought so*, or awe type of smile, nothing. Instead, she held me, pulled me to her bosom and let me cry. *Uzimmie! Uzimmie! She truly saw my heart!*

"Jemina, you're not horrible. You're human."

There was something so good and decent about being understood, of someone letting you be weak without being made to feel small.

Patience wiped my face with a lacy cloth. "He rescued us from Bedlam and has helped us in so many ways. One of us was bound to fall for our hero."

I started to laugh, but in my head the images of that day in Bedlam danced. "He whisked us from evil. It was so dark, leaving under shadows of the melancholy stone angels of the gate. I stumbled and he caught me. Up in his arms, our barrister carried me to his carriage. The first time I'd seen the moon in two years. The first time in two years a man held me, and I felt safe."

"It's fine to like Ashbrook. You do no disservice to Cecil St. Maur. Your husband would want you to move forward."

"How do you know, Patience? What if he were mean or selfish—"

"Or sick, like my first husband." My friend picked up my sketch, a bowl of mangoes. "You may never know. But we have confirmation that your husband is gone. You're free, Jemina."

"Am I, Patience? I can't stand that I have feelings for a man whose proven again and again he'll hide things to protect me. How am I to trust myself if he reminds me that I'm feeble?"

She put her hand to my cheek. Soft coconut radiated from her skin. "Then he's not the one. Busick taught me this. If Ashbrook doesn't make you feel as if you can have the world and be yourself, then you have to get over him. I'll help any way I can."

The tension in my neck felt like fire. I didn't want to not think of him and his rare smile. "Maybe these feelings will pass. I should draw more fruit. Maybe that will soothe me."

"What about flowers? Trumpet-shaped pink hibiscus or bright orange poincianas with their furry green leaves. You're a good artist, Jemina. My sister, Charity, she was a good one too."

Never did I ever like it when shadows filled Patience's eyes, so lost and sad they became. As if I were Ashbrook, I distracted her, whipping jet-black charcoal under her nose. "Such a chalky, ashy smell. It amazes me that it can create such wonders. I might have been trained. My fingers seem to remember."

"You had to be amazing. Your watercolors of fruit are the best."

"Watercolors? No, I'm better at sketches." I tapped my nose. "Wonder if I should tell Ashbrook I want to paint. I should write to him about my new goal."

Patience put down my sketches. "He's bothered by your suitors, especially Willingham."

"What? Ashbrook is jealous?"

"Yes. I asked him." She fiddled with the sash of her robe. "He's forthcoming when asked a direct question."

"Direct? He'll just distract me, like always."

"Maybe you'll get another hug." Patience rolled up one of my flopping tendrils. With a tug, she pinned it back in place. "Your curls must be beautiful, bronze and scarlet and draping about your neck. More suitors will be calling in the morning."

"Suitors, men coming for my twenty-thousand-pound dower. That's Ashbrook's fault too. He mentioned it in front of Lady Bodonel and now all of London knows."

"It stopped my mother-in-law's vicious treatment of you. I think he did it to protect you but underestimated the consequences of the town's largest gossip knowing you have a fortune."

"See, everything comes back to Ashbrook."

Patience folded her arms. "I guess this means you're not going to give up on him."

"Can't I deny liking him till the end?"

Her sigh was heavy—a smidge sad. "Alas, some things can't be denied. Oh, how the duke makes me fret sometimes."

Her tone sounded very sad, and it rocked me, spinning like a boat beat by waves. "What has happened? You and the duke aren't fighting?"

"Lord, no. Well, no more than our typical complaints, but my husband conveniently forgets I'm not one of his secretaries or lieutenants. And I'm not his recruit."

"That's normal Repington. What's the matter, Patience?"

Her eyes became misty and distant. "He's doing too much. He's in the middle of some new operation, probably for Wellington. He so driven. I fear for him sometimes."

"Have you told him?"

"How do you tell a commander anything? He likes a salute, a yes, a no . . . and again."

Her face fevered anew as if she hadn't meant to say that, but the duke and duchess's care for each other was so obvious and thick. The duchess loved her stubborn husband very much.

She sat at my desk, moving my sketches. "I even asked his friend the viscount to intervene, but Lord Gantry is still hunting his wife. He's not much use. I'm so sorry for him. He's desperately in love with a woman who's run off."

The viscount was a tall steady man who wore his chestnut hair too long and tied in a ribbon. He always frowned. He had no secretive gap between his teeth. "Hopefully things will be resolved."

"If he were unattached, he'd be a good match for you."

"Noooo. He's so close to the duke, it would be like marrying a brother. Not for me."

"You don't have to leave us, Jemina. You're a sister to me. To the duke too."

My heart whimpered, and my eyes were hot. I loved Patience. She was my family. I knew I'd lost family. I had that feeling so often when I dreamed, but this love of Patience was a miracle. I was ever grateful.

She yawned and stretched. "I'm never this tired. Chasing Lionel and now the duke has exhausted me. Lady Bodonel will visit tomorrow. She wants to be a part of my husband's life, but he has so little trust of her."

"And you do?"

"Someone has to make her easy. If I keep her from pestering Busick and teach her how to treat her son, then all will be well. It's the least I can do for him."

"You're an odd one, Patience. You lead me and the other widows in so many ways, but you defer to the duke. How do you do it?"

I lowered my chin. "Maybe that's too personal of a question to ask."

Her soft, warm-coconut-smelling fingers lifted my chin. "It's not. And the answer is I don't know. I merely trust in his love. And he reminds me that I can trust in me."

"That simple? That's the secret?"

Patience yawned again. She looked so tired. "Yes, just like that."

"Your Grace, go to bed. Go on to the saluting saint. The duke need's his top recruit well rested."

Patience stood and drew me into another hug, and I put my head onto her shoulder. "Busick is far from sainthood. We warred in the beginning. We butted heads, but I never doubted the man he was, how honor and protection for me and my son were his top priority."

She released me. "Figure out what you want. If you never recover your memory, what will make you happy?"

Ashbrook's question again.

"Good night." She left me with my divergent thoughts of liking and not liking Ashbrook. Climbing into my comfy bed, the left side, I pulled my woolen blanket up to my chin.

Though he's been turning down my invitations, I'd write Ashbrook again, until he agreed to see me. Surely we could strike up a peace. I'd be sweet to him, and then that earl would tell this girl all.

CHAPTER 12

DANIEL—A LETTER FROM A DETERMINED WIDOW

Holding the door, Daniel let the Lord Mayor out of his office. The tall, slim man with his hair, full white and thinning, grimaced as he passed. "I have to assign you another case for the Crown. The argument you will use sounds logical. I think you will do well."

Daniel held his breath for a moment, his speech had to be said without emotion. Yet how could he not, swallowing such condescension. "My lord, I've tried many cases for the Crown these six years, so many before your tenure."

"My appointment is new, and I want the highest conviction rate possible. You can understand."

Of course Daniel did. He understood that he was the only one of his colleagues questioned in this manner, not even the more junior ones. "Yes, my lord."

The Lord Mayor left, and Daniel wished the man would fall down the stairs.

As easy as he could, he closed the door and forced air in and out of his lungs. The man did this to make him quit. Daniel wasn't the type, but neither did he want to be taken down in disgrace. Everything the Prince Regent had done, and even Lady Shrewsbury's faith, would be in tatters. Which is why his anxiety increased about the Widow's Grace operations.

Just because he didn't know about them didn't mean they didn't happen. He eased into his chair, reminding himself he'd always been careful. He'd always followed the letter of the law and just overlooked things. And Lady Shrewsbury was brilliant. She'd not be caught.

But operatives who injured themselves on roofs were another matter.

Mrs. St. Maur sent another letter. He'd scooped it up this morning at breakfast. Her earlier ones were easily ignored. Daniel had no intention of getting into another argument, or worse, admitting to things about her past that would hurt her.

Yet, how could he not respond to this one?

> *Finchely House*
> *London, July 12, 1814*
>
> *Dear Lord Ashbrook,*
> *I thought I needed answers, and I assumed you*
> *were the man to help. Alas, you are not.*
> *Sad.*
> *This lowers my esteem for you. A man who loves*
> *poetry should be placed in high regard. Why else*
> *would I have spent my mornings writing to you every*
> *day these past two weeks? I am not one to beg.*
> *If I were it should be for something else, something*
> *substantial, like a perfect lime or pomegranate. I*
> *decided that I want a pomegranate. I will admit I*
> *was in the wrong for slapping you if you were able to*
> *procure one for me.*
> *Yes.*
> *That has to be the remedy for us. If you are not able*
> *to share your secrets, a pomegranate shall suffice,*
> *don't you think?*

I was called away on something, something I'm not supposed to tell you about.

Sorry. Forget that I mentioned anything.

As I return to this letter, I see it sounds particularly harsh. I understand why you would not want to visit. Nonetheless, you do not seem to be a man easily daunted. If you change your mind and come with a pomegranate, I will allow a visit. I promise to be mostly understanding.

Sincerely,
J. St. Maur
Sandlin Court, London

Daniel folded the letter. The absurdity made him laugh, laugh out loud. She was neither harsh, nor mean. Reading the apology line and the request made him chuckle all over again. The tension in his shoulders lessened. He'd be able to face the Lord Mayor in court more at ease because this woman wrote him a ridiculous letter.

Mrs. St. Maur deserved a response and a pomegranate.

CHAPTER 13

JEMINA—VISITING SUITORS

Another glance out the parlor window of Sandlin Court revealed the same empty Davies Street as five minutes ago. This offshoot of Grosvenor Street was quiet, nerve-rackingly so.

No Ashbrook yet.

His short note saying that he'd visit left me spinning. No explanation of why he ignored my other letters. Yet, I knew this one might do something to stir his inquisitive or protective nature. He might want to check if our impasse had driven me mad.

Well, maybe I was a little otherworldly. I was searching for him when I had a perfectly good suitor here.

"Ma'am," Mr. Willingham said, "what is out the window? You keep looking."

I turned fast, letting the sheer curtains fall from my fingers. "Nothing, sir. It seems such a nice day. Perhaps you should climb into your landau and go for a drive."

"A drive without you? I brought the landau to entice you."

The blond Adonis with his pale blue eyes seemed impassioned about courting me in his fancy vehicle with its top down. Almost as enthusiastic as he was devouring one of my freshly baked chocolate biscuits. "You must come, Mrs. St. Maur."

"No, I shall stay here at Sandlin Court. It was nice of you to visit." I headed to the door and held it open. My sleeve snagged on the molding. "Shouldn't you be going?"

"Nonsense, Mrs. St. Maur. I don't have an appointment at the docks for another hour. It seems like I just arrived."

No, he'd been here long enough to devour a plate of cookies and to crowd me twice on the couch.

Tugging free, the gray lace ripped a little. So much for looking perfect for the earl. Resigned, I walked back to the window and adjusted the curtains, so I could see out the window when I sank into one of the newly upholstered chairs. A dark yellow tapestry, almost jonquil in color, covered them. I wrapped my cream shawl about me and sat. I wasn't cold, but I needed something to do with my hands. They seemed nervous and sweaty, but that was from my fretting about all the biscuits being eaten up before the earl's arrival. He liked treats. The sweets would get him to stay longer.

Willingham looked at me with big eyes.

I glanced at the diminishing pile of biscuits. "I know you're a busy man, Mr. Willingham. I don't want you to tarry too long and deprive others of your company."

The man guffawed. "You're funny. Good sense of humor."

He was a nice-looking fellow whose eyes brightened when he laughed, but he wasn't laughing anymore. His stare was too strong. There was longing and something else in his face, but that had to be his desire for my biscuits.

Patience's recipe for the treats turned even my clumsy hands into a wondrous baker. Could I have been . . .

I lifted the silver tray to Willingham. "Another, sir?"

His mouth pursed as if he wanted to say something, so I pressed it into his hands.

"You seem to enjoy these, sir. Please have another."

"Well, if you insist, Mrs. St. Maur. You are a dear." He scooped up two.

I'd used dies to cut a fleur-de-lis on the surface of the dough,

and the heat of the oven deepened the pattern. The light chocolate coating on the back made the treat more refined, adding
sweetness to the buttery texture. I thought they'd be enjoyed by
Ashbrook as he teased the information I wanted.

Now, I doubted there'd be any when he arrived.

Crumbs on his lips, Willingham kept chewing. "These are excellent. Do you remember how to cook other things?"

"Glad you like the biscuits, Mr. Willingham." I ignored his
question like I did all questions about my lack of memories.

"I didn't mean to offend you."

"You did, but have another biscuit."

The Adonis stature faded the more I glared at Mr. Willingham.
He wore his hair too long. It curled over his ears like fur. His coat
hung upon him like it was two sizes too big. The man had the
money for a haircut and a tailor, didn't he? Or was he looking for
a wealthy wife to maintain such upkeep?

"These are good." He talked with food in his mouth. "I should
probably save some for your other guests. You do have other company coming?"

The sheepish look was slightly endearing, but there wasn't
much of a draw, nothing to compel me to prefer his company to
any other man with broad shoulders.

The notion of choosing a new husband based on looks made
me want to snicker. My new fortune offered me vain reasons to
be picky. It was liberating to be so capricious, but I didn't need to
choose. Patience said that I could continue to reside with her.

If I wanted a new husband, he had to look at me as the duke
did his wife. When he thought no one saw, his whole face lit
when she walked in the room. It was something to see a hardened military man amazed by her grace, her smile.

I wanted that type of love, all-encompassing, even over-
powering.

My gentleman caller scooted along the couch. He sat closer to
my chair. His knees in beach-colored breeches almost touched
mine.

I think I liked him better far away.

"What is it that you intend to do while you are in Town, Mrs. St. Maur?"

"Visit with friends."

Mr. Willingham glanced at the biscuits and then me.

Another awkward silence settled.

Not wanting to break it by talking, I crumbled a sweet biscuit onto my tongue.

"Mrs. St. Maur, I hope it is a good while that you stay in Town. I'd like to keep visiting you."

"You wouldn't come if I resided in the country?"

His face pinched as if he considered it. "It's more difficult. My business is at the ports."

He rubbed at his neck, upsetting his thick cravat. "You haven't seen all the good things in Town. You said you and the duchess where going to the market. Perhaps I can escort you two."

I shifted and hid a little more beneath my shawl. "No, that's fine. Our plans have changed. I . . . We are staying in today."

His brow raised as if he had questions to ask, but he nodded and gobbled another biscuit. For a moment, I pictured a settled life with him at the breakfast table looking at my biscuits with such affection.

What happened when the treats ran out?

"Well, maybe tomorrow, Mrs. St. Maur. I could escort you two then."

"I'll have to check with the duchess. She may have plans."

"Let me know. Don't forget . . . I mean remember to . . ." He took up another biscuit.

I let the crunching of the crispy treats encourage more silence. Perhaps I should ask Willingham to leave so I could check on Patience.

She wasn't feeling well this morning. She hadn't looked so well, not for the past week, very pale in her tawny skin.

Did she hurt herself climbing and keep the injury to herself?

Did she think I'd get worked up and decided to keep the secret from me . . . and the duke?

He'd be highly upset.

And I'd be sad, sad that she was hurt and thought it necessary to treat me so carefully. Everyone should be clumsy like Mr. Willingham and just say whatever awful thing they meant.

"You've gone quiet on me again. I didn't mean to . . ." He stood and wandered about the room. The warm paper treatment of the walls, the suit of armor in the corner. It was a mesh of the duke's and duchess's styles—formal, militaristic with color.

Willingham stopped and stood in front of my watercolor painting Patience had hung yesterday.

It was bright, reds and burgundies, my best fruit bowl.

"This is lovely and new. Did the duchess get it from a vendor at the market?"

The man had his hands on hips as if he readied to be a model for my next drawing if I drew people. Did I draw people?

"No, sir." I didn't feel like explaining or enjoying such false praise. I was just beginning in watercolors, and Willingham wasn't my muse. Pomegranates were.

"I rather like this room, Mrs. St. Maur. A very comfortable situation. You said the duchess redid this room. What color was here before?"

"Pink. I think it was called dead salmon."

The man laughed as he circled the couch. "The duke's last decorator had a since of humor."

But that was how the color was described, dead as in flat, salmon as in fish pink. I stood and swept to the window. Tugging the curtain wider, I witnessed nothing new, still a lone street. Still one carriage, Mr. Willingham's.

"Are you looking for someone?"

"No. No." I drew the airy panels shut. It was foolish to hunt for the earl. His plans could've changed.

"You seem to be lost in thought, Mrs. St. Maur. What if we go for that drive? My carriage is outside. See the spirited set of four? They can carry us away. It's such a lovely day."

This wasn't what I wanted or who I wanted.

Mr. Willingham wasn't for me. As sweetly as I could, I moved from him and fluttered to the fireplace. "I'm not up for a drive."

"I suppose I should've asked in advance. A lady like you certainly appreciates planning."

"I do like plans."

He followed me like a bee, staying close like my jasmine-yellow skirts were petals.

"You are beautiful, like a gentle—"

"Flower."

"Yes . . . My gentle flower."

That sounded sweet, but it made me feel delicate and easily crushed. I wasn't that, at least I hoped that wasn't me anymore.

"Maybe I'm not being direct enough in my admiration."

Mr. Willingham picked up my hand and puts his lips to my wrist. His grip was strong. It would be a fight to wrench away.

I didn't like his forwardness or the feeling that he would take advantage.

No raising my voice or anything to anger the big man. I coughed something awful and throaty.

Taking a handkerchief from his pocket, he released me and offered me the monogrammed cloth. "Do you need water, Mrs. St. Maur? Let me get you some."

Patting my mouth, I smelled salt of the sea, even a tinge of fish in his handkerchief. Willingham must spend a great deal of time at the docks.

Coughing, I waved and nodded. "Yes, please."

The fellow went to the table and rushed back with a goblet of water. "Here, Mrs. St. Maur."

Mr. Willingham was looking at me as if he'd done something wrong, but at this moment, he didn't crowd me.

Perhaps he wasn't so terrible.

Then he advanced and hung his head over mine. Again, I felt his breath on my brow. Hovering. Biscuity and a tinge tart.

"I've been invited to Lady Shrewsbury's ball next month."

Another cough crossed my lips. I took two steps from Willingham. "Yes, it should be a great event. I hear she holds it once a year to honor widows." I wouldn't mention the dinner outing that preceded it. He was not to be my partner.

"Perhaps we could go together or be seated together. I want you to have my special attention."

Light blue eyes twinkled as if the admission should make me swoon.

It didn't.

It kept me pining for the grandfather clock to chime, for this visit to be done.

"You need more tea, sir, to go with another biscuit. I should send for some."

He grabbed my hand. "No. Don't go. There's much to say."

Was there? Where was the duke? Half an hour should have passed by now. He promised to interrupt in Patience's stead to keep any prospects from gaining ideas. Willingham had my hand and ideas.

"Mrs. St. Maur, I don't think I'm doing this right, but you need to know I'm developing feelings for you."

"How? How is that even possible?"

He blinked at me.

In his confusion, I drew my hand away, looking at my shiny band. "You're rushing things."

He had my hand again. "I'm overcome with your beauty. You must marry me."

"Why? I mean, you don't know me."

"I know enough. The Duke of Repington brags about how smart you are. His dear friend the Lord Gantry says so too."

"I'm pleased that these men you've spent a minute of time with have talked about me and think well of me. That is no reason to marry."

Looking up into his flustered face, I knew I had to get rid of him once and for all. He didn't have the patience to allow me time to love him or even to consider him as my future. "No marriage. Not now."

"I'm sorry." His head hung, his face souring. "But every young woman should marry. Every widow should wed again."

The outer door to the town house rattled open. Oh, please let that be anyone who might need the parlor.

"Mr. Willingham, you should be going."

The parlor door opened.

Silver livery gleaming over his military boots, a footman entered. He had to be one of the duke's former soldiers. "Lord Ashbrook to see you, ma'am. Shall you receive him?"

Thank Jah. Jove delivered. My head bobbed. Dapper in his well-fitted tailcoat and holding a delightful bouquet of ransoms and lilies of the valley in his arms, Ashbrook crossed the threshold.

My pulse raced. It doubled when I heard Mr. Willingham groan. It tripled when I caught the earl's half grin and the pomegranate under his arm.

CHAPTER 14

JEMINA—USEFUL, TERRIBLE BARRISTER

Ashbrook had finally come. He stood in the parlor with gifts, looking like the perfect suitor, the perfect pomegranate picker. Yes, perfect to dissuade Mr. Willingham.

I rushed to the earl. "My—my lord, the bouquet is lovely. The duchess will enjoy them. Oh, and is this for me?"

"Both are for you, Mrs. St. Maur." His voice lowered as his head dipped to my ear. "To make amends."

The pique I had at Ashbrook lessened, maybe evaporated entirely.

A little stunned, a little touched, I stroked a petal and palmed the pomegranate. "Thank you, my lord."

The partial smile, the beginnings of that rare one disappeared as Mr. Willingham loomed closer.

"I didn't know you'd have company," Ashbrook said, his gaze burned on me. "I thought it would be the two of us."

"Mr. Willingham just stopped by, but he's leaving."

The Adonis stuck out his hand to the earl. "I don't believe we've formally met."

Ashbrook didn't shift the flowers to engage. He merely dipped his chin. "No. Not directly."

The earl gave me the flowers but kept my hands. His fingers lingered on mine, strong and warm.

"Lilies of the valley and ransoms are such special beauties, resilient and fragrant, a little like you, Mrs. St. Maur."

I dampened Mr. Willingham's handkerchief and wrapped it about the stems of the flowers. "I like them. Thank you."

"Wait," Mr. Willingham said as he crowded me, "Jemina, Mrs. St. Maur, you and I were visiting."

"I suppose both of us are here for the lady." Lord Ashbrook pulled at the paper and exposed more blooms. Then he made a show of claiming my fingers again and putting his mouth to my knuckles.

The touch was soft, as was his lips. "Chocolate, my dear? Is that what I taste?"

His cheek quivered. Was that a suppressed laugh?

Ashbrook cleared his throat. "I'd like to finish our conversation in private, ma'am."

My hand became lost in his palm. Though there was strength in his hold, he didn't tug me. I wasn't uneasy about him, not like I was with Willingham.

Like they had a mind of their own, my fingers tightened about his.

Had I ever held Ashbrook's hand before?

Then I remembered him rescuing me from Bedlam. Yes, he held my hand and gave me his shoulder for support. My legs were weak from the shackles used to restrain the crazed. Then he whisked me into his arms when I stumbled.

My heart beat hard.

"Mrs. St. Maur?" Mr. Willingham's shadow crowded us. "Sir, you are intruding."

"I have an appointment, Willingham. I believe you are lingering."

I pointed my first suitor to the door. "Thank you for visiting, Mr. Willingham."

When I turned back, my gaze tangled with the earl's. He

wasn't letting go, and for the briefest moment, I didn't want to box his ears.

Yet, this was Ashbrook, the barrister who forgot to tell me he had a piece of my life hidden on his desk.

"Hmmm." Willingham coughed.

The earl hadn't moved, hadn't changed his position nor lost my gaze or fingers.

"Lord Ashbrook, is there anything you wish to ask my other guest before he leaves?"

He sighed and released me. "Is shipping a good business, Willingham, or is it still recovering with the war just ending?"

"Very fine, your lordship. The recovery from 1812 and the Peninsula War have been challenging."

Ashbrook had a distant look for a moment.

"My firm has many ships," Willingham's tone boomed. "All full of business. I can provide very well for a new bride."

"Can you, sir? That's nice to hear." Ashbrook turned and motioned me to the watercolor. "Mrs. St. Maur, is this new? I hadn't noticed it on my last visit, but we were occupied."

Why did his stance, hand on his hip, tailcoat open showing the fine buttons of his bottle-green waistcoat, feel territorial?

Maybe because it was.

Ashbrook was a preening rooster, but if Mr. Willingham could learn anything from the earl, it would be how to command the floor without hovering, how to display his strength and not be domineering.

My barrister could be very condescending, but he always allowed me the space to object, to speak my mind.

I liked that about him.

Willingham followed me to the painting. "You visit here often, Ashbrook?"

The earl reached out and touched the canvas. "This needs a frame. Yes, Mr. Willingham. Now and again, when Mrs. St. Maur or the Duke or Duchess of Repington require my advice."

Willingham snorted. "Sorry to hear about your uncle. He was one of my dearest friends and clients."

The well-fitted gray sleeve of the earl's tailcoat crinkled. The muscles underneath seemed to flex. Though his expression remained blank, his pupils shrank and became fully jet. There was no mourning in Ashbrook, nothing but tension.

Pushing away from both of them, I set down my pomegranate and straightened the lilies, sniffing the sweet fragrant ransoms. The white flowers looked like lace. They needed color, maybe some blue or purple.

My nostrils filled with the scent, my chest with their peace. To keep this ease, I had to take charge.

"Mr. Willingham, the earl is my former, well, actually, current barrister. There's business we need to discuss. It was nice of you to come this morning, but you must leave."

Willingham stepped closer to the earl. "Tell me, Ashbrook, do you always bring flowers to clients?"

"Only the pretty ones with freckles."

Willingham turned beet red, and his hands fisted.

I set my flowers on the table near the few remaining biscuits. Locking arms with Willingham, I started him toward the door. "Time for you to run along, sir."

"Mrs. St. Maur," he said in low grumbly voice, "a drive, the two of us."

"That would be a no." Ashbrook's low tone wasn't a whisper. It was loud enough for servants in the hall to hear. Then the peacock barrister sat on the arm of the couch as if he owned it.

He mustn't know how much pleasure I'd have seeing him wobble and fall but kicking Mr. Willingham out of Sandlin Court was a higher priority. "Good day."

The man stepped into the hall. "But, a drive? Another moment?"

"Good day, sir. Thank you for coming."

With all my might, I closed the door on him, then sighed and leaned against it, placing my whole weight on the handle and trim, but I pinched my finger. "Ouch."

"Bravo, Mrs. St. Maur. He's gone, but you needn't hurt yourself evicting the shipper."

Ashbrook chuckled, but his face sobered as I shook my stinging hand. "You did hurt yourself?"

"My palm. My thumb is all red."

"I knew Willingham was only capable of bringing you pain. Has he been here every day making a nuisance of himself?"

"He wasn't the only bird waving feathers here. You know it's male birds that do that the most."

Shaking out my reddened palm, I took a few steps toward the earl's side of the couch. "Did you have to antagonize him? I thought you saved those special feelings for me."

"I must distribute my disdain with an even hand." Ashbrook now wore a full smile, not his half-committed one I'd seen so often. No gap showing yet. "Let me look at your fingers. This male bird, or *cock* or cack, has other special talents. Me no cack mowt kill cock."

So Ashbrook wasn't going to say something to convict himself. The rooster's mouth wasn't going to kill him. His small entwining of patois and humor tugged at my frown. Thumb stinging, I balled my fist. "No special assistance is required. I'm fine."

The man tugged on the chain of his watch fob. He was stylish sitting in dark buff breeches. His starched cravat was snow white.

The more I looked at him, the more I saw his eyes weren't unfeeling or lumps of coal, but crystalline and shiny like cleaved obsidian stones. There were even bits of gold and maybe bluegreen at the edges.

"You're staring, Mrs. St. Maur? What is it that you are trying to determine?"

I folded my arms and pretended that I was affronted by the accusation, but I was guilty of peering at him, of wanting his rarest smile.

He was handsome.

His deeply tanned skin, glowed of warm sunshine. The high-sculpted cropping of his hair—smooth on the sides, curly on top—held tiny waves. His thin mustache and well-trimmed beard framed his wide face, making those strident eyes something a girl could get used to having them upon her.

"Must be good thoughts, Mrs. St. Maur, since you seem at a loss for words."

Pumping my hurt hand, I looked down at the lilies and Mr. Willingham's cloth. "I'll have to return his handkerchief, but what new aggravation would that cost?"

"Mr. Willingham is no longer a favorite?"

"I have no favorite, but he's persistent. He makes time to see me."

Ashbrook's smile disappeared. He became silent and looked toward my painting.

I liked the jovial version of the earl better. "Thank you again for the flowers and the fruit, but it's not enough. You think you can come here and talk me into forgiving you?"

"I'm an officer of the court. The flowers are no bribe."

"Bribe, maybe not, but you are trying to influence me. Between the two of us, sir, you possess the most secrets. I'm trying to decide if your long silence was on purpose or if you are using it to torment me."

"You're very talkative. I can see how silence is a torment."

"Did you deem me unworthy of knowing about the *Minerva*? I think your reticence is a type of empowerment."

"You strung together all those thoughts by glancing at me, ma'am?"

I flung my palm, spreading out my fingers. The pinched skin still stung. "Yes. I must be a pawn to you, to be set aside or squished like a bug."

"No. Not all." He approached. His hovering, unlike Willingham, smelled sweet like cedar and starch. It wasn't odious or fishy or salty.

"Hand me your hand, Mrs. St. Maur." He lowered his cupped palm. "Please."

I touched his fingers for a few seconds before I jerked away. "What are you going to do?"

"Examine your injury."

"Why? Are you a doctor now?"

The heavy sigh leaving his nostrils made me nervous. "Mrs. St. Maur, please. I won't hurt you. I'd like to make it better."

"Fine." I lifted my palm to his.

"We need to be in more light." He adjusted his spectacles, then led me to the gilded sconce by the mantel. "You're in possession of a splinter."

"A splinter?" I drew my hand away and studied the redness.

"Yes, ma'am, let me remove it. You keep talking to distract yourself. Ask me questions."

This was hard with the earl touching my palm, poking at the soreness.

"Umm. Why have you waited until today to come?"

"My court schedule is very busy. I also wanted you to calm. I'm not partial to being slapped."

Yank. He tugged the sliver out.

It hurt but much less than having a wooden stake beneath my skin, but the tingle or shock coursing through me remained. Ashbrook still had my hand.

"Keep it balled up tight. It's very red."

I did, and he went into the hall and asked Mr. Gerard to bring him a glass of brandy. A few minutes later he returned with a glass of the duke's fine liquor.

"You were thirsty?"

"Goodness no. Not this stuff. This is for you." He took Mr. Willingham's handkerchief, dipped it in the glass, then sopped the cloth across my palm.

"Ouch. It burns, you fiend."

He held my arm, kept my hand from slipping away. "Easy. It will clean the wound and keep the soreness from festering."

"Oh. Thank you, I think."

He closed my fingers, then spread them. "Do that a few times. Tell me if you feel anything. I want to make sure there is nothing more."

There was plenty to be felt, with the warm, rough feel of his skin on mine, the short puffs of heated breaths from him blowing on everything that stung.

My heart gonged. Could he hear the cymbals banging in my chest? "You." I swallowed. "You act as if you care, Lord Ashbrook."

"Is that such an improbable thing?"

"I wish you weren't so confusing."

"Well, ma'am, if you understood me, you'd find I'm rather dull. But you? I've pondered your letters. The anticipation of what you'd write next crossed my mind more than I care to admit. Made me actually hope to hear you say you forgave me."

"Are you asking to be forgiven? That would mean that you heard my objections and acknowledged them as facts."

"Cute. Legal talk. But you are right." He stroked my palm along the red veining. "I am sorry. The physicians said you must remember on your own. Nothing forced. I could say I was swayed by them. That would be a cowardly admission and mostly not true."

He stopped in midswirl of his finger, right on the lifeline vein. "I wanted to protect you. I know what I lost on the *Minerva*. If I could spare you that pain, any pain, I would."

His voice became a warm whisper, easy and soothing to my ears. "I don't want you sad, or aggrieved. Forgive me, Jemina St. Maur?"

It was affectionate, even passionate, the way he asked. To say yes, did that mean I'd lose my power? I had to be powerful, to engender such words.

I shrugged and moved to the lilies. "These flowers should have water."

"That doesn't sound like you are ready to consider my apology. Should I return another time?"

"You're forgiven if you will tell me more about the ship. Do you know how many nightmares I've had that now make sense?"

"No. Tell me about them."

My throat felt a little dry.

Ashbrook closed the distance between us. "You remember being on the *Minerva*? Tell me all about it, Mrs. St. Maur. I'm listening."

"I'm confused, but that's a common occurrence when I think of my past."

His lips pursed. His eyes darted. Of course, he liked me this way.

I went to the door and opened it. "You may leave. Thank you for the flowers and the doctoring. And the pomegranate. It looks ripe."

He crossed his arms and didn't budge. "It is ripe, with its flesh taut and ready for you. The seeds should be bright red, red like your cheeks when you blush. Please close the door. I wish for a few more minutes."

With such a description of a pomegranate, how could I refuse? I yielded and closed the door, this time without a splinter.

The earl played with a button on his coat. "Mrs. St. Maur, I hadn't ever expected to speak of the *Minerva* again. I want to forget losing . . . so much. I apologize. I remember the anticipation of counting the days for my Phoebe to arrive, then waiting for weeks to see the mast and flags of the ship. The crowds in Portsmouth . . . I wore lignum vitae pinned on my waistcoat for her. So she'd see it and know me."

His powerful voice dimmed. The wave of sorrow in his words rushed at me like a hurricane.

This man was still in mourning. I hurt for him. "I'm sorry."

"I suppose it's silly to hear me speaking of such. It's been two years . . . feels so fresh."

As if he needed something real and tangible to ground him to now, he again clutched my hand and massaged it. "You remember nothing of Cecil St. Maur, none of his habits or dealings?"

With a slight shake of my head, I opened myself up to Ashbrook's condemnation. My husband died on that boat, the boat that killed the barrister's wife.

He felt everything, and I nothing.

Shamed, waves of guilt dragged me down. The tears I'd locked away began to slip out.

A swipe at each eye did nothing but smear salty tears along my face.

Oh, Lord, I was falling to pieces in front of him.

"I'm sorry, Mrs. St. Maur. This is not what I wanted. I never wanted to make you cry. That's why I hadn't said a word. I take full responsibility. I did this. Please. Please accept my apology."

"You've seen me at my worst, in chains, my hair matted. My chemise ripped and dirty. What's a sobbing fool to her barrister?"

"No fool. Just human."

His arms wrapped about me, drawing me from the waves. I held him tight. I couldn't drown in these emotions if I kept my head up, if I threw my arms around him as I'd done the ship's mast.

A ship's mast? A new memory.

Ashbrook drew me closer, fitting me to his chest. "This isn't working, woman. I can't bring you more pain, not when we are both tied to the *Minerva*. Mrs. St. Maur, it's best we both forget."

His strong embrace fell away. A chill coursed over me with the heat of him gone.

Yet, he stayed near and patted my arm as if that was the sensible way to end this moment in which loss had united us.

"Sir, you could've quoted poetry again."

His half smile became full and I saw the little gap.

The door to the parlor flung open.

It was Willingham. "I forgot my handkerchief. Mrs. St. Maur, you've been crying. Lord Ashbrook, what's going on in here? I demand to know."

I held Ashbrook's gaze and did the one thing I could do to send the bothersome Willingham fleeing forever.

"Help me, friend?"

Tugging on Ashbrook's perfect cravat, I drew his head to mine.

Then I became the girl who kissed the earl.

Chapter 15

Daniel—The Danger of a Kiss

Withdraw, Daniel.

Turn away.

Stop kissing this woman in the duke's parlor. The mad Duke of Repington who let his troops exhibit with cannons in his grand hall.

Daniel and Mrs. St. Maur weren't courting or promised to each other. Until this moment, had they even liked each other?

Yet his hands pulling her off-balance said he had. That war of where her freckled nose would go versus his larger flared one ended. He went left, she right, harmony in a delicious kiss.

This was better than arguing or teasing her. She filled his arms and he enjoyed all of it, all her curves, all the beats of her passionate heart pressed against him.

"Ashbrook, unhand her!"

Mrs. St. Maur leaned back. "No, his hands are in the right place. Leave, Mr. Willingham."

She laughed and kissed Daniel again. Her fingers sought the tight waves of his hair, forcing a part where there was none. The touch didn't seem like curiosity, but maybe it was. Yet, it was hard to ignore her nails, the hunger in them, each of her languid strokes.

Huzzah.

This time, he caressed her fully, savoring the hints of vanilla and chocolate in her breath.

He'd admired her spunk. Hell—

Willingham pounded closer. "Ashbrook, I said let her go."

Daniel broke from their kiss but nuzzled her ear, the lobe, such supple skin. "Mrs. St. Maur, whose orders do I follow?"

Even as he asked, his hand slipped to her side, beneath her shawl . . .

Her eyes went wider, the darkness of her irises sparkled, reflecting on his slipping lenses. "I require another kiss before we talk about the papers."

"As you wish. Sorry, old boy. Duty calls."

This time Daniel went for it, earning moans, deep sighs, the reward of inspecting her backside. It wasn't so flat. It was surprisingly firm. Climbing buildings does a body good.

Willingham was certain to strike him, so this needed to be worth it.

And it was.

And . . . it . . . was.

The world would explode if he moved from this moment.

Warm. Passionate. Chocolaty. Jemina St. Maur was a force of nature. Whipping a storm of desire, a full-blown cyclone about him.

Not right.

Not in her best interest.

Not—Hell, did she just moan his name?

A fist slammed into his back. "You, bounder, I told you to leave her alone."

Daniel took another blow and protected Jemina. He eased her to his side, so the jealous buffoon didn't accidentally strike her.

"Mr. Willingham," she said, "I chose him. You need to leave, leave for good."

Willingham took off his coat. "You're confused. Time to teach the fancy earl a lesson."

Daniel caught Willingham's fist and powered him backward. A

regular at Gentleman Jackson's 13 Bond Street classes and trained in pugilism by his friend Richmond, Daniel had technique and used the strength he built living on the streets, surviving for months, all alone.

"You don't want to do this, Willingham," he said. "I don't want to hurt you. You must go."

"No, half-breed, you should and leave this woman to a real man, a pure one."

"Pure? A glorious widow, a man of the world, a buffoon in shipping. Not sure of your definition. Maybe Mrs. St. Maur is pure, not remembering how men roughhouse. Let's take this outside."

"Gentlemen, *tan tedy*, please. I mean *stand still*, please. I asked you to leave, Mr. Willingham. You're not welcome."

"He's confused you, the slick-tongued devil. That's what they do." Willingham balled up his fists. "I'm going to enjoy knocking you down, a lot."

He charged, but Daniel had sized him up weeks ago when he'd seen the man hovering about Mrs. St. Maur while sending inquiries to confirm her dower payment.

Daniel ducked the fool's blow but grasped the man's weaker arm and twisted it behind Willingham's back.

Willingham jerked and twisted but couldn't buck free. "Ashbrook, let me go, so I can punch that nose."

"Why would I indulge that? It would inhibit future kisses from my favorite client."

"You pompous—" Willingham tried to wrench away.

Leaner than the brute, Daniel was strategic and twisted the fool's arm until Willingham squealed like a pig. "Let go. Fight fair!"

"All's fair in love and war. You're intruding, Willingham. Stop being a boar."

"Jemina, the fast-talking devil has bamboozled you. That's what they do."

Daniel crushed the fool's fingers within his palm. "They? You mean barrister? Good barristers give our clients what they want. I'm very good. I'm what she wants."

He shoved Willingham forward toward the door.

The fool charged back again leading with his left.

Daniel punched him in the jaw, delivering speed and power. Richmond would be proud, but all he had to do was imagine the sneer on his uncle's face when he kicked Daniel, the boy, his heir, to the streets. With his bottled-up anger, he could beat Willingham or any man into the ground.

The fool squealed when Daniel caught him again and led him out of the parlor. "Do you understand, Willingham? You're no longer welcome to Sandlin Court or to Mrs. St. Maur."

Mr. Gerard waved at a footman. The front doors opened wide and Daniel flung the fool outside.

Picking himself off the ground, Willingham rubbed his arm. "Watch your back, Barrister."

"Have your tailor watch yours. That's a poor fit." Daniel tossed the poorly made jacket at Willingham's head. "Good day."

The shipper stomped away to his carriage.

The doors closed.

Old Mr. Gerard tugged on his dark coat and stepped into Daniel's way. "Do you know what you're doing, your lordship?"

The man's stare settled on Daniel. A thousand unsaid words of caution transmitted between the them.

"Getting rid of a pest for Mrs. St. Maur, Mr. Gerard."

The old man, the old Blackamoor man, frowned. "Well, at least you chose the good heiress. Keep your head, sir. The mad ones seek revenge. They don't like their noses tweaked by us or earls."

What Mr. Gerard said was true. The realities of society life—knowing acceptable behavior and one's place—all lay etched in the butler's tired face.

"I'm an officer of the court, Mr. Gerard. I'll be fine."

"If you say so, sir. I'm rooting for you. My shillings are on black."

Mr. Gerard proceeded into the grand hall while Daniel returned to the parlor.

The unpredictable widow found a vase for the lilies. She had the pomegranate in her palms. "I shall sketch this."

"If you are wondering about Willingham, he's gone. Been wanting to do that for a while. Goodness, that felt good."

"What? Kissing me or beating on Willingham?"

He caught her gaze, those incredibly reddened lips, that teasing cupid's bow.

Her tresses had come down, big reddish-brown braids had unraveled from her chignon. Her eyes were dark, like fiery polished agate with bits of jade swirled in a sea of coffee-brown.

"Lord Ashbrook, I asked which, the kiss or the punch?"

"The . . . I know you only made a show of things for Willingham. Right, Mrs. St. Maur?"

She didn't say anything, just glanced at him as she often did like he'd done something wrong.

Had he?

Maybe he should say he wanted her back in his arms to savor her mouth as much as her chocolate breath. If he were crazed, he'd tell her he craved the feel of her clanging heart against him and that he'd dream of it, of her tonight and every night until his blood cooled.

Not a word of this uttered from his lips. He merely stared.

"At least you didn't apologize, sir. I think it would be very hypocritical to enjoy a kiss, then kill its memory by saying you didn't mean any of it."

"Technically, I returned your kiss."

She glared at him and ducked her fists under her shawl.

"Never mind. My fault, ma'am."

"Lord Ashbrook, I grabbed you to drive Mr. Willingham away, hopefully for good."

"You make a very sound argument, Mrs. St. Maur. I think it's best we never mention it."

He started to the door.

She gave chase, then reached forward as if to straighten his cravat, but she slapped him.

It didn't hurt as badly as the one at the Lincoln's Inn. She hadn't even put any power to it.

"Ma'am, you're losing your touch."

"That was for you, to pretend to be outraged by my scandalous behavior. I put myself on you, but you're too much of a gentleman to complain."

"So you slapped me to pretend I'm slapping you?" He squinted at her wondering if both of them had lost their way. "Well, your touch was light. You're too generous to yourself. Good day, madame."

"Wait, why did you finally come?"

"Folly, I assure you. I wanted to talk of the past with someone who'd understand, but between your violence and need to kiss me, I'm not sure it's wise."

"You wouldn't be abused if you weren't so pompous or so noble. I have amnesia. I don't need to be protected. I chose to be kissed. I chose you."

"That, ma'am, is the most frightening thing anyone has ever said to me. Good day."

Out the room, he fled before those passion-stained eyes saw into his soul and saw all the lies he told himself about not wanting her.

Safe on the other side of the door, he leaned against it and straightened his mangled cravat.

"You still there, Ashbrook?" Mrs. St. Maur's voice, low and sultry, seeped through the door and touched him, vibrating along his wavering spine.

"Ashbrook, I hear you breathing."

"Yes, ma'am, I'm here, but not for long. My cravat needs to be fixed before I'm seen in the world. Can't let anyone know that I've been in a brawl or compromised."

"I don't mean to confuse you. I do thank you for your help."

"You're welcome. Any time . . ." What was he saying?"

"Your pomegranate will be my next artwork. Will you visit to-morrow, so we can discuss what you came to say? I won't kiss you. I promise."

Those had to be the second worst words a pretty woman had ever said to him. "No, I'm busy for the rest of my days."

As he turned, he nearly banged into the Duke of Repington. The man pushed his invalid chair closer, rolling the big front wheels near Daniel's feet. His back must be aggravating him.

"Ashbrook, you're here? Have you rescued Mrs. St. Maur from her suitor? My meeting ran a little long."

How not to appear guilty? "Yes. I . . . I helped."

The duke leaned forward. "Is everything well, Ashbrook?"

Mrs. St. Maur opened the door, every hair in place. She looked pristine.

Daniel tweaked his lenses. This escapade was starting to feel like a Widow's Grace exploit. Or a dream, something forbidden and sweet.

"Your Grace," she said, "is your back hurting you?"

"A little, Mrs. St. Maur. Too much crawling with Lionel and horsey. My son said Papa before his nap. Tell my duchess he said Papa, not Wellington." He brought his thumbs up to his lips. "Is everything in order here?"

Daniel said nothing. The duke might not be at his best today, but a bullet from his side arm didn't need to fly that far. He peered at Mrs. St. Maur, almost begging her to say nothing.

"Your Grace, would you mind seeing Lord Ashbrook to the door? I'm going to check on Patience," she said, her tone even and calm. "Ashbrook, we'll finish our conversation later. I'll find you."

Not willing to think about the implications of her *finding* and *choosing* him, he buttoned his lips and nodded.

She curtsied and went deeper into the house.

"What does that mean, Ashbrook? She'll find you?"

"Women, Your Grace. What does anything mean?"

The duke leaned back and looked up with narrowing blue

eyes. "You're in trouble, Ashbrook. I don't do trouble here, not with my wife's dearest friend."

"Understood. Good day, Your Grace."

Daniel bowed, then retreated to the outer door. A footman had readied his top hat and sleek onyx gloves.

Tugging them on, Daniel stormed out, never looking back, never intending to come back. He kept his head down until he stood by his carriage outside Sandlin Court.

As he climbed up the step and plopped onto the sleek tufted seat, he laughed at himself. Jemina St. Maur had won this round, getting him attacked by Willingham and further ensconced on the duke's suspicions list.

Daniel's orderly life had no need for an unpredictable widow, even if she tasted of fire and chocolate.

CHAPTER 16

JEMINA—BARRISTER SURVEILLANCE

I kept my head low in the hedgerow, peeking out at the lone estate on Finchely Road. It looked the same in the moonlight as it did the day I first visited—big, fanciful, so many windows.

Never would I forget that night the barrister freed me from Bedlam. He took Patience and me here, fed us pheasant and fresh bread while we waited for Lady Shrewsbury to arrive. The roast was juicy and the buttery shortbreads with caraway seeds and currants so crisp. My tongue hadn't known such delight in two years, maybe more.

Had I ever thanked him?

No.

Instead, I kissed him to drive away a suitor.

A noise like a crunch sounded close, but I saw nothing, so I turned back to the house.

The lower level had darkened but not the second floor. It glistened with light.

Odd for this time of night, well past ten.

Odd for me to be out too, but I needed to learn about him. I'd sent him notes all week. He didn't reply. He knew more. I needed to find out what. My dreams had become too vivid.

The nightmares were getting worse. This time I saw things so clearly, I felt a chill in my bones. I struggled to stay afloat, twisting up the bedsheets and blankets.

The crackle of a leaf, a snap of a twig—I wasn't alone. I crouched lower in the hedgerow and waited.

A leather glove covered my mouth. My heart seized.

"Shhh, Jemina. It's me."

Readying to fight, I lifted my gaze, my hands.

Patience had me.

"You scared me." It was all I could muster. Too many lumps in my throat.

She squatted down beside me. "You scared me first. Jemina, you accompanied the duke and me to Town. You said it would be a change of pace from the country. You didn't say you'd be running out in the night. What if we had a mission?"

"I have a mission."

"The countess told you to come by yourself?"

"Not a Widow's Grace mission, a Jemina St. Maur mission."

"I don't understand. Help me understand."

Her whispers sunk into my skull, but my caution was spent. I held her tight, my fingers tangling into her thick cape, knocking off the hood. "Help me. I'm dying inside."

"I will, Jemina. I will."

She rocked me, embracing me, anchoring me to now, the present. "Talk to me."

"Patience, I'm in a dray going down a street. The street, King Street runs North and South. Two-story houses with wide verandas line the view. Green and yellow structures with green and white shutters. It's peaceful with palm trees and purply lignum vitae in yards."

"You remember Jamaica?"

"Kingston, I think. The streets are dirt, pounded flat by all the travel. The air is hot, the wind whips the palms and wide guango trees. The sky is red and blue, magnificent. Then I'm boarding a boat."

Patience rubbed my shoulders. "You're remembering."

"That's it. I can't see anyone else. I can't see . . ."

"See what, your husband? That's fine, Jemina. Remembering a little—"

"That day Ashbrook brought us here. You and I ate pheasant and shortbread. Such a treat. Then he left us with Lady Shrewsbury when a baby cried. That shriek was so loud."

"Yes, Jemina, that must have been his daughter."

"Nothing felt true or lasting until that moment. That child's wail, that little voice was like a trumpet heralding to me that things were going to be different."

"Yes. It made me ache for my Lionel. When I saw him again—"

"It made me remember that I lost my child."

"Jemina! On the *Minerva*?"

I pounded my head. "I don't have all the pieces. I didn't see a child's name on the list, but maybe in Jamaica. Maybe I left the babe in Kingston. Could that be possible? Why does it have to mean disaster? Does my babe have to die like Cecil?"

She kissed my brow. "I'm so sorry."

"I'm hunting a child in my nightmares, Patience. I know it. Every time I get close, I wake up or I'm in Bedlam screaming for my baby until I'm hoarse. And every man is telling me he doesn't exist."

"Don't torture yourself like this, Jemina. Don't. The memories could be of a niece or nephew or cousin back in Kingston. Maybe you were a governess to a wealthy fam—"

"The earl in there said I'm an heiress. I have a fortune. Why would I work as a governess?" My tone was hot with bitterness. I was grateful to have means, but what is money to a lost son? "The baby who haunts my dreams has to be mine. If my child was still in Kingston wouldn't the family I left be looking for me?"

"You sure, Jemina? The sinking of the *Minerva* could be mixing up your recollection."

"I didn't ask about my husband, Patience, because I didn't remember him, but I remember singing to a child. My song was loud and proud. You know my lullaby. '*Il était un petit navire. Il était un petit navire.*' 'There was once a little boat. There was once a little boat.'"

My eyes ran with water. "I sang that to my baby. I have to know the truth."

Patience.

My Patience sobbed.

I'd hurt her heart with my story. I had to put her back together and hugged her tight. "I would sing it again, but it would probably be too loud."

"Blubbering and laugher doesn't mix, Jemina." She swiped at her eyes.

"This could be a mistake. Some twisted nightmare that I've made true. Just because I remember fighting the water and the *Minerva*, that doesn't make the rest true. But it feels true."

Patience snort sniffled. "We'll figure it out, but answers surely won't come from sitting outside Finchely."

"Ashbrook knows my past. Rather rude of him not to share."

"Let's go ask him, or are you going to kiss him instead?"

My cheeks heated. "No, unless you think that will get a confession."

"Jemina?"

I nodded. "I know, but he has evidence in there. Has to."

Patience glanced toward the house. "This place is smaller than my Lionel's Hamlin Hall, but it seems spacious. Plenty of places for children. I hear Ashbrook's a good father. He dotes upon his daughter. Loves her something fierce."

"Why are you telling me this?"

"There's many ways to get into that house, Jemina. I know you to be excellent with children. Maybe offer to help the bachelor."

"You think he'd let me, a woman locked in Bedlam for two years who now thinks she has a child, be around his?"

"Jemina, you're harmless, and do you think he'd let you kiss him if he thought you were insane?"

"He's a man. He says I'm pretty. None of this requires a physician's proof of sanity."

"If you think that physical attraction is all there is between you and Ashbrook, go for it. Have at him. That would get you in the house."

I pulled away shaking my head. "You're teasing."

"Yes, I am. Let's corner him and ask direct questions. Lady Shrewsbury's dinner at week's end. He has to be there for his aunt."

"That doesn't sound easy, questioning a barrister."

Patience threaded her hands with mine. "You don't have to do this alone. I'll help."

"You're wearing yourself thin fretting about the duke and his meetings with the War Department. He's doing too much, remember?"

"Not too busy for you. You're a sister to me."

She put our hands together again. Her white gloves, my bare hand—we looked the same in the moonlight. We were sisters, sisters of Bedlam, sisters of love.

"You and I have a bond, Patience. That must never be broken." I rubbed at my temples as if I could jog something loose. "I may need Ashbrook's unwitting assistance to learn more."

"His what?"

"Unwitting assistance. You know, burglarizing his things again until we find the truth. I need to know. I deserve to know. No one will stop me this time."

"You're angry, like someone is keeping you from the truth."

She spun my face toward hers. Could she read my thoughts?

"Jemina, who do you think is against you? The Widow's Grace?"

"You said it. Lady Shrewsbury controls everything. She loves her nephew, and he's hiding the truth."

"Lady Shrewsbury . . . the countess and her network have freed us from Bedlam. Ashbrook drafted the papers. How could they wish you ill?"

"We've worked so many operations. You've seen what happens. We get the intelligence first about a cheated widow. Then we talked with the widow and put together a plan. Then we act."

"Yes, you and I have become quite good at this."

"That didn't happen for us. No one asked anything of us. Ashbrook said I was free, but I wouldn't leave you. He came back hours later and had the paperwork to free you, too."

"I am so grateful to you and to him. I—"

"*Ku ya*, Patience! Look here, my friend, he did it. We were not a Widow's Grace operation. We were a Daniel Thackery project. He's the one with the reasons and the truth. Lady Shrewsbury has to be covering for him."

"Why, Jemina? Why would he rescue us other than him being a good man who recognized your name on a list?"

"I don't know. In my heart, I know he's not evil, but until I have all the answers, I'm lost. Every nightmare is pushing me closer to him or back to Bethlehem Hospital. Bedlam. Bedlam."

"You're not going crazy. I'll not allow you to return there. The Widow's Grace is meant to save widows in dire straits. You're safe. You're with me. I'll help you any way I can."

"Then help me get to the truth. I don't know what else to do. My baby's waiting for me when I close my eyes. I have to know his name or tell her I miss her. I have to know my baby."

Patience stood and brushed leaves from her cape. "We'll get answers. Widows have to be smarter. And with the clever barrister, persistent and lucky."

She stretched out her hand to me. "Take my arm. We'll get you another audience with Lord Ashbrook."

"But I wrote him. He hasn't accepted another meeting."

"Keep writing him. If you stop, he'll suspect a new tactic. We don't want him suspicious."

I squinted at Patience. "You've been putting many things together about me and Ashbrook."

"Anyone who kisses you in my parlor and brawls another suitor has my attention. But I don't want him to hurt you."

"I did get hurt. I had a splinter. Ashbrook made it all better. Then I kissed him to be rid of Willingham."

Her mouth opened, then closed, then opened again. "I suspect you keep him on edge with your humor."

She tugged on her cap, her face full of love and laughter. "We'll start by getting him to come to Lady Shrewsbury's dinner."

"I've been watching him every night; he never goes out. The only visitors are his card-playing buddies."

Shaking her head, she walked me back to where I'd hidden the horse I borrowed, the duke's Shire, Zeus. She patted her hand along the silver mane. "He's a good one. The duke's stables are the finest."

"Where's your horse, Patience? I'll wait."

"No, I took a carriage. I'm still not feeling myself. Summer colds are the worst. I'll get Lady Shrewsbury to ensure Ashbrook comes to the dinner. You'll clear up the confusion. Maybe then he will set an appointment to discuss everything. But we must be careful. Gossiping Lady Bodonel will be there."

I'd watched him playing with his daughter or reading in his study. Why did he have to be a man with secrets? "I'll keep writing him."

"Jemina, trust me. You'll have truth and anything else you want. You made my dreams possible. It's time for yours to come true."

"I don't want my dreams, Patience. I want to be wrong. The only part of my life that I can recall can't be loss."

She held the reins steady, readying for me to mount. "The truth will be yours, Jemina. I'll be here to love you through it."

If Ashbrook wouldn't cooperate, I wasn't sure what to do next, but sitting around waiting wasn't something I could stomach anymore. I didn't know what I was capable of, but the truth wouldn't be denied, even if I had to become ruthless to get it.

CHAPTER 17

DANIEL—WAITING FOR PAPA

A sigh laced with doubt steamed out of his soul. Daniel sat back in his carriage, hoping Mr. Anthon could hurry his arrival to Finchely. It was ten thirty.

Missed story time, and Hope could be balling in her crib.

The Lord Mayor again had Daniel in his chambers for two hours. Rumors were rampant about illegal releases of patients from Bedlam. The man browbeat Daniel and three other barristers.

The Lord Mayor could piece together Daniel's involvement with the Widow's Grace if more noise was made.

Who was stirring up trouble?

He stroked his watch fob, then looked to the darkened road. It would be another ten minutes before he arrived at Finchely House.

"I have a capable housekeeper. I just employed a diligent nanny-nurse, one who Hope seems to take to. My little girl is fine."

Well, his daughter sort of ignored the new nanny after her first day of employment. She didn't want to share her toys with the woman, which was highly unusual for his moppet.

Yet, with two women managing his household, perhaps it was time to find something for himself. Or perhaps doing something about the widow who stayed on his mind.

Jemina St. Maur.

Her notes kept coming, even after their kiss. Her latest note made him fret, then laugh, then enjoy the fact that he'd been caught in a rumor as a rake. The carriage lantern illuminated the stationery that he pulled from his pocket.

> *Finchely House,*
> *London, July 26, 1814*
>
> *Dear Lord Ashbrook,*
> *I will say sorry in advance.*
> *Lady Bodonel, the Duke of Repington's mother*
> *came to tea. She delighted in gossiping about an earl*
> *and his widowed client. It was horrible keeping a*
> *straight face as she said we'd had at each other and*
> *rolled all over the floor.*
> *You seem to do good work standing. Why would a*
> *floor make for better gossip?*
> *The Duchess of Repington and I are going to the*
> *market. If you were thinking of coming to Sandlin*
> *Court to help strategize our way out of the rumors, I*
> *suggest that you wait another day.*
> *Mr. Gerard told me in confidence that the butcher*
> *confirms you and I are having a raucous affair full of*
> *mirth and decadence. I'm not sure how to end this*
> *faux alliance or if we should, since we seem to be hav-*
> *ing so much fun.*
> *Surely that wouldn't be right.*
>
> *J. St. Maur*
> *Sandlin Court, London*

Her words, the irreverence of them lingered like sweet flowers or heady perfume. If only she were a different kind of woman, one that would enjoy raucous but discreet trysts with a hermit who needed to fit their appointments on his way from court to Finchely.

Perhaps a town house on the northern edge of London would do. Then he'd have only a thirty-minute drive to home. Hedonism and efficiency.

The notion sounded ridiculous.

A hermit could dream.

Another glance out the window showed he was at least five minutes from Finchely. No fences or hedgerows or forests with ironwood trees sprouting blue violet lignum vitae.

The ache of missing Phoebe, the guilt of her not being by his side wasn't quite as strong as before. Liking Jemina, thinking of that woman who was here in London writing Daniel notes—did that shake something free in his chest?

He sat back and reread Jemina's letter until Finchely's fences, the lumber ties showed. *Almost there, Hope.*

He grasped his fob and fingered the deeply etched *T* on the surface. "Lord, let my tot sleep through the night."

Was it fine to pray for such things within moments of contemplating debauchery?

Being a hermit and dealing with the Lord Mayor's suspicions had surely driven him mad.

The carriage stopped.

Daniel stuffed the letter in his coat, grabbed his hat and gloves and ran through the hedges, up the drive, and into the main door.

Then he heard the sound of terror. His little girl wailed at the top of her lungs. It shattered everything in his chest.

He tossed his things. His valet's warnings could go to the devil as he flung his jacket to the polished floorboards and leaped up the stairs.

Arriving to the second floor, Daniel slid across the indigo-blue carpet runner on the landing.

Flinging open the door, he found his little girl standing in her crib. Her eyes were big and red as if she'd cried a river.

With two big chunky silk braids falling down her back, her wet face lifted, and she raised her hands to him. "Pa-Papa!"

His soul broke and mended as he scooped her up. "Papa's here, Hope. I'm here, princess."

She put her soggy little palms about his neck. "I thought . . . thought you gone! Gone like Mama."

He lifted her apple face to his forehead, so she could see his resolve. "No, dearest. Never. The Lord Mayor . . . Long day working."

Hope blinked twice. Her sobs slowed. "Pa-Papa here. Papa, no leave?"

"No." He held her tight, snuggling her to his chest. "I have you. I'll always be here, maybe just a little late."

Daniel rocked her and looked toward the hall. "Where's your nanny? She's not supposed to go until you're asleep."

Hope's long dark brown lashes closed. She cried harder. "Gone."

"What? The new nanny left? Mrs. Gallick. Where's Mrs. G?"

As if his questions had summoned her, his housekeeper entered the nursery holding a tray of tea and raspberry biscuits. "Sir, you've returned."

Still bouncing Hope, he pivoted to Mrs. Gallick, a woman who'd known Daniel since he was born. He took a breath and mustered up his practiced calm. "I have, Mrs. G. Where's Hope's nanny? She's not supposed to leave my child alone at night."

The sturdy, graying brunette, a woman of good temperance and judgment frowned as if she wanted to spit. "The deplorable thing is gone."

"See?" Hope wailed anew.

He put his hand to her head, stroking the curly tresses that framed her face. "It's not that type of gone. Right, Mrs. Gallick?"

"No, sir. She's terminated."

The bitterness in the woman's voice didn't sound as if the nanny had died, but that his housekeeper might have wanted her dead.

"Do explain, ma'am."

"The foul harlot is gone." The woman dropped her gaze as if the tea were the most interesting thing. "I terminated her on your behalf, lordship."

He adjusted his spectacles and counted to ten before starting again. "You terminated Hope's nanny. Why? For what reason? She's been a good employee these last weeks."

"I don't want to say in front of the child."

"Gone, nanny dead, too."

"No, Hope." He made eyes at his housekeeper to help. "Please. Out with it, Mrs. G."

"She was in your bed, naked. Not a stitch of clothes on her. I told her I had to run errands. She must've thought I'd be gone for the night."

"What the . . . naked? Truly, not a stitch?"

"Naked as a bird. I made her fly away."

He felt his face stretching trying to hold in his laughter. "Why would she do this? I'm not that type of employer."

"The woman was waiting for you, an attempt at a compromise. She's an on-the-shelf wallflower with connections. Lady Lavinia Nell stopped by almost at the exact moment. I think they were in on it together. The beastly women were determined to make everyone think that the new Earl of Ashbrook was horrid. Maybe even trying for a harem."

His mouth surely dropped open and hit the floor, maybe crashed through down to his study. "Was she, were they drunk?"

"Calculating shrews." Mrs. Gallick rotated the silver tray in her hands. The cup and teakettle wobbled. "I tossed the nanny out as soon as she could lace on her corset. That evil woman won't be made your countess and break your mother's heart, God rest her soul."

"And I dealt with Lady Lavinia."

That voice. If he wasn't holding Hope, he'd stand up straight, at attention. "Lady Shrewsbury, I didn't know you were here."

Mrs. Gallick passed him and headed deeper into the nursery. "Your tea, ma'am."

The woman stopped in front of his rocking chair by the window—the one occupied by his aunt.

His heart stopped for a moment, but rage made it beat again. "Mrs. G, you didn't say we had company."

"We do, sir. She came to help with the dismissal and to take care of Lady Lavinia." The housekeeper pivoted back to Lady Shrewsbury. "It's chamomile like you like with a little bit of spirits."

She winked, and the two laughed.

But Daniel fumed.

Mrs. Gallick had sent for his aunt to ensure there we no ramifications of a half-naked woman and a gossip scheming at Finchely.

This was his sanctuary with his daughter.

This was a violation. He tightened his hold on Hope. "Aunt," he said, "take your tea. Wait for me in my study. I'll get Hope settled, then we'll talk."

Lady Shrewsbury, the blond cherub nodded. "Of course, Daniel. There's much to be said."

She took her cup and left with Mrs. Gallick.

When the door closed, Daniel moved to the rocking chair.

Hope flopped onto his lap and he settled her against his waistcoat.

"Nanny not dead, but no—no come back, Pa-Papa?"

The woman needed to be imprisoned for pulling such a stunt, but stupidity wasn't a crime. "She's probably a little chilly but very much alive. She'll not be back."

He sank against the wooden spindles of the seat. Slowly, he started the motion Hope liked, back and forth, not too fast, not too slow.

"No like her. Pa-Papa, just need you."

"You have Phoebe's heart, don't you? She wrote that she just needed me." He hoped that part was true. So much had been left unsaid.

Hope closed her eyes. "No more anyone go, Pa-Papa. Stay."

It was hard to be so small and understand big concepts like death and termination. The little girl burrowed deeper into his arms, grabbing his pearl buttons, some of Mr. Weston's, London's elite tailor's best.

Daniel kissed her brow and kept the chair rocking until his little angel became a sleeping, drooling sprite. Nothing seemed better or more perfect.

Too much was at risk from scheming women, daring widows, the Lord Mayor's inquiries, and Hope's nightmares.

Yet Daniel might be his own worst enemy. With his increasing fascination with notes from the rumor-torturing, lovely St. Maur, things were bound to spin out of control. He needed to take charge or be caught in the cyclone, the maddening desire of a Creole Jamaican woman. *Chubble. Chubble. Trouble.*

CHAPTER 18

DANIEL—TEA WITH LADY SHREWSBURY

Pocketing the sleeve buttons for his cuffs, Daniel took a final look at Hope. The child lay in her crib, sound asleep. Her arms locked about Mrs. Feebs, a wooden doll with big glass eyes. She looked peaceful.

He tiptoed to the hall and swatted the polished oak balusters of the railing forming the steep stairs. Slowing his steps, he crossed the pristine whitewashed hall and remembered with whom he was about to deal.

Lady Shrewsbury could smell weakness. She thrived on people underestimating her to gain full advantage.

She taught him everything he knew.

It was why his court prowess was hard to rival, why his losses were rare. He pushed on the crystal knob and stalked into the room.

A chill swept through him.

Mrs. Gallick and his aunt had pulled chairs from the dining room and lined them about the stone hearth, just as they did when his mother lived. They even left a seat as if she was expected to join them.

His aunt didn't fight fair. He refused to move closer and fall into the emotional web she'd laid. Yet, Daniel couldn't help thinking of his mother's last days. At eight, he gave her a proper burial, then returned to Finchely only to be turned away by his uncle. The man used some legal scheming to wrest control. That was the day Daniel purposed to know more of the law than anyone.

He posted at the threshold, becoming a fixture as much as the burnished paneling covering the walls. "Lady Shrewsbury, have an exciting evening? Not often do you discover a naked nanny in cahoots with my former mistress."

Mrs. Gallick must've heard the edge in his voice, one Daniel rarely ever offered. She sprung up, wiping her hands on the white apron atop her blue checked gown. "I'll leave you two to chat. Always a pleasure, Lady Shrewsbury, Lord Ashbrook."

His housekeeper fled as if her termination was next.

The woman should know that was impossible. How does one terminate Mrs. G, a second mother, one of his three counting Lady Shrewsbury?

He shut the door with a thud. "I could've handled things."

"Daniel, you're upset. Your mother always said to relinquish hard feelings before sunset. It's why she kept forgiving my wayward brother, your father."

"Well, since it's past midnight now, I've gained over fifteen hours to stew until next sundown."

Aunt padded the arm of the chair next to her, inviting him to sit . . . in his own study. "Daniel, the art above the mantel, that's new. The waters look so true."

"A local artist in Covent Garden made it. An abandoned woman, the poor pregnant lass was trying to make income. I'm drawn to the colors of the blue water, the oranges and reds of the sunset of Port Royal, Jamaica. This painting is what the artist imagined of the city before an earthquake and tidal wave destroyed it. Sort of a Sodom and Gomorrah in the Caribbean."

Arms folded, he moved a little closer. "Beauty before wrath. You look lovely tonight, Aunt. Banishing infidels agrees with you."

"You have a right to be angry, Daniel, but at whom?"

"What did you do to the exhibitionist in my bed?"

"The naked nanny, as you put it, was taken to her father's. The baron was mortified, well he *exhibited* mortification. I made sure that the incident would never be mentioned. Lady Lavinia and I came to an understanding. Your reputation is safe. She still gets to come to my dinner and the Widow's Ball."

"Safe? So, even though I was not here at the time, you believed I would get blamed?"

"Maybe, maybe not. You're an amazing barrister, a very good man."

"Apparently popular too. It's incredibly frustrating to have principles and standards and still be held under an air of suspicion."

"You're triply blessed, my boy. A scandalous father, an unprincipled swindler uncle, and—"

"And skin darker than a Corinthian gentleman?"

She offered him her polite, encouraging smile. The same one she gave when she asked a street urchin to join her for an ice. Daniel accepted. It was the best decision his nine-year-old mind had made. And she was patient to undo the damage and rage living a year on the streets did to his soul.

He sighed and rubbed at the tightness in his neck. "I must be doing something right to earn a naked nanny gambit and Lady Lavinia's attention."

He flopped in the chair next to Lady Shrewsbury and began untying his slippers.

Maximilian, his beloved pug, came from under his desk in the corner and sank at Daniel's feet. "There you are, Max. You could've chased them off. Right, boy?"

After petting his pug, fluffing his curled tail, he shrugged. "Perhaps people will remember that I possess the Thackery temper too. I can break things as well as I'm given to protect."

"Daniel, my love, you are many things, but impassioned enough to be cruel, I've never seen."

She tugged on his arm. "That's not a bad thing. It's what we wanted, what we hoped for."

His aunt said, we . . . Lady Shrewsbury still honored that missing seat. His mother feared for Daniel, being a boy of mixed race in line to inherit a fortune and a peerage.

He dropped his head to back of her chair. "I know Mother would be proud, and she would laugh at these antics."

"Gertrude would. She'd be glowing at all you've accomplished, starting with regaining her house. You've restored it these five years to such grandeur."

"Uncle's fault. He gambled too much. I was able to buy it from his debtors at a bargain."

"Well, the man tried to lose all the Ashbrook holdings when he realized you'd inherit, and there wasn't a thing he could do to stop it but live forever. Making arrangements with your father's card-playing friends to take the fool for what they could for a commission was brilliant."

"Aunt, your attempts at distracting me won't work. I'm not Jemina St. Maur."

"You fussing with her again? I heard that you two had warmed up to each other. Rolling about in fun."

Daniel didn't want to sort through his feelings for Jemina with his aunt. That was for his vingt-et-un gents, not that he'd ever bring up the mysterious woman to them. "Let's try another problem. Why did you let Hope cry? You were wrong for that."

"I was right there. She was safe. It's a tough thing to let them cry it out, but—"

"No. No. No. She's not even four. I won't have her bottling up her feelings so soon. She has to be free for as long as she can."

Lady Shrewsbury put a hand to her mouth. Her face reddened. "Is that how you feel, dear? Bottled up?"

Caged at times.

On display at others.

He released a long soul-emptying sigh. "I haven't minded becoming a hermit. But don't tell me I'm coddling Hope. Don't tell me I'm not a good father."

"Never. I can't conceive of how you've become such a good one. Neither of my brothers were decent enough to you. Your father tried, but his fondness for drink took a toll. My older brother, the late Lord Ashbrook, I can't conceive how the two of us are even related."

"Nice character testimony, Aunt, but this is my judgment. My Hope will not cry it out, she'll not be made a man at four or six or eight. She's been through too much."

His aunt stood and took the kettle warming in the fireplace and poured herself another cup.

She offered him one, but Daniel declined. not knowing if it was the doctored brew she'd shared with the housekeeper.

With her graceful movements, Lady Shrewsbury could've been a theater performer, as her oyster-colored gown trimmed in pearls floated and sparkled in the glow of the hearth. No one would ever suspect such a little woman was an evil mastermind, well not evil, not until this evening.

"I'm sorry, Daniel. It's your right to raise Hope as you see fit, but I will still offer suggestions."

Lady Shrewsbury never backed down.

Never.

This must be a new tactic.

Daniel moved to his sideboard and checked his reflection to see how hardened of a grimace he wore. His eyes looked black and beady as night behind his spectacles. His bottling up of his anger had failed.

The decanters of liquors he kept on display to offer guests held a gleam. Fear was in those potions, but Aunt had slayed most of his demons. Daniel had used the law to kill the rest.

"Brandy is your favorite, Aunt. I think it's cream for your tea."

She smiled at him with rosy cheeks, then he sat again, this time settling into his mother's seat. Very comfortable and honorable, and very much missing.

"Thank you," Lady Shrewsbury said as she set the kettle on the hearth. "Why is your mood so foul?"

"Everything. The Widow's Grace business, the Lord Mayor's suspicions. He believes someone at the Lincoln's Inn is helping in a conspiracy. I thank you for not needing me for your capers as of late, but have you considered in the smallest way stopping?"

Aunt rubbed her finger along the wrought iron poker as if dust dared to show itself in a house run by Mrs. G.

"No." Lady Shrewsbury sipped her tea, leaving the crackle of the fire to echo her resistance.

"Well, I thought I'd ask." He shook his head at the stubborn woman. "I'll ask again before one of us is carted away to prison."

"Why were you kissing Mrs. St. Maur at Sandlin Court?"

"Rumors? Aunt, I didn't think you listened to such."

"Why you are so fickle, Daniel? First Lady Lavinia, now Jemina?"

Well, if Aunt wouldn't answer his questions, he'd be selective too. "I'm not interested in Lady Lavinia, particularly now."

Lady Shrewsbury heaved a long breath. "I was concerned when I saw her eyeing you. She's looking for a fourth husband. The debts from number three have been staggering. Your elevation and fortune make you an appealing candidate."

"I was appealing to her before. I'm not exactly a new mark for that one."

Sherry eyes rolling up, she poured more amber cream into her teacup. "This I know, but now she wants to be your countess. She probably showed to save you from the nanny, a compromising witness for your character. You deserve better than a leech."

"That's a cross between a naked nanny and a hard place." He chuckled. "It's amazing how the matchmaking forces who once eschewed their daughters from dancing with the dark barrister of the courts have no qualms about my swarthy tan or ancestry now. Progress?"

"It's twisted. Your brilliance and spotless character should be enough. But let's talk about Jemina. She does fit with your collection of art and lost souls.

He pushed back against the chair's spindles. "What?"

"Collector, Daniel. The stray dog you saw begging outside the Old Bailey."

He petted his beloved hound. "Max is a loyal beast. And you don't collect, Aunt? Don't you save downtrodden women everywhere?"

"That's the Widow's Grace. But you hire a sixteen-year-old pickpocket after you've convicted him."

"Mr. Anthon was wrong, but he paid his due. Now the lad is eighteen and has become the best man-of-all-work around. He even keeps my horses exercised and with a ready saddle in case I have to ride off to keep one of your widows from the magistrate."

"And Jemina?"

Daniel glanced at Lady Shrewsbury. There was such love in the woman, but he'd been making his own decisions since Eaton. He wasn't coming to hang on her skirts now.

Leaning closer, he patted her hand. "Rest assured, Aunt. I have done nothing that she hasn't wanted. But I must break your rule. It's only fair. You didn't adhere to mine."

"What rule is this that?"

"The one about your widows. I intend to take a mistress. I want it to be Jemina St. Maur."

Lady Shrewsbury's sherry eyes widened but then lowered into a casual glance. "No, Daniel, she's delicate, unsettled in the world."

He laced his fingers with hers and kissed her hand. "She's unsettled my world, and it's your fault for sending them to burglarize the Lincoln's Inn. I have no choice but to distract her with kisses and anything else she will allow."

"Daniel!"

"If the only way for her to forget about the *Minerva* is to be my mistress and be involved in a secret all-consuming love affair, it's a sacrifice I'll make."

Her smile dimmed. "What's at risk, Daniel, other than your vanity? You haven't told me all there is about the *Minerva*."

He bit his lip, then decided to confide in her. "Hope, her safety, her growing up free, is my concern."

Aunt grasped his arm, her nails digging into his white linen sleeve. "What are you talking about?"

"You sent the Widow's Grace to the Lincoln's Inn. They stumbled upon the one time in my life I bent rules for me. I forged documents, lied, everything to keep that baby safe, so I could raise her for Phoebe."

Lady Shrewsbury mouth hung open. "You lied?"

"Proxy marriages are not legal in England. Phoebe and I were to leave Portsmouth and be married here at Finchely that night. Instead, I held a memorial and created the proof needed so that I would become Hope's rightful guardian."

Aunt clutched his hand. "You'll find no condemnation from me, but how does this affect Jemina?"

"Searching for the records of the *Minerva* will not improve Mrs. St. Maur's lot. It can only awaken the awful Dunns to Hope's existence. They will demand my daughter be sent to their sugar plantation. I hate to think of her lot there, a girl slow in speech, one still learning to walk at age three."

Aunt dipped her head. "You have done well for my niece. But this time, Daniel, we're on opposite sides. Jemina St. Maur is a member of the Widow's Grace. She's owed the truth. She must find it."

"If she's distracted, she won't care. Then she won't be climbing buildings or getting hurt. You must admit this a winning set of arguments. Aren't you always saying the great good outweighs the means?"

Her head shook as if it would wobble to floor and be a ball for Max.

"Aunt, it's out of my hands. She said she chose me. What am I to do but oblige her choosing."

He grinned, but Lady Shrewsbury didn't share his humor. It didn't matter, the *Minerva* business would stay a secret, he'd ensure it. A woman with passion consuming her heart wouldn't keep digging for ghosts of yesterday.

For the first time in a long time, Daniel knew what he wanted and that was Jemina St. Maur.

CHAPTER 19

JEMINA—A DINNER WITH SASS

Lady Shrewsbury's in-Town estate was exquisite, and so different from the remote locations she typically occupied. My eyes soaked in the grandeur of the large dining room.

Crystalline sconces were everywhere, each sparkling with candlelight. Gilded molding banded the top, middle, and bottom portions of the walls and glittered when one walked by. More golden trim befell the arched entryways.

The paint wasn't white or blue. It was something in between, and it felt as if wishes were reflected in the creamy hue.

I had a wish.

I wished Lord Ashbrook would end my suffering and tell me his secrets. I wanted answers tonight. And I hoped he wouldn't be too angry at my hurting myself on yesterday's mission.

Lady Bodonel grabbed my bruised wrist. "This dinner is just a taste of how grand the ball will be. Are you not excited?"

"Yes," I said with a wince.

She looked over my head and waved her fan. "You are an excitable one."

I watched the slim woman float away in her cream dress, light catching on the seed pearls decorating her cap sleeves. The woman accosted the Lord Mayor's wife.

Patience's mother-in-law was an interesting person. She seemed lost sometimes, but the minute you wanted to help her she'd revert to the caricature of an unfeeling creature looking for stature and greener and greener fields.

Where was Patience?

I should be able to see my friend. Where did she go? We came in together.

My frets drowned in the music.

Beautiful violins.

My comfy slippers made time with the string quartet. Tap. Tap. One of the musicians looked a lot like Ashbrook's card-playing friend.

The melody, soft and soothing—this would be a wonderful dance.

Skipping wouldn't be appropriate, but my heart did so.

Maybe I was a dancer.

Maybe I was graceful and twirled about the room with ease. Maybe that's how Cecil St. Maur and I met.

I took a step and found my slippers missed the beat. My ankle twisted a little. Well, maybe not a great dancer.

Still, the music felt good; it hit deep in my soul, lifting me. Last night's dream, I faced the nightmare, the howl of the endless winds, the sheer panic of trying to keep to my head and hers above water.

I was sure it was a girl in my arms.

A little one.

She was small, for I could hold her in the crook of my arm and the mast at least for a little while.

"Jemina, are you all right?"

"*Mi den yah.* I mean, I'm here." After a few blinks, I saw Patience's face. She looked beautiful in her cream gown with an overdress of sunny garnet.

But her smile was gone, her lips pressed too tight.

"I just left Lady Bodonel and her group of *friends*."

She stepped to my side, and I took her arm. "Do you need air, Your Grace?"

"No, too much time with my mother-in-law. She can't be tolerated in long settings. Goodness." She rubbed her brow. "We still have to get through dinner."

We moved from the crowd and made our way closer to the middle of the room. We stopped at one of the long tables. Each hosted twenty. Elegant pressed tablecloths shrouded them like snowy doves. Bisque-colored tureens sat at the ends. The air around the pots felt hot.

A peek inside exposed white soup with the heavenly scent of toasted almonds. I loved white soup. Lady Shrewsbury served this to the Widow's Grace at the end of successful missions. It was her chef's specialty.

"The colors tonight, red and white, seem to be a trend." Patience put her hand on the red chairs. Her pinkie skirting the shiny brass nails tapped into each.

Smoothing my lacy bodice, I felt sick. "Then I was meant to stand out in dove gray."

"You're still elegant, Jemina."

I toyed with my thin gloves, wishing I had waited for Patience to retrieve the sparkly pair she thought would go well with my gown. "I'm sort of overcast skies. I shouldn't have come."

Gently, she picked up my bandaged wrists. "We have to find better ways to get into places. I'm sorry you got hurt. I should've been with you."

"Patience, the duke needed you this week. I should've been more careful. Widow Cultony's not good with knots. She'll get better. I'll be better. Nothing broken, just very sore."

"Well, your glove hides most of the wrapping. Follow me," she said. Patience had me sailing through the crowds. Several of the soldiers or former soldiers that I'd seen visiting Sandlin Court were here.

"Do you think the duke sent them, Jemina? I'm not sure what

he's up to these days. I find him whispering to Lionel and Gantry in his study more and more, then he starts to treat me as if I'm fragile."

I pulled Patience to the side beneath a big urn cascading with roses and ransoms. "Dear heart, why are you given to doubt?"

"Jemina, I know he loves me and I him, but this world of London, it's not me. I'm not sure it's him. Do you know how he longs to shoot off cannons or march with his troops? You can't do that in Mayfield. Well, not easily."

"True, Mr. Gerard can't keep hiding the balls."

"Our butler and my lady's maid are the only two servants in the household who aren't in the military, but he's made them give reports too. What can they be reporting? Laundry, stockings inventory?"

She sighed and held her elbows. "I don't know if I like the people we are when we're here. I don't want to bring up Lionel under this scrutiny. I should talk to Lord Ashbrook. He might understand and have suggestions."

Him, not me? I squinted at her. This was the first time, the first moment I felt distanced from her.

"Jemina, don't frown, I didn't mean it like that. But you fit in this society more than I ever will."

When we discussed the slights she faced, we never asked if the woman I was before the *Minerva* might have been one of those heartless women who made a point to be cruel to Patience because she was mulatto. I hoped old me wasn't awful. I didn't know.

Patience lifted my hands. "You're the dearest. I love you, but some things are difficult to express unless you've walked my path and know how carefully I must always tread."

I searched her pretty dark eyes, shimmering in the light and saw a smidge of something I hadn't seen in a long time. Fear.

She stroked my arm. "Let's see whom we shall be sitting with. Lady Shrewsbury won't let us be together."

I let the moment go. I didn't know how to ask her to explain why the small slights of strangers made her feel low or of the lingering hurt of being singled out because she was different. I couldn't let her remember that pain, not when she needed to focus on smiling and getting through this evening.

We moved back to the grand tables. Servers added silver chargers to hold the bone-white plates. They topped each with crisp starch napkins. The sweet starch made me think of the earl.

I picked up the card that read *Lord Ashbrook*, then put it down as a footman lit the candelabras. Polished to a mirror shine, they sat on the tables every three or four feet. One centered on the table was the tallest, with arms like a starfish holding ten-inch beeswax candles.

I touched the smooth metal. "No tallow for Lady Shrewsbury."

"Not tonight, or for the Widow's Ball, I suspect." Patience's frown, thin and wan, returned. "I'm going to get some air, Jemina."

I started to follow, but she held up her hand. "I need a moment alone. I'll be right back. Please stay. Find the earl. Clear the air. Fix the rumors running rampant for his sake and yours."

Knowing what it meant to want your own peace, I let her go but would go after her if she took too long.

A rumble of a laugh fell to my left.

The hair on my neck pimpled. I turned. The handsome Earl of Ashbrook stood near, chatting with the Lord Mayor.

With a stiff stance, Ashbrook nodded and offered a jest, some legal scholarly joke.

At least he was here, and I can personally thank him for the roses. Twenty-four long stems, with petals the color of fiery red. Mr. Gerard said they'd arrived from the finest hot house not a bunch purchased from a flower seller in Covent Garden.

That meant it wasn't a whim but something deliberate. Ashbrook had thought of me. Didn't know what that could mean.

He caught my gaze and looked as if he'd move toward me, but his aunt took his arm and led him the other way.

It was hard not to stare. My hands had nothing to do but to fold and refold the napkin in front me.

Lady Shrewsbury and Ashbrook made what appeared to be small talk, complete with him laughing and her tapping him with her silvery fan. Such a dazzling pair—his height and nice broad shoulders to the demur countess, pretty Lady Shrewsbury with her thick shiny pearls dangling about her throat, her cream-colored dress.

The earl wore dark pantaloons and an ivory waistcoat with gold-colored threading that made X's or crosses.

"Buckles?"

A little startled, I held on to the seat back. "Excuse me, ma'am."

"Buckles, that is you. I recognized those ugly slippers from the Lincoln's Inn."

"I'm not sure what you are talking about."

"Buckles, don't be ashamed. I've gone after men myself. Stowing away in carriages, presenting myself like Cleopatra all rolled up in a rug. You do what you have to do to gain their attention, and once you have it, you don't let go. That was my mistake with Daniel."

"Excuse me. I must—"

"He didn't tell you? I'm his special friend, Lady Lavinia Nell. It must've slipped the earl's mind. We were quite comfortable for a while, but then I left him and he married. He's quite alone now, unless you've claimed him."

The woman was fishing. I'd give her enough string to choke. "Well, he's my barrister. Such a strong dependable man."

"So the rumors are true? Buckles, you are his new mistress. Well, you're not one of those sugar plums in white. Though tonight, white was called for."

"What?"

"Didn't you know that a white or red dress was the fashion for the evening? You decided to be the lady in dark gray. A little gloomy, don't you think?"

"We stand out in many ways." I said, grinning. "I'm sure you know this."

Lady Lavinia winced. Her sparkly ivory gown, low cut in the front, jiggled with iridescent beads. "Sarcastic little thing."

She folded her arms and paced half around me. "Well done, Buckles, you'll stand out, but next time do wear something more than a simple muslin gown. It does you no credit to be dowdy. You need something to combat those freckles."

Was my mouth open?

It had to be with such venom. I put my slapping hand to my side. "That's not a very nice thing to say."

Her eyes squinted, and she seemed to peer over my head. "You can say more than a few words. Our earl isn't close enough to overhear."

"Overhear what?"

"My warning. You leave him alone. His world, the world of the *ton*, is too much for you. He needs a savvy woman, someone to guide him, not a dowdy amnesiac. He could be a judge over the courts, a magistrate, with the right influences."

"I don't think he needs your influences or your mean spirit. Or did you plan on poisoning him with your wretched perfume until he submits?"

"Cute, Buckles, and here he comes. I'm winning him back tonight or there will be hell to pay."

"I have no need to win him back."

I meant because I never had him, but Lady Lavinia's face became a prune, shriveled and purple. "Stay out of my way."

She left, and I didn't stop her. Nor did I go running to Ashbrook as Lady Lavinia might've expected. The anger in me exposed that I was lying. I didn't want answers to my past alone. I wanted Ashbrook, too.

My hands felt sweaty in my blush-colored gloves. I peered at my gown. Yes, it was dark gray with Mechlin lace on my bodice—a gown perfect for half mourning. I intended on saving my best for the upcoming Widow's Ball. I hadn't thought that I needed to be shiny to keep vipers away.

With my back to him, I heard Lord Ashbrook greet Lady Lavinia. There were mutual chuckles. For a moment, I wondered if they laughed at me.

Ashbrook wouldn't do that. There was more compassion in him than most. I knew him to be a good man, even if he had secrets.

Yet, the man stayed with the viper.

They kept laughing.

The earl could fend for himself. I needed air, away from the poison. Maybe I'd find Patience, and we'd both beg off.

Left then right, I traipsed from the room.

"Jemina," Lady Shrewsbury said, "are you well?"

I nodded, for there were no words but jealous ones to express how I felt.

"You look like you've had words again with the earl."

"No, ma'am, we haven't spoken."

Her eyes widened, and she nodded that *I see you struggling* nod. "My dear, don't let my nephew get you confused. That's his talent."

"So, his intentions are to confuse me?"

"You and perhaps himself. He's been different since he lost his wife. He loved her so deeply, all through letters. Then he lost everything before they could build their dreams. I'm sure he doesn't know what he wants. Don't get caught in a trap, thinking and hoping for one thing and he means something else."

"You don't approve of him and me?"

"It's not my place. Just be able to handle the consequences. Men don't get consequences, not like women."

"Can you say it plainly? My head is beginning to ache."

She patted my hand. "Widows have to be smarter, even with men who seem upstanding. A man has to be willing to change his whole world to secure his happiness and yours."

Since my world was only two years old, upheaval didn't seem so bad, but Ashbrook had lived a whole life.

With her sherry eyes sweetly looking at me, maybe even praying for me, Lady Shrewsbury released me. "Do head back soon. White soup will be served."

The woman went into the dining room, but I pressed down the hall through the maze of doors. I think I walked in circles, but I finally found the patio.

Patience wasn't out here, but I wasn't ready to return.

The air had a slight chill, but it felt so much better than being in the dining room with all the light and the scrutiny.

The door opened and shut behind me.

A tall form joined me in the dark. I didn't have to look to know who was behind me, not with the way my heart started to beat. I was the girl who the Earl of Ashbrook had followed into the night.

CHAPTER 20

JEMINA—AN OFFER AND
A GENTLEMAN

My pulse pounded, beating like the duke's military drums.

Ashbrook walked closer. His footfalls tapped the patio's cobblestones. I should turn to him, thank him for his flowers, and then leave this dinner.

Yet, I stayed frozen, trapped by the scent of him, clean cedar and sweet lilies, and starch.

He stood behind me.

It wouldn't take much to fall back against his chest, just to breathe a little more of him.

His hand lifted to my shoulder. It sent a spark, a deep shiver to my skin, the little bit exposed by my square neckline.

"Is all well, Mrs. St. Maur?" Ashbrook's voice. "I saw you leave in haste."

"I'm quite well, my lord."

"Something has to be wrong. Your voice isn't loud."

"Well, I'm not speechless." I glanced up, searching the cloudy sky for stars. "Not quite a full moon, you know. That's good. Strange things happen when the moon is full."

"That's what they say, Mrs. St. Maur."

His hand became a little more demanding. He turned me to face him.

I complied and enjoyed his fine appearance—trimmed beard, thick sculpted hair with waves of curls on top, sparkling brass lenses, and those eyes, shiny and jet. "Thank you for my flowers. They are beautiful, displayed in Sandlin's parlor and my bedroom."

The lift of his lips turned a little wicked. A smirk attached to the corners of his kissable mouth. The gap between his teeth peeked. "Your bedchamber, you say? I was hoping you'd write with details."

"To tell you of my bedchamber?"

"Anything. I am open to anything. I miss your notes."

Lifting my sore wrist to him, I tugged at my glove and showed him the bandage. "Been a little too achy to write. I hope you accept my compliments and gratitude."

My wrist became captured by his palm. I heard an angry grunt, then something mumbled about the Widow's Grace.

Releasing me, he moved to a lit torch a few feet away. The light blazed, illuminating the gardens of the house. "I came of age here, riding horses every day until going off to school. I always liked the way Lady Shrewsbury kept the grounds."

A secret.

The barrister seemed poised to tell one. Like a moth, I was drawn to him. Standing close to the torch, the hot, smoky scent of burning pitch whipped around us. "I'm here."

His head dipped to mine. His black eyes were glittering crystals, and I waited for what would come next.

"Mrs. St. Maur, you could've sent a footman or Mr. Gerard for me. I would've come."

"I'm fine now. I'll be able to write in a week."

"Are you in pain?" He ripped off his thin dinner gloves with his teeth and placed the balled white fabric into his pocket. Pressing thumbs along my wrist, he worked a light massage.

I coveted this easy touch, and I wished it was on my neck at the point of my spine where tension gathered.

"Mrs. St. Maur, you had me so concerned."

"You care? Some of your friends dislike me, particularly my freckles."

"Then they are fools. I love freckles. I also love your hair. I want to see it undone, out of these wondrous braids, hanging to your waist."

I reclaimed my wrist from his massage. "Don't burden yourself on my behalf."

"It's no burden at all. I quite like thinking of it, of you and your waist."

"Ashbrook, I asked if you cared about me. That part you did not answer."

"Of course, I do, as your barrister I feel—"

"You feel nothing. You left me to figure out everything. You offer no aid. Go now, before I do something crazy."

He leaned closer. "Like kissing me again?"

Drawing my hand away, I stepped back. "No, I hadn't thought of it."

Ashbrook followed. "I've thought of it, Mrs. St. Maur. I've rehearsed in my head how you blush, how you taste, the way you shiver when we kiss. But then there's the awful matter of your sending me away with a slap. Please. Please, just tell me what you want. Don't send me away."

I folded my arms, holding tight to my forearms. "Then stay."

A cricket chirped in the distance. It was hidden in the dark. The landscape had become like ghosts, with a trace outline and shadows confusing what was there and what was not.

His hands clasped my shoulders. His thumbs traced circles on my neck. "What happens if I stay?"

"Nothing. Everything. I don't know."

Ashbrook's breath on my neck tingled. He hadn't decided to embrace me. Perhaps he needed poetry for that.

"My lord, I should let you enjoy the moon, sir, while I find the Duchess of Repington."

"She's chatting with my aunt, and your moon disappeared behind the clouds. That means you will leave me for no reason."

He went forward, a little deeper into the garden. "Jemina, I wish you wouldn't go."

His tone was low. If I hadn't heard it in that instance, I probably would never have. My slippers moved me to his side. "I'm listening."

"I love your letters, they bring me great joy."

"Lord Ashbrook, I know you tossed them in the rubbish bin."

"No, Jemina. I've kept them all. They show an attachment between us."

"There's always been an attachment since you rescued me. But you, my lord, you've ignored that."

"Not true. There's no ignoring you." He lifted his arm to me. "Come to dinner with me. I don't want you left alone out here. This isn't the place to say all I wish. We must meet tomorrow."

"I'm not ready to go back. The density of the hypocrites and the hypocritical is too high."

"Ignore the elite's whispers."

"How? They hound Patience, who is perfect. They come for me because I'm comfortable in dark gray. You can go laugh again with Lady Lavinia."

"Mrs. St. Maur, I admonished Lavinia in joke for a nasty little trick she tried. Never would I find any humor in a woman's choice of dress. You're a vision in a sea of white."

"You have gold threads, fine embroidery on your waistcoat. You're very fashionable."

"I am, but I still get whispers. We need to head back in. We can talk tomorrow." He started to retrieve his dinner gloves, but I stopped him and clasped his fingers, my bare palm to his.

"I won't do you the disservice of saying I understand how you feel. I just know those whispers are wrong."

He glanced at me over his spectacles, then kissed my hurt wrist. "Thank you for that. I do recall you being handy with a needle and thread with a costume for the duchess, but you have the money to hire a modiste. If you slowed your Widow's Grace pursuits, you have the talent to create fashion."

"You think a new dress will stop all the talk about me, the girl with no memories, the girl released from Bedlam with a fortune?"

"Technically no one says the latter. That's our secret. See, we do have one."

For a moment, I saw all the conflicts of his spirit dancing in his eyes—part desire, part a wish to remain distant, part the danger of what this attraction meant.

When his hand slipped to my waist, I assumed he went with desire.

"Mrs. St. Maur, what if we make the rumors of our romance true?"

His lips pressed to mine and my arms skated about his neck. In the dark, with the fire of torches reflecting on his spectacles, I let my flame for this man unleash. I burned in his arms as his kisses descended, smoldering like lava.

My breath came faster as the pressure of his hands changed.

I was in danger, falling into that scary place of wanting him, wanting him terribly.

It took everything to step away from fire. I wasn't quite sure if I could survive being burned. I smoothed my wrinkling lace. "Gossip is wrong. Why reward them, making their lies true?"

"The reward would be ours. I like thinking of you under my protection as a benefactor."

He folded his hands under chin. "If I purchased your gowns like a proper benefactor, I'd have you in a satin lace, high about your neck, for I noticed how much more comfortable you are in those fashions. The gown must have short puffed sleeves that allowed your arms to be free, and shots of silk about your hips. You have hips."

My cheeks felt hot. My face must be red. The crazy knocking in my chest sped up. "That's not a terrible dress you described, my lord. It sounds lovely."

"Only on you, on your hips. My mother would call those birthing hips."

My heart stopped. Did Lord Ashbrook know about me, that I had a child? Was his flirty statement confirmation?

"Mrs. St. Maur, I'm ready for the whispers. I'll smile when I hear how beautiful you are, how lucky I am."

"See? Your plan doesn't work. There still will be talk. Let's go back to your original plan of teasing me until we argue. Everyone will assume it's a break, and the rumors will be done."

"How can you be an operative of the Widow's Grace and not know the difference between a man struggling to avoid you and a man cross with you?"

"The results are the same. Frustration, always wondering if I'll see you again."

"So, this impasse is my fault?" His chuckles started. "It's always the man's fault in your world?"

"No, just London. That's all I have an understanding of . . . the two years I can remember. You wouldn't even give me the copy of my marriage contract. Maybe it smelled too much of Jamaica. Can't have me empowered with all my memories."

His lips depressed, flattening to a line. Yet, there would always be one separating us, him who knew all, me who knew not enough.

I laughed at myself for getting so worked up. "I suppose it's silly to quibble about such things when we're having a jovial affair. I do think you are right. I should travel to see if there is a place where a frugal wife is considered an asset."

He reached for me, then dropped his hands to his sides. "Dinner. We should go."

"A frugal wife is not in demand somewhere, Lord Ashbrook?"

"I have no opinion on wives."

"Something we can agree upon. I've had this name St. Maur for a short season. Seems a shame to get rid of it."

He picked at the buttons of his waistcoat. They glimmered in the torchlight. "You don't want to marry either? Good."

Ashbrook crossed that invisible divide and lifted me, twirling me around and around before taking me into a deeper embrace. "I surrender."

His head dipped, and I claimed his kiss.

Better than before. It was a true dropping of his caution. His mouth was hungered, endless in its searching. The razor-cut feel, slight and bristly, of his beard sent tingles over my face.

I surrendered too. In his arms, I found myself. I was a girl desired and sheltered by the earl, the man I fancied.

"Jemina, I don't want you married either. I want you for myself."

His tone was rushed. His hold on me was everything. He was a mast, a stronghold in my storm.

"Let me be your benefactor. Be my mistress. Let us explore these feelings between us. We'll have an affair to remember."

A temporary love, that was what he wanted?

Now, I was speechless looking up at Daniel Thackery, the Earl of Ashbrook, the man who made my heart race and break at the same time.

CHAPTER 21

DANIEL—DANGEROUS LIAISONS

At the Old Bailey, Daniel knew when he'd argued his point successfully. He felt it in his bones when the jurymen would decide in his client's favor.

The cold look in Jemina's eyes let him know he stood on the verge of failure. "I think we should return to dinner, Lord Ashbrook."

"Dinner has no appeal. I'm hungry for nothing but you. Tell me you don't feel the same."

She didn't agree, but she hadn't stormed away either. She was a breath away, smoothing her bodice.

Maybe there was a chance to fix whatever he'd gotten wrong.

"Perhaps you need reassurance of my intentions. I've thought about this, about you. If the *ton* has convicted us as lovers, we should be guilty."

"Ashbrook—"

"Let me say this better. I think I adore you, but you're wild. You're not ready to be shackled down. You're still learning who you are."

Her eyes widened, and he decided it was better to keep her moving as he explained his plans. He took her hand and waltzed her around the patio.

"I've been looking at property. I found a town house at the start of Finchely Road. It's halfway between your residence at Sandlin and mine."

"You bought another house? Something closer to aid in surveillance?"

"Such a sense of humor, you have." Daniel dipped his head and kissed her brow. "We could be discreet, if that is your concern. We'd meet in the afternoons. A beautiful, convenient solution that is amenable for two consenting adults who are set against marriage."

He nuzzled her neck. "Goodness, you smell nice."

"Jasmine is in my lotion, I think."

"Wonderful." He brushed his lips to her cheek. "I love this fragrance."

"You thought of this plan, to find a love nest, a temporary love nest?"

The squeak in her voice didn't sound like passion.

"We need a place that's discreet. Somewhere we can become better acquainted. We can be everything to each other—better friends, lovers, everything."

"You've actually contemplated this and came up with this argument to sway me, all by yourself?"

Of course, but it was Bridgetower's idea of buying a town house nearby, but he'd keep that to himself. He twirled Jemina around. "Tell me what I should say. Tell me how to win you."

Her silence didn't indicate she was in agreement. Her irises seemed small, but the blush on her cheeks looked of rapture.

He kissed each hand. "A man in my position, a man of the world, secures the comfort for those in his care. Then when all is done, he thinks of his own needs. I'm tired of mourning. I've wanted a mistress, but no one has captured my interest. You have. I want you."

"I can't recall ever receiving such an offer." She patted away his fingers. "Lord Ashbrook, I must decline."

Panic filled his chest. Daniel wiped at his mouth. "I must be

doing this all wrong. Let me change your mind. I'll send you flowers every day. I'll ply you shameless with paints and canvases, even pomegranates, everything I know you like. Please reconsider or at least think on it."

She shook her head. "You truly shouldn't listen to rumors."

"The one of us filled with rapture rolling around on the floor. That one?"

"Rapture and moments pass, my lord. I've had too many things pass me."

"We can have our moment, over and over again. Then when this affair cools, Jemina, we'll return to our lives with wonderful memories. Is that your concern, committing to me too soon?"

"I don't want to be the next Lady Lavinia. She has such wonderful memories of your moments she's threatening perceived rivals."

"What? She threatened you? I'm disappointed in her. I'll make sure she never harms or bothers you. You'd never be like that."

"Are you so certain? Just as certain that our passions won't last?"

He shouldn't have emphasized the ending part, but she needed to know everything before agreeing. "I'm being honest. I can't promise forever. We both know tomorrow isn't promised."

"Then, I'm pretty sure that we shouldn't be spending our last hours in a dalliance. Good evening, my lord."

He caught her arm, her unhurt one. "Jemina, no—"

"Ashbrook, is it the title that makes you like the rest, a heavy-handed peer who assumes every woman wants him?"

He'd ruined it by saying too much, but she had to know everything. "I don't want anyone but you. I'm certain we'll be good together."

"As certain as you were with Phoebe Dunn?"

Her high-pitched tone hit him like a punch to the gut. Daniel dropped Jemina's hand. "I was very certain about Phoebe, but she is gone. A man must move forward."

Her eyes, the windows of her soul narrowed more. The passion they'd had drained to almost nothing.

He decided to take the little bit of invitation left in her eyes and kiss her.

Mid lean, her hand flew up and caught his chin, stroking his beard. "I'm curious about the length of this proposed affair. A week, a month, a year?"

Honesty dug a hole beneath his slippers, deep enough to be a decent grave. He'd never mislead her or have her hoping for something he couldn't give. "Jemina, we'll have a glorious time. All you have to do is agree to be mine."

"Yours for the moment, then passed on to another. Is that how Lady Lavinias are made, disdain from a partner?"

"She discards and chooses her friends too. It's not always the man's fault."

"Lord Ashbrook, I don't know what to say about this proposition other than no."

"Well, the fact that you haven't slapped me is positive. Jemina, I should've been more polished. I should've practiced this speech."

"I'd hate that this was something you'd practiced. It seems awful to convince yourself that your feelings for me won't last."

He groaned as she shredded his words. "This is rushed. I hadn't given into temptation in a long time. I'm clumsy."

"It's a temporary infliction. Heals up nicely like bruised wrists."

This trial was lost. Was there anything he could say to the jury for an appeal?

She tapped a patio stone with her buckled slipper. "I suppose this foolhardy offer means you feel something for me. Good to know I wasn't crazy."

"You're not, and what I feel won't be done in a day or even a few weeks. I'm in deep waters over you. Jemina, I've debated saying anything, but the spark between us burns up my caution.

I'm admitting things horribly, but I don't know how else to say how much I desire you."

"You're right. This is a horrible way to ask someone to be your mistress."

He lifted his spectacles and rubbed the bridge of his nose. "You confuse me, but that might be a part of your charm. I want you, Jemina, but a mistress is all I can offer. I'm not marrying again. You just said you weren't marrying either."

"I meant right now. I'm sorry for you. The limitations that you've placed on your life are terrible. I don't intend to remain joined to loss."

"I'm not sure about the future, and I don't know if you want to fit into my world. There are rules and expectations that you'll not want to follow."

"Because you're a man and a peer?"

"Because I am a man, a peer, and a Blackamoor, and my child is Blackamoor."

She hugged her elbows as if what he said hurt her. Nothing he spoke was untrue.

"Why even ask me to be your mistress? I'm not a peer like Lady Lavinia, and I'm not a Blackamoor, though that condition doesn't seem to be a consideration for your affairs."

"I'm sorry. Let me try once more." He cleared his throat. "Jemina, you dazzle me, but my walk is very narrow. I'm dull, somewhat chained to my profession. My daughter is my priority. She needs me home to read to her, to put her to bed, to tell her all will be right in the morning."

"A woman needs that too. So, it was no jest to be your afternoon lover?"

"I was honest."

"In your world, that's honesty?"

She wanted complete honesty; he'd tell her his fears about her. "We both know that temporary may be all that you can offer."

"What?"

"Jemina, who you are right now could go away tomorrow. That's the risk about you. You could wake up with your memories returned and be someone else. I don't want to become a man you're loathed to touch."

Now her eyes widened. Again, he'd said too much.

"A temporary mistress situation is my fault? You tell me over and over that only tomorrow matters, to forget the past, to go for what I want. Now you fear my yesterdays." She clutched his collar. "Who was I, Ashbrook? What type of woman was I that I'll want nothing to do with an honorable man? Tell me what you know."

His defense should've rested. Instead, he'd ran amok. He rubbed at his face and prepared to destroy her peace. "Here's what I know. The St. Maurs looked at Blackamoors, at those of African descent as chattel, things to abuse and sell. They heavily financed the slave trade between Africa and the colonies until the transport became illegal. Now they run the intercolonial slave ships. That's what I discovered."

Hurt flared in her eyes, like volcanoes spewing ash and molten rocks. "That's not all, is it? Finish me."

"That's all I know."

"Was I a slaveholder?"

"I don't think so. I could find no records on you, but Cecil St. Maur was."

"Cecil? I'm going to be sick." She knelt in the grass and her stomach erupted.

Daniel held her shoulders and braced her against his legs.

She vomited again, and he kept her chignon from falling into her face.

When she finally soothed, he helped her up and offered her his handkerchief.

"I'm sorry, Jemina. I should never have told you."

She coughed and wiped at her mouth. "At least you gave me something that was true."

Daniel held her. "By far, this was the worst proposition I've ever made. I am so sorry."

"I must find out the rest. Perhaps you can help me contact the St. Maurs. They will know."

"No, Jemina. They let you be committed. They left you to rot. Your past is gone. No one but you and I know what I've discovered."

She wiped at her mouth. "I have to know if I held those views. I have to know if I can make restitution. I have to know—"

He had her by the shoulders. "Nothing more, Jemina. It's done. The *Minerva* is done. Don't stir up trouble."

Daniel closed his eyes, took up her palm, and slapped himself. "What was that for?"

"It was coming. I just wanted it silent."

"Ashbrook, you're not the only one with connections and plans. I'll take whatever risk is necessary to regain the rest of my missing pieces."

"It's gone, Jemina. You're different now. I'm asking you to stop."

"You just told me you found evidence of my past. That means there's more out there. Thank you for your offer to distract me with leisurely afternoons, but I will be busy figuring out the rest of my history. It's obvious I have to save myself."

Daniel had ruined this. There had to be a way to salvage this, to protect her from a life that couldn't possibly be hers, not now. She wasn't the woman who left Jamaica. He couldn't let her be of that world again.

He spun her one more time, his hands guiding her waist. They were one, in a rhythm of the violin. "I know you possess the same crazy feeling about me. Your heart is beating hard against my chest. Let me distract you. I could be so good to you."

"Good would be helping me find out every last fact."

She pushed away, and he let her go.

"Dinner should be getting ready to start," Jemina said. "I'll pretend we had a horrible tiff. That should spur rumors of our break."

"I apologize, Jemina . . . Mrs. St. Maur. Seems, I'm always apologizing, but I'll protect you from hurting yourself."

"Like a restraint at Bedlam? My ankle still has marks from those kindly chains. I just hate that the man I fancied thinks I'm too fragile for the truth."

"You've chosen who you are every day. The past doesn't matter."

"It's my past. Mine. It matters to me." Stomping to the threshold, she turned. Her face was beyond pain. It was beautiful with rage, raw and red with that avenging anger that comes from the breath being knocked from someone. "Tell your aunt I couldn't stay. Enjoy the white soup. It's delicious."

"Forget my offer, Jemina. Let's go back to being friends."

Her fingers tightened on the doorframe. "We were never friends. I would remember being friends with you." Head held high, she left him on the patio.

Maybe not friends, but he was her benefactor in ways she must never know. A hurt Jemina St. Maur was dangerous, dangerous to herself, to his secrets and his heart. Daniel needed to protect her someway, somehow before all was lost.

CHAPTER 22

JEMINA—PLAN B

Sandlin Court was quiet as our carriage arrived. Patience had that distant look on her face, and I had Ashbrook's offer ringing in my head. Why did he have to be so thick and yet kiss so well?

Mr. Gerard greeted us at the door. "Your Grace, Mrs. St. Maur," he said, "I'm glad you've returned before midnight. I think that prohibits something called plan B from coming to fruition."

"Plan B?" Patience's cheeks glowed, her lips wiggling into a smile, her first of the night. "That's serious."

Part of me wondered what would happen. Deference to her husband's concerns should be expected, but I couldn't help thinking this was all unfair. We should be out late if we wanted, and I should expect the truth, even it was awful.

I tugged and straightened my wrinkled skirt. "My silk has wrinkled so badly. Ashbrook's fault."

"From what I saw from my walk of the grounds, you helped."

Chubble deh a bush. Oh, so much trouble. "Your Grace, we must delay inspection." I put my arm about Patience's. "May I see you a moment?" I spun her from the light fawn painted walls of the hall and headed her into the parlor.

"Jemina, are you finally going to confess?"

My sleeve caught on a rough part of the door, and I thought of Ashbrook caring for my palm, each embrace, each kiss.

"Jemina, you're all red in the face."

"If you saw us, did you hear what was said?"

Patience sucked in a deep breath and nodded. "That he wants you to be his mistress, that your Cecil St. Maur was an investor in the slave trade, and the St. Maurs owned people who looked like me."

Speechless and shamed and sickened to my stomach, I bent over like my stomach had been kicked in again.

Then I felt coconut-scented fingers lifting my face and holding me, like I was still good, not a part of the evil my soul detested.

"You listen to me, and you listen well. I don't care who you were, but I know in my heart who you are now. I would trust my Lionel to you." She brushed back my flopping curls, found a spot on my brow and kissed me. "You are my sister. Nothing changes. I choose you like you chose me. Nod if you understand."

I nodded.

Then I wept.

And I felt loved, like I'd never felt before, vibrating deep in my bosom, in my bones.

"Does it dishonor you, us, if I keep digging to know who I was?"

"No, Jemina. It's your past. Knowing what or who you were is your right. I know you will always be good. There's too much good in you for you to be any other way."

For one last moment, I held on to Patience, heard her pure heart, and knew, like I hadn't in a long time, that everything would be all right.

"Dry your eyes. His Grace should think we came from a mission, not had a sentimental talk. We must keep him guessing."

We started for the door. "And have some charity for Ashbrook.

He deeply loved Phoebe Dunn. The mistress business was the wrong thing to ask, but he did. He's moving forward. That's something."

He knew all of this and still wanted me. "I suppose it is."

"Jemina, Ashbrook is the keeper of secrets. If you two were more sure of each other, I think he'd be more forthcoming."

I smiled, for Patience was right. The man knew more. I'd have to figure out how to get it out of him. "You think he's a pillow talker?"

She shook her head and laughed with me all the way to the duke's study.

Mr. Gerard stood at the door. "Your Grace, hurry in. Plan B will be loud. It might involve those canons you asked me to store in the basement."

The duchess held her breath and opened the door. "We're . . ."

Peeking over her shoulder, I saw such a sight.

The duke's notes were scattered across the floor like snow on the sleek dark mahogany. Baby Lionel was swaddled in His Grace's arms as they both slept on his leather tufted sofa. The man was baby happy. From the content look on Lionel's little face and that snorting button nose, the baby was duke happy too.

My friend sighed and hummed my lullaby. " 'There was once a little boat.' "

She tiptoed and went to her son and lifted him. The boy's whistle snores sounded lovely and light.

"Jemina, the duke has even put on a fresh napkin."

"How can you tell he did it and not a maid?"

"There's a medal pinning the ends together. I'm not sure if I should salute my son or fret about him soiling the red ribbon."

"Salute." The duke's sleep-warmed voice rumbled.

Patience dimpled as he pulled his watch from his pocket. Then he pushed up on his crutch and kissed her.

"Ah, my beloved. I see Lady Shrewsbury let you escape early. By Jove's hand, it's a miracle. It's not quite eleven."

The man put a hand to the middle of Patience's back, his noble chin resting on her shoulder. He looked at ease in a simple shirt, waistcoat and breeches, not his garnet-colored regimentals with his chest lined in medals.

Patience kissed his cheek and ruffled his ash-blond hair. "You have done well, my love. I'm sure Lionel's been no trouble, but your papers—"

"Crawling practice, my dear. Yes, I know my boy is only nine months, but he's quite advanced. In his eyes, I see greatness."

Holding Lionel close, Patience curled into the duke's chest. She fit perfectly alongside him. "Yes, I see it too. You're the perfect father for Lionel."

With a second kiss to his cheek, Patience sang. "'There was once a little boat, a little boat. *Ohé! Ohé! Matelot. Ohé! Ohé! Matelot.*'"

The duke sang too.

Their voices light and dark blended about the words.

Lionel seemed to smile wider as he slept.

My empty insides warmed, and I backed out of the room and neared the sapphire-carpeted stairs that led to my bedchamber.

Still smiling at my friends' love, I thought about what I wanted. My mind was empty. Until I knew all, how could I figure out what was for me?

I knew I deserved joy, someone calling me beloved, looking at me like I was his world forever, not a week. I wasn't surrendering my truth for anything that didn't last.

Enduring love and family was only offered by my friend, not the man I fancied. There'd be no future for me, nothing certain, not without Ashbrook telling me all that he knew.

CHAPTER 23

DANIEL—NO PLAN

"Pa-Papa."

Daniel had taken only a step inside Finchely when Hope spied him.

Mrs. Gallick's held his princess's hand. "Pa-Papa!"

She wobbled a little as she ran toward him before Mrs. Gallick caught her arm, keeping his little girl from falling.

"Hope's still getting used to those legs, sir. But she'll get 'em."

Her progression was slow, but she'd improved at holding her balance. The child survived so much. Difficulties were to be expected.

Clad in gray breeches, he knelt a few feet in front of them. "Can you make it to me?"

Arms stretched wide, he waited.

Hope's grin became serious. She let go of Mrs. Gallick's hand and took a step forward, then another, tottering until she was just about in his arms.

Then she fell, bam, onto the marble.

His heart stopped.

Hope rolled over, laughing. "Almost, Pa-Papa, almost."

Then he could breathe. She had to have Phoebe's spirit. From the letters they exchanged, she was always sunny and looking for joy.

Was it awful to think marriage and love fleeting institutions because his first try was tragic? Well, Phoebe hadn't trusted him enough to tell Daniel about her baby. What could he have done better?

Had he learned enough to do better now?

Putting his disastrous proposition aside, Jemina should trust his opinion. She needed to leave the past alone.

"Pa-Papa, I made a watercolor just like yours. May I show you?"

"Yes, my sweet." He scooped her up and put her on his shoulder.

Mrs. Gallick smiled bright like a shining star. "I'll go get your dining room ready for your friends. And then you and I will play, Miss Hope, then get ready for bed."

The child started to frown but then smiled her toothy pout. "Pa-Papa can still see picture."

He took off his brass spectacles and slid them into his pocket. "I can do that, but Mrs. Gallick will do story time at ten."

His housekeeper was running herself ragged. A new nanny needed to be installed.

Daniel climbed the stairs with Hope holding on to his ears like a horse's reins.

Across the pink swirly tapestry rug, he bucked and played a stallion until he approached her table. When he stepped over her collection of wooden toy ponies and saddles, he dropped to his knees, then lowered Hope. "Show me what you have created."

"Look, Pa-Papa."

Centered on the small ivory table was a piece of paper, glossy and wet.

He took out his spectacles again. "A seascape? But it's mostly pink?"

"It's better. Pink is better. See, Pa-Papa."

Her little eyes, brown glassy gems quivered.

"Oh, yes, I see that now. Striations of rose and blues and jade, jade green and pink. Yes, it is lovely."

"Yeah, Pa-Papa."

Pushing aside her two carved horses with rockers under their feet and shaggy string for tails, he squatted on the carpet. Hope sat on his thigh as he carefully picked up the art.

"See, like yours but more colors. The good ones."

"You are an incredible artist." He set the paper back on the table catching a drip of pink into his hand. "So talented. My little girl the painter. We will let this dry, and I will have it framed and hung. Next to mine."

"No. Next to Mama. Then, she can see it."

"You mean the sketch I have in my bedchamber?"

"Yes."

Guilt churned. "Next to the sketch of your mother? You remember her?"

"Next to Mama's picture. You said that was Mama."

He kissed her brow. "Yes, it will go in my bedchamber."

"And it will keep Mama company when you work or when you read to me."

Speechless and guilty. He looked for something to wipe the paint from his fingers.

Hope must have taken his palm as an invitation. She poked her pinkie into the paint. Then painted lines on each side of his mouth.

"Am I your next work of art?"

"Now, you always smile."

Paint stains, inky fingers, he didn't care, he pulled Hope into a tight embrace. "I'm happy because you're happy. I'm always happy when I'm with you."

"What about when you work? I'm not there."

"Work makes me happy."

"Mrs. Gallick says you used to ride real horses."

"She did, did she?" He sighed. Paint smears were on her pink pinafore and on his formerly white shirt. "There will be time for all of that . . . when you are older. But maybe we should try a nanny again."

"Don't like nanny."

"Not the last one, Hope. A good one, who will be your friend."

"Smile more? I like Pa-Papa smiling." Her little arms ensconcing his neck felt wonderful.

Just because Jemina wasn't interested in his offer, it didn't mean he should stop trying to move forward. It would be hypocritical to suggest she forget the past if he stayed stuck in his.

Cards flipped out to each of the men at Daniel's table, he stared at his hand. Max jumped about, adding to his distraction, but not as much as Richmond's grin.

"What's the matter, Barrister?" he asked as he signaled for another card.

"Nothing." Daniel wasn't concentrating. The solicitor representing the St. Maurs had contacted him, this time formally by letter. The digging widows must have awakened the beasts.

Mr. Mosey from Tonbridge—the solicitor asked how to contact Jemina for important business. With her continued poking around, it would only be a matter of time the solicitor found her. Doesn't she realize the St. Maurs would've let her spend the rest of her life in Bedlam?

The Dunns were business partners to the St. Maurs in Jamaica. Coffee exporters. They could be alerted to Hope with the chaos surrounding Jemina.

But the dear woman was more at risk. The St. Maurs were her closest kin. They could gain legal guardianship of her affairs, if somehow she was again proven unstable or unfit.

Mr. Gerard reared back in his chair. "From the rumors, it sounds as if his brief affair with an heiress went awry at Lady Shrewsbury's dinner."

"My wife," Richardson said, "overheard from her cousin the butcher at the marketplace in Covent Garden that it was an awful ending."

Daniel sighed. "You can't have an awful ending if there was no beginning, gentlemen."

"So it's worse, you never sampled the nectar. Sorry, old boy."

Richmond laughed and stroked his thick, high hair, fully ebony though nature had made it recede. "Truly sorry. You have to be sure of the woman when you cross that line."

The line was the racial one, which rose like a brick wall when black and white danced hand-in-hand. It fueled hatred, spun up the mobs with talks against abolition, and the awful othering of mixed-race offspring.

Daniel lived this daily and the hate his parent's marriage bore. This friction was something he wanted to avoid, which made his courtship with Phoebe, a beautiful West Indian girl more palatable.

"Oh, you have it bad. A moping Ashbrook." Richmond shook his head, then signaled for another card. "Book smarts don't lead to wise choices."

The subtle dig was a reminder that Richmond was happily married to a beautiful Irish lass. He paid for that the first year of their nuptials. The man fought every day with every man in his village, all who taunted his wife for "marrying a devil."

Daniel stroked his chin, analyzed his cards and the risks he wanted to take. A few shillings at this table were the stakes, but outside of Finchely it was his heart and his daughter's happiness at risk.

Was that it?

His affairs with Lady Lavinia and other oat sowing was in the shadows.

In court, he defended many things, so how could he not defend a relationship with Jemina?

No. That wasn't his hesitation. It was the fear of losing her like Phoebe. When their lives were set to begin, Jemina would disappear within her restored memories. He'd lose again.

It was bound to happen, her awakening from amnesia. She was too hungry for the truth.

Richmond looked at Daniel and flipped a card to him. "Just helping you decide. You're taking too long with your choices."

"It's difficult sometimes." Daniel oversold his hand. He lost.

His friend offered a knowing smile. "There aren't enough eligible Blackamoor women in London. We kid you, but it is difficult. Those women of age, who are educated with a dowry, are sought after by second sons of the *ton* or peers and merchants looking for wealthy brides. Very competitive to gain *da empress*."

"Your Mrs. Richmond is a queen." Mr. Gerard swept up another card, then tossed his set back. "I'm over too." He stretched and went to the sideboard and forked another cut of the juicy roast. Then slathered honey and butter over two biscuits. "Ashbrook tried. It's done. It's for the best."

Still stewing, Daniel waited for Richmond or Mr. Anthon to hit vingt-et-un. "Can we move on from my private affairs and hurry the game? I need to win more of your shillings."

The fellows nodded and feasted and hummed as the play continued.

With their advice now switching to politics, Daniel shifted his gaze between his cards and the door, and that wretched, unescapable sense of loss.

His fears didn't stop him from thinking of Jemina. When he closed his eyes at night, he no longer saw the sketch of Phoebe or the docks of Portsmouth. It was the widow, the one who got away that filled his dreams.

Jemina and the heady kisses.

Jemina and the heavy ticking feel of her heart.

Jemina and the hurt in her eyes as she walked away.

After winning a set, Daniel returned to scanning the doorway. Hope might crawl by with Mrs. G. chasing. The lady was likely tired from managing his daughter and his household.

He'd have to keep looking or listening for commotion; the brave little girl who wasn't supposed to come down those stairs might try.

"Huzzah." Mr. Anthon slapped the table with a three of clubs, seven of spades, eight of hearts, and three of hearts. Twenty-one.

"What, no court cards? A jack or queen." Daniel smiled at the young man and passed him the deck and the pot.

Bridgetower came in; his face looked cross.

"Not another broken soul." Richmond tossed in his cards. "You young people should be lucky in love and do poorly at cards. I need to take my winnings home."

The violinist adjusted his thick onyx cravat like a taut bow-string. "Ashbrook, do you know there's a woman in your hedge-row?"

"Clothed?"

He squinted at Daniel. "Yes. Like would she not be?"

"It's been an interesting month, friend, sit."

He pointed to the door, then shrugged. "Well, fully dressed as far as I can see in a green cloak. Pretty, peeking at Finchely with theater glasses."

Jemina's cape was emerald. It made her eyes a more intense hue. "By herself or are there two spies?"

"By herself. Umm. You're not going to go see about that?" Bridgetower's lips formed a flat incredulous line. He pointed to the door. "You sure?"

"Nope. When she's ready for a formal visit, she'll come to the front door, just like you gentlemen."

His friend shrugged and began filling a plate from the meats on the sideboard. Adjusting his tailcoat, he sat astride. "You're a strange bird, Ashbrook."

Strange and patient.

Daniel was all of that, and maybe lucky. If he was still a Widow's Grace operation, then he might have another chance to take a risk and fix things after all.

CHAPTER 24

JEMINA—BURGLARY AND A BARRISTER

A week of surveillance of Finchely House proved nothing to me other than Daniel Thackery, the Earl of Ashbrook, liked to stay home, often in the comfort of his friends. Not even the duke's invitation for dinner made him leave.

A daytime investigation was the only thing I could do. Ashbrook would be in court. I stood at the rear of his property. In the woods, a familiar scent, the sweet smell of blue and purple flowers made my head swim. A torrent of memories swirled in the breeze. I had an hour or less to accomplish this mission, to find whatever evidence he had here.

Then I could let Ashbrook go.

Thunder crackled. My hand rattled the assegai iron hook I clasped. I could do this by myself. It was heavy, but there was no better tool to climb. Patience was so good at this, but I couldn't involve her.

The windows on the second floor at the rear of the house possessed no view of the road. Blessedly, the earl kept minimal staff. I should be able to do this undetected.

Whoop. I cast my rope. I missed, and the hook crashed to the ground. My confidence faltered for a moment.

On the third try, my assegai caught the edge of the balcony. Twenty tugs convinced me that it would hold.

Closing my eyes, I pretended it was night and Patience was ahead of me, steadying the rope. Boots clawing into the vined trellis, I pulled myself higher. When I dared to look, I was at the top with my hand curling over the stone wall of the balcony.

I threw one leg over, then the other to pull myself over the wall. Safe on the floor, I hugged myself. I made it and had a new appreciation for wearing breeches.

Lightning sizzled behind me. The need for speed pressed. I knelt at the door and jiggled the handle. Whether it was my pressure or luck, the door opened, and I entered the earl's bedchamber.

Very masculine furnishings greeted me—a dark walnut bed with one single pillow.

Ashbrook wasn't a softie, so why would he have a lot of fluffy things for his head?

The room was neat. The bed and night table of cedar smelled of polish. I tapped my fingers on the footboard.

The man who said he wanted me—I was in the place where he closed his eyes.

At night, was he sleeping? I wasn't, too many thoughts of him, not enough of my past.

Pulse ticking up, I pulled back the bedclothes, the thick linen sheets, and peeked under the frame. Nothing, not even a speck of dust. Rounding the bed, letting my palm rise and fall with the curves of the footboard, I looked for notes or documents, but none were in the open.

Where would Ashbrook hide secrets?

After searching drawers of a tall mahogany chest, I stopped at his bare night table. The pictures above it caught my gaze—a child's painting and a beautiful charcoal sketch of a woman with freckles.

She wore a turban to cover her hair. A ringlet of curls crowned her temples. Stunning. "Hello, Phoebe Dunn." It could be no one else.

A sigh steamed out of my lungs. Her smile would stay in my head. With such joy on her face, there was no wondering why Ashbrook still loved her, why his heart had no room for anyone new.

The other painting was a watercolor. I wasn't sure what it was, but it was bright, streaked with pink and orange and blush red.

Again, I softened. The extremely neat man had put his daughter's painting in a place of reverence. I could picture him smiling, fully smiling, hanging it.

Focus, Jemina. Focus.

"Where would the earl hide papers?"

Tiptoeing from his bed, I opened the door of a closet.

My mouth dropped open.

This wasn't a tiny thing. It was a room, a room with deep shelves stacked all the way around the perimeter. Waistcoats, breeches, tailcoats of many colors—blue, green, and brown were folded flat and separated by tissue paper like ladies' gowns. His court frills—white starched collars he wore for trials hung on hooks.

I touched one. The pleating bounced back. The smell, that sweet starch made my heart thunder like the worsening weather.

A window, large with six glass panes, exposed gray and black clouds. If it were sunny, I knew it must be beautiful to dress in here, basking in the light.

It would be wonderful to make sketches so far above the world.

Putting my thumbs together, measuring, I tried to view everything from Ashbrook's viewpoint. A stable and carriage house mews sat farther from the house, then those gorgeous woods with the lignum vitae. That's what the blue flowers were called. I remembered.

Focus.

With my hands still lifted, I turned back and spied a wooden box on a high shelf.

"What do we have here?"

Crossing the tapestry of red and gold threads, I reached on tiptoes to get it.

"Those are Mama's. No touchy. Pa-Papa, doesn't let me play here."

As slowly as I could, I rocked back on my boot heels. "Well, we wouldn't want to disobey."

When I turned, a gorgeous little girl crawled to my knee. Her coloring was deeper than Patience's, with more red in her brown skin.

"Freckles, you have too," she said.

Stooping, I met her at eye level. The sweet little thing had wide sparkling eyes, not quite topaz or chestnut, something in between.

"Hello."

"You new nanny? Pa-Papa said he might get one. Mrs. G calls her nurse. Don't want either."

I wasn't going to lie, but I'd be vague. "I'm a friend of your father's. He hasn't decided on a new nanny, yet. I thought I'd look around to see if he truly needed one."

The little girl nodded. "Don't want one. Not nice."

I straightened the collar of her blush-pink pinafore. "They can be good."

"The last one not nice."

Looking at her serious frown, her poked-out lips, I wondered what the last nanny had done.

Ashbrook's words fell into my ears—chattel, abuse. I felt sick. This precious little girl should never see how mean people could be.

"You can't touch the box. Mama letters in there. No touchy."

"Then, I won't, but do you know where else your father hides secrets?"

The grin spreading across her face blessed my soul. She took my hand and stood.

She wobbled but led me out of the closet. "I'll show you."

Time was ticking away, but I liked the feel of her hand in mine.

The little girl stopped and pointed to the pink painting. "See."

"I like the art, sweetie. This one is yours?"

Her lips bubbled with a little spittle, and she erupted with glee. "Yes. Pa . . . Pa-Papa say I good."

"What's your name? I've seemed to have forgotten."

"Papa calls me Hope and princess. I like Hope."

"I like that name too. Though you are pretty, pretty like a princess. Pretty like your mama."

The child's lip trembled. "Mama . . . She gone."

Before I could stop myself, I was again on my knees, hugging her, winding her little body up in my arms. Her head flopped against my chest.

It was the most natural thing to embrace this babe.

And the most hurtful.

My loss fell upon me, anew. My daughter, the one I lost on the *Minerva* would be about this age.

Though Ashbrook thought it unwise to contact the St. Maurs, that they may try to lock me away in Bedlam again, I just might try. They would at least know my baby's name.

Then when I prayed, I could tell her I loved her, that I would've died for, should've died with her.

"Don't cry, nanny friend. Don't cry."

Hope tugged on my ear, then locked her little arms about my neck, I held her and wanted so badly to have what Ashbrook had, a sweet girl with a name who painted pink streaks better than any.

Ku ya! *Look here! No falling to pieces. The secrets. Rally, woman! No tek yuh time an' nuh rush di wuk. No more dallying.* I had to be thorough.

The earl would be home soon. I swiped at my eyes. "Hope, you were going to show me where your father keeps secrets."

She shook her head. "Not if you cry." She tugged at my hair, a falling curl. "What does Pa-Papa call you?"

Brushing at my face, I put her back down on the floor. "Friend. I'm a friend."

The little girl had a tighter grip on my hand. "Let me show you, Friend."

Hope tugged on my breeches. "Can you ride horses? My dolly, Mrs. Feebs can't ride my toy horses. She needs to dress like you."

"I do ride horses, but you don't need breeches. You can ride in a dress."

"Show me. My dolly's in my room. Wanna see her and play?"

There wasn't time to and not get caught. Yet, another look into those wide eyes made it almost worth it.

"I'm supposed to play in my room, Friend."

"But where does your father not want you to go? The kitchen, his study?"

"Not on the stairs or the study. I'm not supposed to touch his desk."

"Hope, that sounds like a good place for secrets. You go on to your room."

"No, I show you." She took my hand and led me down the hall. Her balance was very unsteady. The child was at least three. Shouldn't her legs be a little stronger?

Now, I felt worse making Ashbrook's daughter both a witness and a fellow conspirator.

She stopped at the newel post of the stairs; a great carved pineapple topped the thick baluster.

"It's this way, but I'm not supposed to go by myself. We need to wake up Mrs. Gallick. She's napping in my rocking chair."

"I can help you, baby."

She dimpled as I picked her up.

Something changed when I held her, when she put her little face to my chest. My heart raced. I'd break into Ashbrook's house a hundred times to hold this girl and have this feeling.

"Down the stairs, Friend."

"Yes." I was here for burglary not hugs.

We went and I counted all the sconces, at least six. Forgot to notice how this child drew my breath into her lungs, how her head fit right in the crook of my neck as she clutched the ribbons of my hood.

"Put me down now. Miss. Miss?"

"Friend." I said, "I'm your friend, remember."

That notion pleased Hope. She offered the best toothy-one-tooth-missing grin. "Down now."

I didn't want to, but I set her onto the floor. Wiggly, wobbly, she held her balance, then clasped my fingers.

"Papa's study here."

We passed a footman, but I acted calm, like I was supposed to be there, and hid beneath my cape, tugging up my breeches to show stockings.

No one moved, and soon we were safe in the study. I lifted my gaze from Hope and studied the burnished paneling, the picture window. This was the room I'd seen him pacing within from the hedgerow.

I glanced at the painting over the hearth, a seascape of a sunset. The buildings green and white. The sky was reds, oranges, and yellow.

"Mine looks like it but pink."

"It does. It also looks a lot like my home, I think."

Then Hope tugged me to the desk behind a chair and ottoman—all next to a big window. "Pa-Papa keeps locked, but the key here."

She pointed underneath the desk. Before I crawled to get the key, she pointed to letters on the velvet ottoman. "Friend, more secrets."

Some notes looked like my stationery. The other were from a solicitor's firm in Tonbridge.

"If those are from my mama, could you read them? Pa-Papa won't read."

So, Ashbrook was difficult to all the women in his life. I drew my hands to my side. "Your father knows best. I'm sure he'll read them later when you are older. Let's check the desk."

Pounding . . . I heard the pounding of slippered heels, hard and loud. Ashbrook?

There wasn't a place to hide. My barrister shouldn't be mad at both of us. "Sweetie, your father's home. Go to him, run."

"But he says not to."

"Just this once. Go greet him, Hope. Run fast."

The child squeezed my hand and then dropped to the floor. She crawled out the door.

Something was wrong, but I had no time to discover it or the earl's secrets.

Moving to the window, I stared outside. The earl's carriage headed toward his mews.

In another moment, the front would be clear of people. I'd jump down into the hedgerow, and then figure out how to get to my horse in the back of the property.

Lightning zipped. I leaped out and landed on my bottom.

But I'd left the window glass open.

The observant earl would detect that someone had entered his home. I needed to be gone before he or the rain came barreling down.

CHAPTER 25

DANIEL—IN THE RAIN

Mood foul like the coming weather, Daniel stormed into Finchely. He'd lost a trial at the Old Bailey, earned sneers from the Lord Mayor and a lecture of useless warnings. No barrister was perfect, and one who's client lied to him and his solicitor only to confess on the witness dock did prohibit a win.

Days like this made him question Prinny's gambit if Daniel was to be judged by a standard no one could uphold.

"Papa, you're home."

He looked down at the sprite, so happy in her pink dress. "You're not supposed to come down these stairs by yourself. These stairs are steep."

"I was careful, Papa. Friend helped me."

Yawning, Mrs. Gallick met them in the hall. "I suppose you left, Miss Thackery, because I wanted you to wear blue?"

"Don't like blue, only pink."

His housekeeper yawned again. "You in for the evening, sir?"

"Yes. I am a little early."

She smiled at him. "Well, you get changed out of your court robes. It's time for Miss Hope's nap."

"But Pa . . . Pa-Papa just came home."

He knelt on one knee. "I'm not in good mood, but I promise

that once you have your nap, we will play. We'll have a good time of it, just you and me."

"You promise, Pa-Papa? You've been sad all week."

He hugged his girl. "I promise. You make me happy."

With a kiss to his cheek, he gave Hope's hand to Mrs. Gallick's.

"Sir, I have to be out this evening, in an hour."

He yanked off his collar frill. "I truly have no plans."

"Why don't you change and see if Max might need some attention? He's barking a lot today. Come on, Hope."

Her bottom lip stuck out, but she went up the stairs.

His girl wobbled but took each step like a knight charging a hill. She was fearless.

Daniel felt proud. She wasn't going to let anything stop her.

Fingering his watch fob, he thought about getting Max and riding. That might relieve his tension and give his sandy pug some needed exercise. Why else would he be yelping?

When he entered his room, Daniel noticed the door to his closet ajar. That was odd. His valet always closed it up tight.

He scratched his head and went inside. Taking off his robe and ebony tailcoat, he put them on the proper shelves and hooks in his closet.

Tugging on his hunting jacket and boots, Daniel heard Max's heavy barking.

His pug wailed at something.

The bark became more insistent. When he went out onto his balcony, Daniel found a rope and hook wedged onto it. Then he saw Max chasing someone . . . some widow . . . some Jemina St. Maur.

He tugged on the rope and thought about using it to leap down, but he wasn't ready to fall. He had a widow to catch.

In a blink, he crossed the hall, jumped down the stairs, and tore out the rear door. "Get her, Max."

At top speed, he flew across the field.

Even at a distance he could feel the panic in her. That made him run faster.

Veering a sharp left, he went into his stables. Heaving, breathing furiously, he found the horse Mr. Anthon always had ready.

Daniel hopped on his mare.

Thunder warbled as he peeled out and headed straight for the best pug in the world and that wicked widow. "Give up, woman."

Max had her cape in his teeth. His boy was strong and kept Jemina from moving forward.

She untied her cloak and his dog became a tumble of emerald cloth.

"Stay where you are, Mrs. St. Maur!"

Her fearful grimace turned to a smile. She charged into the woods and climbed onto a horse.

No side saddle for her. She rode like a man and rode well.

"Of course you'd be a natural on a horse, Jemina."

Those girls from the islands, they weren't wilting doves. "Slow down, there's a fence. Probably trees that need clearing."

"Catch me if you can." She laughed, the wind making her voice sound maniacal.

There was a break in the fence with a log that came down. She jumped her horse.

Daniel wasn't taking chances and aimed for a proper opening. "Jemina, the weather's picking up. This is dangerous."

She held her seat and leaped over fallen trees, even a stream.

Jemina didn't know his land, didn't know the twists and turns of the field.

But he did.

He used that knowledge to gain ground.

She ducked down and crossed a creek. She'd get blocked by the thick of bushes. Jemina would have to double back.

Daniel had her now.

Speeding up, he charged at her. "You know you're caught. Surrender."

"Not until you have me, Barrister."

She bent her head and pushed toward him.

The woman was crazy. If she thought he'd back down, she was very wrong.

He aimed straight for her. At the last moment, he shifted, held out his arm, and wrenched her from her saddle. "Arrested."

He let the horse beneath him ease into a trot and held the squirming woman fast. "I'm not letting you go."

Her face lifted to his.

Their gazes locked.

Then her arms went about him. "You better not."

He wouldn't. He couldn't.

When he clicked his tongue, Max caught up. "Watch that other horse, boy. What his name, Jemina?"

"Zeus. Don't drop me."

"Then you better hold tight."

Daniel tugged her higher onto his saddle. Those wily arms of hers curled about his neck. Her breath was heavy against his throat.

"You know, Hope believes in hitting her doll's head against a saddle. Maybe she's on to something."

The smell of rain filled the air. Then the drops started.

"I'm not going to think about why you are here, Jemina. I'm not going to ask anything. I need to kiss you. Hate me later. Good plan?"

She sat up straighter, closed her eyes and nodded.

With his thumbs, he trailed the droplets falling upon her lashes. "I need those eyes open. You need to see me, Daniel Thackery. I need to know it's me you want."

Squinty agate eyes that looked of chocolate and jade blinked at him. "Yes."

He raised her chin and claimed those lips.

In the rain, they kissed. His heart drummed in unison to hers. That crazed rhythm in her bosom was everything, everything he felt, everything he couldn't say.

The rain fell harder.

But he wasn't moving. Not from this.

He'd be grumpy and fussy at how crazy she'd been or the clear burglary of his house—later.

Right now, he'd be a young fool kissing the woman who drove everything in him to a fever.

CHAPTER 26

JEMINA—CAPTURED

I was his prisoner, my mouth on Ashbrook's in the rain. Thunder moaned and so did I. My hair had fallen. It was a soggy slick on my neck.

But I was in his hot arms, dripping wet, being kissed by this man like I was air. Maybe he was air, for I gulped him up, too.

His dog's barking picked up. Zeus might be wandering.

Yet, I held Daniel tighter and let his hands wander, exploring the soggy fabric of my shirt, my corset.

He took a deeper breath and just embraced me, fitting me to the hardened muscles of his chest. His voice whispered words that dug into my soul.

> *The pealing thunder shook the heav'nly plain;*
> *Majestic grandeur! From the zephyr's wing,*
> *Exhales the incense of the blooming spring.*

"More poetry? I love your voice, but what does it mean?"

"It's Phillis Wheatley, a negress poet from the Americas. I find it calming when my heart is about to explode." His fingers twirled a lock of my hair. "Maybe it will soothe yours. It's riotous against me. And I only want it closer. I hunger for so much."

He began again.

> *But the west glories in the deepest red:*
> *So may our breasts with ev'ry virtue glow,*
> *The living temples—*

I kissed him. Didn't need him painting words about the communion of human temples made to worship flesh and flurried desire. I had too many images in my head of him and me and sweet abandon.

The rain worsened. Groaning, he quit me and motioned his horse. "Back to the house. We need to get out of these . . . I mean we need to get you good and warm."

I was warm, and he knew it. The question was what to do about it and all our secrets.

He rode over to the Shire horse and grabbed his reins. "You didn't steal this too?"

"No, he belongs to the duke. Are you going to turn me in to the magistrate?"

"Jemina, I don't know what I'm going to do with you but sending my would-be mistress to Newgate would be an awful scandal, especially with the talk about us dying."

He clicked his heels. "Come on, boy. Come on, Max."

We crossed his grassy-green fields splashing puddles and headed into his stables, an old building made of thick timbers.

Daniel jumped down, and then jerked me from his saddle.

With his hand firmly locked onto mine, he turned to his groom, a young man of eighteen or nineteen. "Mr. Anthon, once you get these horses brushed down, there's an emerald cloak out in the field. Can you get it, beat it clean, and send it up to the main house?"

"Yes, sir, Lord Ashbrook."

The young man stared and smiled as he took the horses from Daniel.

Not letting go, the earl marched me up to Finchely.

Max followed, and then jumped up onto my hip, trying to tug us apart.

"Down, boy. My prisoner's not going anywhere. Inside with you, Jemina. We'll get you freshened up, then I'll ship you back to the duchess, or should I say the duke? I think Repington will be better at coming up with a punishment. I'm sure he's court-martialed more than one or two within his command."

That didn't sound good, and that wouldn't help Patience. "Please, Daniel. Let me be no trouble to them."

"Just trouble to me? Inside."

In the threshold of Finchely House, I dripped from head to toe. So did Daniel. He flung out his spectacles.

He turned to a footman and jerked off his coat. "Can you retrieve some towels, maybe a blanket?"

The fellow in a light blue livery disappeared and then returned with a pile of linens. Daniel took them and towed me into his study. "Sit. Sit here by the fire."

Rain continued to come down. Thunder crackled and shook the roof.

He worked the logs in his hearth and started a blaze.

The heat felt good.

He dropped towels on my head.

"If I'd kept my cape, I wouldn't be so wet."

Max lay beside me at my boots. I dropped a towel on him and started drying the crooning hound. "Bad dog."

"Max, this is Jemina. Jemina, this is my pug, Maximillian. We call him Killer. Good dog, catching the bandit."

The earl wiped at his spectacles and then took a towel and wrapped my dripping hair.

"I must look odd to you."

"No comment, Jemina. Let's get you dry."

Maybe I had a face like Phoebe's and could wear a turban.

"Jemina St. Maur. Wild woman. Do I need to list the ways you could've been hurt. Max, who's letting you rub his belly and purring like my aunt's cat, can be vicious."

Another tickle of pug's thick neck, and he rolled over whining. "Yes, I feel threatened."

"He must be off duty." Daniel barely contained his laugh. After stoking the flames again, he took the sheets and wrapped me and the chair.

The door opened. "Sir . . ."

"Yes, Mrs. Gallick."

"I, aaah, I'd changed my mind on heading out, my lord. The weather is so bad."

The housekeeper stared at me. I was sort of glad the sheet covered my breeches.

Daniel sighed. "Hope's napping?"

"Yes. Sir, is all well here?"

"Yes, my friend here, Mrs. St. Maur, was caught in the rain."

"The note writer? Ahh. I'll go get you some tea." She left the room and eased the door closed.

Daniel pushed up his lenses and rubbed his beard. "Why? You could've come and asked to borrow sugar. That's a good excuse, not outright burglary."

"You don't tell me anything unless you're cornered. And I only entered your bedchamber without permission. Well, you sort of gave me permission to be there."

"No, not at Finchely, not where my daughter is."

"Hope welcomed me to the rest of your house. She thinks I'm a nanny candidate."

"Don't lie to my daughter."

"I didn't. I told her I was a friend. I think that was more appropriate than saying I'm your father's mistress. Well, his mistress candidate."

"You turned down my offer, though those kisses in my fields says there may be room for negotiation."

His head bent to mine. I lifted to his lips, ready to taste, to surrender—

A scream.

Piercing and infinite, the shriek filled the house.

The child's cry ripped at my chest, slashing my recovered heart to ribbons. Sheets and all, I dove out of his study. Hope was at the top of the stairs, wobbling and crying. "Mama! I want Mama!"

Everything slowed.

My ears exploded with the crash of thunder, with seeing her fall.

I leaped and had her in my arms, but the tangle of sheets, made me crash and roll. It was my shoulder, and then my head that felt the impact of the treads. I tucked Hope deep against my ribs so my arms, my legs, my spine hit each step.

When the world stopped. I saw my baby being taken from me again, and I screamed and screamed.

Then I let go and sunk to depths with the *Minerva*.

CHAPTER 27

DANIEL—THE STAIRS

Pacing back and forth outside the bedchamber adjacent to his own, Daniel waited on the landing.

The stairs, twisting and steep, lay to his right. He loved going up and down, counting the polished balusters, sweeping his fingers over the carved newel posts.

They'd always been a danger. He just thought he'd been clever enough, guarded enough, to keep disaster at bay.

None of this was supposed to happen. Hope was supposed to be taking her nap, secure and safe. Thank goodness she was well and sleeping in her room. Dearest Jemina—he wasn't fast enough to save either.

He swiped at perspiration on his brow. Jemina had protected Hope, but his favorite widow burglar, she lay hurt behind the bedchamber's door, unconscious. He stared at the knob, the inset panels. Memories of hearing his mother sob in that room constricted his heavy throat.

Someone in that room needed to come to him.

Someone needed to tell him if Jemina opened her eyes.

Just a word.

Just a mention from the physician that all was well.

Just a peep from Lady Shrewsbury about Jemina's breathing.

Just a hint from the Duchess of Repington that their friend was still the Jemina they knew, the woman they both loved.

He wasn't supposed to feel this way again, not about her or anyone. Love meant being vulnerable. Every moment he paced it became clearer. Daniel was about to lose the second woman he ever loved.

It wasn't fair.

It wasn't right.

Holding on to the rail, his sanity, he had to keep his wits for Hope. He needed a little more hope. He called out for something bigger and stronger to save him from his doubts, his growing despair.

The duchess slipped from the room and stood by his side. Her frown shook his awakened heart.

"We can't lose her." His voice was a strained whisper.

Her grace nodded. "She's a miracle. To have lived when so many others didn't. The *Minerva* took everyone, her husband, all her family."

Daniel looked to the window, to the falling rain. Nothing to do but wait, wait for the rest of his world to be destroyed. If he closed his eyes, he'd be at Portsmouth, standing in line, holding fast to his dreams until it was his turn to hear the horrid news.

"Your Grace, I always thought I was good with waiting, you know . . . with my uncle, with trials. Maybe I tolerated it, foolishly believing that good triumphs, that in the end I'd win."

The duchess blinked her topaz eyes heavily. "All is not lost, Lord Ashbrook. We can't think that it is."

Jemina's sacrifice kept his daughter safe. He owed that woman everything. She needed everything, more than he'd ever prepared to give.

The woman, his friend, had to live so he could make good on the promises burning up his soul.

* * *

Close to midnight, the rain had finally stopped. A purple inky sky framed his windows, and Daniel sat on the landing waiting, feet crossed, arms folded, staring.

Nothing. No news. No awakening. Nothing.

The door to Jemina's bedchamber opened. Daniel leaped up, holding his breath, prepared to be kicked in the chest.

Patience rushed to him, grasped his arm. "She's awake. She is awake. She's going to be well."

It took a moment to fill his lungs, for her words to register. His posture sagged as steam blew out of his nostrils. Jemina lived. Again, she was a miracle.

Lady Shrewsbury came to them. "Patience, can you come sit with her. I need to leave for a little."

The duchess nodded and sailed into the room.

The door closed.

The feelings of triumph warred with the fear that the woman he loved might be again that woman on paper who married into a disreputable family.

His aunt took up his hand. "Daniel, she's improving. And as you can see, she doesn't need a Widow's Grace operation to become injured."

"This is a really bad time to prove a point, Aunt."

She put a hand to his shoulder. "No points. Just trying to tell you that life is short. When you find what you want, it's fine to take risks."

He asked Jemina what she wanted, but he hadn't asked the question of himself, not for anything longer than a season.

His aunt kissed his cheek. "I'm going to check on my niece before I leave."

Before she could turn, he scooped Lady Shrewsbury up in an embrace. "Thank you," he said to her silvering blond curls and lacy mobcap.

"What's that for, Daniel?"

"A great many things. And an admission that I still welcome my aunt assisting in some of my problems."

"That's a big admission for you." She smiled at him. "Will you also admit that you see the need to continue the Widow's Grace?"

"If you are asking if I will continue to assist you, I can't, but I can still look the other way as long as you can keep your ladies from danger and running amok. Can't convince you to retire with me?"

"Retire? Daniel, you are in your prime." She held on to his hand, "You are thinking about making radical changes again?"

He didn't know what he wanted other than to walk into that bedroom and see Jemina's face and know she recognized his. "I might think about a house in the country with no stairs. Maybe an estate sprawling with land for horses."

"Daniel, why not go make your guests something to eat? I think Mrs. St. Maur is hungry. I told her a story about your mash."

With a nod he trotted down the stairs to the kitchen. Even if he had to court her all over again, he would. For Jemina St. Maur was the woman who needed to be his mistress, his wife, and new mother to his child. The order of titles was the only question that remained.

CHAPTER 28

JEMINA—A LITTLE HOPE

Patience finally went to bed. She hovered about me, washed my face, working herself too hard.

I barely opened my eyes when Ashbrook came in with his sweet-smelling bowl of fruit. I sent him away. I didn't want his lecture about how reckless I'd been.

I knew it was careless and foolish, to run in a tangle of sheets.

If he understood what it was to lose a child, your life, your future, then he'd know I couldn't bear to see it happen again.

Maybe men couldn't understand. Maybe—

The bed shook.

I looked in the low candlelight expecting to see the earl's pug but saw Hope. She'd crawled inside my room.

"Are you better, Friend?"

Putting one hand to my head, I massaged the lump on my crown. "A little."

"Good. Not gone. I don't want Friend gone."

The child should be in her bed. I wasn't steady enough to take her, not that I knew where her room was. Would Ashbrook be considerate and have floorplans lying about?

"I sorry, Friend."

Her little face held such a deep frown.

It ached to do so, but I lifted my hand and waved to her. "Why don't you come up here with me?"

She crawled fast, then pulled up, holding on to the blankets. She took the doll stuck under the crux of her arm and handed her to me. "This is Mrs. Feebs. She watches over me."

"Please to meet you, Mrs. Feebs." Setting the doll—a beautiful wooden one with brown yarn hair, and dots on her face—by my side, I stretched and lifted Hope to me.

She snuggled into the blankets but instead of lying near, she snuggled onto my stomach with her head on my chest. "I like your heart."

The sweet little thing yawned and fisted the buttons of the nightshirt I wore.

Once the small thing went to sleep, I should call to Ashbrook or Mrs. Gallick.

Instead, I hooked my arm about her and went to sleep, silently sobbing, coveting the feel of her little warm body next to my bosom.

CHAPTER 29

DANIEL—AMBROSIA

'Twas too much for this night. Daniel tied his robe and hunted for his daughter.

That feeling that she was hurt or scared whipped through his horrible sleep. Now to find her missing from her crib was abominable.

Running from the nursery, he glanced at the stairs. Nothing. Nothing was below.

Then he heard noises.

Crying.

Not a child's whimper, but a big girl.

A light spread from under the bedchamber adjoining his room.

He tapped lightly for show but barged inside.

Jemina lay propped up on pillows. Her finger was to her mouth silencing him.

Then he saw little Hope asleep in her arms. "I guess Hope chose the order, mother first."

"What, Ashbrook? What did you say?"

"Nothing." He played with the belt of his robe. "Hope had me fretting. She should be in her bed."

"My lord, she's fine."

"We're back to formalities, Jemina?"

She pushed back a curl from her cheek. He was right. Her loosed locks did reach her waist, those hips.

"If you're going to lecture me about risks—"

"Why would I do that when you're not given to listening?" He moved to the footboard. "Lectures are the last thing on my mind. Your health and safety are everything."

She blinked at him, and he hungered to know what she thought, what notions danced in her lively head. "Do you need anything?"

"I can't move."

He clutched the bedpost. "What? Do I need to get the doctor?"

"No. I meant I don't want to disturb this little one. She's sleeping good. How old is she?"

"Four in October."

"Her balance?"

He bit his lip, then unbuttoned them. Hope's hero needed to know. "She's a little slow developing her balance, but she's getting better."

Her eyes were filled with tears. His throat clogged a little but he didn't know how to move forward.

Then he spied the uneaten bowl of ambrosia mash on the bed table. "You don't like cherries or pineapple? Too light on the coconut?"

She stroked Hope's cheek. "My hands are a little full, not that I mind."

Daniel was never this indecisive, but he hadn't felt like his whole world was before him either. Humor. That and arguments were how they'd distracted each other.

"I think if you tasted my ambrosia, Jemina, you couldn't resist it."

"Daniel—"

"No. I am quite serious." He took a step, forcing his feet to the table. Sitting on the edge of the mattress, he filled a spoon with his mash and waved it under Jemina's nose. "I suppose I will have to feed you like this one."

"It's not necessary."

"It is absolutely necessary." He put a finger to her lips and smoothed that cupid's bow with his pinkie. "Open."

When she did, he put a spoonful into her mouth.

A cross between a laugh and yum squeaked out. "You didn't say there were bananas and pomegranates too."

"I'm unpredictable when it comes to mashes." He fed her another and another until a third of the bowl was gone.

A touch of juice drizzled down her chin. The urge to dip and sip the offering pressed. Jemina was seductive, and she wasn't even trying.

"You're an expert. Not too much on the spoon, just the right amount. An expert and a good host."

Good host maybe, but he was no saint. The path to sin and a cupid's bow was too close to his child. Yet he stared at her glancing back at him, remembering him, even desiring him with her lovely eyes.

Daniel bounced up. "That's probably enough."

She pushed at a frizzed curl. "I must look awful. Lord—"

"Daniel. It's Daniel to my prisoners. Be intimate with my name."

"Daniel, do you have curl papers?"

"Hmm. No. Ribbons. Pink ribbons, I'm sure I can find those. Pink is Hope's favorite color. She fusses something terrible when forced to wear another color."

"Rebellious in nature so soon. I love her."

His heart stopped. Then it started as his swallow went down slowly. Hope really had chosen. Any fear of Jemina not wanting to be a stepmother was extinguished.

What should he say, now that he knew what he wanted?

"Daniel, I'm going to tell you my plans. I'm not going to hide. I want to contact my family. I should know why the St. Maurs put me away. Did they blame me for the loss of their son?"

Nothing good could come from her digging into the *Minerva* or the St. Maurs. "What if we wait until you're better before we talk about the past?"

"There's never going to be a time for you to help. Will there be, Daniel?"

He rocked back and then looked down at Hope. "My child is getting to know you. She likes you. She'll expect to see you. If the St. Maurs have power over you . . . I don't want you taken from us because of terrible people. We almost lost you tonight. Can I please have a week or two of not fretting about you or Hope?"

Her forehead wrinkled. "Must you always think the worst will happen?"

"I'm a barrister. I've seen the worst, but tonight you've stopped the worst. You saved my Hope."

"You gave me hope when you rescued me from Bedlam." She settled deeper into her pillows. "Well, what do we do in this period?"

"I'm a patient man. We can have a torrid affair later, and it will be long and torrid."

"How long? How torrid?"

"Very long. Very torrid. In the interim, let's have a truce and work on the question that we struggle with, friendship. Let me be your friend, Jemina. I don't want you to ever question it again."

"I'd like to be your friend, Daniel."

"Excellent." Like at the Old Bailey, he turned his back to her as if she were one of the jurymen.

He paced and put together a good plan to cement their friendship. "Next week, you should be feeling better and you should come to court. Your colleague, Widow Cultony, has her hearing then. My colleague, a fellow barrister, is still in the dark about her knowing his strategy. I assume by now Aunt has amassed countering witness statements."

"That sir, I cannot disclose. See, I can be discreet."

He laughed and shook his head. "You are unusual."

"And you are out of ambrosia. If you are going to be up watching me and Hope, the least you can do is make more."

He leaned close, peering down at the empty bowl. "You're not the type of girl who would leave me nothing?"

Her palm went to his jaw. It was rough, a little calloused. Probably too much rope climbing. "You look so serious, Daniel, fretting over a little ambrosia between friends."

Retrieving the spoon, he dropped it with a clang into the empty bowl. "I'll see what can be arranged."

If she kept touching him and stuck to the present, he'd give her the world. He'd give her forever too, merely for the way Hope clung to her.

He kissed his daughter's brow, then Jemina's too. "I'll return with another bowl."

He headed to the kitchen. An odd comfort filled him. That sweet picture of Jemina and Hope turned in his head.

If she could trust him and leave the past behind, then Daniel would know he'd found the woman for him and his daughter.

Gaining her trust fully was going to be difficult when danger and Jemina seemed entwined.

CHAPTER 30

JEMINA—OLD BAILEY FRIENDS

My nerves seemed tight, stretched like a canvas readying to pop as I stood at the entry of the prestigious Old Bailey. The curved marble of the bricked facade looked daunting, so aloof and strong.

When I walked inside, a little boy waving nosegay went past me. The sweet herbs of whatever was in his pot ushered in peace, which lasted until I saw Daniel.

He came from a room up ahead. With a slight dip of his chin, his perfectly trimmed beard looking elegant, he turned but not before I saw the look in his shiny jet eyes. The seriousness in his face, like a man possessed, it made him look older, almost haunted. With a coarse silver wig and the white frills about his neck, he looked like the world was upon his shoulders.

This image was at odds with the gentle man who fed me mash and laughed with his whole soul.

"Woman, look where you're going."

I'd bumped into a lady wearing a feather turban. She had that look of old money or the appearance of it with her shiny satin blue pelisse.

"Sorry."

An arm looped about mine. "Don't mind her, Buckles."

Lady Lavinia, spry with her brunette curls coiffed and bouncing under a bonnet that pointed to the side like a pirate's, spun me around. "Come for the show or the earl?"

"Maybe a little of both. I hear court can be quite dramatic."

"Not as dramatic as the little fight I heard you and our Daniel had. He seemed quite inconsolable through Lady Shrewsbury's dinner. I had to work extra hard to cheer him up. Don't go twisting him up now because you want him back."

Lady Lavinia thought me stupid or that I hadn't been recovering at Finchely. I had no doubts about how Daniel chose to spend his time.

The femme fatale definitely didn't know this girl had been hand-fed by the earl. I grinned at her. "Keep up the good work. We need him happy."

"He'd be a lot happier if he was more like his father and not so serious."

"Lady Lavinia, I think the earl is fine as is."

"His drunkard father was more fun. Always singing, always one to count on to do something outlandish."

Daniel never mentioned his father, not once, and I knew the barrister hated outlandish. "Excuse me. Court must be starting."

As I turned, she grabbed my elbow again. "You're not bothered that he's with us both? You're not frustrated that he won't publicly acknowledge either one of us?"

"Discretion is a good quality. I thank you for giving him comfort. A little bit of advice: he doesn't like loud women."

The woman faltered for a moment, but her smile recovered. She released my arm and walked with me deeper into the building. "You're a strange one, Buckles."

"It's a gift to be contrary."

She looked away, adjusting her calf leather gloves. "Go marry the dowdy shipper. Lord Ashbrook is not for you."

"I know, but a girl should enjoy the services of an earl, a handsome one at that, at least once. Excuse me."

Her stained perfect mouth hung open. Those painted cheeks darkened as I left her to her scheming.

Making my way to the gallery, I took a seat by a column, near a face I recognized from Lady Shrewsbury's kitchen table meetings.

Brunette, lithe from fretting, Mrs. Cultony looked at me and I her.

We weren't supposed to acknowledge one another in public. No one was to know. But I clasped my hands in prayer. In a clear voice, I offered a whisper just for her. "The holy habitation is the protector of widows, providing relief and favor. Favor in the courts."

She nodded, and then faced the barrister's table.

I felt deeply for Mrs. Cultony. The custody of her girls would be assured if this cruel charge of theft was gone. The Court of the Chancery would have to see how loving and good she was and how wrong her husband's family had been in taking the children.

If my babe had survived the *Minerva*, I'm sure the St. Maurs would use my amnesia to deny my rights. I felt it deep in my bosom. Daniel must suspect this too, that they'd use my condition to harm me. It had to be why he was so protective.

A man costumed similarly to the earl with a wig and black robes approached the high desk at the front of the courtroom.

"New evidence has appeared, Lord Mayor," he said. "After discussing with a colleague, I suggest the charges against Mrs. Cultony brought forth by the Cultony family be withdrawn."

The Lord Mayor, a thin man in a robe of scarlet and donning a horse wig full of curls half down his back, craned his neck. He looked over his high desk. "What are you speaking of?"

"Several witnesses have come forward to dispute the claims. The missing items were found in the family's possession. The Cultonys are now saying this was a tragic misunderstanding."

"A misunderstanding?" The Lord Mayor guffawed, uttering an annoyed nasal sound from his lengthy nose. "Let your clients know what a grievous problem it is to have misunderstandings waste the court's time."

"They do," the barrister said, "and they extend every apology."

The crowd and my fellow widow sat like stone, like marble statues.

So did I.

It wasn't done until the man in red said so. All the Widow's Grace knew this. Cultony needed the law and facts to marry with favor—all had to be on the same side for this to be a win.

The Lord Mayor picked up his gavel and held it for at least twenty seconds. "The charges," he said in a huff, "are vacated. Remind the Cultony family if they ever waste the court's time again, they will find themselves in Newgate. Call the next trial to order."

The barrister bowed and headed back to the table, the half-circle-shaped desk where Daniel sat.

My fellow conspirator, my fellow widow grasped my hand.

Her face was still fully forward, but she squeezed my fingers, three quick pumps, all hidden beneath my creamy shawl.

Then she tiptoed out of the gallery of spectators. The Widow's Grace had done good.

But I didn't budge.

My barrister stood. He seemed a little taller than the other men. The ebony color of Daniel's robe made his skin seem darker, so much warmer than the others. He was wonderfully tan, golden, like the sun had found a way to touch him through the large windows anchoring the court.

Daniel leaned over the table and flipped through papers. "I, Lord Mayor, have an instance of true theft. This will be a prosecution of fabric."

"Showy fabric? A case meant for you, Ashbrook." The Lord Mayor snorted a chuckle. "Proceed."

The tone he took with Daniel . . . a little harsh, even condescending, made me cringe, but the earl didn't flinch. He turned to his papers as a man was brought by the bailiff to the prisoner's dock.

Shackles. Dull metal on his hands. It looked so heavy.

For a moment, I closed my eyes to it, until I heard Daniel's perfect diction, crisp and calm. "This is a theft of convenience. Sometimes proximity can cause things to go awry. Sometimes it's a gift."

Heat rose to my cheeks as if he spoke only to me.

He made a point with hand waving, then he raised his gaze to the spectators ringing the courtroom.

Did he see me?

Did he wish, like me, that it was only him and I alone in this room?

Then he could be as carefree as a man on a horse giving chase, not chained to protocol or other's expectations. Then I'd share my secret of how I liked being under his protection last week. How I craned my ear to hear him return to Finchely, seeking out me and Hope. I'll never forget our final dinner together, all of us sitting in his dining room, his full smile showing between courses.

Daniel moved in front of the jurymen. "I will prove that Samuel Towl took advantage of proximity to abuse his employer."

"Proceed, Lord Ashbrook." The Lord Mayor flipped a page on his crowded desk. "Do get on with it."

"Samuel Towl," Daniel said. "You've been indicted for the felonious crime of stealing the property of John Gray. Is that true?"

"Yes, they charged me, but I didn't do it."

Daniel picked up a piece of paper. "Have you ever worked for the linen draper, John Gray?"

The fellow in chains slapped his hands against the rail. "I worked for 'em. He fired me and lied on me to get me charged. How's a man to feed his family when you rich do-nothin's tak'n' everything?"

The crowds sighed and hooted, but my eyes locked again on the prisoner's chains. Iron links to hold you down, to keep you away, to make you comply. The St. Maurs dumped me into Bedlam. Why? What threat was I, or was it punishment?

Someone was to blame for my husband's and daughter's deaths. They decided I was to pay?

I blinked and focused again on now, the present.

Daniel raised his palms, and the room quieted. "Why would Mr. Gray do this? You seem a decent man, a family man."

"Do I have to answer this Blackamoor's questions? If I'm going to Newgate, let it be done with my peers, the good ones."

The place became noisy again.

Many laughed, but Daniel, he didn't look upset. Nothing had changed in his blank expression—his stance remained unbothered. Nothing.

"Mr. Towl," he said, "you will answer my questions, or you can confess right now to being so foolish as to steal from your employer in the middle of the day."

"I'm not foolish. Can he say I'm foolish, Judge?"

Daniel went in front of the prisoner box. He whispered something.

All leaned in, but I could tell that he said something that wiped the smug smile from the defendant.

"Last chance to confess." Daniel's voice boomed. "Save yourself a further embarrassment, Towl."

The chained individual pursed his lips as if to spit, but the barrister flicked a finger and a quick-moving guard whacked Towl on the leg.

"All right, my lord, call off the dogs. I'll answer."

Daniel still seemed unemotional, like stone. "What time did you get up on April third?"

"Same as always. About seven."

"How did you decide upon what to wear?"

Towl shrugged. "Just pulled on what was clean."

"Hmmm, how sad." He moved from the prisoner's dock. "When did you arrive at Mr. Gray's employ?"

"About nine, same as always."

"Describe your place of work. Is it elegant?"

"Yes, I see more of those Mayfair types comin' and goin'."

"And you work hard. Look at your hands. Calluses. I can tell you work very hard."

"Yes, I do. I slave for Mr. Gray. You should know about sl—"

"Must burn you up." Daniel leaned in again. "To work day after day with little to show for it."

"Yes, you rich fancy people don't understand."

Daniel marched back to the barrister table and moved some pages around as if he were looking for something. "The fabrics at John Gray's are beautiful. I hear there's true gold threads woven into some of the most expensive cloth." He held up a fragment of silk.

The cloth shimmered in the candlelight.

"Dare I say, there's gold in the weft of the material." He set down the remnant. "That must be mighty expensive, Mr. Towl."

The defendant wiped at his mouth like he drooled. "Yes."

"I can see that even these scraps have value. An industrious fellow could do something with the bits and pieces, but you have to have some sort of talent to piece things together."

"Mr. Gray didn't care about the scraps. I could take those and make something good out o' 'em. I've made a purse out the material."

"So that's what you did. And you've done it before." He held up three ribbon-bound documents. "I possess three witness statements saying that two ladies and an elderly gentleman all purchased items from you. Such an industrious fellow to make beauty from scraps."

"I am indust—Industri . . ."

"Hardworking? Is that a better word, Towl?"

Daniel's tart comments set fire to the silent spectators, stirring them to chuckle.

"But you received a big order. One large order would set you up right. No one would know. Scraps and a bit more. It was nothing to Mr. Gray's other deals."

"He wasn't going to miss it."

A gasp rushed over the Old Bailey.

Daniel had made the man confess. Brilliant.

"You admit you did it, Towl? I need you to be very clear. The

court needs to hear you." He lowered his hands like he'd con-
cluded a dance.

The crowds hushed.

Was I leaning forward?

"Towl, I need you to think very carefully. Say the truth and appeal to the court's mercy. Or do I need to bring the witnesses, the
man who saw you take the bundle of new cloth under your arm?
Or the other noble soul who tackled you with goods still clutched
in your meaty palms?"

The man gripped the rails and hung his head. "No. I confess.
I ask for mercy."

The weight of Daniel's questioning made the prisoner crumble. The men in the jury area whooped and hollered again.

That's when I saw the earl's half smile, his shoulders falling
back as he turned to face the judge. "Lord Mayor, you've heard
the confession, I ask that we forgo burdening the good jurymen.
I move you sentence the defendant and offer leniency. He's
given his testimony and thrown himself at your mercy."

"Yes, sir. I throw myself like he said."

The Lord Mayor put on a dark cap and pounded his gavel
along his desk. "Agreed. I will sentence him now. Mr. Towl, you
will be whipped at sundown and then confined in Newgate for
three months."

Ashbrook raised a hand, then drew it back slowly to his side.
"Lord Mayor, must Towl be whipped? He confessed. Mercy—"

"My ruling stands. Lord Ashbrook, know a win when you hear
it. The trial is over. Waste no time with me."

The earl nodded, but the man's harsh tone made my stomach
burn. Daniel did a service to the Crown and the judge was condescending to him. That wasn't right.

The diligent barrister took it without complaint.

Why?

A glimpse at Daniel's hand showed it fisting about his papers.
He did have emotions. They'd been buried. The man riding,

chasing after me on horseback, hid nothing. This one in court was forced to hide everything.

I understood him, better than I ever had, the show he had to maintain. The hurt he had to hide. If I'd understood sooner, we would've quarreled less.

The Lord Mayor left his bench.

The bailiff led the angry, bucking prisoner out of the court.

The Old Bailey cleared.

Daniel drew a crowd. Women. Wealthy women in fine dresses, the kind with lace and pleats that took hours to press, fluttered about him.

Lady Lavinia passed me, tipping her bonnet before leaving. She must have thought it unwise to threaten all the ladies who waited for the barrister.

I wasn't trying to compete for his affections. Maybe I vainly thought I had them, but I hated tension between women more. Maybe that's why I loved the Widow's Grace, women helping women.

Still, I didn't want anyone helping themselves to Daniel.

I started down the stairs to reach him. People rushed past me, but I was determined.

Left. Right. Somehow, I became a little turned around in the hall. The crowd flowed one way, but I swam against it.

Upstream, I waded in the entry to the prestigious courtroom.

Empty, the benches for the barristers, the jurymen, bared.

Silent and cold, the air scented with dying nosegay teased my head.

I put my hands on the barrister table, the spot where Daniel had stood, had won.

"Madame, who are you set to defend today?"

That voice.

Rich, shiver inducing, Daniel.

"Mrs. St. Maur?"

Like a magnet, I spun toward him, feeling the draw to his dark eyes. That crazy heart of mine raced. "I think I should defer the defense to you."

"Well, I have a pretty good record of wins when I am not distracted."

"Your lordship, I seem beset by distractions."

"Then let's have the perfect afternoon, friend. My carriage is outside."

He'd changed from white and black to another stylish waistcoat of emerald and a jacket of deep indigo. But on his head remained the powdered wig.

Before I could stop myself, I was at his side with my hands in his hair, fingering the fine thick bouncy waves. I pulled off his court wig.

"Can't keep your hands off me. Can you, Jemina?"

Nodding fast, I swallowed hard. "Where's the box? You must have a box for this."

He held out his arm. "It's in my carriage, along with an afternoon of adventure."

"Adventure, you say, Lord Ashbrook? Is this before you rush home?"

His smile showed and a tinge of the gap in his teeth. "Alas, friends and mistress candidates have to endure my schedule. Are you game?"

"Yes." Holding his wig like a reticule, I wrapped my arm about his. This was an invitation I couldn't refuse.

CHAPTER 31

MARKET DAY

With his palms on her waist, Daniel guided Jemina into his carriage. He hurried, not that he was opposed to holding her, but the Old Bailey was a central point of gossip.

This wasn't the discretion he'd followed since beginning his practice. Yet, not touching, not helping her wasn't an option.

Jemina sat opposite him as he put his wig away in the leather-trimmed box where he stored it.

"You're mighty silent, my lord, for a man who won his trial."

He waited for the carriage to start, for the two of them to be away from this stiff showy world. "It's a ritual of quiet reflection."

"Oh." Her head turned to the window with thumbs up, moving in and out.

The carriage turned the corner. He relaxed and stared at his companion, her buckled slippers and simple lavender dress. "What are you doing?"

"My ritual."

Fresh-faced without the artifice of rouge or heavy perfumes like the typical spectators at the court, the woman was a welcomed change.

"You're never boring, my dear."

"Daniel, you say that as if you are."

He sat back with folded arms. "Quite dull, except for my aunt's escapades and my vingt-et-un nights."

"Oh, the card game with your friends."

His smile bloomed. He couldn't help it. "You can't help watching me, can you?"

Jemina leaned forward. "You could make things a great deal easier if you just confessed all."

"I'm not a defendant, Jemina."

"A hostile witness then to my secrets."

Lifting off his spectacles, he took his handkerchief and wiped his lenses. "Why not leave all this law business to me? I'm quite good at it. Alas, I'm just a servant, serving at the whims of the Lord Mayor."

Those thumbs of hers kept moving, opening and closing. "You make yourself sound so small."

"Rest assured, I'm a big lad . . . ready for all challenges." He rubbed at his face. "You want to tell me what your ritual is all about?"

"I don't want to disturb you."

Well, that was annoyingly considerate and wrong since they were conversing.

Those hand of hers kept moving. A dance? Some sort of code?

It definitely was a tactic to confuse him. It worked and left him staring at her perfect oval face, her smooth cheeks loaded with freckles. Those dots foretold a love of the outdoors. He could definitely see Jemina frolicking in the sunshine or barefoot on beach sand.

Her palms rested on her lap, the beginnings of her hips.

"Done with your ritual? Jemina, I can honestly say I was wrong about such formalities."

She put a finger to her lips. "Shhhhhh."

Then her hands lifted again, moving close to the window, thumbs sliding together then parting. Close. Parting, close.

He reached out and grabbed her wrists. "You will drive me insane. Do you do this on purpose to confuse me or to make me think about you constantly?"

"Maybe this is how I distract myself from thinking of you and the secrets you are silent upon."

"We both need hobbies, Jemina." He pulled her fingers close to his lips, enjoying how her eyes grew large with anticipation. "Or maybe we need to admit that friendship for us is not enough."

Her eyes grew wide. That sweet mouth of hers parted. "What are you saying? You're not going back to that ridiculous offer?"

He wasn't, but it wasn't ridiculous for two consenting adults. . . . Goodness, she had him defending what he didn't want, well not all that he wanted. Hell.

"Marry me."

"What? You jest."

Daniel released her and shook his head. "Not a joke, more a plea. My offer is not why I asked you to join me today. I wanted to cement our friendship, but what better way than in matrimony. Then I won't have to fret about you crossing the hedgerow to ravish me or burglarizing Finchely because it would be your home."

"Are you always joking?"

"Only if you say no. Oh, and I forgot, marriage takes care of your concern about the longevity of my affections. As you can see, I intend them forever."

She lowered her eyes. "I see."

That was it? He blathered and bared his soul for nothing. "Jemina?"

"If I asked you something would you tell me the truth?"

Daniel wanted to say it depends, but he found himself nodding.

"Tell me of your parents, their marriage. Lady Lavinia indicated it was not a happy one. You've told me Lady Shrewsbury raised you, another indication of something unsettling betwixt the two. I want to know why ours would be different."

The balance of this blurted gamble depended on what he said. The intimacy of his mind to hers, the openness is what she craved. He tugged at his cravat and coughed, waiting to see the desire in her eyes turn to pity. "My mother died young."

"I'm sorry, D—"

"Of a broken heart. My father drank too much spirits. He always left and was always in his cups. He had no control. I heard he died from too much drink, choking. . . . Finchely was my mother's. She grieved his loss and then died."

She put her hand to his knee, and he covered her fingers.

"I make sure never to indulge. I'll never be him. Never will Hope fret about me not coming home. You wouldn't either."

"You'd never do that, Daniel."

"If you knew the shame he brought to my mother, you'd be fretful every time I left out the door. Some things are in the blood."

Her carefree smile faded. The slight curve to her posture from her years put away from society seemed more prevalent.

"As I said, I'll be home to you and Hope. And I'll work hard to fill your life so that you never hunger to look back."

Their gazes locked, sending tremors of longing and more through him, tightening like a vise about his heart. He bottled up his own caution, fearful that the wrong words, the wrong look, would make her turn. "Say yes."

She bit her lip and kept his hand. "There's much to consider."

Considering wasn't dismissal, but it wasn't yes.

Fingers lacing with hers, he sat back. "I can be patient for now. Jemina, think on it. Today, I will show you how to pick a ripe pomegranate."

"A pomegranate?"

"Yes. The way you gobbled up my mash, I feel honor-bound to teach you how to make your own, starting with a perfect pomegranate."

Those pretty lips parted. "Yes, perfect."

Mr. Anthon stopped them at busy Covent Garden. Everyone

came to shop or take in all sorts of entertainment. Daniel and Jemina would blend in, and his coins would take care of vendors who stared too much. Lady Shrewsbury took him here often in her efforts to help Daniel feel more comfortable in society. At times, he felt like a feral cat learning to live indoors.

Lifting Jemina down from the carriage, he was careful with his hands on her waist, the small of her back. "Rituals."

The serious lines and counters of her cheeks disappeared as laughter filled her face.

With her arm tucked about his, they started into the group of vendors, a large array of makeshift stands clustered in the field.

The first merchant they approached had a flat board set atop stacked stones forming a table. Upon the thick piece of pine lay three baskets of produce—apples, pears, and red grapes. No pomegranates.

Daniel guided her to the first.

The merchant eyed them with a harsh, cross look, but when Daniel pulled out his coins, the woman softened. Seems silver continued to banish judgment of his arm entwined with Jemina.

But Daniel steered her to another table. More tolerant vendors would gain his money.

"You're used to the glances, Lord Ashbrook?"

"Yes. Either they haven't seen such a stylishly appointed gentleman today, or they're wondering whose bastard I am."

She blinked at him with wild large eyes. "How can you joke about such?"

"It's been asked, and it's better than trying to modify my behavior to suit people I'll never see again."

He towed her to another stand, this one with beans the color of her eyes. "Maybe they are wondering who works for whom? The heiress and her butler. The steward and the head housekeeper."

She tweaked his cravat, straightening the knot. "Maybe they are wondering where the heiress found such an exquisite lover."

His mouth dropped open, and she laughed.

"I must be reminded that you take no prisoners with your jests, Mrs. St. Maur."

Ignoring his ramping pulse, he pointed to a fruit seller. "Apples. Fine apples for a penny, my dear."

Jemina squinted; her gaze narrowed in the bright afternoon sun. "They look delicious, but it's not a pomegranate."

"This is true. Let's continue the hunt." He navigated her past two more tables. "This is busy but more orderly than Swansea Market. There are cows among its vendors, but I doubt Swansea has your pomegranate."

"Why marry now, Daniel?" Her lips thinned to a sad line. That cupid's bow drew him close. "I mean, you were married before. Was it successful?"

"Wasn't long enough to tell." Daniel faced the vendor. "How much for a pound? My daughter, she loves green beans."

Her hand gripped his shoulder. Her nails digging into the wool, sending a sweet complicated shudder through him. "I didn't mean to upset you. Don't hide from me."

Her tone was low, meant for his ears, but how could he answer?

"That would be a tuppence," the old man said, and tugged his thick apron.

Pulling out his purse, he paid and waited for the man to portion out the green beans onto a scale and then scoop them into a sack.

Jemina collected them. They kept walking. Her silence gnawed at him.

"We corresponded two and a half years. I did love her. Yet, I don't know if I truly understood her or she me. Sometimes, I reread her letters looking for anything I missed, anything I'll be able to tell Hope."

"What makes you doubt your love or hers?"

He couldn't say it aloud. He'd told his aunt about the paperwork he'd forged, but not about Phoebe Dunn never saying a word about Hope. That was dishonesty, and she cheated Hope out of her name and a story or two that he could share with her child.

"Daniel?"

"I wish I had something for Hope. I don't want her to forget Phoebe. We go every year on Hope's birthday to Portsmouth and cast flowers, lignum vitae into the sea."

"That's beautiful, Daniel."

Jemina's eyes became glossy. Reminding her of the *Minerva* had made her sad. As quickly as he could, he spun Jemina like they danced a reel.

"I do not think we'll find a pomegranate today. We'll have to come another time."

"Keep distracting me. I need you to, Daniel."

He twirled her and kept her moving. The man who never did anything to draw attention, found himself dancing Jemina in public back to his carriage.

With her lifted inside, he instructed Mr. Anthon to head to Sandlin Court. Then Daniel sat beside her. "Tell me your secret, Jemina. I know you remember something."

She clawed at his lapel. "I lost a child, Daniel. At some point in my life, I don't know when, but I did. And I feel her sometimes. And I miss her."

"Jemina?"

"Don't ask if I'm sure, or when or even her name. I don't know. You want Hope to not forget her mother. How horrible is it for a mother to not remember her child?"

Daniel pulled Jemina into his arms. "I'm so sorry."

She trembled against him. "Distract me. I'm tired of mourning."

"No. I'll not distract you. I'll mourn with you. I can understand grieving missing pieces."

She put her head to his shoulder and melted into him.

"Marry me, Jemina. It will let things die down, all the rumors and commotion about the new earl or the new heiress. Then I'll dig up something for you. I'll find a christening record, something. I'll find a name. I promise."

She reached up and kissed his cheek.

"At Lady Shrewsbury's ball, the Widow's Ball, we'll announce our engagement. That's the purpose of her celebration, for widows to start anew. I think it should be a new start for a widower too."

"Let me think on it, Daniel."

It was a long silent drive, but she remained in his arms, and he whispered poetry and his vision of a future at Finchely for three.

When they arrived at Sandlin, he led her to the door. "The ball is in two weeks. That should be plenty of time to decide. In the interim, should you need an escort to the market, I'm at your disposal as long as it's a light day at court."

She locked her hand with his. "Our little disagreement at Lady Shrewsbury's dinner was of great interest. With an engagement at her ball, the scrutiny upon us will be intense."

"Ahhh. I sense someone has made up her mind."

"Daniel."

"The earl and his volatile heiress will make believers out of the *ton* of opposites attracting. And I want to dance with my betrothed out in the open with music and candles. I never did that."

"What if I need more time?"

"Hope and I will give you more, but she doesn't want a nanny. I think a mother will do."

Her eyes grew wide, such lovely pools of the best, the most delicious chocolate, with minty bits of jade.

"This widower comes with a little girl who thinks the world of you. She hasn't stopped asking for you. She's even started calling you Mother. I'm tired of correcting her."

Tears streaked Jemina's cheek. "I love her too. How could one not?"

When he kissed at her wrist, he felt her hand tense. "Jemina, I know this to be right. Put away your questions of the past, just for now, for a little while. Focus on what's in front of you. Find me at Lady Shrewsbury's ball. Let there be a yes upon your lips."

With a nod, she ran inside. He didn't give chase for that proper kiss he wanted. He could wait, for he knew Jemina would come to the same conclusion as him, that they were meant to be, that they would be good together.

Hope would have a new mother, and he'd have a mistress and helpmate, all in the right order.

He whistled and boarded his carriage. Daniel could wait for her answer, for he was sure Jemina would say yes.

CHAPTER 32

JEMINA—THE WIDOW'S BALL

The Lady Shrewsbury's dining room now seemed endless, open in all directions. Every inch of it, including the chalked floor for dancing dazzled in candlelight. It took my breath.

Yellow and orange petals of trefoils cascaded silver vases on tables about the perimeter. These were common flowers that Lady Shrewsbury had us pick in the fields. Such a simple act, and it was amazing to see them displayed in places of honor. This was Shrewsbury's symbolism, that all, no matter our backgrounds or story, could be renewed and made wonderful. The common could be resplendent like ashes God blew upon and made into beauty.

"This is spectacular," Patience whispered. "Some widow will have an offer tonight. They will write a new chapter to their lives."

Could Patience read my thoughts? I hadn't told her of Daniel's offer. She'd been sick, and the duke had insisted that she rest.

I nodded. "Someone will catch the romance of this place and be inspired."

A footman in silver livery passed with goblets. I wasn't thirsty for ratafia or any spirited drink. Patience waved him away, and he soon disappeared, swallowed by a hall.

Arm in arm, my dear friend and I journeyed further into the dining room and stopped at a refreshment table. Crystal sconces shed shimmering stars of light onto a table of sweets—perfect molds of colorful jellies shaped like crowns, cakes, large and small with fruit and bliss icing.

Spinning around, I saw beautiful women, our fellow widows of our secret society. My fellow conspirators as Daniel would call them, the ones who gathered around Lady Shrewsbury's kitchen table, wore gowns of many shades—cream, pinks, blues, greens, everything but mourning black.

Shining silver bands—the rings the countess, leader of the Widow's Grace, had given us to replace what was stolen—glistened on hands about the room. I think I was ready for a new ring and new promises.

"They are so lovely." Patience clapped; her long pearl-trimmed gloves matched the luster of her bronze-green gown. "Lady Shrewsbury is a mastermind and the perfect hostess."

"Our friends, Patience, all so brave and ready to start anew."

"You're brave too, Jemina. You should think of what you want and seize it."

Before I could tell her that I agreed, Lady Bodonel, the gossip, stepped in front of us. "Your Grace, I don't know why you didn't insist on the duke coming with us. You should've demanded it. He could surely dance a bit with his stump."

I closed my eyes in anticipation of Patience exploding, but none came.

"No. My husband will do what he wishes. I support him as he supports me."

Lady Bodonel was viscountess, lower in station that my friend the duchess, but one would never know from her manners. Her waving fan of ivory lace came too close to Patience's cheek. "I only want the best for him, you know?"

I looked at Her Grace, and she at me, perhaps waiting for

which of us would tell the Lady Bodonel the truth, that no one, absolutely no one thought she wanted the best for anyone but herself.

Patience was kind, but no fool. "Show the duke." Her tone was stern, deliberate with an edge. "Show his family and friends too. Support his wishes and let him be."

Lady Bodonel frowned as if she ate sour lemons and then charged away. Hopefully it would be the last we saw of her until it was time to return to Sandlin Court. She was staying with us while something was painted at her residence. To avoid her, the duke seemed to lock himself in his study.

Looping her arm with mine, Patience moved us in the opposite direction. "The duke and Lord Gantry have decided to stay at Sandlin Court to discuss strategies. That means they'll smoke cigars and read maps. Sounds as if Gantry is planning a trip."

"Maybe that is what the duke's been up to, helping his friend."

She laughed and shifted in time with the violin and harp music playing. "I'm not sure. His tactical planning is not for Wellington. I might have had Mr. Gerard shuffle Busick's papers and he saw nothing from that commander."

This time I took her hand and swirled her around to distract her. "You and the duke are too sweet. He's as concerned about you as you are about him. A perfect match."

"Buckles?"

That voice. I cringed and turned to greet Lady Lavinia. "Evening, ma'am."

"Do you have any other shoes?" She shook her head at me. "Why do you wear them everywhere?"

"I like these slippers. They are comfortable. Lady Lavinia Nell, this is Her Grace, the Duchess of Repington."

Patience folded her arms. "Oh, yes. I heard about you."

Lavinia took out something that looked like opera glasses and gawked at my friend. "You are rather pretty and such a nice necklace."

Fingering the ruby the duke gave her, Patience nodded. "Thank you for the assessment, I think."

"I was just telling Buckles here that I remember seeing those slippers in a certain barrister's office. I thought the women here were upstanding."

Patience stepped a little closer. "How would you know about seeing slippers if you too weren't at a barrister's office?" She pointed at Lavinia. "I hear you are known to be a scandal with or without your slippers."

"Rude even with that slight accent." Lavinia sputtered, her smile dropping away. "Just tell Buckles to let everyone have a shot at the rich earl and see who wins."

I shook my head. "Lady Lavinia, the earl is an independent thinker. He'll give sway to whom he pleases. Why are we women fighting over him?"

She huffed again. "It is his choice, but the man does not know what's in his best interest. There are ways to fix that. Excuse me."

I had a bad feeling that Lavinia had horrid ideas on how to fix Daniel. That couldn't be good. I hadn't seen Daniel in two weeks. Though we'd exchanged letters every day, he hadn't ventured again to see me at Sandlin Court. He wanted an uncompromising yes. He wasn't settling for anything less.

I think I was ready.

At the front of the room, a footman said, "Lord Ashbrook."

Warm and tingly, butterflies flew in my stomach.

This was a formal ball. Men wore black breeches, white shirts, and waistcoats. Yet, the earl's cravat seemed whiter than snow. His cream waistcoat had silver threads that sparkled like his eyes. Even the fabric of his breeches held hints of silver in the hem. The man shimmered like a star fallen to earth.

Did he see me?

I hoped he did.

I wore the right color, a beautiful airy cream dress with an overdress of sky blue. Nothing about me was mournful. My spirits rallied. I would indulge in now and accept his proposal.

My eyes locked with Daniel's.

As he started for me, Lady Shrewsbury scooped him up and led him to widows who'd brought their daughters, then to other members of the Widow's Grace.

Then to Lady Lavinia.

The mean woman towed him off to dance.

I thought Daniel was coming for me.

I thought we'd finally dance in the open.

Jealousy spread like a slow rolling boil in my stomach.

Patience tugged me toward the desserts. "You look angry. Are you all right?"

"I think I just made a decision."

"You're staring at Ashbrook. Are you back to being enemies?"

"No. I just hoped I haven't waited too long."

She put an arm about me. "What is for you is yours. No Lavinia can take it from you."

I shrugged. With everything being stripped from me, I simply didn't know.

"Still looking for the earl?"

Mr. Willingham stood beside me. "You should choose better than him."

"Who do you think I should choose? A man who treats me with dignity or one who thinks he can push me to marry him?"

He rubbed his jaw. "You're fiery. Maybe a bit crazed. I hear you do crazy things outside of Sandlin too. Perhaps the earl can explain it. Perhaps he should suffer for encouraging you."

Patience pulled me from Willingham before I slapped him. She must have sensed that I'd do something rash.

"Be careful, Jemina. I think the duke has men here spying. The last thing we need is for a brawl to start and more rumors to fly."

Fear struck my middle, not over making a scene but that something bad would happen. Willingham was baiting me on purpose. Why?

Lady Bodonel came to us. "Jemina, I want you to come and meet some people. I think they could be good candidates for you. Then you can have your own house and move on from the duke's."

"No, Lady Bodonel," Patience said, "it will be you moving on, not visiting. I thought I could stand your sniping for the duke's sake, but you've pushed too much. Jemina is always welcome. You're not, not anymore. Return to your paint fumes."

I couldn't let my friend's evening be ruined because of me. "Lady Bodonel, the Lord Mayor has come. You should go meet those important people. I think he knows the peers who've been recently widowed."

The lady turned without uttering another word and disappeared in the crowd.

"Jemina, is that true?"

"It's a rumor. One I just made up."

Patience smiled, but her face looked very green. "I need some air."

"I should come with you."

"No, stay, Jemina and catch your earl."

"I need to tell you something."

"Later, Jemina." She moved away, and I let her go. Maybe Lady Bodonel was right. I needed to move forward and turned to spy Daniel.

He'd disappeared.

Maybe that was for the best. It would give me more time to think through how to tell him I wanted to marry and that I was silly for delaying.

Then maybe, I'd be brave enough to say there was love in this crazy beating heart for him. He should be the first to know.

CHAPTER 33

DANIEL—JUST LIKE HIS FATHER

Daniel spent what he thought was an appropriate amount of time dancing with Lady Shrewsbury's widows and making small talk. Now it was time to collect Jemina, whisk her away and kiss her until she accepted.

It was a difficult two weeks, just sending notes, not seeing her, or giving in to the temptation of letting Hope's cute pouting face melt her resistance. His daughter asked about Jemina every hour. That week of recovery at Finchely changed everything in his household. It couldn't change back.

"Ashbrook," the Lord Mayor called to him.

Daniel groaned but went dutifully to chat with him and his law colleagues. Jemina signaled with her fan, but another man took her hand and led her to dance.

Torture.

He groaned at himself for making her dower so high. Her charms and his stupid incentive would make the draw to her beauty that much stronger. It was one of his secrets, as she'd called them, one that went awry.

If any of those men ever spent time with her and she didn't slap them, they'd know that the fire in those eyes were true. Her soul was lovely. She bore the face of the mortal Helen, the queen Nefertiti, or the goddess Aphrodite.

Daniel fingered the *T* etched on his pocket fob. It was time to stop all these social rituals and spend the rest of the evening and the rest of her life with her, no other.

He glanced up from his conversation with the Lord Mayor and noticed that Jemina was nowhere to be found.

"Excuse me, Lord Mayor. I think I should—"

"Get some refreshment," Lady Lavinia said. She clutched his arm and gave him a good excuse to move.

"Here," she said as she handed him her glass. "Now take me for air."

Still no sign of Jemina.

Perhaps she was getting air.

"Fine, Lavinia."

They shuffled through the crowds and down a quiet hall.

"The parlors? I thought we were headed to the gardens."

"No, this is the way to your girl. Buckles is your girl, right?"

He coughed a little and sipped her punch.

It was fire. Foul brandy.

"Here, this is definitely yours."

"No, dear, it's yours. Sorry, darling."

"For what—"

Two men stepped from the shadows.

Slam. One hit him in the face.

His spectacles flew. Before he could get his bearings, a man struck him again.

Such pain. His eye felt three times its size.

The two knocked him to the ground, his head banged against a table leg. Daniel writhed on the floor as they kicked him.

The men held him down, elbow in his chest. They ripped away his father's fob.

Daniel gasped for air as a hand cut across his throat.

"I'm really sorry, darling." Lavinia said, "but you are too strong and too clever for me. I had some friends help."

She tipped her glass.

Splish, splash, splosh.

Poison dripped onto his forehead, into his eyes, down his cheeks. Criminals kept him pinned. He couldn't move as the brandy filled his nostrils, burning.

Then Lavinia brought the glass closer and spilled fire down his throat.

He fought as he gagged. He couldn't help but swallow. They ripped his fabric as he drowned in liquor.

That smell.

That was his father's smell.

The weight upon his limbs relented, but he couldn't figure out how to move.

"Willingham, let's leave him for a few. Let's let him grapple with his darkest fear, that loss of control. The brandy will make him incoherent. Then, I'll be back for part two of my plan."

She stuffed his spectacles in his tailcoat pocket. "Daniel, in time, you will forgive me. I promise to make all the scandals go away. I'll make it up to you."

He sort of heard her chuckle. Then the shadows disappeared. The music became loud, mockingly loud, reminding him of the fights he thought he'd won living as a just man.

No.

Not a winner.

They left him bloodied, stewing in his own drool, smelling like a drunk, stripped of his threads, his armor.

Barely clothed, just a torn tailcoat, waistcoat, and shirt, he'd become the scared boy of eight readying to sleep his first night on the streets, the streets that killed his father.

Daniel's head dropped to the floor. He couldn't escape.

CHAPTER 34

JEMINA—A BABBLING EARL

I had to stop looking for Daniel. More than an hour had passed since he arrived, and we still hadn't talked.

Must he be a social butterfly when I felt as if I'd burst?

That must be his role for Lady Shrewsbury tonight.

I understood, especially with the Lord Mayor and several of his fellow barristers attending the ball, he needed to circulate. He was an officer of the courts as much as a peer, but I needed his smile, any part of it.

My pride wouldn't let me chase after him like I was Lady Lavinia.

So I danced with a banker. Then a baron. Then a knight.

Time passed.

The punch bowl lowered.

The heat of the ballroom became oppressive. Maybe if I went out and let the night air touch my face, I would feel better.

This house was a maze. Nothing looked familiar. A suit of armor here. Left then right. Then I turned around and back.

With a shake of my head, I headed for quiet. This was as good as being outside.

My eyes drew to something shiny on the floor.

Scooping it up, I saw it was a fob, his fob with the etched T. Broken glass, hands stopped a half hour ago.

Tick. Tick. Tick. That noise should be his watch, but it was my heart pounding through my bodice. Daniel?

Then I saw naked legs, bare feet.

Chubble! Chubble! I screamed trouble in my head, but nothing came out of my mouth.

Those legs gained a torso. The moonlight from a near window made this man's waistcoat sparkle.

Daniel.

Charging forward, I pressed, shaking.

I dropped to my knees.

His face—bloody. Swelling consumed an eye. Beaten?

Why was he missing pantaloons?

Shaking hard.

Couldn't hear anything but the violence in my chest.

I pushed at his sleeve. Too unsteady to sense the thud of a pulse.

Cupping my hand to his bloody nose, I felt air.

Alive.

I fell upon him. "Daniel. Daniel, wake up. Are you much hurt? Where are your breeches?"

One eye opened to a slit.

And I smelled something I never smelled on him. Brandy.

After putting his fob in my reticule, I touched his arm, his sides, and he winced like a rib was broken.

Then I realized that he'd been beaten. Someone wanted to make it look as if he'd drunken himself into a stupor.

And to steal his breeches was to embarrass him. "Sorry, Daniel."

"The voices started again. Make them stop, J."

"Daniel, I need to get you up."

"I'm sorry, Jem . . . You're a gem."

He slurred. He sounded drunk and adorable.

His hand touched my cheek. "So pretty. Don't slap me too."

"No. Now cooperate, Daniel."

I tugged his arms and made him sit.

"Whoa. Oh. This hurts. And the world is moving. You feel it?"

"Come on, Daniel. You have to move. Help me. We can't explain this."

"You need help? You know I'd do anything for you."

If he weren't inebriated, out of his mind on brandy, I'd put his words in my heart. "Then help me. Stand up."

My pulling started his moving, but at a pace slower than a snail. His limbs didn't seem to be under his control. He lunged forward, and I popped up under his arm to prop him up.

So heavy. So much taller than me. His arm wraps around my face. "I helped, sweetest?"

"Of course, Barrister. You're late to court."

"Court. Never late."

He started wobbling and moving like he knew which way to go.

Clinging to him, I guided him. "Can't take you back to the ball without breeches and slippers."

"Who stole them? Jemina, tell the judge. I saw the Lord Mayor somewhere."

Daniel was so obliviously in his cups, no one would believe he'd been set upon. They'd blame him and call Daniel a drunk. They'd compare him to his father. This was a nasty trick.

This couldn't happen. That would cut Daniel too deeply.

I heard people coming.

"Daniel. Daniel, help me into this . . . this room."

"Yes."

He leaned almost too far, but I kept him upright until we made it inside.

We both fell back against the closed door with a thud.

"Ohhhh, J."

I covered Daniel's mouth.

He kissed my fingers as I waited for whoever was in the hall to leave. Maybe I could get him out of here through the large window.

"Is it time to go home? My fob is gone. They took it. Only thing I have of his, 'cept his name. Don't like it."

"Daniel's a beautiful name."

"Hmm." He swayed.

I held him up. "Come before someone catches us."

"J. I have to go to Hope. Hope likes you."

My heart tripled its beat. I had to save Daniel, not just for his reputation, but for Hope too.

Though the hall sounded empty, I knew this wasn't over. "We have to hide."

The room was small and smelled stale. Sheets covered the furnishing. The arrangement appeared to be a couch with a table behind it. A candelabra missing three limbs sat on top.

Using both hands, I held Daniel up. His head, his battered face rested on my brow.

"What are we doing?"

I covered his mouth. His voice boomed like it had in court.

"You are too loud, Daniel, like you tell me."

"J . . . You're not that loud. I said that to make you mad." He chuckled. "It worked. But I don't want you mad. I want you to like me. I want you to . . ."

"To what, Daniel?"

"Jemina," his lips vibrated along my brow, "what are we doing?"

"We're hiding until I can figure out how to get you back to Finchely."

"Is that all? I thought we were liking each other." He opened his arms wide. "Be my love."

He started to sink, and I wrapped my arms about his waist.

"Jemina, dearest."

"Yes?"

"Pantaloons, did you take 'em?"

"Don't be concerned. Can you stay here and be quiet? Let me go get Patience."

He swayed again. "She can't see me. No pantaloons. Not prop-proper."

There was no leaving him, not like this.

"I don't feel so good, J."

"Dance with me, Daniel."

"Of course. That's what a gentleman does."

He straightened, clasped my palm in his, and spun me in a reel.

It was dizzying and we veered like a maddened top. Fast, then slow.

Part of me wanted to laugh. Maybe I did. Controlled, always in control, Daniel Thackery, was the madman earl.

No longer did I wonder why we ended up here. We were both balancing on the edge of crazy and joy.

His leg hit the sofa, and he fell over taking me with him.

Flat on the couch. Dust flew, and we both breathed heavily.

"I'm going to cover you up, Daniel. Maybe I can hide you and go get help. You have to stay put."

"No. Don't leave me. Please don't. Don't want to be alone."

He clasped my hand. His palms were sweaty. "Someone has tampered with my drink. I think."

"Yes. You wouldn't do this, not to your aunt, not to yourself."

He wrapped his arms about me. "Don't tell Hope. She can't fear for me like I did Papa. Don't tell her. Please."

The light sneaking in from the window exposed blood in his nostrils, about his eye. My poor love.

He slumped into the dusty sheet but held me fast in his arm. "Don't tell. Can't disappoint."

"I won't, Daniel."

Blinking, he touched my cheek. "You have a lot of freckles."

"And you don't like freckles?"

"No. Love 'em. Hope has them too. Lovely."

Oh, he would be one of those sweet talkative drunks. "Who did this?"

"Who didn't?"

I searched his tattered shirt and found bruising on his arms. "Do you hurt?"

"Yep."

"Where, Daniel?"

"Everywhere you haven't touched."

Petulant, he kicked his feet. "This is not good. I want my pantaloons. They were new."

"Shhhh," I said again. "You're too loud."

His beautiful waistcoat had spots. I was pretty sure it was more drops of his blood.

One dark eye was swollen, the other a slit.

When I touched his jaw, it felt puffy. Somebody beat him badly. "Who hit you?"

"Willing-Wiling hhhhmm and Lavinia and others."

"Lavinia?" That's what the shrew meant. She'd planned to compromise and ruin Daniel. Never. I wouldn't let them.

"Make the world stop. I'll tell you everything. Like how beautiful you are."

His head flopped back again.

"What was their plan? Did you hear what they were going to do next?"

"Hate doesn't need a reason. Jealousy either. I should've known better than to come to such a public place to woooo you."

"Daniel, you're not making sense."

"You. Your fault. Why did you make me want you? Want you, near you."

That sorrowful look in his countenance captured me. "I should get Patience; she can help me get you out of here. We'll get you home to Hope."

"Don't leave me. I'm not quite myself. I don't feel like me, and it's dark. Cold. I'll sing to keep from being afraid."

He started to hum like a little schoolboy's ditty. Then he switched to something like a hymn. "My rock . . ."

A ton of footsteps sounded outside. I clapped his mouth. "Shhh."

"Lady Lavinia, you're saying you were attacked?"

It was Lady Shrewsbury's voice. That witch Lavinia was using Daniel's aunt to set him up in a compromise to force him to marry her.

"Yes, someone grabbed me. Who was he? I don't know. I was terrified."

She had them looking for Daniel.

She wanted a compromise. I'd give them one.

I tugged the dusty sheet onto Daniel, making sure he was covered, we were covered.

If he was going to be caught, it might as well be with me. I worked an arm out of my sleeve and undid the ribbon of my stays to look as seductive as possible.

"Whoa, J. What?"

I yanked down my hair. It fell onto his face.

He blew big breaths that moved my curls from his cheek. "Stop, J."

"Trust me, Daniel. I'm pretending to be the mistress you wanted."

"I don't want just that." His fingers went to my shoulder. "Did you know your skin is so soft? What else are you hiding from me?"

He giggled and stroked my chin and my lips.

But he stopped. "I can't, J. Can't take advantage of you, not like this."

Daniel was under me. I was half in the sheet with my dress falling, but he thought he was still in control. "We have to make this look good and loving."

He squinted up at me. "Loving you is easy to do."

I heard doors opening. "They are getting closer."

"Let me up. Let me explain."

If Daniel talked, they'd know my fake lover was the Earl of Ashbrook. "If I keep you covered in the dark, then the scandal is mine alone."

"I object, J. Let me up. I'm supposed to take care of you."

"Why do you have to be noble now?"

Thinking I could quiet him, I kissed Daniel. He had the wherewithal to kiss me back.

He tasted of bitters, like medicine for a cough or the shakes. But I gave into the sensations of his hands, the one on my waist, the one thumbing circles on my naked shoulder.

Tremors slammed through me.

"Jemina, be mine."

I leaned in close to his cheek. "We have to make this look good."

Daniel kissed me. "Good, I need you."

That line of pretend and not pretending was right at his fingertips, right at his tracing my bosom.

"J, you're everything. You and Hope."

His words seared my throat.

"We should stop, Daniel." But he kissed my neck. And the music was all around us.

I was way past needing him.

I wanted him.

But this wasn't right.

No words had been said between us, and maybe they didn't have to be since he'd proposed, but I knew we both had to be in our right minds to move forward.

"Oh, let me up, J. And put up your sleeve. Find my pant-a-loons."

He fussed again. Again, too loud. He would be understood. This deception would be found out, and he'd be a laughingstock.

No.

I grabbed the candelabra and whacked him across his head.

He fell back unconscious.

CHAPTER 35

JEMINA—RESCUING THE EARL

Chubble! Chubble! I must be crazed, laying on top of silent Daniel on a dusty couch.

The candelabra I used to make him quiet fell from my hand. The hit was hard, but he breathed. It was for his own good. Sorry!

This masquerade to keep Daniel from a compromise had to look good. With me kneeling on his thick thighs, I flung down my other sleeve, then, half naked, hovered over his chest.

Daniel was not moving, not touching me, not making me laugh.

But my goodness, he slept beautifully, bruises and all.

The door flung open.

I laughed a haughty sneer and stayed low with my loosed hair covering him.

"Oh, my lord, you are amazing." I screamed and laughed as a crowd gathered.

As quickly as I could, I yanked more of the sheet up around me.

Dust flew everywhere, but now Daniel was fully covered. "Do you mind!" I said. "This room is occupied by the baron . . . by two consenting adults. Very consenting. Please leave."

Lavinia gasped, wiped her fake tears. Her reddened cheeks

said it all. "Oh, I see this room is occupied. Carry on, Buckles. We'll have to look for my attacker elsewhere."

The awful thing, a head-shaking Lady Shrewsbury, and a crowd of others left.

The door slammed.

Both Lavinia and the Lady Shrewsbury knew it to be me, but neither would say my name. Lavinia wouldn't risk her hand in the conspiracy, at least not tonight. Lady Shrewsbury wouldn't identify me. I was still a member of the Widow's Grace.

Daniel was safe for now, but rumors would spin.

I caught my breath and uncovered Daniel.

There was dust his beard, on his mouth.

I wiped those beautiful lips of his with my pinkie. Full, soft. "We did it."

My heart beat so fast. For a moment, I collapsed atop Daniel. The buttons of his waistcoat dug into my bosom. His beard tickled my collarbone.

Pulling up my gown, I ran to the door and locked it, and then returned. Fishing up my sleeves, I wanted to laugh at myself. This almost felt like a Widow's Grace exploit.

"Daniel, if you can hear me, I've bought us time. We still need to get you home to Hope."

He didn't move. Did I hit him too hard?

With an ear to his chest, I heard *drum-drum, drum-drum*, not the crazy beat of my heart.

Daniel would be fine. He needed to sleep off the brandy and my hitting him with a candelabra.

Goodness, I hoped I hadn't made him lose his memory. I hoped the knot on his head didn't make him forget me.

I heard my name, but it was not from Daniel's lips.

My conscience?

"Jemina, let me in. It's me, Patience. Lady Shrewsbury said you needed help cleaning up."

I sprung to my feet and let her inside. "Daniel's in trouble."

She held my hand and walked me to the couch. Lightly snoring, he turned his head.

"Jemina, where are his pantaloons?"

I tugged the sheet across him again. "Lady Lavinia, Willingham, all of them are trying to set him up for a compromise. The woman wants to marry him, but he asked me."

She put her palm to my face. "Oh. I'm so happy. But we have to get him out of here."

"They can't get away with embarrassing him. They need to pay for this dirty trick."

"Focus, Jemina. Focus." She put her cold hands on my hot cheeks. "We'll plot retribution later. We still have to hide him and the crazed widow given to lewd exhibition. That's what the Lord Mayor just said."

My face dropped into my hands. "Well, it's now acknowledged publicly, I'm a lunatic."

"You're not crazy. You did what you always do for people you care about, selflessly saving them. That's what you did for me at Bedlam. That's not crazy, to lay down your life for a friend. It's honorable."

The love in her voice, the understanding, calmed those notions of doubting my own sanity.

"Patience, Daniel has helped so many of the women out there dancing. They need to help lift him out of here. The Widow's Grace needs to save our barrister."

"How do you hide a man, Jemina?"

"Like Cleopatra. Let's get something thick to wrap him. The carpet."

We pushed the couch and the table aside to free the tapestry. More dust flew, but this would work.

Patience grabbed his arms.

I took his bare feet and eased him to the floor.

Then we rolled him in the carpet, kneading and threading him into the tapestry like bread with a yummy center.

I put my ear to the rug.

Daniel's breaths were muffled, but I heard them.

"Stay here, Jemina. Your face will detect too much attention. I hope the earl knows how much you love him." Patience charged out the door.

I couldn't think about that now, not until Daniel was safe and with his treasured reputation intact.

It took ten minutes, but Patience returned to the parlor with five fellow members of the Widow's Grace, including Mrs. Cultony. Each lady was elegant in their gowns, their pristine chignons and pearl pins, and those shiny silver bands Lady Shrewsbury gave us.

"I have his carriage pulled to the rear," Patience said. "We just need to take this carpet out back."

The ladies spread and took a position about the Cleopatra roll.

In a blink, we had Daniel in the air. Covered by the music of violins, we strained and hauled our barrister out of Lady Shrewsbury's house.

Mr. Anthon jumped down and brushed past the women who'd set down the carpet. "What did they do to him?"

I clasped the young man's arm. "He's fine. They played a mean trick to compromise him. We just have to—"

He began pulling at the layers. "Why is he in a carpet?"

"He's fine." I turned to the Widow's Grace. "Ladies, go on back in. Thank you."

Everyone but Patience returned to the ball.

Mr. Anthon stepped closer. "Mrs. St. Maur, what did they do to him, ma'am?"

His voice shook, then I remembered how close this young man was to Daniel. I had to reassure him. "He's fine, sir, but they stripped him half naked and poured brandy down his throat We got him out of there. No one saw him. He'll be safe once we get him in the carriage."

Daniel's man-of-all-work trembled, his face twisting with rage.

"What is it, sir?" I called after the fellow as he advanced on the house. Fists balling, the young man looked as if he wanted to set everything ablaze.

I ran and caught his arm. "Mr. Anthon, we have to go."

"They have to pay, ma'am."

"It was a trick. We'll plot—"

"No. Mrs. St. Maur, they didn't just set a trick. They wanted him ruined. They strove to take away all he's worked for. They don't want him to matter."

The heat in his voice, the strain in the muscles of his neck, hurt my heart. "Mr. Anthon, calm down. We have to get Lord Ashbrook away."

He shook his fist at the house. "Ma'am, you don't get it. They wanted everyone to believe this good man was a criminal attacking women. Compromise is what they call bad behavior by one of them, the accepted sons of the *ton*, not a Blackamoor earl."

My anger at Lavinia was already hot, but I needed to burn. I had only thought this a trick to force him to marry Lavinia. I forgot about those who held Ashbrook in suspicion, the whisperers who cast aspersions on the *dark earl*, those who wanted to believe the worst about him because of his skin.

My mouth dropped open. "Patience, Lavinia called it an assault. *An assault.*"

"I saw the wetness on her cheek." My dearest friend groaned and covered her mouth for a moment. "Let's get the carpet in the carriage. We need to get him out of here."

This was the part of Daniel's walk he didn't think I'd understand.

Until this moment, I didn't.

Mr. Anthon pushed forward. "No. They have to pay. They have to."

Patience stepped in front of him. "Ashbrook can fight this tomorrow, if we get him away from here. Keep your head. You know what our barrister would want you to do."

Wiping at his face, the young man nodded and returned to the carpet. He hoisted it in the air, and I guided the carpet into the carriage.

"Thank you, Mr. Anthon." I touched his hand, my shaking one to his gloved one. "Please, take us to Finchely."

With glassy eyes, he agreed and closed the door.

Patience whipped it open and stuck her head inside. "Are you sure you are going to be all right?"

I wasn't, but I nodded my head anyway. "I have my carpet. I'll see him home and make sure he's safe."

"You stay safe, Jemina. You're red and flustered."

"Go inside. Keep your mother-in-law from gossiping."

She murmured our mantra of the Widow's Grace, our prayer, then added, "May the duke's Jove be with you, Jemina."

Mr. Anthon again shut the door. Soon, the carriage was off with a lurch.

Putting my arms about the end with Daniel's head, I steadied him on the carriage floor.

Yet, I wanted to go back with Mr. Anthon and set everything on fire.

CHAPTER 36

DANIEL—THE HORRIBLE, NO GOOD HANGOVER

Loud voices.

Daniel heard them, then nothing. His face hurt. A terrible headache rattled between his temples.

His whole body felt as if he'd been bested in the ring by Gentleman Jackson at his Bond Street boxing rooms or that Bill Richmond had decided to take his vingt-et-un losses out on Daniel's skull.

He tried to reach his jaw and couldn't. Something heavy was on him. Heavy and dusty.

Good Lord. Attacked and now stolen? Everything was moving? Or was that just his stomach?

Daniel punched and twisted to break free and found he couldn't much move. He lay in a cocoon. His inner fears of ransoms, of being impressed and sold to a ship or worse raged. He pushed away and summoned his dry court voice. "Release me!"

"Daniel?"

Jemina? Sweet Jemina. "J, are you here too? Did they hurt you?"

"I'm well, and I'm here, Daniel. Sit tight. I'm getting you to Finchely."

"What? How do I get to you?"

"Daniel, I have you. I'll take care of you."

He needed to see for himself. He had to free his arms and fought and coughed. "Let me out."

"Daniel, we rolled you up in this carpet."

A what? "J, let me out. I am dusty. Jemina, don't go. Pleeeeeasse."

"You're singing again. I didn't know you could sing so well."

He coughed again. "It's nothing I admit to."

"You're a rich alto, maybe higher."

"Let me out. It's dark in here. I'll sound better. Promise."

The ride became bumpy, and the cocoon banged up and down, side to side.

"Good God. I'm going to be sick. Don't let me choke."

"Daniel, I'm sorry. Shift a little, Daniel. Wiggle your way out."

"Hope wiggles and wobbles. I don't. Oh, my face hurts."

Jemina tugged at the carpet, and he rolled onto the floor. Dust went everywhere, but he was finally able to sit.

"I'm dusty," he said. "My lungs feel heavy, like I breathed yarn, and I'm dusty, Jemina. I'm never dusty. Can't stand anything untidy, unclean like it's been left to the streets."

He hit at his torn jacket. A spray of lint filled the air. "My poor coat. It was ebony. Now, it's sand. Aunt's staff has been neglectful."

Jemina knelt beside him and put her hot palms to his cheeks. "Do you know who you are?"

"I appear to be a dusty man in a carpet on the floor of a carriage."

He peeked inside the folds and saw the truth, his naked legs. Kicking, he felt the weave chafe against his toes. His feet must be bare, too. "New evidence. It appears I'm dusty with no stockings. Make it all go away."

She stretched and hugged his neck. For a second, he flinched. "No more hitting. I'll be good."

Jemina kissed his cheek, then his bruised eye. "Sorry, sorry, sorry."

"You don't mind kissing a drunk, a skunk drunk, drunk skunk?"

"Say your name. Please. Say it."

The fear in her voice cut through the throbbing in his head, his chest.

"P. Daniel Thackery, the Idiot of Ashbrook. From a line of idiots. Done. Now stop everything from spinning."

She mashed his face into the comfort of her bosom. "I have you. I'll make you better. This has to be my fault."

"Sure, your fault." He started to chuckle. "It's not like you hit me and made me drunk. Did you steal my pant-pantaloons? You don't have to give them back, just wanna know."

"Well, I didn't do most of the things on your list, and I didn't steal anything. I'm taking you home. You have a closet full of pantaloons and breeches."

"My closet. I love my closet. It's big. It hides secrets. Oh, you are comfortable, but I'm getting dust all on you."

"It's quite fine. When you're home, I'll get you all cleaned up."

"Remind me. Tell my aunt her people didn't clean under the rug. Dusty."

"I'll do that, Daniel."

"If I put a white glove to this rug, it would fail. Maybe you couldn't see it, my glove being white and all."

He pushed and tried to climb up to the seat, but her grip was too tight. "Sit still."

"Hey. Hey. You're scared. Your heart is beating for two."

He wrenched around so he could see her eyes, pretty eyes and those lips with the cupid's bow that needed kisses.

"I'm scared, Daniel. I found you lying in the hall. I was terrified."

He sagged against her. "Don't you fret. And you are comfortable. We need to go home to my little girl, actually our little one. She's claiming you now."

"What, Daniel? What are you talking about?"

He gripped Jemina's hand. "Oh, Hope. She can't see me like this. She can't know I'm a drunk."

"You're not a drunk. This isn't your fault."

"I'm not my father, you know, J. At least I'm going home to my little girl. I'm going home with you."

"You're a talkative and loud barrister."

"And a singing one." He started to hum the song Bridgetower composed to get Hope to settle. "That little girl, such an unexpected blessing. I have to tuck her in. How am I going to do that? She's going to know."

His arms felt too heavy to lift. "My head so fuzzy. Who hit me? Did I hit back?"

"Yes, champion. They're all knocked to the floor."

"Richmond, my friend the pugilist, he'd be proud. He said to fight for you."

"Daniel, if I hadn't found you—"

"You did, and other than a very queasy stomach and a head about to explode, I'll live."

"Well, I'm not fine. You could have been hurt worse. It's my fault."

Blurs shot through his mind. Sensations of skin, of touching Jemina, but how did any of that make sense?

"Wait. What happened? Did I . . . Did we . . . Oh, God, I missed heaven."

She positioned herself in front of him and put her palms to his shoulders. "What do you remember?"

"None of the good stuff."

She shook him. "Talk to me, Daniel."

"Stop moving. I went looking for you, but Lavinia found me and some buffoons, her buffoons and Willingham. I guess he's still mad about me kissing you."

Her soft fingers pried open each of his eyes. "That's your second mistake."

"Wait, doesn't a first come first?"

She rubbed his neck, the base of his skull. "You should've been with me this evening. You should've been by my side, dancing with me. That was your first mistake."

"Oh, that's nice." His sighs burned. "Then everyone would know there was some truth to our rumored affair."

"Oh, they're more rumors now. They won't stop talking about me and a baron."

"You and who? Who do I have to duel?"

"You were the baron."

He shook his head. "No, J. I'm an earl. I'm sure of it. My uncle." He chuckled. "He tried everything short of killing me to stop it. I kept my head down and bought and sold all the assets he thought he'd sell on the cheap. Made a fortune off his foolishness."

She kissed along his jaw. "You're babbling."

"I used the money to help people, to help the Widow's Grace. To help you."

Her forehead creased, knitting together her brows. "Um. You sit still until I get you to Finchely."

Daniel counted his fingers. "One. Two. What was the second mistake? We are up to two, right?"

"Believing Lady Lavinia would do anything good is a great blunder."

"Well, you are right in that matter. Somehow, she and Willingham . . ."

He fisted his hand, and then immediately stopped. The pain in his head tripled. "Did they hurt you, J?"

"No."

"Good, I couldn't stand that, not that I can stand much."

He fidgeted, crossing his arms. Then he picked dust from his sleeves. "Am I getting you all linty?"

"No, I'm fine. I just need to breathe."

The carriage lurched, and so did his stomach. This was trouble.

"Jemina, I don't feel so good."

He touched the lump on his skull. "Did you see who hit me? Willingham?"

"Um, why don't you close your eyes and rest until I get you home?"

"Will you make me tea and biscuits?"

She nodded, and he felt the knocking of her heart as he pressed against her bosom, one he decided was perfect and taut like ripe pomegranates.

"Beautiful. Your gown cream and blue, so lovely. Now dusty."

She put his head to her shoulder. "I went to your tailor's suggestion for a dressmaker."

"Good. Next time, I'll ignore everyone. Just dance with you. Follow you like Max."

"You are sweet when you talk too much, Daniel."

"Fine, if you were mine." He took up her wrist. "You wouldn't have to hit people if you were mine. Why aren't you mine?"

"It's your drink talking. Your house is very far—why don't you rest?"

"Can't rest well. Not fine, you're not mine."

"Daniel, don't say anything you'll regret."

He smirked so wide his cheeks hurt. "You mean like exposing yourself to save me."

"What?"

"I wasn't quite as passed out as you thought. I did see the swell of you, good pomegranates. You're delightful and crazy, J."

She pulled away and took her cupid's bow.

He wrapped his arms about her. "I didn't mean it like that. I meant you shouldn't have to debas ... debase ... debauch. Don't do it for me."

"Not my finest hour. Lady Shrewsbury and a dozen others had such a show, including the Lord Mayor. No one looked at you."

"Did it for me." He kissed her cheek. "You saved me."

Putting his hands, all of them on her waist, he tickled her. "How about another go? I promise to remember this time."

"I need you sober and in possession of your brilliant mind, Daniel. You're a protector. Someone needs to protect you."

"If mine, you'd be fine." He yawned and blew into her hair.

It had fallen; wild ruby- and wheat-colored locks that tickled his nose.

"Mine."

He liked that notion. He held on to her and waited for the world to stop moving.

CHAPTER 37

DANIEL—IN THE FAMILY WAY

Max whimpered a gut-curling howl every time Daniel put his face in the basin. In his bedchamber, he lay half stretched out on his mattress, half over the side.

He heaved again.

Lunch, dinner, for at least a week, a year flew out of him.

Lavinia was a wizard, an evil one. Nothing of mythical lore, but the type that needed to be burned at the stake. The wench made her trolls dump poison down his throat.

What if that taste was enough to control him?

The wizard tried to turn him into his father. What would Hope do if he couldn't come home? What about Jemina?

"Jemina!"

Nothing, no one responded. Maybe she did leave after all.

Daniel wouldn't blame her. With Lavinia's nasty tricks, it seemed he couldn't keep friends or nannies.

Slow and easy, he sat up and blinked his eyes. Yes, he truly was at Finchely, not in a ditch, not an alley. His hands were clean, not dirty.

Jemina brought him home like she said she would. He was fuzzy-headed over the details, but he was sure she'd thwarted a scandal or compromise or crime—perhaps all three.

He tore off his ruined cravat, and then slipped out of his jacket and waistcoat. His legs were already naked and dusty. "Those pantaloons were new. Wretched wizard."

Everything was so dusty. His waistcoat held spots of his own blood. He hadn't been in a fight that broke a sweat in years.

All his rigor or rituals to be proven a worthy father, all shattered. Did Lavinia want him as a husband that badly that she'd ruin him, his good name? Was Willingham that mad over Jemina that he'd commit a crime to eliminate competition? None of this made sense. None. It was crazed.

He pushed at his skull, then brushed lint from the lapels of his jacket. Jemina rode in on a literal white horse and rescued him. She risked everything.

Reckless, full of zeal, slightly erratic. Jemina.

Her reputation had to be embers, but it showed what he knew. She cared more about him than herself. No more questioning her methods or her heart. Any doubts of her or why he'd fallen for her evaporated.

"Oh, Hope."

His little girl needed him. He didn't tell her good night. That never happened.

Holding his breath, he stood and waited for Max and the world to stop moving. Then, he scrubbed his teeth and tongue and started to wash his face and hair of dust, but they were already clean.

Jemina and Mr. Anthon had done that. He sort of remembered that, in between holding his head over the basin.

Ugh. He needed to go to his daughter. Then write Jemina a long, long, long note.

Wobbling to his closet, he tossed his jacket, shirt, and waistcoat to the floor. They'd receive a proper burial later. He struggled to find his night shirt and robe, an onyx dust-free robe. He pulled each on, and then tied the silk sash.

Crossing the hall, the blazing lights of the sconces blinded him, but he wobbled his way inside the nursery.

His heart, it danced at the sight.

Hope and Jemina, each asleep.

Each adorable.

Each needed to be his. Well, technically one was, but the other survivor of the *Minerva* had to be his, too.

He slid Hope from Jemina's protective arms and cradled her. Sleepy brown eyes opened. "Pa-Papa better? Mama said you were sick."

"Mama? Mama said that? She came to you in a dream?"

"Yes, Mama's heart is good to hear again."

He wasn't sure what she meant but took it as a sign. "Sweetie, go get in my bed. I'll be there shortly."

Hope yawned and took off crawling. Only during the worst thunderstorms did he let her sleep there, but now he needed a chaperone when his lady joined them.

As gently as he could, he scooped up Jemina. She was a very sound sleeper.

Daniel staggered, but it was his duty to protect the woman who saved him.

When he made it back to his bedchamber, he caught his daughter bouncing on the mattress.

He waved at her. "We can't disturb Jemina. We'll wake her. That's not good."

The child stopped, almost freezing in mid bounce.

He laid Jemina down and took off one of her slippers and then the other.

No attempt would be made at removing anything else. His intentions were noble, mostly. They needed to stay that way.

Yet, the memory of clasping her naked shoulder, of Jemina fuzzy and wild and alluring, hovering over him, awakened his dulled wits.

Goodness, he needed her.

With her and Hope under the covers, he lay on the floor. The floorboards were good and cold and not moving.

His daughter settled down. In another five minutes, the wiggle worm snored.

Max draped across his feet. Then he bounced up into bed, probably taking the spot that should be Daniel's.

The mattress shook. Jemina bolted up, gasping for air.

Achy, he sat up. "Easy. It's all right."

She looked at him so lost with wide darting eyes.

Instinctive like a warrior, he raised his arms, and Jemina dropped into his arms and bumped his head. "Sorry."

"Fine. It's fine. All of my face aches anyway." Daniel wound an arm about her. "And my hero can't be scared."

"Yes, she can be. I can."

Leaning against the side of the bed, he cradled her smoothing her back, fingering the silky satin of her wrinkled dress.

"Daniel, I'm sorry. I hit you pretty hard with that candlestick."

He rubbed the lump at the top his head. "So you did hit me? We should stick with kisses. Yes, I think kisses."

She pushed a little from his chest, then melted against him.

"For all the reasons I wanted us to marry before, you know we must wed now."

"Daniel, let's talk of this tomorrow when you are better."

"Between Lady Bodonel and Lady Lavinia's forked tongue, your reputation will be in tatters. Blessedly from what I can remember, you've been compromised at least once tonight. And now you're in my bedchamber and our chaperone is asleep, this has to be a second compromise."

"I'm not concerned about my reputation."

"That's obvious, but fret about mine. Rumors circulated about all these attempts at seduction, and still I fail. The fellows will tease me mercilessly at vingt-et-un. Not good, ma'am."

She chuckled. He loved her loud laugh.

"My ego, Jemina. It alone demands that you be ravished and pleasure sated by now."

"Daniel, you're making light of tonight. I know what they tried to do to you. It has to be my fault."

He didn't want to think of it or how everything might have been ruined if Jemina hadn't rescued him. He reached up and traced her nose, connected the dots between the freckles on her cheek. "You. You made the storms go away. That tells me I'm lucky."

"Willingham struck you because of me. My fault. I made you vulnerable."

"Well, there's one thing that is your fault. I can't stop thinking of you. My daughter can't stop chattering about you." He sought her face, "I trust you with all of me. Here's my secret. I don't want to go on without you."

"You need to sleep, Daniel."

"My child calls you her mother. Only my wife can be Hope's mother. She wants you. I want you. Can you want us, too?"

"You don't think I'm too reckless?"

"Yes, you are, but I need you. I need you here with Hope and Max snuggled in my bed."

"I had decided to say yes. That's why I hunted for you. I spent two years in Bedlam. After this night, at least half the town will think I need to be admitted."

"The Duke of Repington found his wife there. Bedlam must be where all the good women are."

"Be serious, Daniel."

"I am. You saved me. You made sure I was safe. You made sure Hope was too. There's no better woman to trust."

"Hope's nightmares are almost as bad as mine."

"But look at how she's sleeping knowing we are both around."

Jemina raised up and looked at the mattress and covered Hope's feet. "Do you want your lone pillow?"

"No. I want you to return to your original yes. If we are both off the marriage mart, London will be safer. The lunatic practices will have to die down."

"Daniel, what if I willfully participated in my late husband's deeds. What if I'm guilty?"

"Forget him."

"I did that." Her voice lowered. "I'm scared."

Risking his headache doubling, he pulled her cheek to his. "Choose to be the wife of Daniel Thackery, the new Lady Ashbrook, Hope's new mother. I know you lost a child, Jemina. Nothing can fix that loss, but I'm offering you a chance to raise mine. Join our family. Make Finchely a better home."

"Hope's mother is a nice title."

"You like that one the best? Well, she is the cuter Thackery. And she is already calling you her mother. Don't make my girl a spreader of falsehoods."

Jemina brushed at a tear dripping her cheek. "I don't want to hurt you or her."

"Too late for that. You've whacked me with a candlestick."

"Candelabra."

"Technicality. I don't want you to suffer for what you've done for me. Women always fair badly in scandal. You've seen it with the Widow's Grace. Let me protect you as you have me."

So many shadows filled her eyes. How could he draw her back to where things were safe and warm?

He put his hand into her glorious tresses that hung to her waist and smelled of strawberries. If he said he loved her, she wouldn't believe him. She'd think he said it just to tip the scales.

Daniel could read a jury and how Jemina's emotions shifted from indecision to no. He'd win this trial only by admitting to what she could accept and think true. "Love will come for us, Jemina. I know it will. I will treasure you."

Nodding, she didn't say a word but burrowed deeper into his chest.

He took that as yes.

Jemina's tears wet through the lawn fabric of his shirt down to his shoulder.

This wasn't a sign of happiness but a sort of resolve. Perhaps it was goodbye, goodbye to everything in the past that could hurt Jemina and unwittingly Hope. Daniel had his future Lady Ashbrook in his arms. He purposed to turn all her sadness into morning joy.

CHAPTER 38

JEMINA—WEDDING JITTERS

My wedding day arrived at Sandlin Court.

Daniel and Hope had visited almost every day, these past three. My skeptical heart had become convinced of the rightness of this union. I was now desperate to see the earl's half smile and Hope's full one. She seemed to miss me so much, more each time.

A knock to my bedchamber made my heart jump and spin in my chest.

"Come in."

Patience did, with a big box in her arms. "Mr. Gerard has your package back from the jeweler and your intended is here, and he's asked me to bring you this."

That means my present for Daniel had arrived.

"I don't need another gift. He's sending me ransoms and lignum vitae flowers every morn."

Patience smiled wide, her *I know best* smile, and pushed the box into my hands. "He insisted. He said you'd understand."

Now I was intrigued. My fingers slipped along the big red bow of the white package. The satin ribbon slid off with an easy tug.

I wondered what his dry humor had erected. A peek from the corner said the gift was wonderful, but I promised myself I'd not weep anymore.

The dress was silver with lace up the neckline and crystals along the hem. They caught the light when I lifted the skirts from the crinkling tissue paper. The beauty stole my breath.

A note lay in the bottom.

> *To my bride, my future,*
> *My tailor is better than yours.*
> *I ordered this first day I asked for your hand.*
> *This is right.*
> *D.*

That was weeks ago. He was so sure of us. Fine. I wept.

Patience held me. We were both sobbing sacks.

"Come now. How are we, capable women, made weepy by sentimental men?"

"Ashbrook can sing a little, just like the duke. I'm done for."

"Jemina, you love him. You're very done."

"I want to be the good woman he sees wearing this gown. The woman Hope calls Mama. I didn't think I deserved a second chance, not after letting everything go with the *Minerva*."

Patience wiped at her tears. "The disaster wasn't your fault. You deserve every happiness. And so does Ashbrook. He and Hope are the lucky ones. They captured your heart."

"I should tell him, Patience. He should know that I love him before we marry."

She grabbed my arm. "But you're not dressed."

"This can't wait."

"Yes, yes it can. When he sees you next, it will be as his bride, one with hope on her lips and in her heart."

Patience was right.

Always right.

"Dress me. Make me pretty."

"Easy task."

"I'm all freckled and red."

She steered me to the vanity and held the gown to my chin. "Beautiful, especially with those freckles and such glowing cheeks."

The mirror reflected my growing smile. Even my eyes had a bubbly grin. I was pretty sure I loved the man I was to marry. I respected him greatly. I already loved Hope. When he called me her mother, it healed a little of my heart.

Just a little.

This time, no matter what, I wasn't letting go. As long as I kept my head above the waves, I'd hold on to their light.

CHAPTER 39

DANIEL—WEDDED DISCLOSURES

In the formal study of Sandlin Court, Daniel stood with Hope at his knee, staring at the duke and his stepson, Lionel.

"Pa-Papa," she said, ducking and hiding, playing peekaboo with Repington. "He's nice."

"Little Miss Thackery, don't tell anyone," the duke said. "It's our secret."

"Princess, I will take you to the parlor. I think I must have a word with the duke."

"No, Ashbrook, she can stay. I like little girls filled with curiosity. I'm blessed with this boy, but a little pretty girl added to my battalion would be delightful."

Hope stood up and wobbled until she made it to the duke's chair. He picked her up and put her on his knee.

She promptly swatted and jiggled the medals hanging from his scarlet regimentals like Lionel did.

This gruff duke, who'd been nothing but suspicious of Daniel, was pudding to Hope, smiling more than he'd ever seen.

The duke patted her head, then lifted Lionel higher in his arms, "You're going to marry my little Jemina?"

Daniel straightened as if called to attention. "Yes."

Repington unpinned a medal and gave it to Hope.

She swung the gold medallion by the ribbon, reminding Daniel of how he swung his watch fob. Willingham and associate took his. There was no replacing it.

"He's marrying my mama." Hope clapped her hands.

Lionel gurgled and drooled, perhaps approving the statement.

"You're very sure of this, Ashbrook? I was under the impression that you two were at odds. I'm not convinced this is right."

"You're claiming Mrs. St. Maur now too, Your Grace? I thought she was a grown woman who knew her own mind."

"The woman is family. She's like a sister to my wife. You know the duchess has lost hers."

"On a boat?" Hope peered up, her eyes big like hot-air balloons.

"No, Miss Thackery." The duke's voice softened. "They were lost in a land far away. My inquiries have come up with nothing. Ashbrook, Jemina St. Maur might as well be a Strathmore. Maybe we can exchange for another . . . like Lady Bodonel?"

Fidgeting, Daniel flicked at an alabaster button on his jade waistcoat. "Pardon, Your Grace? I don't understand."

"Never mind, Barrister. There's probably no legal precedence for swapping relatives." He drummed the side arm of his wheeled chair.

Lionel followed suit, clanking his medals and offering a one-tooth grin. "Pa." He bubbled spittle. "Wel-ton."

"No, but close, son." The duke beamed as if the babe were a prized cannon or a vanquished enemy or the duchess's famous coconut bread. "Here, Ashbrook, hold Lionel a moment."

He offered up the boy, and Daniel took him. The boy was tanned with ears that looked a little like the duke's. What would a son between Daniel and Jemina look like?

This would be a full marriage. Potentially, there could be more Thackerys.

Setting Hope to the floor, the duke stood. The articulating knee of his carved limb made a slight click as he lifted to his full height. He stuck out his hand. "You will be kind to her. I can still muster an army if needed."

"Repington, I think I'm more afraid of your wife and my bride teaming up for revenge. They are fast masterminds."

"Then you understand. You have my blessings."

Daniel didn't need anyone's blessing but Jemina's, though having the duke's was good.

"Come, I think they have set the nuptials for the parlor."

Repinning his medal from Hope, the duke led the way. Daniel's little girl tried to march, then flopped down and crawled behind him. Her pink dress with the rosebush-red collar looked marvelous and festive.

As they moved to the grand hall, the person he'd been waiting to arrive entered the house.

"Lady Shrewsbury," Daniel said, "just on time."

The whirlwind came straight toward him. "Daniel, may I see you for a moment?"

"I've already given him my consent, Countess," the duke said. "No changing his mind. We have too much cake to not have a celebration."

Daniel gave Lionel an affectionate pat on the head, scrunching the fuzz atop his skull and offered him back to Repington. Then he turned to face his aunt. "Duke, may we borrow your study, so I may have a word with my aunt?"

"Of course, but no fleeing through the widows or tampering with my swords. Only the duchess has permission for those."

Daniel bent to Hope. "Follow the duke and be a good girl. Help him with Lionel."

The little girl stood up again with his help. She wobbled farther and made it to the infamous parlor.

Lady Shrewsbury took Daniel's arm, and he whisked her into the duke's headquarters. Closing the door, he put his back against it.

"I see you received my note."

"First, you disappear from my party. Did you know Mrs. St. Maur was caught in the throes of passion in one of my parlors with a baron? With the confusion, only one of my other widows received an offer."

"Well, two if you count my bride-to-be."

"You don't mind that she was *flirting* with another?"

"Aunt, she was with me. Lavinia tried another compromise, this one left me quite incapacitated. Jemina rescued me and damaged her reputation to keep mine from ruin."

"So that was you? Your twitching feet under the sheet?"

"Yes, and your people need to dust the spare rooms."

"Well, I thought . . . Lavinia said . . . Lady Lavinia must pay. I can't believe she enlisted me in something to ensnare you." She drew the duke's sword, the one hanging low on the wall.

Daniel whipped it from her hands and returned it. "Aunt. I don't need to represent you on charges of murder."

"Very well. Jemina's loyal to you, Daniel, but are you comfortable with her past? We know definitively that the St. Maurs were a party to financing the slave trade."

"She doesn't remember any of it. I won't convict her of that. Aunt, you know Jemina, how gentle and kind she is."

"I do. She is a good woman." She backed away from the weapons. "Is she ready to be a stepmother to Hope? You told her what you've done in case the Dunns ever make trouble?"

"She will be a great mother to Hope. They've bonded."

Lady Shrewsbury raised her hand then dropped it. "That's good, but you didn't answer my second question. Does Jemina know that you assumed custody of Hope and created a will and guardianship papers to keep her?"

"No." He turned away for a moment, then stood up straight, chest puffed out. "No one need know anything about it. The Dunns haven't questioned. With Jemina no longer making inquiries because she has a new life to occupy her, no one need ever know."

"Daniel, you're starting this union with a secret, a big one."

"I shouldn't have told you. You're going to look at Hope and me—"

"No, Daniel. I'm going to trust that you know what you are doing. You are a great judge of character. I merely think that the woman with whom you wish to share your life should know everything. No secrets."

The fear of losing everything by admitting to anyone but Lady Shrewsbury the truth about Hope was too great. How would he explain that he was different from his uncle if Daniel implemented a scheme to retain custody? Merely having good intentions didn't make wrong right. "I want this forgotten."

"Truth has a way of coming out, Daniel."

"The only truth that matters is that I can make Jemina happy and that she makes me happy. And Hope. I've never seen my daughter with such joy."

"The woman you brought to me from Bedlam is trustworthy. Don't you know that?"

"I know who she is, Aunt. We'll face our future together, everything. No looking back. Give me your blessing on this."

"Daniel—"

The door opened, and Jemina came inside.

She wore the silver gown he'd had made for her. She sparkled as she moved, like a beautiful light fit for a chandelier. The woman was a vision. His vision.

He clasped her hand. "You look lovely, Jemina. My aunt was just giving me . . . us her blessing."

Lady Shrewsbury looked up at him, then she nodded. "Yes, I have. Take her hand, Daniel."

Wrapping her arm about his, he tucked her fingers within his palm.

His aunt looked at him, then her gaze lowered toward their entwined hands. "You stay happy, Jemina, and you keep Daniel and Hope safe and loved. Promise me that, my girl."

Lady Shrewsbury came forward; she took a ribbon pinned on her hat and wrapped it about their wrists. "You two are bound together in so many ways, the *Minerva*, Bedlam."

"Pomegranates," Jemina said.

She must've noticed the pomegranates and cherries, symbols of sweetness and fruitfulness, embroidered in the lace of her sleeves.

Aunt squinted and shook her head. "Maybe this was inevitable. And who am I to stand in the way? Be good to each other. And above all, you're still both members of the Widow's Grace. No long wedding trip."

"We're in the middle of the Season. My trial load is large. I haven't purchased a country estate yet."

His bride-to-be squinted at him. "We don't need to go anywhere but Finchely."

He sort of forgot to mention his thoughts on retiring. He'd postpone that for now. "You're absolutely right, Jemina. See, I'm already taking to this agreeable husband role."

"And this is my gift to you." From her pocket she pulled his watch fob. "I found it that horrible night. I had the glass fixed and springs repaired. It shall work now."

Daniel grasped it and the tips of her fingers. His throat felt a little thick, and the man who loved words was speechless.

Mr. Gerard poked his head in. "The minister's here. It's time to begin."

Putting the Thackery treasure into his pocket, Daniel clenched her hand and then claimed his aunt's.

"Shall we, ladies? I'm not sure how long the duke and baby Lionel can keep little Hope occupied."

"Mr. Bridgetower is in there," Mr. Gerard said, and held open the door. "His music is keeping your daughter entertained."

The butler led them into the hall.

Strains of the violin punctuated each step. The tempo raced like Daniel's heart. Palms still clasped, he slid his thumb along the soft flesh at the crook of her hand and they stepped into the infamous parlor, where everything changed.

With the special license in hand, Peregrine Daniel Thackery, the Earl of Ashbrook, would take his vows with Jemina Monroe St. Maur, the woman who stood beside him.

This marriage was true and right. He took away the sliver band Aunt gave to her widows and offered her a gold and ruby one.

A distant look overtook the joy in Jemina's eyes. She held the license and stared at him. "Peregrine Daniel Thackery?"

"Yes. Like my fob, a parting gift from my father."

"Peregrine?"

The sooner his bride was enrobed in wedded bliss, the safer and happier they'd all be. With the exchanging of their vows, the past was done, buried at the bottom of the sea.

CHAPTER 40

JEMINA—THE WEDDING NIGHT

Sitting at the vanity that my new husband said was mine, in a room that was mine with a tiny closet full of new gowns, I stared in the mirror.

"Not a ragamuffin today." Not that I thought I ever was, except in hospitals.

The faint glow to my ruddy cheeks remained. I held up the new band on my finger, shiny gold with a pomegranate-shaped ruby, round with fiery facets.

I was Lady Ashbrook, Daniel's countess.

He said Finchely was ours. That Hope was ours. When would it feel that way, not borrowed, which meant it could be taken?

One stare at the girl in the mirror rallied my spirits. Though my past was a blur, I deserved joy. I deserved more of all the good things. I wouldn't disqualify me from life, not again, not as long as I had breath.

Daniel opened the adjoining door to his bedchamber. "Good, you're not asleep. That second wedding breakfast might be enough to make you tire."

He chuckled with hands behind his back in a dark emerald robe. No nightshirt. I saw bits of chest, chiseled, sun-warmed and brown, tufts of hair as fine as the curls on his head.

"My lord, I liked meeting your friends, the Richmonds and Mr. Gerard's granddaughters, and so many others. I felt welcomed."

I loosened the ribbon Patience had threaded through my braids. They all came undone. Springy tresses unwound and fell about my pink robe.

With one hand behind his back, Daniel came forward, scooped up my silver brush and swooped it through my slacked braids. "Soft. A little like Hope's. I believe she too will have a lot of hair."

He bent a little closer. The dark hue of his robe drew out tiny flecks of green in his black eyes. "How do you find your room?"

"Perfect," I said. "But I do remember this room from before. The incident on the steps, that is unforgettable."

"I wanted you to stay forever then." His smile was full, gap and all. With a quick slip to my neck, his palms skimmed my throat, and he set down the brush. "Does my Lady Ashbrook require anything? Something to nibble."

"I'm full from the feasts. I'm fine."

"Just fine? I think I know how to make time perfect. Close your eyes."

My middle clenched. My pulse sped. I latched my eyes tight. Well, almost so. I had to peek.

He knelt and slipped a bowl from behind his back. Taking a shiny spoon from his pocket, he scooped into it. His pomegranate ambrosia danced on my tongue.

I gobbled it. I loved it. I reached for him, and let my kiss say what I wasn't brave enough to voice.

He had suggested that I was too loud sometimes.

Daniel tasted of cherries, sweet and tingling to my tongue.

The bowl found a home on the vanity, and I went into his arms. He stood, lifting me with him, kissing me, backing me across the boundary between our chambers.

Against the footboard of his bed, we settled.

Daniel had his strong hands on my face. Everything was *purr-fect*.

Then he stopped.

Across my lips, he brushed them with his, then whispered something.

I didn't hear. My heart pounded too hard.

He bent to my ear. "That noise, Jemina?"

"Nothing, darling." My arms settled against his shoulders.

His hands worked away the knot of my sash. I caught his thumbs. I was a widow, a grown woman. Yet I only possessed two years of memories—none of them was this. Nothing had my heart spinning with the anticipation of being loved by this man.

This next kiss was soft. His words against my throat felt like flames.

> *Elated with hope, you no longer mourn,*
> *My soul expands, each grateful touch of you, your bosom burns,*
> *While in my hands our pleasures we behold*
> *The silken reins, you shine supreme.*

His voice wrapped about me. His nimble fingers undid me, my ribbons.

"More Wheatley, Daniel?"

"Technically, yes, but a little of my words."

"I suppose this means you like me."

"Um. Yes, Jemina."

A second kiss took hold, followed by a third.

Then he stopped. He seemed hesitant.

A first time, a first memory with a man I felt so much for, who I mostly loved and definitely wanted, shouldn't fill me with nerves. Nor should it cause my husband to withdraw. "Be with me, Daniel."

I stood on tiptoes to encourage him.

But he lifted his head. His eyes had lost their sparkle. The heat of his body went away. "That's Hope. She's crying."

My hands fell to the footboard. I finally heard her screams over my heart. "Yes."

Daniel was out the door almost as fast as me. He caught me at the nursery.

Hope's scream echoed. "Mama! Mama, the water!"

I reached out to her, but my vision blackened. My feet were on the *Minerva*. I tried to hold on to the mast, tried to keep our heads above the water. Ours. My baby and mine.

"I'm here, Hope."

That was Daniel's voice.

"Your papa's here."

When I blinked, he had his daughter in his arms, bouncing her against his chest. "Hope, please. Wake up. You're safe with me. Your papa's here."

I didn't know what to do, but the words to my lullaby came from my insides. "'*Il était un petit navire. Il était un petit navire.*'"

Hope reached over Daniel's head. "Mama, save me. Get us from the water. Mama, please."

My husband looked helpless, but he turned and put the little girl into my arms.

Snuggled against me with her toddler arms clutching my robe, Hope calmed. "Water's everywhere. So dark. No let go."

No let go?

My heart broke.

One glimpse at Daniel said his secret. Hope had been on the *Minerva*, too.

This wasn't my nightmare.

This was our truth. "Hope survived the *Minerva*?"

Daniel stared at me for a moment, then nodded. "Phoebe brought Hope with her from Jamaica. She's a miracle, just like you."

"Why didn't you that say, Daniel?" My voice grew louder and louder. "Why?"

Daniel bit his lip.

Now I knew he purposely didn't mention it. He kept this secret from me.

"Mama. No go. No go no more."

Hope's grip was so tight. I couldn't think of anything but reassuring her. "I'm not letting go of you. Never again."

"Jemina, everything about the *Minerva* should be forgotten. It's too painful. Look how it hurts her. I wish no one would think of it."

"Some truths shouldn't have to be begged to be acknowledged." My voice was tight. I strangled in my hurt. He hadn't been honest.

Hope's curly head leaned deeper onto my bosom. "Mama came back for me."

"I'm not—"

Daniel puts his hand to my lips. "You're her mother now. Now is all that matters."

The way he said it, so confident and assured.

What more did he know and not say?

"Mama."

Hope melted into my arms, falling into the crook of my elbow right under my bosom. I went to the rocking chair and sat.

The more Hope and I rocked together, the more I accepted the truth she'd been trying to tell me.

I wasn't her new mother.

I was her old one.

I did save her from the water.

We did survive the sea together.

My heart rejoiced. Tears and joy and betrayal warred in my breast. I had my daughter in my arms, but Daniel . . .

He stepped close and put his palm on Hope's head. "Give her to me, Jemina. You rest. It's your first night in your new home with your new family. I wanted it to be special."

His tone wasn't repentant. It was a mesh of sadness and practicality.

I refused to let go of my miracle. "No, I have her. I told her I wouldn't let go. I won't be a liar."

His palm went to his mouth. "I want you to rest and get use to us, Finchely."

He sounded concerned, but all I could think was if I'd known this before, I would have been here every day. How many nights had my daughter cried herself to sleep, when I could've had her in my arms?

"Jemina, you don't look well. Your cheeks are scarlet."

How do I tell him how angry I was and how grateful I was to find my baby? But who would believe a woman from Bedlam? One with no facts, nothing to prove it but a feeling so deep in my chest I might burst.

"Jemina?"

"I'm well. I'm sane. Don't touch her."

He jerked back like I'd bit him. Maybe I had with my tone.

"Jemina?" Daniel stooped beside the rocking chair. "What's wrong?"

How was I to say this and not be condemned? I couldn't. I held Hope tighter. "I'm upset with myself for not hearing her cries. I'm selfish."

An easier breath left him. "No, not at all. You've proven yourself so giving over and over." Daniel kissed my cheek. "We'll get you used to our routine. Then, we'll find time to be selfish. Now, Lady Ashbrook go to bed. I'll comfort my daughter."

"No. No, you go rest. You have court tomorrow. I have her. You trust me with her, Daniel?"

He nodded, but those eyes of his seemed to assess me. Surely, he knew I stewed. How could I not?

What was the truth?

Had Daniel lost both Phoebe and her child with the *Minerva*? Had all his hopes been stolen by the hurricane that sunk that ship?

Or was I Phoebe? And he saved my baby.

I kissed my Hope's head. "Go to sleep. When she falls to sleep, I'll put her to bed."

He brushed her curls but seemed hesitant to move.

"Go on, Daniel. I'm her mother, remember?"

My husband, keeper of secrets, stood at the door. The man looked truly lost, but the way Hope held on to me, I'd never put her down.

I'd just found what I'd been looking for. It merely came with a husband I could no longer completely trust.

CHAPTER 41

DANIEL—LADY ASHBROOK WHO

A week of marriage had passed. Daniel wouldn't exactly notice a difference from his old life, the one he had two years ago.

Alone, estranged from Jemina, he crouched low on the floor outside the nursery.

Well, this was different, sitting on the tapestry in the hall. Two years ago, he'd be in his study reading Phoebe's letters before preparing for vingt-et-un with the fellows and waiting for the day the *Minerva* sailed into Portsmouth.

How did marrying change everything?

His wife, his wife in name only, sang her lullaby. She made it loud over Hope's cries until the child soothed. His daughter's nightmares came every night, and Jemina was the only one to calm her.

He tried so hard and in so many ways to get Hope to again sleep through the night, even towing them all into his bed. If she wasn't in Jemina's arms with her head to her chest, the babe sobbed miserably.

Knocking his skull against the wall, he couldn't fathom what had shifted, changed. Marriage was to make them a family.

How could wedding Jemina turn her from a friend to a nanny? Not even a naked one.

Something had broken. Finchely was broken, a broken home. And he was here after court, not out carousing or becoming a belligerent drunk.

Now, he felt like an outsider, and Jemina's eyes held so much hurt that Daniel might as well have been his father.

"Your mother's not leaving you, Hope. Know this." Jemina's voice was loud. Those were the words she'd said on their wedding night.

Maybe she didn't know she was a good mother without wearing herself to tatters like torn fabric.

Maybe if Daniel wrote her notes again and told her this she'd listen.

Mrs. Gallick came up the stairs with two mugs on a tray. She offered him one, and then sat beside him, squatting on the floor.

"Sir, there's another letter from that solicitor, Mr. Mosey. I put it in your study."

The gossip of their marriage would bring those devils working for the St. Maurs.

He eyed the mug and groaned. Why wouldn't the past stay gone?

"Thank you, Mrs. G. Don't let the countess see them. She's taken on enough."

"I won't, sir." Mrs. Gallick collected one of the cups. "That one is a natural mother. Hope will grow out of this. You just have to trust."

The contented smile on his daughter's face when Jemina responded to her as her mother made him happy, but something wasn't right.

Mother?

Did Hope figure out something he'd missed?

His baby was brilliant.

Their baby was brilliant.

Had he found Phoebe and didn't even know it? When Daniel stepped into the room at Bedlam to free Jemina St. Maur, wasn't that what he'd hoped? Hadn't he wished that tragic accident had become his miracle—Phoebe alive and with amnesia and falsely called Jemina St. Maur?

"Lord Ashbrook, I'm going to get more cream for my tea. Do you want anything, else? I know you don't like my cream."

He shook his head, and she left. His face no longer bore swelling but he had tasted enough spirits for a lifetime. "No cream."

But Jemina was not the Phoebe described in letters. Unless her deception was greater than not telling him about her daughter. Was this a mistake of the London bankers he'd used to find a freeborn Black or mixed-race daughter of their investors in the colonies?

Innocent mistake?

Creole women of Jamaica were considered Black if they were less than three generations from Black blood. Creole mulattoes were considered white if their bloodlines were beyond three generations.

Was that it? Jemina's diction sounded as if she'd been educated in England. The red in her skin, could she be Creole or Sephardic Jew? There was no hint of Portuguese in her tongue, just the distant slip of Jamaican patois when he teased her or she didn't think anyone listened.

No mistake? Fraud?

Would a West Indian widow desperate to have a new start with a wealthy husband lie about her race? This explained the Dunns' insistence that they marry by proxy before allowing Phoebe to come to London.

He knocked his head against the wall.

His housekeeper rushed up the stairs. "Sir?" She sat beside him again. "Want to talk?"

He picked up the toasty mug. The calm of the citrusy chamomile wafted in the steam. "Do I look like I have something to say, Mrs. G?"

"I know you don't want to hear this but your daughter will cry out her nightmares. Both you and Lady Ashbrook should be out here letting the girl learn to pacify herself."

With a slurp, he let the hot liquid burn his throat. "Pacification? That's one of the things we want, do we mean it?"

"You have it bad, sir."

"Have what bad?"

"You're in love and mad at the same time? I'm not sure what Lady Ashbrook did, but I think she deserves every consideration. Her heart is large, and she's been so supportive of Hope. Not all women would do that."

No, not all women would risk a fall on stairs for a toddler or disgrace themselves to save an earl. He rubbed his forehead and conceded to Mrs. G's wisdom. "She's special."

Jemina's amnesia was true. If Hope was right, the woman he married, the new Lady Ashbrook didn't know.

"Talk to her, sir. Tell her everything you have swirling in that brilliant mind of yours."

"Everything?"

"Yes. Everything. I think she'll understand and be reassured."

Is that what was missing? A way to reassure her that no matter who she was, or what she'd done, that Daniel loved her.

He drained his cup, every last bit as if it were his last. "Nothing matters but now. I've said that so many times. It's about time for me to act like I believe it."

"Excellent, sir."

His housekeeper clinked her cup with his as if they'd made an agreement. Well, maybe they had. The woman knew him too well.

"I pray that the air is cleared soon. Lady Ashbrook loves that baby as much as you. Do what you have to do to keep your family."

The family he somewhat created, the one thing he'd always wanted and coveted and promised himself. Why should something like the truth stand in his way?

It hadn't before.

"Well, look at that, sir."

"What, Mrs. Gallick?"

She waved him to the door of the nursery.

"They're both asleep, sir."

It was a sight. Jemina, so beautiful. The reddish braids of her chignon spilling down her shoulders. Hope with her thumb in her mouth nestled against his wife's gray walking gown.

"I should do something. My Lady Ashbrook is wearying."

"Sir, that one was meant to mother a child like Hope, one tortured by memories. She's the right one. Don't get confused. This is right."

"Thank you. Good night, Mrs. G."

She walked away, leaving Daniel to stare into the nursery. Hope and Jemina, the two of them, both pieces of his heart, both finally at ease.

Tempting fate, he picked up his beautiful little girl and set her in her crib. The doll, Mrs. Feebs, he put in the tot's arms. "Mrs. Feebs, you keep Hope company tonight."

Then he turned to Jemina.

Daniel didn't lose trials often. When he did, he learned to accept what he knew and move forward. Trying to figure out what was right or more in the right was unfair. Jemina still had no memories to even counter a single suspicion.

In the end, this was his fault. He stopped looking for answers. He let his heart become tender to both Jemina and Phoebe. One in the same, or not, it didn't matter. This was the family he created, the one he'd defend, the one he'd never give up.

As gently as he could, he lifted Jemina.

Her cheeks seemed thin. The woman was worn out.

"I let go. I can't." She put her arms about his shoulder, clutching him like her life depended upon holding him. This was her nightmare.

He kissed her brow. "You're safe. So is our Hope."

Daniel sat in the rocking chair and held his Lady Ashbrook. That's who she was right now. They'd stay in the nursery. If Jem-

ina fully awakened, she wouldn't be startled searching for his . . .
her . . . their daughter. "Siphon some of my strength, my love.
Nothing else matters."

Hope snorted but did not cry.

She knew her papa loved her. Maybe it was time to let her
mama know the same.

CHAPTER 42

JEMINA—WHAT DOES HE KNOW?

I laid on the mattress in my bedchamber, my head floating on a pile of pillows. Wasting most of the morn staring at the sealed note Daniel scooted under my door, I decided to open it and see if he'd confess.

Finchely House, London, August 30, 1814

> *Dearest J,*
> *I wondered if you'd smile at me just once. I didn't mean for your role as "mother" to become so exhausting.*
> *I miss you.*
> *I miss everything.*
> *Please tell me a secret. Tell me how to make things better.*
> *Your servant,*
>
> *D. Thackery, Earl of Ashbrook*
> *Finchely House, London*

Daniel's letter sounded miserable. I was miserable, fretting about Hope and twisting myself up about the lack of trust between husband and wife.

My eyes and face felt puffy from poor sleep. I burrowed deeper into the bedclothes, bundled in a gauzy bronze robe.

The lacy cuffs, the sash embroidered in gold, another of Daniel's gifts, seemed meaningless compared to having my daughter. How did I tell him he's raised my girl for two years? I was committed to Bedlam because no one believed my child was alive. I screamed for her until I was hoarse. No one listened. They only wanted me to admit I'd lost all.

I hadn't.

My daughter was taken. How did Daniel get her? Did he help those who took her?

This was my secret; one I could not share. Not without proof.

I knew in my soul Hope was mine.

But I remember nothing else, not her birth, not her true father. A Blackamoor child couldn't be Cecil St. Maur's child.

Covering my eyes with my pale hands, I laughed, laughed like a loon. I had no facts, no proof to offer. Daniel would think I was crazed. He'd wish me to Bedlam, not his bed.

Lord Ashbrook, a barrister of the courts, could send me away. As my husband and a peer, who would stop him? No one would believe this girl over an earl.

My heart beat fast, whirling in my chest.

My breath a full-blown cyclone. My safety, my relationship to my daughter all hinged on a man versed in the laws, laws which were always used against women.

With a knock on my door, Mrs. Gallick brought a tray with a shiny silver dome, a teapot, and a cup. Letters were stuck under the crook of her gingham-checked arm. "Lady Ashbrook, you are up."

"You didn't have to bring me breakfast."

"I had to, ma'am. You're not to waste away, not under my care." Mrs. Gallick said with a smile. She set the tray on the night table by my large window. The housekeeper fussed with the panes and let the warm air inside.

She turned, wiping her hands on her white apron. "This room hasn't been used that much. The master's late mother enjoyed it. She insisted on sunny yellow walls and for this window to be open every morn to let in the fresh air.

Mrs. Gallick parted the jonquil curtains wider.

The strong sunlight shone through, but there were clouds in the offing.

She bent to uncover porridge and slices of bananas. The letters slipped.

I scooped them up before she did. One had my name, well my new title. The script wasn't Daniel's.

Mrs. Gallick's eyes widened more. "Let me have that. His lordship doesn't want you distracted with anything but eating."

Palming the one for me, I handed over the others. "I'm not hungry."

She took them and put the letters into her apron. "Mouse bites. That's all you've done all week. A grown woman can't survive like this."

"I've survived worse."

"Suggest to his lordship how to make things better. I think he'll do anything for you."

The well-meaning housekeeper offered me a sad smile and left.

I missed what we had too, but he had secrets and I had mine, and neither of us seemed willing to share. I broke the seal of the wax on the correspondence.

Finchely House, London, August 29, 1814

Dear Lady Ashbrook,
Congratulations are in order. There are assets
formerly belonging to your late husband that need
your attention. I have a buyer willing to pay a fair

*penny for these assets. I have written to Lord
Ashbrook a number of times to no avail.*

*Blessings to you on your nuptials, though I must
warn you, there are members and advocates of the
St. Maur family who believe that you are under
duress, perhaps of a diminished capacity. If this is
wrong, please communicate at once. It would be in
your best interest to resolve the matter as soon as
possible.*

*T. Mosey, Solicitor
Sleck Building, Tonbridge*

Diminished capacity. That was fancy learned speech for "other-worldly," "a loon." The St. Maurs had an interest in me now. I resided in Bedlam for two years, but they wanted me now.

My abdomen lurched. The St. Maurs or my husband could return me to Bedlam. I'd lose Hope again.

Never.

Shaking, I hugged myself, and tossed on my shawl.

Then I remembered me. I wasn't a victim anymore. I'd scaled buildings. I'd fought a hurricane and won.

No more waiting for someone to come with answers.

No more wanting Daniel to save me.

I pressed on the adjoining door and went inside. I'd check for more Mosey letters before I went to Daniel's study. The sketch of Phoebe no longer hung on the wall. Only Hope's drawing remained. I hadn't noticed that on our wedding night, but I wasn't paying attention to much but Daniel.

Phoebe's notes. Daniel's secrets—they would tell me what he knew. Going into the big closet, I breathed Daniel, sweet cedar and lily of the valley.

On the shelf close to my hip was the waistcoat he wore at our wedding. The white tissue paper cradling it made it seem so delicate, so fragile.

His voice, the memory of it, rang in my ear. His vows to honor and keep me sounded clear and crisp. Could he be part of a conspiracy or just another victim to it?

My hook and rope were on the floor in the corner. Good to know where it was if a fast escape was needed. Yet, I knew Daniel would let nothing happen to me. How could my mind war between him being good or part of the world who took my baby?

I heard a noise outside the closet. Daniel?

Then nothing, no valet or Mrs. Gallick.

My whimpering heart raced but not from fear, from anticipation. I still wanted Daniel despite the secrets.

Toes flopping on the smooth tapestry of red and orange, I passed the window. The sun burned through the panes and fought with a gaggle of clouds. The gray was gaining. Hope might startle from the thunder.

Torn between going to her and finding secrets, I took down the box that Hope told me not to touch. My fingertips felt fire as I pulled out the first note, then all of them.

A quick scan of one had me laughing at the jests Phoebe offered. Tears welled when she mentioned the loss of a brother. Phoebe Dunn was a brilliant writer.

Soon I'd read them all, and none, none of them mentioned a child.

There was a reference to Max in the last, obviously in response to something Daniel had written about his loyal pug. Yet, there was no evidence that Phoebe Dunn had a child or would travel to London with one.

She could've omitted Hope in one or two letters, but how could a loving mother never talk of that precious girl?

Phoebe couldn't be Hope's mother. I definitely couldn't be Phoebe Dunn. If that notion had rooted in my head, it disappeared.

Patience. She'd understand and would confirm my thoughts. I needed to get to her. She needed to see these.

Stuffing the letters into my pocket, I turned, readying to dress, hop into a carriage, and get to my friend.

But I froze.

Daniel stood in front of me and from the look in his eyes, he wasn't letting me go.

CHAPTER 43

DANIEL—THE CLOSET

Thunder barked. Lightning scattered outside his window. His grand closet that let in the proper light shined it on his Lady Ashbrook.

She stood before him, wide-eyed, awake, in the translucent dressing gown he thought would make her eyes radiate.

"You're home early, Daniel."

"I had a conversation with the Lord Mayor that made me need to leave."

"Oh." She fingered a long braid that shifted in color from wheat to red with each flash of light.

He moved closer. "My, my, what a nice surprise, my wife with my favorite things."

With a finger to his nose, he posted in front of her. "If I wanted to visit with my wife, I just needed to find her in my closet?"

"It's a lovely place. Very big, bigger than mine."

He leaned down to kiss her brow, but she backed into a shelf.

"Um. *Chubble*. Um. I like your tailcoats." She touched his favorite indigo jacket with the smartly cut revers. "The fabric is so nice."

"Yes, I do have a very fine tailor." He closed the distance, putting his hands on either side of her. "I think Mr. Weston should make you a pelisse or a new cape. I think your emerald one has weathered a great deal."

Lightning flashed.

"Does that mean you don't like me as I am, Daniel? Do you want to change me?"

Her tone sounded short and defensive. The workings of the female brainbox were elusive, Jemina's particularly so. Nonetheless, he determined last night how to fix things, by sharing his heart.

"No changes. Why change the woman I love?" He reached for her hand and imparted a kiss to her palm. "I love you. I love you so deeply. That has to be what's keeping us apart. I haven't assured you of my affections. My household has cast such demands upon you. It hasn't been fair."

Her mouth, cupid's bow and all, popped open. "How can that be? You don't know me."

Harsh and loud and definitely not convinced, Jemina's voice cut through him.

"Don't know you?" That must be the Phoebe Dunn business. She must remember something. Was that shame scorching red her cheeks?

"*Cack mowt will kill cock*. Jemina. This rooster won't kill with my words. I will choose them carefully to tell you my thoughts. Then you have to believe me."

Daniel put his hands to his mouth praying for the words to heal this rift. "It is true. I don't know much of you, how you grew up, your circle of friends other than the Widow's Grace. You left from Jamaica on the *Minerva*. You could've been friends with my late wife. You and Phoebe could've been close, thick as thieves. I don't know. Nothing of the past matters. Now is what matters. It's the only thing that does."

Her gaze lowered to her sleeves. Glimmers of lightning reflected in the gauzy fabric silhouetting her waist, hips, her trim legs. "I like this place. I think it would be good to draw in here.

It feels safe, like I can say anything in these walls. Maybe you won't think me crazy if I said what is in my head."

"Having conversations in my closet is not crazed. I often recite case law here while my valet finds something suitable."

"You're making fun. I can't say anything unusual without you laughing or fearing for my sanity."

As if she stood on the witness dock, he stepped to her with his ready question. "Like that you could be Phoebe Dunn, a woman initially reported as rescued?"

Her eyes whipped up. The sassy jutting out of her chin screamed no. No, she wasn't Phoebe.

Daniel put up his hands. "I assume that . . . I mean I know you not to be her. You are you. And I love you."

Her face held shadows, but she hadn't slapped him. Her fingers unfurled and clasped her elbows. "The rain is falling. The sun has lost this battle."

"Rain is needed too, Jemina."

"I saw a note from the solicitor, Mr. Mosey. The St. Maurs think I'm of diminished capacity. He hinted at having our marriage dissolved. Would you ever want that?"

"Jemina, I want to hide things that will distress you, but it's not from thinking you cannot handle the strain. It's me. I want to protect you and the family we are now."

"Just like that. The past is gone? Everything is made right? How generous."

He wasn't being clear, and her fears were twisting what he said. As gently as he could, Daniel put his arms about her. "My mother said to not be angry after sunset. But I have been. I'm angry at myself for not keeping us focused on the miracle we are."

She grasped his fingers, which had begun to find paths to her soft skin hiding beneath her shawl.

"I'm still at the place where we pledged everything to each other. Surely that meant being husband and wife in or out of this closet."

"You didn't tell me that my baby . . . that Hope was on the *Minerva*. You don't trust me."

She pushed his hands away. "Daniel, you're not ready to listen. You've come home early. You should rest before dinner."

Her tone was dismissive, perhaps this was an attempt to diminish her pain.

How could he encourage her? "Help me know what to do."

"You've said what you had to, Daniel. Change from court."

"I used to say you were too loud, Jemina. I don't like you quiet." He locked his hands to his crown. He still wore the stupid court wig. He took it off with care and put it on its proper place, its box on the top shelf.

Her smile disappeared. She seemed almost panicked.

"Do small spaces bother you?"

"Daniel, this is not small."

"Then what is the problem? We aren't leaving here until I'm convinced everything between us is good."

"We could be in here a long time, *Peregrine*. Someone might think we've gone missing."

"See, we're not fine if you need to address me with such a horrid name."

"It is pretty horrible, but Peregrine and Phoebe sounds pretty."

Was that a confession? The blood rushed his ears, but her blank face reduced it to a trickle. No confession or stray memory, just Jemina's delightful turns of phrase. He could play too. "We don't know everything. Your middle name might be Phoebe, then we'd still be such a match."

He let fall a ridiculous laugh that made his chest feel freer. "I miss our teasing. Let's purpose to fix us."

She put her hand to his cheek. He tensed, but for naught. No slap. By the cravat, she grabbed him. "You want a dutiful, submissive, believe-everything-you-say wife. Fine." She leaped at him, kissing him into a corner.

Court frills fell and a dulled hook pressed into his spine.

"Whoa, Jemina. That's not fixing. This isn't talking. It's the opposite."

"We talk too much." Wrapping him in her arms, she sealed her lips to his.

Her passion this time backed him into a wall of shelves.

"Jemina?"

"Daniel, I've been told I'm too loud."

"Then I should close the closet door."

She wound her hands underneath his coat. "Let's go back to our wedding day, when I believed everything you said. When I knew you trusted me."

Her teeth raked along the veins of his throat, sweet and seductive, but her words possessed a ruthlessness. He didn't know what to listen to.

"Jemina, I may waiver or dither, but I come back to bare facts. I know you and I are meant to be together. In the end, that's all that matters."

"If you say so, Daniel."

Something was wrong.

Jemina kissed his frown. Deep with raw, bitter passion, she tasted of sweet, swirling confusion.

Catching his breath, Daniel put distance between them. "Let's go for a ride. Get caught in the rain and rebuild whatever has broken."

"What if I told you that your failure to disclose to me that Hope was on the *Minerva* has made me question what else you'll hide from me, Peregrine?"

He stopped looking at the hurt raging from her eyes. He owed Jemina the truth. "I did fail you, because I don't want to remember how I almost lost everything. That day on the docks waiting for news of the *Minerva* was harrowing. I searched for news of Phoebe, then little Hope was put in my arms because they thought she belonged to me. A Black man coming for a Black babe. If I'd been late the lieutenant was going to dump Phoebe's daughter at a brothel."

He cleared his throat, wrenching at his cravat. "I don't want to know how close I came to missing the most wonderful little girl in the world."

He ran both hands through his hair. "I don't want to think of it anymore." Clasping her fingers, he led her to the door. "Go get dressed. Let's ride. Let's ride in the rain."

"Daniel, you saved Hope. They couldn't find her mother."

"Phoebe was gone, and all I had left was that angel. I vowed that day on the docks to protect her and love her like she was my own flesh and blood."

Something lively danced across Jemina's countenance. A smile warmed her face, the first since their wedding night. She embraced him about his waist. "Oh, Daniel, you're a hero. Let's pretend you've caught me in the thunderstorm."

Jemina kissed him and slipped his waistcoat to the floor.

Her shawl fell away, and they undid his cravat together. "Let's get out of these *wet* clothes."

The play in voice had returned, and he noticed the uptick in her heartbeat. In his. "I do love a woman who knows what she wants."

"I know now. I'll focus on how lucky I am you saved my little girl."

She kissed his cheek.

He cradled her chin, angling and positioning the best route to heaven. He'd learned which way the noses went, straight ahead, so her passions met his strength.

They became a tangle of desire and laughs.

And he loved her all the more.

CHAPTER 44

JEMINA—CRAZY LOVE

I must seem crazed to Daniel, kissing and keeping him in this big old closet. In here, he wasn't the man who hid things. He was the man who saved Hope. The hero who made possible a reunion with my child. He kept my daughter safe, and he loved her when I could not.

With my hands to my temples, I stopped all the noise in my head and admired my husband unbuttoning his shirt. The man was finely built, smooth and muscular, sun-warmed brown on a cloudy day.

"Ball it up, Daniel. Drop it to the ground. Be untidy."

"It will wrinkle."

"Do it if you can, dearest. Be free and reckless. Or is P. Daniel Thackery unwilling to be wild?"

The hesitation was palatable, but he did it. "If it makes you laugh. Don't tell my valet." He neared and slipped the sash away from my robe. "Huzzah. Unwrapping a rare gift done up in this maddening sheer."

The robe slipped my shoulders and rested in the crook of my arms.

"Will you, Jemina, make a show of casting it to the floor?"

Doubts rushed in and crowded the space between us. I toyed with my cuff.

"No. Don't, Jemina. It's too pretty, the way it sculpts you, your hips." Daniel lifted my chin and filled my emptiness with his kiss. I surrendered to the notion that he was more good than wrong, more understanding than not. I couldn't hold him to a perfect standard when I was sure I hadn't been perfect or right.

No more fretting. No more shattering truths meant to divide my scarred heart. I gave in to this yearning and returned his passion. It was freeing.

My fingers slipped to his neck as I cinched my hands about him.

"Love you, Jemina." Spinning, he lifted me high. We shivered together with the rain streaking the window, hiding our embrace from the grounds below.

His skin heated mine to an inferno. His hands touched my buttons and hooks, unfastening them.

He spun me round and round in his closet. My nightgown fell away as if caught in a cyclone.

My love of him rushed like a hurricane's wind.

Still twirling, still finding the joy of his lips on my shoulder, I became dizzy.

Blown away, almost breathless, I clung to Daniel. He was solid and whole like the mast of the *Minerva*.

No letting go.

No letting go.

Bang, his arm hit a shelf.

The tissue separating his colorful waistcoats scattered.

The sound of crinkling paper shifted under his feet.

Then everything slowed.

Caught in the eye of this storm, everything quieted but my heart. Arms locked about my waist, Daniel had me and put my slippers again to the floor.

Dizzy, I held on to him as he kissed my neck, the hollow of my throat, every curve.

My pulse, each vein vibrated like zips of lightning.

"I love you," he said, "Peregrine Daniel Thackery loves you." Breathing hard, with his hands to my cheeks, he took my mouth.

That was the beginning and closing argument from the best litigator I knew.

It was enough.

The tingle of his beard on my ear had me begging. *Take me, take me up in your arms again.*

I kicked my stays away and stood before him, bared of everything. I reached for my husband, my friend.

No letting go, not this time.

Tissue and waistcoats flew as we sank to the floor. The scents of boot polish and soft bay was heady and comforting.

Kisses. Hungry Kisses.

With his smooth lips on mine, that feeling of survival and satisfaction merged.

He rushed me to the tempest, that point where the clouds burst into a war of colors, where the sea surges overhead and *you* die, drowning in the deep, the deepest surrender.

Together, Daniel and I, we died to love.

And was I happy being his, for he was mine. I merely had to ignore how my heart longed for my husband and the truth.

CHAPTER 45

JEMINA—WHICH HEART BREAKS

Patience paced in her parlor, and I waited for her judgment.

"Am I insane?" I asked again. "Or am I right: Hope is my daughter? Which do I tell Ashbrook?"

Her mouth opened, then snapped shut. Her rich complexion looked ashy, and Patience was never that unless there was a shortage of lotion.

"This is too much, Jemina."

"What's too much? Marrying a Cecil and a Peregrine? Yes, that does seem unfair." I pulled my cape about me and slumped on the sofa, swarmed in pillows. "Do I tell Ashbrook about Hope?"

"Are you going to explain why you left Finchely, climbing out a window in your husband's pantaloons? Can't the man keep them? Someone's always stealing them."

"I had to get to you, Patience. I needed you to tell me what to do."

She sat next to me and picked up a bone-white teacup. With a lump of Demerara sugar, she stirred and sipped.

This was her ritual, and the silence left me numb. Patience must think I was crazed.

"My stomach is a little upset, that is all," she said, and set the cup down next to the platter of untouched coconut bread. "You left Ashbrook sleeping and scaled a two-story height? You hate heights. Why didn't you walk out the front door?"

"Must you be logical?" Tying my bronze sash tighter about my borrowed clothes, I shrugged. "I was rash and—"

"Impatient."

"Yes. You've grown on me, but I trust you."

"And I you. I'd trust my Lionel with you. If anything ever happened to me, you must promise to see to him."

My dearest friend was troubled. Her voice held a little tremble. That wasn't Patience.

Hugging her neck, I hoped my confusion hadn't rubbed off. Patience was strong, the strongest person I knew. "You know I'll do anything for you, for Lionel and the duke."

"That gives me comfort." She embraced me so tight I knew something was wrong.

"Patience, what's wrong?"

"Nothing much, nothing at all. As your friend, I'm telling you to return to Finchely and tell your husband everything."

My hands dropped to my lap. "You don't believe me."

"That's not it, Jemina. This just feels wrong."

The sun setting outside burned in the window. It did shine when the rain stopped, and the rays illuminated everything left standing. I had love but no answers.

"Help me reason this out before Ashbrook awakens or Hope wants her bedtime story."

Patience smoothed her shaking fingers over the front of her mulberry walking gown. "Why don't you trust the man you just married?"

Shoulders shrugging, fingers tensing, I sipped my chamomile tea. How did I say I crept from Daniel's arms as he napped in his big bed with his lone pillow? Daniel. He was beautiful and spent. Together, we listened to the rain. He quoted me poetry in a house that was calm and quiet. As a couple, our hearts had found peace.

But my soul had none.

At Finchely, the rain stopped, Daniel snored, and all my hunger for truth returned.

"I need to be sure before I break his heart. How do I tell him he lost everything, that Phoebe's child is mine?" I handed her the letters again. "Read these. Tell me I'm wrong."

"Jemina, you've brought me Ashbrook's private correspondences from his late wife! I'm fearful to read such personal thoughts."

"We've done so for others, Patience. Every mission we do."

She frowned from her lips to her topaz eyes. "That is for the Widow's Grace. There was a culprit who'd wronged a widow. Who's the culprit here, Jemina? If you are right, Ashbrook lost everything, his wife and stepdaughter. If you are wrong, you've violated his trust."

"I know what I feel inside, and if I go to Ashbrook without proof, he won't . . ."

"He won't what, Jemina?"

With my napkin, I wiped my fingers, then pulled the other letters from my cape pocket. "I took these, too. Six notes from the St. Maurs' solicitor. Each question if I'm of diminished capacity. Ashbrook hasn't said a word of these. If I tell him I'm Hope's mother without proof, he won't trust me. He might think this man is right. He'll put me in Bedlam."

"The earl would never do that. He rescued us from there. Have you no faith?"

"Patience, you just said the two outcomes. When I tell him he has nothing of the woman he loved, he'll be devastated, or I'll lose the trust he has in me. I can't lose him."

My headache felt worse. Shaking, I wanted to be back in Daniel's bed, hiding in his embrace. "Ashbrook's one of the best men I know. He'd fight for truth if he were me."

"Jemina, stop. Breathe."

I'd twisted my sash about my wrist so tight I'd frayed the edge.

"If you tell me I'm wrong, I'll ride back now. I'll walk through the front door and beg his forgiveness."

Patience put her brow to mine, our foreheads merging. "You're not crazy. Show me how to help you, Jemina. You tell me what we do. You have to drive us to the answers you need."

"Read Phoebe Dunn's letters."

She hesitated, flicking the edges of the worn foolscap. Yellowed and aged foolscap, she held up each. The faded scent of honey surrounded me, then Patience looked up, her eyes locking to mine.

Those lips were a flat indelible line dividing what she'd hoped and the third scenario, that Phoebe Dunn had no child and Daniel knew.

"Say it. Say it so I know I'm not otherworldly, not a loon."

Patience nodded. "Never mentioning a child in more than two years' worth of letters to a fiancé is wrong. I don't think that a woman would leave Jamaica and travel across the world and announce her child to her new husband on the docks of Portsmouth."

"In her last one, she writes of bringing a surprise. Was it a baby or some innocuous lovers' token?"

"Phoebe sounds like someone you and I would befriend. There has to be something we're missing." The duchess stood and paced. "The man who freed us, who has helped so many of the Widow's Grace to regain custody, who deals with prosecuting all manner of crime, wouldn't lie about the woman he loved, but could he be tricked?"

I eased back into the pillows of the sofa. Soft and velvet and colorful, like one of Daniel's waistcoats, I felt the comfort, the give-and-take of the padding like lyrics of his poems. "At least I am not crazy, for you have leaped to my conclusion."

Patience sat beside me again. "Ashbrook couldn't have known Hope wasn't Phoebe's, could he?"

Her voice was barely audible, but I heard her. "That's the

question I need answered, but I hope, wish, pray that he did not know. That's why I left. I have to prove him innocent. Someone else is to blame."

"There's a possibility that he knew, Jemina."

Hated that notion, that he'd lied to everyone, including me. My head dropped against the pillows. I pulled one over my eyes. "I heard voices in Portsmouth. Men had decided my fate. I heard them in the hall saying I was a St. Maur. I had no child. They kept prodding and poking me, wanting me to accept that I was crazy and my baby didn't exist. My amnesia left me without defense. Who did this? Not Ashbrook. Who's my villain? Who am I to believe?"

Patience held me and rocked me, soothing me like Lionel. "You have to have faith, that belief in the unseen. You know Ashbrook loves you and Hope. He'd never hurt you or anyone."

"I need to prove him innocent, to acquit him in the court of my mind. My peace is important, because it's mine." Setting down the pillow, I stood. "I'm not going to sit around waiting for my life to come undone. I'm going back to the Lincoln's Inn. The answers are there."

"Lincoln's Inn. Scaling trees?"

"I'm dressed for it." I pushed the hem of Daniel's frilled shirt back into my borrowed pantaloons.

"It's too risky. Lady Shrewsbury says there is too much scrutiny on him because of your rushed marriage. She's fretful of how the Lord Mayor, his superior justice, treats him."

With a shrug, I stood and smoothed his shirt that smelled of cedar and lilies and my tears. "I'm going tonight, by myself."

"You have lost your mind if you think I'd let you do this without me. Someone has to be there to keep you from falling. Let me dress."

I paced in front of my fruit bowl art, thinking of my husband's mash. My faith was low, and I hungered for proof that kept Daniel as my hero, the man who rescued me and Hope.

CHAPTER 46

DANIEL—OUT THE WINDOW

Daniel rolled up the cuff of his Saxon blue robe. The warm bluish-gray cloth took away the chill of his empty bed.

The pillow, the lone pillow he'd entrusted to Jemina when they'd climbed out of his love nest, otherwise known as his closet, looked untouched.

She wasn't there, not on the left side she'd claimed nor the right.

Knocking on her door produced no answer.

Yet, he didn't know what to say.

Had he ruined things more?

He told her how he felt. Was that wrong? Was it foolish to tell a woman he loved her? Was it foolish to let her seduce him?

Noooo, that was his best idea.

This pique made no sense.

Max waggled into the room. His head raised, looking at Daniel, condemning him.

"Max, do your lady friends treat you well?"

The dog sniffed and licked Daniel's toes.

He stooped and fluffed his boy's coat. "Max, I did my husbandly duties well, better than well. There were no complaints. I know that I—"

"Pa-Papa, what'cha telling Max? Story time?"

He bit his lip as Hope crawled, then walked, then scooted closer.

With her doll in hand, she flopped beside him. Was that a sunny yellow pinafore on the tyke? Not pink?

"Tell us a story, Pa-Papa."

"How about you tell me one?" He stretched and sat next to her on the floor. "Did you give Mrs. Gallick any difficulties when she dressed you in yellow?"

"Mama said she liked yellow. She told my dolly, her friend, Mrs. Feebs said the same thing. Right, Mrs. Feebs?"

Hmm, Jemina did this? "You love calling your new mother Mama."

"She's my mama. I told you this."

Hope didn't look confused. She seemed quite certain.

"You haven't seen her in such a long time. You called my wife Friend at first. Does she look the same to you?"

"Don't know, Pa-Papa."

Max yelped as Hope pulled his curled tail.

"No, dear. No teasing Max. He's a boy. Teasing can be very frustrating."

Daniel sighed. "We take flowers to your old mama every year to Portsmouth when the lignum vitae blooms in the woods. She's gone, but I know she loved you."

"But her heart, Papa. It sounds the same. I know it's Mama. No one has that sound." She picked up her doll. "Tell Papa, Mrs. Feebs. Mrs. Feebee, you know my mama."

"Feebee? Mrs. Phoebe knew your mama?"

"Yes."

Daniel bit his lip hard. Everything stung inside like the beating he took at the Widow's Ball.

Phoebe.

Confirmation that Phoebe Dunn didn't deceive him. Phoebe wasn't Hope's mother. Hope wasn't the surprise from Jamaica.

His gut twisted and broke.

He'd made a grievous error. His conviction of Phoebe Dunn for deceit was wrong. His evidence was circumstantial and flawed.

One close of his eyes, he stood on the Portsmouth dock among the crowd waiting for confirmation of survivors. The brown baby was in his arms. No other brown onlookers stood in line. Like the matter-of-fact lieutenant, he'd assumed the little girl was Phoebe's.

He slapped his own skull, hard. He'd been judge and jury that day. Though he saved a child set to be abandoned, that would never make up for depriving this babe her true mama.

That true mama had to be Jemina. "Oh my Lord."

"Pa-Papa?"

He wrapped his arms about Hope. "Your father . . . I did something wrong."

"Fix it." Hope's eyes were wide with trust and belief. "Fix."

A glance at Jemina's closed door broke his heart more. Had she figured this all out and couldn't find a way to tell him? Or had she tried, but he wasn't listening?

"Pa-papa? Why you frowning?"

He sank fully to the floor. "I think . . . I know I hurt your mother's feelings."

Hope crawled onto his lap. "Not good. Fix."

She said it with her soft, sweet voice as if that was something easy to do, repair a disappointed heart. How did he admit to having a hand in Jemina's sorrows?

A chill sliced through him as he looked into Hope's eyes. He had no legal claim to her other than what he'd engineered. His marriage to Jemina had righted it.

Daniel hugged Hope so tightly. He was her papa no matter what. He kissed her brow. "I need to tell Jemina something very important. You and Max stay here. Look very cute, so she'll be more understanding."

She hugged the pug's neck and giggled as if Father Christmas had left her a small gift.

Yet, this was a gift, her true mother restored, and by a miracle they were all together.

Daniel stood and stalled, then stepped slowly to their adjoining door. He knocked and called for her.

No response.

"Jemina?"

A few more light taps yielded no answer.

"Darling, I know you're spent, but Hope and I have something to say."

Nothing.

Perhaps she bore embarrassment. It was unusual finding joy in a closet, but it seemed so right, so completely surprising, so them.

"Jemina?"

No sounds came from the room.

Not even sobbing.

Fear worked its way into his gut, twisting and squeezing as he beat upon the door, harder and harder.

"Jemina. Jemina, please. Let me see your face."

No more waiting. Daniel put his shoulder to the door and rammed it. Finchely was a strong old house. It flexed but didn't budge.

"Woman, I need to see you now. I'll break the door down if you don't answer me. Jemina?"

He took six steps back, then rammed the door, crashing onto her bed.

The mattress sat cold and empty.

The room was vacant.

No wife, no petulant, stubborn, wonderful, beautiful temptress anywhere. Her closet was too small for her to be sitting in there.

Max ran in and barked at the window.

Jemina's rope and the hook dangled from the sill, the hook that the Widow's Grace used to scale buildings.

Hope toddled inside and clung to the hem of his robe. "Mama's gone."

Daniel doubted she was under the bed. Yet, he bent and peeked. No dust, no Jemina. Then he tore the closet door off its hinges.

"No more mama! She went away again." Hope began to cry.

What was left of his heart shattered. "No, sweetheart, Mama hasn't left. She needed to do something."

"She's not going to go away again? She no go to the sea? No go."

"I'll bring her back. I promise."

Hope wrapped her arms about his leg. "Papa, don't you go to the sea too."

She said it clear with no stutter.

He lifted her high. "Mama went to play with her dearest friend, the Duchess of Repington. She'll be back. She will."

Max whimpered as if he knew differently.

Daniel had ruined things, but Jemina would be back for Hope. That he knew without doubt.

"Hold on to Mrs. Phoebe. You'll see, everything will be well."

The little girl didn't move. Like one of the Widow's Grace's tools, she stayed hooked to his leg.

This was horrible. For in his gut, he knew Jemina had finally chosen what she wanted more than anything—more than his love or the family he'd built. She wanted the truth, and only trusted the Widow's Grace to claim it.

CHAPTER 47

JEMINA—CLANDESTINE OPERATIONS

Tonight, the moon shone bright and full. I could see through the trees to the top of the Lincoln's Inn.

"Jemina," Patience said, "you sure you want to do this? You could go to Finchely and try once again to sort this out."

I looked up through the canopy of leaves at the bright stars. "I should've taken Ashbrook's keys. I was in such a rush."

"Let's go and talk with the earl. I'll be with you."

"Talk? To return without proof of anything will make him think I am crazed. He won't see that I'm doing this for me and for us. I don't need protecting. I need the full unvarnished truth."

With a grunt and a prayer, I tossed the rope and hooked it good. "After you, Patience."

She touched my face. "I'll support you."

The night sky was overcast, but I saw shadows in her eyes. She doubted the evidence was here.

I couldn't think that. I couldn't.

She gripped the rope and started climbing. Patience was in breeches. I still wore Daniel's pantaloons with my sash keeping them up. My trusty buckled slippers were ready.

Faster than anything, my friend opened the window. Soon, we stood inside.

She lit candles, as she did that night we first burglarized the Lincoln's Inn.

With more confidence than I had in long time, I went to Daniel's desk and rifled through his stack. I found nothing but more notes from the St. Maurs' solicitor in Tonbridge.

Patience made her way to the sofa and curled onto it. "Wake me when you find what it is you're looking for."

"The complete list of the passengers. That should say who was accompanied by minor children."

"Have at it." Her voice sounded tired.

I felt horrible dragging her from Sandlin Court, but I started again through the pile. This time slower and read a few of the letters from Mr. Mosey. "The St. Maurs are after assets I possess. What could that be? Not my widow's dower."

Patience pulled her arms under head. "Assets have nothing to do with the *Minerva*. Stay focused."

Could people like the St. Maurs think of Hope as an asset?

Would they be so callous as to term my child that? My soul wrenched and twisted about my middle, wringing like a rag on a washboard. Daniel said they were slaveholders. Of course they'd call my beautiful Hope, with her dark skin and eyes, chattel.

Jerking at a drawer, I found it wouldn't open. "Ashbrook locked his desk this time. None will budge. How are we to get it open?"

Patience yawned, "If I were the duke, I'd shoot the lock."

"That's not helping." I looked at Daniel's desk and smoothed my fingers along the face of the drawers. Then I fingered the dustless underside of his desk and struck a piece of brass. Daniel was a creature of habit. I freed the key.

Patience turned over on the sofa. "Smells like coffee was spilled here. That's a nauseating scent."

My friend wasn't herself. "You keep resting."

Jabbing the key in the lock, I twisted and opened the drawer. I could rifle through Daniel's things—his papers, his letter, more half-written drafts to Phoebe Dunn, to me.

Pushing them away as if my touch would make them ash, I dug deeper until I found my marriage contract to Cecil. Scouring each word, I searched for a provision for children, something to confirm that I had a child, evidence of Hope.

Nothing.

I slammed my hand on the desk. Pain shot to my wrist.

"Jemina?"

My face was wet and hot. "The answer should be here. It's not."

"You're crying, Jemina. Crying and burglary don't mix."

"Tonight they do. Why can't I find proof, something that mentions my daughter?"

"Jemina, you have to calm."

"The contract. There's no mention of minor children, no mention of any provision, just my dower, a dower of four thousand pounds. Four thousand pounds is not twenty thousand pounds."

"No, that is correct."

Pushing the paper closer to the candle, I hunted for an explanation. "Why would Ashbrook give me a draft for twenty thousand pounds when it says my dower should be four thousand?"

"I saw the draft, Jemina. You definitely are in possession of twenty thousand pounds."

"It's not St. Maur money, it's Ashbrook's." Everything broke inside. I started to gasp and swatted my stinging eyes. "Another secret between us."

"A generous secret, Jemina. Generous. He's been protecting you from the beginning."

Collecting the pieces of my spirit, my broken belief that my heart and my circumstances hadn't been manipulated, I picked up the contract.

Then I saw it.

Saw it plain and in the open. One of the witnesses to the marriage agreement was M. Willingham. I jumped up and shoved the paper at Patience. "Is it too much of a coincidence that my

Mr. Willingham, my aggressive suitor, witnessed this document? He knew me before as Cecil's wife. He'd know about Hope."

Patience folded her arms over her stomach. "I never liked him, even if he's tall."

"He knew who I was and courted me."

"If this Willingham is your Willingham, I wonder why he would act as if he were newly meeting you?"

"A man. Lying. I think I see a pattern."

My friend frowned. Lionel would be in for it when he grew old enough for mischief and made Patience cross. "Keep looking, Jemina. This will probably be the last time we'll be able to rifle through Lord Ashbrook's things. Look through everything."

"Mr. Willingham is in shipping. The St. Maurs are in shipping. That has to be the connection between the two, maybe along their lines of business."

"Willingham attacked Ashbrook. Jemina, he wanted the earl out of the way. He may be working with the St. Maurs to undermine your position."

Daniel might have reasons to protect me, very good reasons. Stars shined through the window. I thought of his jet eyes. I wondered if he'd awakened. Did he know I'd left? Did he question, like me, if there was enough love between us to protect us from yesterday, every wrong turn or secret that led us to one another?

Looking at the four-thousand-pounds notation on my marriage contract, I wasn't sure.

CHAPTER 48

DANIEL—CHASING AFTER WIFEY

Hope was asleep in his arms by the time Daniel's carriage arrived at Sandlin Court. He snuggled her in one hand and reached for the knocker.

Men in military uniform were at the door, not footmen.

Daniel had a bad feeling.

He tossed his hat on the sideboard and headed straight to the duke's study.

The man was at his desk. Lord Gantry stood at his side; both wore thick grimaces.

"It's about time you showed up." The duke rolled his chair in front of Daniel. "Gantry."

The viscount came to him with his arms stretched out. "Who do we have here? Your daughter, she reminds me of my youngest, when she was small."

Daniel hadn't seen the man smile, but Gantry had a wide grin looking at Hope.

"Take possession of the child, Lieutenant."

Daniel pulled back.

"Come on, old man," Gantry said. "I won't hurt this precious girl."

"Fine." He handed sleeping Hope to Gantry. The fellow cradled her like an expert. The toddler didn't awaken at all.

"Gantry," the duke said, "is the baby secure?"

"Yes, she is. She's beautiful, nothing like you, Barrister."

"Ashbrook!" The duke's shout made Daniel turn back, and he ran into the duke's fist.

The blow knocked him to the ground and bruised his recovering eye, the same spot Willingham and his goons had bested him.

The duke sat back down, then rolled closer. The commander had a maniacal grin. "If my back went out punching you into the ground, it would be worth it. Been meaning to do that for a long time, for the way you enable Patience and the rest of her widows' group."

Daniel sat up, holding his face. "I'm not sure I deserved that, but I'll take it. My wife ran to you, confused, hurting. That has to be my fault. Repington, let me speak with her."

"Can't do that, Ashbrook."

"Duke, you hit me once." Then he looked at the man's balled fist. "I probably deserve a second, but that will wake my daughter. She'll scream like a banshee and wake up your son."

The duke leaned over and offered Daniel his hand, helping him rise. "You can't speak to Jemina because she's not here. She and my wife are missing."

"Is that why you have the Second Battalion at the door and crawling around Sandlin Court? A search party?"

"Yes, they are charged with bringing my duchess home. The stubborn woman needs to rest and avoid any of this Widow's Grace business. It's not good for the baby."

"Baby?" Gantry and Daniel said the word at the same time.

Daniel paced. "I'm happy for you, Duke, but are you sure? My wife hasn't mentioned anything."

"Mine is keeping it close to the vest. But her lady's maid informed me that something is late, seven weeks late today."

Gantry, with his chestnut hair falling out of the poorly done ribbon at the back, looked as if he wanted to knock some manner of sense in the duke. "You had a maid spy on your wife to report such things?"

"Yes. What? That's not normal, to ensure the health of my top recruit?"

Daniel offered a frown to the viscount, who shook his head even as he rocked Hope. "That's your friend, sir. Not that I'm in position to dictate proper care and handling of a wife."

"Ashbrook," the duke said, "I don't need the duchess climbing trees or going to gaming hells or whatever your crazy aunt has her doing when she thinks she's sneaking out without my notice."

A soldier came and stood at the door. "They're burglarizing the Lincoln's Inn again, sir."

"My office again?"

"Yes, Ashbrook. That means they climbed those trees again. Do me a favor, leave a key out so if they have to return, you can at least make it easy."

Face aching, feeling stupid, knowing Jemina was given to falling, Daniel sighed like his lungs deflated. "Why are they breaking into my office? Lady Shrewsbury wouldn't send them back again, not so soon."

"That means their running their own operation. They're rogues." The duke rolled back and then went to his desk. "You know what they are looking for. I suggest you go there and make sure they get it. Then bring our wives home safe. Gantry, you go too."

"But Hope?"

Gantry handed her into the duke's arms.

He waved for them to leave while he hummed Jemina's lullaby. "'There was once a little boat. *Ohé! Ohé! Matelot. Ohé! Ohé! Matelot.*'"

Daniel's nerves eased. The man would do well with a daughter as he did with Lionel. "Send for Mrs. Gallick if you can't handle things. Hope has nightmares."

"Go, I have the maid spies upstairs. Does this one wet too?"

"Only if she's scared. I suggest you smile a lot and sing."

"I can help." Lady Bodonel stood at the door with her jewels and a large feathery bonnet. She was either heading to or returning from a party. "I can help with a girl, Busick, darling. Son, I didn't know you and Patience—"

"Yes, our family is growing unless the earl's foolishness has caused my wife harm."

Gantry nudged Daniel toward the door. "Come on, Ashbrook. You're part of the henpecked club now."

"Cock-a-doodle-do, gentlemen." Lady Bodonel flapped her arms and crowed softly as she looked over the duke's shoulder.

Gantry ran a hand over his scalp, undoing his hair. "You two fools have wives, not minions or sycophants, but able helpmates. Keep them, make things right before they abandon you."

He bent and scooped up his fallen ribbon. His regret mirrored the deep frown lines in his gaunt face. The man suffered greatly. "Let's go, Ashbrook."

Daniel hoped he hadn't made one too many mistakes with his helpmate, his Jemina.

CHAPTER 49

JEMINA—ANY TRUTH WILL DO

Nothing. Nothing was in Daniel's bottom drawer. I rubbed my hands. "I don't see the passenger list. Where would he put it?"

Patience didn't move on the sofa.

"Are you sleep, Your Grace?"

"No, but I want to be. Are we done?"

"Not yet." I slammed the drawer shut. "We don't have answers."

"Jemina, what if there are no answers? What if the truth is down at the bottom of the sea?"

Shaking my head so fast it would surely spin off and bounce on each of the barristers' desks. "No, Patience. I can't accept that. The truth has to be here."

"What if despite our best efforts we find no proof that Hope is yours?" Patience winced, her voice cracked. "Can you live with just loving that child, who is yours again by right of marriage?"

I dropped papers and flew to her side. "Are you in pain?"

"Burning in my chest. I must've eaten something horrid." She wiped at her face. "I am in pain for you. I wish you had answers. I wish I had them about my sisters."

"Patience, I'm sorry." I knelt by her side. "I shouldn't have made you come."

"You're my sister. I have to be here."

I held her hand. "I'm done. I'll take you home."

"Jemina, I have to be fine not knowing what happened to Helena and Charity. I have to have faith that somehow they found joy." She kissed our linked hands. "I will always honor them and keep their memory."

Noises came from the hall. The movement was fast. There was no time to blow out the candles.

The door opened, and Lord Gantry pounded inside. "There you two are."

I was relieved it was only him until I heard tapping on the window.

My breath came fast seeing Daniel gaping at me, slipping on my rope.

I rushed to the window and pulled him inside. "What are you doing? The branch might break under your weight."

"I realized that a little late, halfway up."

He put an arm about my waist, but I pulled free.

Gantry held out his hand to Patience. "Come along, Your Grace, the duke has quartered soldiers in Sandlin Court. Lady Bodonel and Hope Thackery are his captives."

"Is she sleeping? Has my daughter had another nightmare?"

"Yes to both questions, Lady Ashbrook," Daniel said, "but I calmed her. I promised to bring her mother back as soon as possible. Let's not make me a liar."

"No, just a keeper of secrets."

"Give him a chance," Patience said. "And, Barrister, be as good as you can winning the jury of my friend's heart. Your side is sadly behind."

"Patience, keep my room ready. I have a feeling I'll need it tonight. Sandlin Court is perfect, my daughter's already there."

Patience offered me a shrug. "Come along, Gantry. We have a war to stop. The duke must've enacted his plan B."

"He knows of your delicate condition, Your Grace. He's worked up a number of scenarios to try to keep you safe but not clip your wings."

"Busick . . . He knows? That's why he's been working so hard, fretting? Because of me. He knows?"

"Yes, he does," Daniel said. "He's thrilled as any man would be to share a child with their beloved."

Daniel walked to the door and held it open. "Godspeed, Your Grace."

Patience kissed his cheek. "Godspeed to you. You too, Jemina."

I wanted to go to her, to congratulate her. To ask why she went with me to climb trees, but Daniel intercepted me, and the door thudded as soon as Gantry and Patience passed into the hall.

He leaned against it and stared.

Chubble. Defensive words readied on my tongue until I saw his eye.

Bruised and slightly puffy. I wanted to touch it, but being distracted would mean I'd lose my argument to the best barrister I knew.

Jerking my hand down, I retreated. "I'm not done looking through your drawers."

"By all means reach in them. And you're very cute in my pantaloons and favorite shirt."

Back at his desk, I went into one I'd already searched, hoping he'd make an expression to let me know I was nearing the truth, but his beautiful lips stayed pressed in a line.

He sat on the edge of the desk close to his blotter and my riffled stack. "Mind telling me what you're looking for. I might be able to help."

"If I said, Daniel, you wouldn't believe me."

He scooted closer, his breath heated my neck. "Try me. I'll listen very carefully to your testimony."

"My testimony?" I folded my arms and tapped my buckled slippers. "You're going to give weight to what I say? You haven't had a chance to soften it for my delicate ears."

"Your ears are delightful, particularly this spot right here."

With his thumb, he stroked behind the lobe, the delicate skin. "Talk to me."

It was hard to string cohesive thoughts with him touching me. I moved out of reach. "The passenger list. Find it."

"You sound out of breath." His half smile showed.

If it became full, I'd be lost.

"Tell me your secret, Jemina. I'm listening."

"The passenger list. Please."

He nodded and went to his bookshelf and pulled the paper from one of his leather spines. He put it in my hands and held them for a moment, smoothing my wrists.

The page was old and tattered, but the ink remained good and legible. Stepping closer to my candle, I scanned the names and found nothing new. "What happened to your eye?"

"The duke."

"Oh. For a smooth talker, you get hit a lot."

"Only since meeting you."

"Why did he punch you?"

"For hurting you." His palms curled tightly about the desk's edge. "Sorry for what I've done or not done. Said or not said. Tell me, my Lady Ashbrook, how to fix us?"

"You're talking to me? Could be any one of your Lady Ashbrooks. We are interchangeable mothers to Hope. As interchangeable as middle names?"

"No. Technically there's only one Lady Ashbrook. My elevation is a few months old. My first marriage . . . Sorry."

"Technically, we don't know if I am Jemina St. Maur, do we? It's just a name on this passenger list, unless we accept men talking in shadows, the ones who committed me as character witnesses."

"You are Jemina St. Maur. The St. Maur family attested to who you were. Why they never asked about your daughter, I don't know, but they should have. It would have spared you such pain."

He looked up to the ceiling, then down at me. "I know you are Jemina St. Maur. I believe you were on the *Minerva*, one of its two survivors, and I think you are Hope's mother."

My mouth fell open, and I shoved it back onto its hinges. "Have you known from the beginning? I came here believing that you were in the dark, too. That you were the man who saved Hope and then me."

"I am—"

"No. You can't be our hero if you couldn't tell me the truth of my dower. You're one of Prinny's favorites, the smartest. Of course, you knew."

"I did not know, Jemina, not until today."

"Did you do this, claiming my daughter as Phoebe Dunn's? Did you help them lock me away like a raving loon?"

Sighing like he'd sprung a leak, he rubbed at his bruised eye socket. "I must confess. I've always wanted a daughter, someone else's toddler for my own. For my own personal plight for abolition, I sought to kidnap and liberate a slaver's mixed-race child and found the opportunity with the *Minerva*. Mastermind that I am, I kept Hope from being sent back to an uncertain future in Jamaica."

"That's not true? You jest? You're being ridiculous, Daniel."

"Am I?" He tapped his chest. "I'm supposed to be in the wrong, remember? And I surely must be wrong to tend to a precious child, one who I believed until this day was my wife's. To honor Phoebe Dunn, I decided to nurture Hope and garnered her the best physicians to see to her speech impediments and the limbs battered by the waters that sunk the *Minerva*. I'm evil." He slapped his arm. "Evil doings must surely be in my blood."

Moving close, I crumpled the list and tossed it at him. "Don't you ever do that. Don't you ever think I put you in the wrong because of your race. It's the secrets you've kept, that's what ruined us."

He bit his lip and stared at me or maybe through me. "I meant Thackery evil blood, not Blackamoor."

My hand flew to my mouth. "I didn't mean to touch that line, the one between us that you've mastered balancing on the *ton*'s tiny thread. But that very line let you and the rest of the world deny that Hope was my daughter. It cost me two years of my life."

With everything bared between us, Daniel folded his arms and looked at the floor, and I never felt more alone.

CHAPTER 50

JEMINA—NOT WITHOUT MY DAUGHTER

At odds in his Lincoln's Inn office, Daniel closed his eyes, perhaps to shut me out to retain his practiced calm.

The silence was damning and hurtful.

"Tell me I'm wrong. Explain things to me." My voice wasn't loud. It was barely a whisper.

His gaze caught and stroked mine. "You're right, Jemina. I'd do anything to give you those two years back. Two years that Hope missed her mama. Nothing can make it up to you or her."

This was true.

Sad and true. I swallowed the growing lump in my throat. It was bitter, everything I'd lost. "You've had my daughter longer than I. I should be glad of that, but there needs to be a villain. Who is it if it's not you or me? There has to be one."

"There's none, none here. No man controlled the hurricane that battered the *Minerva*. It's late, Jemina. I promised Hope that I'd bring you home. Let's go get her."

"How can we just go on, Daniel? You don't trust me, and I don't trust you. I have twenty thousand reasons to be wary."

His gaze lifted; his rare smile bloomed. "Jemina, I do trust you. I know you'll sacrifice for me. You've proven it. In my bones, I know that there's nothing that you wouldn't do for Hope."

That look, confident and strong but with his heart in his eyes—it drew me. I could feel my knees weakening. I should fall in his arms and forget that he knew secrets, forget that he was happy to let me stay in the dark.

Never.

"Take me to Sandlin Court, Daniel. Leave Hope with me."

"Hope Thackery is my daughter. You're my wife. You both belong at Finchely."

His words were measured, careful and deliberate. The barrister was now the judge, and his pronouncement on our residency read like a ruling of the Court of Chancery.

"You're going to make me and my daughter go with you? You're going to use your rights and the law to coerce me?"

He gulped a long raspy breath. "Please don't make me choose between keeping my family together or watching it disintegrate."

"A family that shouldn't be yours."

His face tensed, every muscle tightening to breaking.

I knew Daniel, how important words were to him, and I knew how to twist them to make him feel my rage. "The Earl of Ashbrook will use the power given to him by the king and the Church and his father, all those men, to command his wife?"

"Technically, it was my uncle. He's the man from whom I received my title." Daniel clasped his buttons, raking them back and forth. "Jemina, let me tell you our secret. You, me, and Hope, we're a miracle. That's our secret. That's why we've come to love each other."

"Love? Do you think my screaming for my daughter made me seem more of a lunatic? Was it pushing everything out of my head to forget them ripping her from my arms, did that make me a loon, perfect for Bedlam?"

"I'm so sorry." Daniel took me in his embrace.

I wavered and rested in strong arms that should be fighting for my truth.

"I screamed for her the moment I awoke. I didn't know my own name, but I knew her. They said she didn't exist. They wanted me to lie, and I refused."

Linking my finger to his, I lifted them. The moonlight and the candles glowed upon our union, light and dark, calloused and smooth, lively and learned. "My daughter and I were apart because no one believed I could be her mother. My face did that."

His embrace tightened about me. "If I'd known, I would've found you, would've fixed it."

My heart believed him. Daniel was my mast, strong and tall and unmoving. I wrapped my arms about him, kept my head up, above the water, above a sea of sobs pouring from my lungs.

Strong, silent Daniel kept me upright and secure until everything stopped pounding, until my pulse slowed its popping in my ears.

My throat constricted, but I had to ask the worst secret. "You only rescued me from Bedlam because you thought I was Phoebe. You wished that it was her who lived."

He stiffened, released me, and moved to the window. Time stood still until he turned back, nodding. "I arrived at Bethlehem Hospital, Bedlam, in January on a mission for the Widow's Grace and saw the name Jemina St. Maur on the list of inmates. I'd memorized that name from the list you crumpled. Then I saw the duchess, her bronzed skin, and assumed a mistake had been made."

"Patience? Of course. My dearest friend rescued me again. She gave me purpose. She listened to me. No one had, not in Bedlam or that other place with echoes."

He wiped at his neck, then completed the motion across his mouth, his trim beard. "I returned to this office and crafted paperwork, like I'd done so many times, and went to Bedlam hoping for another miracle. But the future duchess wasn't Phoebe. She was gone again."

"Oh, Daniel."

He bit his lip. "*Cheated* isn't the word for what I felt. Losing my dream again was miserable. Then I talked with you. It took a minute to realize you were of sound mind. Someone had wrongly committed you. It became my duty to get you both to the Widow's Grace. Knowing what you must have suffered, I determined to do what I could for you, to give you your life back; I just didn't know you'd destroy mine."

"Daniel—"

"You wanted my secrets. Let me finish telling you about the one time in my life I made the decision to break the rules for me. That day on the docks with that little miracle in my arms, I became judge and jury. I awarded myself custody of a babe set to be abandoned. I invented birth registries from a parish in Kingston; I formalized Phoebe's will to legitimize my custody of her daughter. Then I made sure to be convincing, that I knew of the child and was expecting her. This baby had survived a sinking. She wouldn't be ripped away from me. Do you know how many times little girls, known as exotic, are sold to the brothels? Very few victims get their day in court."

Daniel took his handkerchief and wiped at my eyes. "I waited—weeks, months—no claims or inquiries. The Dunns never even wrote back when I informed them about Phoebe."

He took up the passenger list. "No one on this list is of mixed race or Blackamoor but Phoebe Dunn. No children are listed at all. If Hope wasn't Phoebe's, at best, I liberated an enslaved child. At worse, the love of my life forgot to mention she had a daughter and decided never to speak of that angel. I tortured myself rereading her letters to determine if Phoebe thought so little of me to never say a word. Or to find the line I'd written that made her fearful her proxy groom wouldn't accept her if she brought a babe from Jamaica. I would've accepted her child. She was part of Phoebe. How could I not?"

He splayed his fingers down the buttons of his dark waistcoat. "I owe Phoebe Dunn the deepest apology. For two years, I've acted like the most tragic widower so no one would question why a bachelor who'd never met his proxy wife decided to raise her little girl. Then I thanked her for Hope. That child is my heart."

"Is Phoebe's sketch true or part of the act?"

"It's true. Phoebe sent it early on. A friend of hers drew it."

"Is that everything, Daniel? No more secrets."

He sat on the desk. "Since I've said I love you a half dozen times today, even when you ruthlessly seduced me to hide the fact that you took back your hook and rope and stole a pair of my pantaloons, I'm not sure how to conclude this trial."

"You did give me your troth and worldly possessions. I thought you wouldn't mind."

"I didn't. Didn't mind the seduction part until you left. My tailor definitely needs to make you some items. Your shapeliness is quite appealing."

"Daniel, must you joke?"

"It's all I have. You'd rather break into buildings than stay."

"I'm moved, Daniel, by your testimony. But you're trained as a barrister to say pretty words, none of which explains why you now believe that Hope is mine. I have no evidence, just a few faulty memories but this is truth to you."

"You want me to believe that Hope is your daughter? Done. I believe."

"You believe just like that?"

Nodding, he folded his arms. "Yes, when you add Hope's statement. She remembered your heartbeat."

I placed my hand upon my bosom; his palm covered it. The ragged rhythm inside raged.

"It's a very distinctive heartbeat. There's an extra beat when you're happy or excited or scared. I've heard how hard your chest pounds. Hope remembered it and named her dolly, Mrs. Phoebes, after her mother's friend, Phoebe Dunn."

"Phoebe Dunn was my friend. I couldn't have been Lady

Bodonel or worse. Now we don't have to fear learning about who I was."

"There is still *chubble*. Hope could be a baby you decided to raise. She could be birthed from an enslaved woman owned by the St. Maurs. Then she might be the asset the St. Maurs want. I paid your widow's dower out of the proceeds of selling off my uncle's holdings. I wanted to ensure you had a new start independent of that family."

"Ah, another secret. You truly were too generous."

"I was. It's enough for you to live independent of me too."

He looked deflated and hurt in a way I hadn't seen. None of the sneers or what almost happened at the ball, or the harassment of the Lord Mayor, had done this. He was prepared to let us go if I wanted that.

"Jemina, I don't know when my feelings for you changed. Oh, how it bothered me to see you garnering so much attention. Then our kiss in the parlor at Sandlin Court was everything."

It was grand. Every one of his were.

"The answers are so close. Let's get them together. Daniel, we don't have to fear learning more about me. The old me—"

"Married into a powerful family." Daniel's head tilted to the side. "I can't let the Dunns lay claim to Hope. I definitely won't allow the St. Maurs to put you at risk. Let's stop now. No more risk to you or our daughter."

"Again, you want me to stop looking. You want me to be content with crumbs from my life."

"I want you content with *our* life." He wrenched at his neck, spread his feet, and lifted his lamp at me like they did to witnesses at the Old Bailey. "What's the baby's true name?"

"I don't know."

"When is her birthday, Lady Ashbrook?"

"I don't remember."

"How many hours was your confinement? Were the labor pains dreadful?"

"Don't know. How many times must I say that?"

Thud, he set down the lamp. "That will be the judge at the Court of Chancery giving possession of Hope to slavers. We lack answers that can't be found. Who will believe us?"

"Don't you think I hate this?" I hit my hands at my temples. "The facts should be up there, along with those voices in my nightmares, echoing and loud in that hall as I lay on that cot in misery. They might have something, know something to make the memories return. My daughter's name should be restored in my head."

"Her name is Hope, Jemina, but I'm not going to stop you from doing anything. Come home with me to Finchely. Let's give Hope a home for now with a mama and papa conversing about the day over dinner. We can light candelabras, serve food on Wedgwood."

"Like you do for cards?"

"The fellows won't mind those games in my study to offer this vision of home and hearth. Hope loves her pink room, her paints. Let's give her a family." He moved from me to the desk and tugged open his drawer. "You've been in here too."

He retrieved correspondences and made a perfectly squared stack. "These are drafts of my letters to the Dunns, my marriage contract and yours, and a few of Phoebe's letters. There are more of Phoebe's letters at Finchely."

"Actually, they are here." I drew them out of my pocket.

His face dimmed. He twiddled his fingers as he drew his palms together. "You have all I've collected. Let's go get Hope from Sandlin Court and end this evening."

"That's it? No more fighting?"

"No more from me, Jemina. You have to decide what happens next. I want you at my side. I want you safe at home. I can't make you be my wife or force you to stay at Finchely. Hope is terrified that you will return to the sea."

"My daughter doesn't have to fret for me. I'm not going to be without her."

"Please, both of you should stay at Finchely for now. I'll soothe her until you come back from your quest for truth."

He wrapped up my rope. "You widows are good with this tool."

I grabbed his arm. "Daniel, I don't understand."

"Legally, with the paperwork I've done, I'm Hope's guardian, her father. That may be the only thing to keep her from the St. Maurs' clutches. I'll not publicly attest to anything differently, but you can dig and put all the pieces back together. I want that for you. I'll keep her safe in your stead."

"If I don't comply, you've washed your hands of me? Your love is conditional."

With a sigh, he fell to his knees, wrapped his arms about my waist. "I love you. Your bravery amazes me. But what I'm offering isn't enough."

With my arms at my side not clinging to him, his breath steaming my middle, I was adrift, drowning in this man, his hands slipping the hem of my borrowed shirt, smoothing my back, my hips, but my head was shaking no before I could stop, before I compromised my soul for a thirst to belong to him, and his vision of family.

"Jemina." His lips closed tight. He stood and buttoned my shirt placard, which had come undone. "I wish I had put the clues together sooner. I wish I had trusted *us* sooner. My fault. My biggest regret."

Why was he taking the blame? He wasn't one of those shadowy men who determined my fate. He couldn't be in that hall, in that hospital and on the docks collecting Hope.

The distant, broken look in his eyes said it all. Daniel had told me his facts and rested his argument. He made me the judge of our fate.

And I was stuck wanting both, what I had in front of me and the past that I hadn't found a way to leave behind.

He walked to the door. "Let's go get Hope."

Nodding to his blanked face, I followed him out of the Lincoln's Inn. The gap between us widened as he let me lead. He understood, probably better than me, that I couldn't choose between him and learning the truth.

CHAPTER 51

DANIEL—THE MARRIED ROUTINE

Sitting in his study, looking out the window, Daniel watched the sunset and studied the cards dealt to him. He'd moved his vingt-et-un game from the dining room. It provided a much better view of an errant wife's coming and going.

One court card, a queen of diamonds, and a deuce of hearts. That was a long way from winning.

"Playing cards in here is different," Mr. Anthon signaled for a card. "Smaller. I guess that means cozy."

Mr. Gerard dealt him one. "The wife must've wanted the room used for its intended purposes. Nothing wrong with that."

"No. My choice. It's better to see the lane, gentlemen. I don't want to be surprised when Lady Ashbrook arrives."

Richmond laughed. "See, you're settling into married life so well. Soon you'll be a seasoned professional and learn how to tidy things before the wifey fusses."

Daniel feigned a chuckle and glance toward the road. He was already neat and had been that way since he came to live with Lady Shrewsbury. The hardest thing he ever agreed to was letting Jemina come and go from Finchely as she pleased. He had to act indifferent, not that the not-knowing was killing him.

As a husband, a man desperate for his wife's safety, he'd been reduced to a henpecked, a nervous Nellie, who wanted to go box with his pugilist friend and let him beat some sense into Daniel. Well, as Jemina had said, he'd been hit too much.

At least Daniel would feel something other than misery and fear. Mr. Mosey's letters on behalf of the St. Maurs had ratcheted up along with his threats to Jemina's mental state. As he feared, that family would be a problem for his family.

Mr. Gerard tossed in his cards. Daniel's appreciation for the butler had grown, and he liked having access to the duke's spying network. They sent reports that Jemina still took on Widow's Grace missions, but her partner, the Duchess of Repington was now resigned to Sandlin Court and foot rubs.

Patient, patient, patient. Daniel's chant to remind him that this was what Jemina wanted. If to be beset with worry was what it took for her to forgive his secrets, then he'd endure. When they reunited, it would be for keeps.

He could wait.

Hopefully not more than another week. A few more days. Two hours?

Right before the sun sank into his woods, Jemina's carriage arrived. She dashed inside, stopped at his door.

Daniel's breath caught. The indigo pelisse that wrapped her body had a double line of brass buttons. The point of her bonnet's brim shadowed curls falling toward the blush on her cheeks. The bluish-purple gown underneath reminded him of the ironwood flowers, lignum vitae. Like the meaning of the flowers, Jemina was life and joy, but she cruelly stood out of arm's reach.

To keep the peace, he let her.

"Daniel . . . Lord Ashbrook, I see you are busy. Never mind. Good evening, gentlemen." She dipped her chin and backed away.

The tapping of her shoes, those buckles up the stairs echoed, echoed all the way to his empty heart.

"Was that your wife, Ashbrook?" Richmond asked, finishing his plate of cheese and ham.

Daniel picked a card, a three of spades. "Looked like her."

"You going to stop and go greet her properly? It hasn't been more than a month since the wedding."

"Things are well at hand, gentlemen."

Richmond stood and waved to the fellows. "Let's help Prinny's brain. Go take care of business. When Mama's not happy, it makes things difficult."

Daniel stared at Richmond, wondering about Papa's happiness, but the gentlemen were already heading to the footman for their coats.

Max whined and trotted around the empty chairs.

The dog was right. His friends were right. It was time to see if *Mama* was ready to be happy with him.

"Should I clean up, sir?" Mr. Anthon returned and leaned on a chair that needed to be taken back to the dining room.

"Yes, down here. I think it's time for me to clean things up once and for all."

His patience was spent. A man dying for the love of his wife could only be so calm. He had to appeal this unemotional, passionless sentence.

Daniel was ready to risk Finchely's fragile peace.

Maybe he was a little like his uncle after all, ready to gamble for a big win, the restoration of his marriage.

Through the half-open door, Daniel watched Hope and Jemina.

His daughter was at her table, painting something in her signature pink. Jemina held the top of the paintbrush ensconced in their daughter's little fingers.

"There you go, baby. That's the perfect way to paint pink flowers. Same technique for fruit."

"Mama, help me draw Pa-Papa's big head here. And work on his smile. I want to show him so he'll remember more."

"Sure, baby." Jemina's voice sounded heavier and wet.

Coughing, he stepped into to the nursery and looked at the picture. The brightest pink hue and red slathered the page.

"Amazing, princess." He kissed the top of her curly head, atop her ginger-brown braided chignon. "Just beautiful."

He caught Jemina's gaze as Mrs. Gallick entered.

"Someone needs to be cleaned up," the housekeeper said.

Jemina took off her pelisse. "I'll help. I haven't had enough time today." She scooped up Hope and held her to her beautiful gown, right at the bosom, getting pink paint on her buttons.

"Sorry, Mama."

"Never. I think it makes everything perfect." Jemina hugged her again.

Daniel reached for Hope's paint-stained fingers and traced a pink smile to his lips. "Seems you ladies have all in hand."

"Pa-Papa funny."

"At week's end, I'd like to take you both to Portsmouth. The lignum vitae are blooming. Let's take some to the sea."

"No sea, Pa-Papa. None."

"Hope, we will all be safe going and coming. I think we need to go together, and then we'll all return to Finchely."

Jemina nodded. "Yes. I want to go with you, Daniel, as a *family*."

His cautious heart raced at her use of the word that was supposed to solve all ills. He didn't react to it, didn't show the naked need that bubbled under his skin. Daniel hadn't proved to his wife that he trusted her mind as much as her heart. "Very good."

"I'll pack you all a picnic basket," Mrs. Gallick said, "with plenty of your shortbread, sir."

Mmmmm. Currant and carraway shortbread. His favorite thing. Readying to dip his hand in the basket, he stopped and glanced at Jemina, loving the joy in her face.

Then his appetite waned.

The trip would be terrible. Her smile wouldn't last. It was set to disappear once he took her back to the beginning. Yet, there was no other way for them to start over.

"Ladies, I'll let you get to things, then dinner in the proper room."

"Daniel, you didn't have to make changes at Finchely for me. Your gentlemen friends looked very crowded in your study."

With a smile, he nodded and wiped off the paint in his beard. "Dinner in a few."

"Yes," she said, and turned to the housekeeper. "Let's get clean, Hope."

They squealed and started splashing water in the basin Mrs. Gallick brought.

Daniel left. He had a great deal of work to do accessing his resources to craft a mission of his own. He needed to discover the missing pieces of Jemina's journey from Jamaica. When the HMS *Belvidera* pulled into port, how had she ended up hours away in Bedlam?

Helping Jemina regain a piece of her truth had to be enough for them to start again.

It had to be.

CHAPTER 52

JEMINA—THE FAMILY TRIP

Leaving Finchely filled me with nervous energy. We hadn't been in a carriage all together since my burglary at the Lincoln's Inn. "Mrs. Gallick packed a big basket brimming with bread and cheese, roasted goose, a jam or two, and shortbreads."

"She always makes a good luncheon." Daniel smiled a little, then took papers from his leather case. The stationery looked like correspondence. The urge to look over his folded hands, past his bluish-black tailcoat and shiny buttons, to peek at his letters pressed.

The carriage rolled on. Hope bounced on the seat with Mrs. Feebs naming things that she saw in the window.

Our handsome chaperone remained quiet and contemplative.

I thought when he suggested Portsmouth that we'd clear the air and maybe I could ask his opinion on normal things like dinner menus. He loved supping with us at Finchely. I missed him and hated those awkward pauses when we both wanted to spend time with Hope. He loved her so.

This journey was for Hope. She knew he wasn't happy. The pleasantries, his holding the basket, helping me onto my seat were to show our daughter the family was well and getting along.

Her nightmares had diminished. She slept through the night

more and more, especially after we started joining Daniel for dinner.

Bored of looking out the window, Hope danced onto my lap shaking Mrs. Feebs at me. "Show her how to ride with a dress.

"Sweetie, you didn't bring your wooden horse."

"But Pa-papa did. He always does. Where you hide it, Pa-papa?"

"Hide something? Me?" He put his hand to his waistcoat of dark, dark emerald. "Do I look like I could keep something from you?"

"He's silly. He always does that when we go visit other mama. Where's the horse?" Hope pointed to his top hat. "There."

He put an index finger to his lips. "This hat? Are you sure?"

"Yes. Yes."

He waved his hand and lifted his hat like he was a showman. "Try again, princess."

Hope tapped her nose and wiggled in her pretty pink coat with lace at the collar. I'd braided her shoulder-length hair and pinned a proper chignon. A crown for our little princess.

"Umm. Your papers, Pa-papa."

"No." He fanned them. No toy, just letters that looked like they were from Mr. Mosey. Why did Daniel bring those?

"No horse," Daniel said, and folded his arms. "I hope he hasn't escaped."

I laughed at his antics and he chuckled. I hadn't seen him laugh in forever.

My daughter pointed to the compartment at the bottom of the seat.

"No. Those are where the big boys' and girls' toys reside. No wooden horse."

That's where he stashed weapons and things to ward off highwaymen, but it was a good place to hide a toy.

"Princess, try one more time." His gaze locked with mine. "It's always good to try again, until you win."

Daniel knelt before us, and my heart fluttered, a slow beat that matched his blinks.

Hope bounced into his arms, and he snuggled her under his chin. His eyes, shiny and jet stayed on me. "At times, I know I don't deserve what I have, but I am grateful. So grateful."

He raised her high, making her soar. "One more time, Hope. Where did I hide the horse?"

"Mmmmmm." She giggled and shook. "Pocket?"

He brought her back to my lap, his hands molding to my knee, warming the thin wool of my carriage gown. "You are correct." He reached inside his tailcoat. The smart brass buttons jingled as he pulled out a new wooden toy. Chestnut brown with a rouge-pink saddle painted, the horse looked perfect and a match to the other two horses in her room.

Hope clapped and laughed with such glee as Daniel made horse *whinnies* and trotted the toy across the seat, across my lap, and into Hope's arms.

"Thank you, Pa-papa."

Daniel's rare smile bloomed. He brushed up against my legs, his hands settling close to my hips as he reached up and kissed Hope's forehead. "Enjoy. We have a few hours to go.

He zipped backward to his seat and dove into his papers.

I played with my daughter showing her how Mrs. Feebs could balance sidesaddle. We kept at it until my moppet's eyes grew heavy.

With her head snuggling beneath my bosom, my angel, Daniel's princess, slept.

The carriage became quiet again like our estrangement at Finchely.

That one time we went to Covent Garden, Daniel was animated after I gave him time to relax after court. How much time did he need today?

Another hour slipped by.

His head didn't lift from his work.

I didn't like him quiet. Couldn't tell what he was thinking. I was miserable.

Miserable because he didn't look at me, not once. Daniel Thackery—the only man inside the carriage, the only one in the world whose attention I wanted—sat across from me only lifting his gaze to Hope.

They had a way of glancing at each other like it was a special language. What was he telling her before she slept? Why did she always laugh and smile like he'd made a joke?

Now, the handsome man stared out the window like it was more interesting than frustrated me. What did it take to gain his attention, to hope he'd say my name and again ask to start anew? I'd tried to find answers without him. There were none, none that I and the Widow's Grace could locate.

Fumbling with the correspondence, the ribbon-bound parchment in his case, I saw my husband frowning, such a waste for perfect lips.

With his head down and the thick waves of hair out of my reach, I wished I drew people, but then I realized no artist could capture this feeling of loss simmering in my bosom. Was this what he felt when we left Hope's room and he went to his bed and me mine?

How did I tell Daniel I missed him? How did I share this secret?

He sat across from me, right there, less than a heartbeat away, and I felt lost and small.

That made me fussy and miserable.

Yet, there were times like now, on my third glance, when he finally saw me staring.

When it was too late to turn.

Caught, I wanted to reach my hand to his. I needed him to pull me into a tight embrace and hold me like we'd never fought, like he and I knew we were to be one—here, here in England, everywhere on the earth.

He should believe me. I didn't want anything else anymore, just him.

But he didn't know my heart.

I hadn't been brave enough to say my secret.

I was miserable.

CHAPTER 53

DANIEL—THE PORTSMOUTH MISSION

Mr. Anthon pulled Daniel's carriage into the long drive of the Royal Hospital Haslar, a structure built on the promontory overlooking the dangerous sea.

"Where are we?" Jemina's brow had crinkles.

Daniel's hands sweated. It tore up his insides to do this, but they had fact finding to accomplish. "I have a secret operation to perform. You are the star witness."

"Witness to what, Daniel?"

"The witness to what happened on October 18, 1812."

Wide, crazy eyes darted, then narrowed on him like he'd betrayed her. She held Hope tighter. "Don't send me away."

His throat constricted. "Never. I need you to trust me, like I trust you. You know the man I am. What I want should be written in your heart, like mine. Put your faith into works and your palm in mine. We have to go inside the Royal Hospital to learn the beginning of your story. How did you go from Portsmouth to Bedlam? Who authorized it? Jemina, it might restore your memory."

She looked out the window at the high brick walls of the building looming closer.

The water splashed as the carriage galloped across the bridge. Jemina put a hand to her chest.

She looked faint, but this is where her nightmare began. They had to come. "I need to give you another piece of your truth. I can't do it without you. I'm not going to pacify you or make assumptions or do anything to diminish your strength."

"Here? I feel the gloom."

"No one can identify you being here but you. You're a brave lass. You stand with me, unless you can't, but this is where the answers lie."

"The Widow's Grace came up with nothing, including *searching* Willingham's office."

"I don't need to hear that." He held his hand out to her again. "Jemina, stand with me."

This time she clutched the tip of his fingers. "Close enough."

"You're not going to commit me, Daniel? This is no trick?"

"No. No trick. And you know I'm loathed to be without you."

She smoothed his pinkie. "Just wanted you to say it aloud. What truth will we glean from here?"

"Jemina, you already recognized the hospital. This is the place injured persons at sea would have been brought. The sailors of the HMS *Belvidera* had to be familiar with it. Many of their colleagues and those in the press gang butchered from the bloody Peninsula War or the battles of 1812 were taken here for treatment."

"You think they took me here?"

"Yes, but we have to be sure. You and I are going to walk inside."

Her heart pounded like a gong. He brushed her wrist. "Lady Shrewsbury has beat us here. See her carriage? She'll sit with Hope while you and I visit Dr. Scottson. Then we will leave together. Is that fine with you? Will you join me on this mission to get answers for my Lady Ashbrook?"

Jemina looked small, so frightened.

"This risk is what you do for the Widow's Grace, scaling buildings, scary things for others." He knelt again in front of her and bundled Hope onto the seat.

With his hands to her hips he scooted her forward, so she'd not miss his gaze, the faith he had in her. "I wouldn't bring you here if I didn't think you strong enough to handle it. You know me, Jemina. I'd protect you before I'd let anything happen to you, but this is something we must do together."

She traced his wide nose, the bridge of his glasses steaming up as he looked at the terror rocking her shoulders.

"Yes, Daniel."

"Repington's contacts were able to arrange today's appointment. His duchess knows you're here, so we are not without advocates, in case . . ."

"What?"

He lifted his hands. "Technicalities. Jemina, we have to go back to where it all began."

Mr. Anthon opened the door, and Lady Shrewsbury came inside. With sherry eyes, dour and a little fretful, she took the sleeping Hope into her arms.

Daniel kissed his aunt's cheek. "We aren't going to be long. I thought if my aunt were here in the duchess's stead, you'd trust that nothing untoward was occurring."

"I trust you, Daniel, but Lady Shrewsbury's presence is welcomed."

"She's my insurance too, Jemina. These aren't places I frequent. And we are far from London and people who know I'm one of the Crown's barristers."

Her eyes widened. Did she understood his discomfort being away from London, where he'd built his power, his reputation? Then he took her hand, remembering how she saved him from ruin. Jemina did understand.

She shot a look at Hope and Lady Shrewsbury, then sucked in a breath and climbed out.

Clouds hung low, churning. The crash of waves lapping in the distance. The soothing sound wasn't loud enough to muffle their footsteps or his instincts to turn them back.

Jemina held her chin up, and they walked through an arcade of trees toward the central reddish-brown building with an arched entry. "It's the biggest brick building in England."

Her fingers tightened upon his. "Wait, Daniel."

Her creamy brow furrowed as they stopped in the shadows.

"That inscription at the top is Portland stone, it's of a woman pouring healing oil on a sailor under the north star."

"You do your homework, Daniel. What's in there? You know."

He flexed his hand to let the blood pump. "Someone who may have seen you. A good number of patients come through here. It's my hope he remembers."

"Three windows at the attic." Her voice was airy, like petals aloft in the breeze. "Three on the second all in red bricks. You don't see bricks, not this many in Kingston. Most everything is wood."

His gut clenched. She'd started to remember, and his fears of losing her whipped his inside. "Ready . . . I'm with you."

Her eyes were vacant, but she tugged him forward. His girl was brave.

His boots hit the cobblestone floor first, after her buckled slippers. The patter and stomp echoed to the mudded ceiling.

People milled about, not talking. All men, some finely dressed, who Daniel assumed to be physicians.

"The wards. I think that is what they called where the beds are." Her voice was low, cracking. "Twenty were in the room."

"Let's keep moving, Jemina."

They did and passed through an area where patients were received and ended up at a massive curved staircase.

Steeper and more twisting than Finchely's, it gave Daniel pause.

"You need a bar at the top of your stairs to keep the *pickney dem*, the little ones, from toppling."

"What, Jemina?"

She grabbed his coat, then wrapped her arm about him. "Take me out of here." Her tone was breathy, the whisper harsh vibrating against his collar. "I beg of you."

Her heart beat so hard, so loud, Daniel feared she'd pass out. "Yes."

He turned her, and they bumped into a tall man with glasses.

She jumped and almost landed in Daniel's pockets.

The physician looked at her. "I know you. St. Maur. The most belligerent patient I've ever had." He glanced at her, hopefully admiring her smart carriage dress, perfectly coiffed chignon, and snappy bisque bonnet. "You came to your senses, I see. Cooperated and were released."

"Something like that," she said.

The physician reached up as if he wanted to touch her head, but Daniel stepped between them. "Excuse me, sir."

"Phrenology, the study of skull structures is my specialty. I wanted to see if the lump on her head was permanent. She was a patient two years ago."

"Dr. Scottson, I remember you."

Fingers entwined with Jemina's, Daniel used the union to motion to the man. "One question. Can you remember who authorized my client Jemina St. Maur to be transported to Bedlam?"

"Yes, never forget. Big man, coat too big on him. Williams . . . no Willingham. Said he was authorized by the family to commit you. Like I said, I'm glad you came to your senses. She wouldn't cooperate. Wouldn't fight for herself or accept the truth. Hope she listens better now."

"No. But that is part of her charm."

The fellow shook his head and disappeared in the stairwell.

Stepping in front of Jemina, he lifted her chin. "So that confirms one piece of our mystery. And that not listening is one of your flaws, mine too."

"You listen better than I do." She crushed his cravat, snaking closer. "Take me from here, Daniel."

This he heard and acted and led her back to the carriage.

"Done?" Lady Shrewsbury offered the drooling Hope back to Jemina.

His wife held her as if she hadn't seen Hope in forever. "Yes."

Daniel couldn't, wouldn't interrupt. Instead, he accompanied his aunt back to her carriage.

"My lovely Ashbrook, was it necessary for Jemina to return to here? She looks so shaken."

He opened her carriage and helped her inside. "It was. Dr. Scottson had to identify her, which the physician did. Jemina needed to see this place and confirm she'd been here as well. She did that, too."

Adjusting her burgundy skirts and gathering Athena, the big snowball Angora cat, Lady Shrewsbury settled into her seat. "That's a lot to risk."

Nodding, Daniel stayed at the door, almost leaning against it, he hid his trepidations with a nod and a shrug. "I needed to show Lady Ashbrook I trusted her strength. It was one of the hardest things I'd ever done."

"Her trauma could've worsened. Such a dangerous thing to do. You're a gambler."

"I'm confident in her. I know she'll fight to keep what we have."

"Keep thinking good thoughts and believe in the collection you've made, your found family." She grasped his hand. "Go to your wife. Gambling is good for you."

"I'll stick to vingt-et-un with the fellows. Thank you for coming to my mission, Lady Shrewsbury."

"Anytime, but be careful, Daniel, my darling. The St. Maurs are influential. You never know whose ear they'll bend."

She had that look as if she knew more, but that was his aunt being the Widow's Grace mastermind. "Well, it's good to have Lady Shrewsbury or her women rush in to save me. See you in London."

"Yes and at Hope's birthday. It's in a few weeks. Will it be a big celebration?"

"A small one. Bring treats. Those currant and carraway short-bread, and stay out of Newgate till I'm back in London." Chuckling, he shut the door, then trudged back to his carriage.

His poor wife still seemed shaken and even more lost. Jemina cradled Hope so tightly, he made sure they both breathed.

"I can only image the memories in your head. You remembered more."

"Daniel, I remember my baby being ripped from my arms. Then everyone told me she didn't exist. I can't remember her name." She kissed Hope's braids. "Why would anyone believe a mother like that?"

Daniel hated what she'd suffered. He left his bench and sat beside her and put her head to his shoulder. "There's one more thing to do before we head back."

"Please let it be something easy."

He wished it was. They had lignum vitae to deliver.

CHAPTER 54

JEMINA—THE MEANING OF HOME

The carriage passed houses of red and orange bricks, then buildings of wood with roofs of thatch or slate. It made a colorful canvas lining their way to the sea.

Daniel held her, even as Hope woke up with all the energy of the duke's blasting cannons.

Salted air snuck inside. It was so much stronger now.

Hope bounced on the seat and peered out the window.

Daniel had that thoughtful look on his face, one that said he understood.

Maybe he did.

I wasn't ready to be weak and cry, not while Hope smiled.

"Boats, Mama. No like sea but like boats."

Nodding, I couldn't risk speaking. My fast-beating heart remained in my throat.

Settling, looking out the window, I watched the crowds gather for ships coming into port. Navy men crowded seaside stands. It looked like chaos. I imagined how confusing the docks might have been the day the HMS *Belvidera* brought in the *Minerva*.

Daniel leaned over and grabbed Hope. "Come on, wiggle worm." He picked up the lignum vitae and put it in her hands. "You wish to come with us, Lady Ashbrook?"

"No. You two go. I'm a little tired."

Daniel kissed my brow. "We won't be long."

With Hope secure in one arm and his blue and purple flowers in the other, he left the carriage and walked to the docks.

On my knees, I crept closer to the window and watched Daniel and Hope at the treacherous water's edge.

They were alone. Even in this place crowded with people, they seemed distant, set apart.

His head bowed for a moment.

The wind had picked up. His tailcoat flapped.

Hope's braids waggled. They dangled and danced in the wind.

The flowers, Mr. Anthon informed me, Daniel had picked this morning from his ironwood trees at Finchely.

My husband and daughter tossed the petals into the sea.

Hope's head bobbled. She must be laughing. Then her arm wound back and she tossed a flower into the breeze.

They did this ritual every year, to honor Phoebe Dunn, or me, or both.

The heavy honeyed smell of lignum vitae lingered on the seat.

The sweetness, I could smell it every day. Sometimes when I closed my eyes, this familiar fragrance conjured up beaches of the whitest sand and waters bearing hues of greenish blue, crystal clear like diamonds.

It had to be my old residence, Kingston, Jamaica.

But that colony didn't feel like home.

Nothing did, not until I found Patience's love and the Widow's Grace.

Now, home stood six feet away, embodied in a man casting flowers into the sea.

Home was a sentimental husband who quoted me poems.

Home held on to my child and was stronger than my doubts.

Home shouldn't be missed anymore.

I pushed out of the carriage and ran to them. Locking my arm about Daniel's, I rested.

With my head on his shoulder, I hoped Daniel understood I wanted to come home for good.

CHAPTER 55

DANIEL—DEFENDING FINCHELY

Jemina rocked Hope and Mrs. Feebs in her arms as Daniel's carriage made the last turn toward Finchely.

She'd cried and sang almost the entire time back to London. This trip might have been too much.

"Taking turns holding Hope is not a bad ritual," he said.

"What?" Jemina lifted her tear-stained face. "Did you say something?"

"Nothing."

"Pa-Papa."

Daniel took the invitation and sat with them. "I'm here."

"Good. Mama and Pa-Papa. Just need Max."

"We're going to him, princess. We're almost home."

Hope smiled, then her little face flopped against Jemina.

He rubbed her cheek, then touched his wife's.

Jemina didn't object. She even leaned a little on his arm like she had at the docks.

This moment was one to savor.

Hope's head fell back, her eyes closed. Her puckered lips held a smile.

Stroking her curls, Daniel sighed. "I think she's tired enough to sleep through the night."

Jemina didn't respond but craned her head toward the window. "You have guests at this hour?"

Her breath came fast. "How could you? You took us away to Portsmouth to have them waiting for me here?"

"Never." He turned her chin to him. "Never. You should know I'd never betray you. When will you ever trust me?"

He doused the lamp and peered out the window. "I know you need the truth; you want it more than anything. That's why I found what I could for you."

She grabbed his arm. "Then why are they here at this hour?"

He'd love to reassure her, but there were two carriages outside of his house. Daniel had a feeling this was his fight, not hers.

His pulse ramped as he shifted to get a better look and made out the Lord Mayor's crest on one of the carriages. "They're not here for you. They've come for me. Down on the floor, Jemina, with Hope. They need to think I'm alone."

She did so, her chocolatey eyes glistened as she rocked their little girl. "Why?"

"Nothing good, Jemina, take Hope and hide in the mews. I'll come for you when everything is safe."

"What? What is happening?"

"This isn't a social call, not at midnight."

She gripped his hand like he had clasped hers in Portsmouth. "We face this together, Daniel."

"No, this little girl will not be ripped from your arms again. You promise me to keep her safe." He jerked open a compartment under his seat. There's money and a knife to help you get away. Big-girl toys."

"Daniel."

"That's the Lord Mayor's carriage. He's here to break up my family. He has the power to take me or you or Hope. Whatever this is, I'll sacrifice myself before anyone can lay a hand on either of you. Please keep Hope safe. Promise me."

She didn't answer. Her gaze said, *Rebellion*.

He edged to the door. "Nothing reckless. Stay safe. Keep our daughter safe. Hide in the mews. If they take me, go to Repington. No one would dare come at him."

"But, Daniel."

"Hope's papa will not be gone."

Jemina released him. She may have even whispered, "Take care."

He couldn't quite hear. The fury building in his chest, the need to punch at something, was ready to explode. He'd strike down as many runners as he could before they dragged him off to Newgate Prison.

When the carriage reached Finchely's door, he leaped out like all was normal with his hat and gloves. "Mr. Anthon, take my carriage to the mews. Stay there."

The young man looked as if he wanted to jump down and fight, but he'd not disobey an order. He kept the vehicle moving. No wife jumped out. Maybe both would listen.

The Lord Mayor's gold crest gleamed with the torch light like it was freshly polished.

No Thackery had actually been an inmate in Newgate.

Would Daniel be the first?

Then he remembered who he was, a peer, a lover of the law, a husband and father who needed to come home each night to his family.

He powered inside Finchely, past a fretful-looking Mrs. Gallick. She wrung her hands on her wrinkled white apron.

He handed her his hat. "Where are they?"

"The study, sir."

The noise of doors opening and closing sounded above.

"The runners, sir," she said in a whisper.

Runners ransacking his Finchely, the place where his family lived.

Daniel stormed the threshold of his study.

Lord Mayor stood near the hearth, enjoying a glass of the brandy Daniel kept for show.

A little balding man sat on a chair while Max growled.

"Lord Mayor," Daniel said, "what is occurring? Why have you invaded my Finchely?"

"Ashbrook, this gentleman has come with some shocking charges."

"Who, Lord Mayor?"

"I'm Mr. Mosey, Lord Ashbrook. I've been writing to you on a pressing matter for the St. Maurs."

When the fool tried to come closer, Max growled. The pug who was never violent looked as if he'd eat a liver, Mosey's.

The sniveling man patted his forehead with a handkerchief. "I received word that you were harboring women, women of diminished capacity here at this remote location. I demanded the Lord Mayor investigate."

"What?" Daniel laughed, something dry and haughty. "Lord Mayor, you let a worm demand you do something?"

The head jurist of the Old Bailey cut his eyes at Mosey. "He brought me evidence that looks horrid."

"Horrid? What can this man who has consistently written to harass my wife possibly have to say against me? Must be good lies to manipulate the Lord Mayor and make him a whipping boy."

The Lord Mayor looked as if he'd choked on his swallow. "Ashbrook, have some decorum."

"I'd have more respect if you weren't making a mockery of my home."

The Lord Mayor gulped his brandy. "He's shown me record after record of you crafting paperwork to have women released from Bedlam. He convinced me that you must be investigated."

"Convinced or confirmed your dark suspicions? I've been in your courts for over a year, at the Old Bailey for six. I've toiled for you and the Crown, and yet you believe lies?"

"Ashbrook, I had to investigate before getting the magistrate to charge you. I could've just let the runners come alone. They've at least not torn your house to pieces."

Two men entered his study. "Nothing, except an exceptional closet. There's nothing out of place in this immaculate house. His daughter's nursery is pink, harmless, adorable."

Daniel waved them toward the door. "Have you searched the property? Perhaps there's a well where trolls claim fair maidens."

"Calm down, Ashbrook. This appears to be a mistake. A tragic mistake."

"It was a mistake to think my years of service have meant something. Have you thought to search the Duke of Repington's house? His wife was freed from an unjust imprisonment in Bedlam too. No, you wouldn't dare go after that peer."

Daniel glared at the man, one whom he'd worked hard to please. "You're worse than my late uncle. At least he let his prejudice be known, never hiding it behind false smiles. The Prince Regent was right about *bastards* in high places."

Lord Mayor's hand shook, and he seemed to search his empty glass for more brandy. "Regardless of my personal feelings, the evidence he had made this a valid claim. Why so many released over the years? There's over twenty."

Ah . . . the Widow's Grace business. Daniel stepped closer. "Unlike you or some of my fellow barristers, I'm known as a fair arbiter. Families come to me and tell me of cruelties done to a missing sister or aunt or mother. In my spare time, I've looked into their plights. I have found many innocent, sane women locked in Bedlam."

Mosey tried to come closer, but Max barked, keeping him against the ottoman. "Sane? Why would they be admitted?"

"Sane women have been locked away because some man in their family has decided it was better to use the Crown's pennies for the widow's care rather than their own. They want them quiet and out of the way to manipulate their assets."

The Lord Mayor turned to Mosey. Perhaps he could see the worm for what he was, an opportunistic tool.

"You're an avenger?" Mosey said.

"If that's what you call righting wrongs, so be it. This inquiry is done. I'm a peer. If I've done wrong, take your accusations to the House of Lords or the Prince Regent himself. I'm sure he'd like to know."

The Lord Mayor looked ashen. His hand trembled as he set the glass on the mantel. "As far as I'm concerned, this is over. It will never be mentioned. Ashbrook, I owe you an apology. I'd heard rumors of your wild associations as of late. I should've judged you by your character. Nothing else. I apologize."

"As of late? I've been Black for a long time. Your suspicions have been with me since the first day you held court."

"Sorry, Ashbrook. None of this will be mentioned from me. I wish you'd do the same."

Mr. Mosey sputtered and tried to gain the Lord Mayor's attention. Then he ran past Max and stood in front of Daniel. "He has to be up to no good. The records? What about his current wife? She's crazed."

"Excuse me, Lord Mayor, this man just insulted my wife." Daniel grabbed Mosey in one hand and punched him with the other. He punched him again until he fell over the study's threshold. "You're in my house. You've wasted the Crown's time. Don't think I'll bear anyone denigrating the woman I love."

Mosey held his jaw. "Where's your wife?"

"You've ransacked my house. You know she's not here. Lady Ashbrook and my daughter are visiting friends."

Lord Mayor sighed, long like he'd swallowed a fur ball. "The runners just finished. They did search thoroughly, Mosey. No one is shackled or abused. This is a normal, comfortable house. Your daughter's room sounds sweet, Ashbrook."

"I've run out of patience. Perhaps I can send word to the Duke of Repington. His men need cannon practice."

"That won't be necessary," the Lord Mayor said. "Get off the ground, Mosey, and let's leave."

"Yes," Daniel said, "all of you leave. Never come back unless my dear wife invites you. She won't."

Mrs. Gallick stopped twisting her hands in her apron. Her smile beamed with pride. "You heard his Lordship. He's been a widower for two years, raising the sweetest child, and now that he's married, evil forces are against him. Shoo."

The Lord Mayor, the highest judge of the Old Bailey court, hung his head as his sad footfalls flopped out of the front door. "Good night, Lord Ashbrook. For what it's worth, I am sorry."

"But . . . My sources," Mosey said. "They say he can't be trusted. He's crazy too. Mr. Willingham says Ashbrook is crazy, too."

"Willingham, that's your source? A broke shipper whose transport business collapsed after the abolition of trafficking, that's your source?" Daniel waved his gloveless hands. "I wonder why he would target me."

The Lord Mayor shook his head. "Mosey, if you don't quiet down, I'll leave you with a man whom you've insulted and brought chaos to his household."

Mr. Anthon ran through the hall. "Sir, do you need anything?"

He glared at the young man. The fellow should be with Jemina and Hope. "No. I'm waiting for these gentlemen to be off my grounds."

The young man held the door open wide. He looked ready to spit fire, but he held his peace. Daniel was thankful for this. It wasn't Anthon's fight. It was Daniel's. "Tell your source, Mr. Willingham, that his harassment must end. I will pursue legal measures."

Mosey pursed his lips, but the Lord Mayor waved a finger at him. "Mosey, not another word or I'll have you at Newgate tonight."

The runners climbed into their carriage and proceeded out of Finchely. The Lord Mayor trotted down the steps and headed to his carriage.

The horrible solicitor waved his fist. "It's not over, Ashbrook. Mr. Willingham and the St. Maurs won't let it be over."

"If I catch you near my house or my wife, I'll make sure you and Willingham pay."

"Are those threats?"

"Promises. I don't break promises."

The fellow frowned and leaped into the Lord Mayor's carriage.

Daniel waited on the steps until the scourges could no longer be seen. Then he walked back inside.

Mrs. Gallick rushed to him. "I was so frightened. But, my lord, I've never heard you so forceful or so angry."

"The Thackery temper does come in handy. This is where my family resides. It has to be safe." He gripped her hand. "Brew some tea while I go get my girls. Mr. Anthon hid them in the mews."

The young man nodded. "Is this over, sir?"

"No. But it will be." He whistled to his pug, and they trotted straight to the mews.

There was no better sight than his parked carriage, black sleek ebony and unharmed.

His groomsmen stabled the horses like normal, as if Finchely hadn't been stormed by runners.

He filled his lungs of the smell of fresh hay and horses' lather.

Jemina and Hope were safe. The three of them survived.

He walked the final distance to the carriage. "Jemina, it's over. We're going to be fine."

No answer.

His stomach clenched as he tore open the door.

The carriage sat empty.

No Jemina.

No Hope.

The family he built was gone.

CHAPTER 56

JEMINA—RUN AWAY

I had my daughter in my arms, and we'd ridden about two miles in the dark. The clouds had shifted. I stopped under a tree to rest, to catch my breath, to think through what to do.

"Pa-Papa was right. Ladies can ride horses sitting."

"He's right about a lot of things."

"Where is Pa-Papa? Why didn't he come?"

Holding on to Hope, I wasn't prepared to whisper lies. "He'll be with us when he can. He'll find us."

"When we go home, Mama? I want Mrs. Feebs. Left her in carriage. My new horsey, too."

"Hope, what about an adventure, just the two of us?"

"No Pa-Papa?"

She grew quiet. Tears fell on my wrist.

"Baby, please don't cry."

The *chubble*, *chubble*, trouble at Finchely had to be because of me. It was dire. Daniel sacrificed himself. Then I ran.

"Mama, don't cry too. Pa-Papa fix. He always fixes. That's what Aunty says."

Lady Shrewsbury, she'll know what to do. "Hope—"

Loud, happy barking surrounded us.

My heart slowed. Those yelps weren't meant for chase. They were our pug.

"Max. Mama, Max has come. He's come."

The galloping closed in. I turned my horse around and saw Daniel flying fast, almost standing in his seat.

Max loped near and ran around us.

Daniel pulled to my side.

"Pa-Papa, you came! We can go now."

"No need to run. All is well, Hope. Jemina, I answered the Lord Mayor's and Mosey's questions. The law continues to think I am a dull and boring man with the best daughter and wife. They don't know my secret, ladies. My family is strong and whole."

He leaned over and reached for me. It was a quick hug, too quick. I reached for him, but he'd circled with his mount.

"Family, let's go home." He took Hope onto his saddle. "Max, lead the way to Finchely."

His horse moved six feet away when he stopped. "My invitation is for all of us. I've sent the evil away. Under my protection, you're safe. No more running, Jemina."

"It's home, Daniel. Isn't it?"

He made his mount come to mine. "Hope, your Mama's still scared. Let's tell her we love her and we understand why she left."

"Yes, Mama. Love, love, love." My daughter yawned. "Mrs. Feebs needs us home."

Daniel reached for my reins. I nodded and let him seize the strap. He led us through the dark, all the way to Finchely's torches.

"Lady Ashbrook, we have a yawner. We need to put this one to bed."

"Me happy, Pa-Papa."

"Me too, my princess. We're going home."

His voice was smooth. There was no anger in him.

Something much worst.

Apathy.

With the Lord Mayor's incursions and my running off, breaking Daniel's trust, I just didn't know how long *we* would be welcome.

CHAPTER 57

DANIEL—WE SURRENDER

Two days without incident, didn't exactly help Daniel sleep, but he was tired.

Long hours at the Lincoln's Inn preparing for an upcoming trial, then coming home to a silent Finchely, did nothing to subdue the restless tension in his spirit. Standing in his closet, he pulled on his nightshirt and thought of nothing but curling into his mattress.

Well, he had thoughts of reconciliation with Jemina, but it wasn't up to him.

She needed to be sure.

The business of the Royal Hospital and the Lord Mayor had made her skittish.

Daniel didn't know how to fix this.

What he wouldn't give for her to barge through their adjoining door wild and crazy and carefree, but she hadn't.

He could be a hermit a little longer. Daniel leaned forward, knocking his shelf of waistcoats and wondered how he'd become so good at lying to himself.

Knocking. Tapping. "Daniel?"

Jemina. Hallelujah. He coughed to deepen his voice. "Come in."

She burst inside and stepped into his closet. She wore a burgundy silk carriage dress with silver buttons and pleating at her bosom. "Daniel? We have a problem."

His heart jittered, but other than a frown swallowing her face she looked unharmed. He tugged on the final sleeve of his robe and determined to remain calm. "You are capable, darling."

He soaked her in, hair up with tendrils coiling at her neck. "Mrs. Gallick said you've been out all day."

"But I came home, Daniel."

He told his pulse to slow, to not fool himself with the soft look of longing in her eyes. "Yes, Hope—"

"This isn't about Hope."

Daniel came to her and put his hands to her shoulders. "Is there new trouble? Something with the Widow's Grace?"

Jemina put her palm on his. "No. It's us. We can't do this anymore. I can't."

The breath in his chest froze, sharp like icicles, piercing his lungs. Schooling his face, he wheezed, then returned to hanging up his court frills. Tell me, Jemina, what can't go on?"

"You're going to stay in there? I want to talk."

"I've heard I do my best work in closets, but I'll move to the bed for you."

Daniel walked past her, breathing a fragrance that was sweet like honey. Then he saw the lignum vitae, blue and purple pinned in her curls. "I like those flowers."

"Hope and I picked some. We spent the afternoon in your woods. I put her to bed and walked again. Mr. Anthon kept an eye on me."

Daniel forced himself to move forward, then he flopped on his bed. "So, what troubles you, my love?"

"Is this how you are when you lose a trial? Resigned and unfeeling."

He was far from unfeeling, particularly watching how the gown draped her curves. "Not sure, Jemina. I don't lose often."

"You're a strange bird, Daniel." She rubbed her brow. "Hope

said that you're going to look at property this weekend for *horseys*."

Fluffing his pillow, he let his head sink into the goose down. "Yes, I'm getting a little bored with Town. A bigger house with no stairs will allow for more horses. They seem to come in handy for fast getaways."

"Finchely is plenty big. If you fix up that barn or put up fencing, you could do that here."

"I could. You could if it pleased you."

"Don't you think you've let me do as I pleased enough?"

With eyes closed, he folded his arms behind his head. "Why don't you tell me what it is you've come to say? I'm listening."

"I surrender."

She sank beside him on the bed then clutched his shoulders, shaking him. "You want me to say it? I'm sorry I ran. I want us again."

His hands slid to her waist, and he tugged her against him. "Must you be violent again? I thought we were past this."

She curled her head into his chest. "I want you back. I want the man I banter with returned. The one always trying to protect me or Hope, even if I don't want him, too. Not a man who's given up on you and me."

He clasped one of her hands, prying it free, nuzzling her calloused palm to his cheek. "It's not going to work, you know. You can't make me fearful, then make me crazy with yearnings, then leave me to my lone pillow. Not falling for it, ma'am. Go on about your evening."

With her tight in his embrace, he'd said the foolish words but hadn't let her go. As long as she wanted him, he had no intentions of ever doing so.

"You need more pillows. One for me, too. Daniel, I surrender." She smiled at him with cheeks reddening. "I hate that you are the most patient man in the world or that you are so confident in our love that you'd let me float about Finchely trying to find my way."

"Well, one—we both know you'd sneak out if I ever tried to dissuade you. Two—your daughter is here. Your affection for me might wane but not for Hope. Three—I'm the only lover you remember, that in itself are points four and five."

Laughing, she collapsed atop him, and he held her as that wonderful noisy heart of hers slowed.

"Jemina, I know you only left to protect Hope. You've already showed me the lengths you will go to protect me. I can expect no less for Hope."

Smoothing the lignum vitae from her hair, he smelled the flowers and put them on the nightstand, next to the letters he and Jemina exchanged, every one. "You're in luck. I'm a little stubborn myself. Once I knew I loved you and that you loved me, it was a difficult thing to even think of giving up happiness."

"I'm glad you chose wisely."

"A wise man knows when he's wrong, and I believe I know how to gain a final answer about Hope. But I will need to reach out to my former mistress for her assistance."

To see the joy bubble in her face only to wither with the mention of Lavinia jarred him. "What, my Lady Ashbrook?"

"I don't want her near you. Give her no opportunity to injure you. We barely survived her last attempt."

His gaze locked with Jemina's, and he drew her chin to his and took her lips. Heaven and sorrow were in the taste of her. Such a shame when she'd had too much of the battle, not enough peace.

Hands to her cheek, he put them eye to eye. "You listen. I know a thing or two about avoiding snake bites. She can't strike me twice, not with you at my side."

"I don't like this. And if she calls me Buckles again . . ."

"Lady Ashbrook, I didn't know you were the jealous type."

He grinned, and she fumed. He grinned more. "Lavinia will be the tool to catch bigger rats, Willingham and Mosey. From the pummeling I took at the ball, she and Willingham are in league. We already know that Mosey wanted to use the Lord Mayor to haul me away and leave you unprotected to the St. Maurs. Willingham had you committed. I don't leave threats to fester. It's time for the united Ashbrooks to finish this."

"He is awful, but I don't want us at risk."

Us, that was a word as good as *family*.

She put her palm to his heart. "And our home."

"Pliny the Elder is attributed to saying home being where the heart is."

"Don't know who that is, but I don't need to. Daniel, I just know I love you."

He released her chignon, letting her curls falling down about them. "I love you, more. Nothing will break us, Jemina."

"I'm glad I only remember you. You're the only one in my soul, Daniel, only you."

That was more to his liking.

> *To shield your poet from the burning day:*
> *. . . fan the pleasing fire.*
> *The bow'rs, the gales, the variegated skies*
> *In all my pleasures in your bosom rise.*

"I tweaked the last line a bit for you and only you. It's a jumble of words about gales and stormy skies. You were blown into my life, Jemina."

"Daniel, I think I know what the poem means. You will share your pillow with me tonight."

Propping up on his elbow, he rose up to greet her. "Welcome home."

Chapter 58

Jemina—No Better Place

My husband held me in his arms for the first time in weeks. It seemed like an eternity had passed between us.

His whispers in my ear, of love, of hope, were not a consolation for not knowing everything about who I was.

It was the prize.

I'd won.

No penalties or past mistakes clung to my soul. I was whole. I found myself, a woman desired and loved for being me. Was there no greater treasure?

Daniel. Strong, patient Daniel, he was my mast in the storm, and I latched myself to him.

" 'His rising radiance drives the shades away,' " I said when I caught my breath.

His black eyes smoked with fire and flame. "Madame, have you been stealing my books?"

"If I can't know me, I'd rather know all of you and your penchant for Phillis Wheatley. You have driven enough of the shadows away for me, Daniel, by being a light, a lamp to show me the way."

"The way home, my love." Fully grinning with the tiniest bit of his gap showing, he took my mouth. He tasted of Mrs. Gallick's currant rolls.

"We will win, J. We will."

"I've won already, Daniel."

A kiss was a start. I needed to know that I hadn't ruined us. Love was so easily broken when you're broken.

But now I was whole.

I found me, I chose me—the me that was a mother and wife and friend of the best man.

Daniel offered me all of his pillow, but I placed his hands on my waist and gave myself to him.

When nothing beyond Finchely was promised, there was no better place to hide than in my husband's deepest embrace.

CHAPTER 59

DANIEL—AN OUTING TO TONBRIDGE

Sitting across from his wife as his carriage made its way to the Sleck Building in Tonbridge, he worked through his arguments for this trial of truth. He needed to be as good as Prinny believed to make sure that Jemina and Hope were never bothered by the St. Maurs again.

Jemina fidgeted in the seat. She looked nervous, and he hurt for her.

"This solicitor business will end. You will be free of troubles, Lady Ashbrook."

Ambivalence had been his weapon, to appear unaffected by the difficulties of the world. Jemina needed his passion and his sense of fashion. Both would keep her focused on what was important: today, love and Hope.

With her carriage dress of bright poppy red and a line of shiny pearl buttons down the front, she made the best-looking witness he'd seen in a long time. "Another smart outfit, Lady Ashbrook. Definitely brings out shades of victory in your eyes."

A smile showed for a moment but then disappeared with her tensing cupid's bow. She looked away, her thumbs opening and closing about an imagined distance in the air.

He clasped those moving digits. "Maybe we should get you an embroidery needle and thread to occupy your thoughts?"

"Oh. Sorry."

"No, it is I who am sorry. I'm not distracting you enough."

"It's hard. Willingham and Mosey and Lady Lavinia are terrible, but they hold the key to so much. And if your friend calls me Buckles, I will stomp her."

"You're ready to fight. That's good but keep your head, dear heart. The law and your barrister are your muscle today."

Daniel moved and sat beside her, putting his arm behind her, then about her.

She relaxed against him, and that distinctive heartbeat slowed.

"For what it's worth, nothing Mosey or Willingham can say will change us, how I love or crave you."

"Daniel, it could be another trap."

"Yes, but I borrowed some of the duke's soldiers as our grooms. Nothing will happen. I like being on Repington's good side. It has advantages."

When the carriage stopped, Daniel helped Jemina down. She looked well on his arm. He was proud to claim her.

Followed by three soldiers, they went into the Sleck Building.

A clerk, a weasel-looking man who looked a lot like one of the men who held him down at the Widow's Ball, sat at a desk penning something. The big snout of this fiend needed busting but Daniel had larger rats to skewer.

"We have an appointment with Mr. Mosey."

"He . . . ah . . . he didn't say you'd be bringing an entourage."

Repington's men in full pomegranate regalia with flintlocks and starched uniforms were impressive. Still, the less witnesses, the better. Daniel tossed a gold coin, hard. It made an impression on the clerk's forehead. "Go away for an hour."

The man put the money in his pocket and rubbed his reddened brow. "Yes, sir. Sorry."

One of the soldiers raised a weapon.

The clerk ran faster out the door.

Daniel coughed, trying hard to keep his laughter inside. "Membership in the Henpecked Club is quite fine."

Jemina squinted at him with deep furrows growing on her brow. "What did you say? What's funny?"

"Nothing." He stepped in front of her and headed down the hall. "Follow me."

"Always, if I'm not leading."

He looked back at his wife, so strong and feisty, ready to face her past. Daniel jerked the door open and interrupted Willingham kissing Lady Lavinia. "Slumming so early in the morning, my dear shrew."

"Lord Ashbrook, your note said to make sure Mr. Willingham was here and not thinking of anything, I took it to heart."

Willingham jumped to the other side of the table backing up against the whitewashed walls. "Lavinia, dove, what is this?"

"I needed to make amends to Lord Ashbrook. I shouldn't have tried to compromise you, Daniel, to gain your money and title. Or let my jealousy of Buckles here drive me to do something so terrible. You've always been decent to me. You deserve better."

"Pretty words from a viper." Jemina approached Lavinia. "And it's Lady Ashbrook, not Buckles. Remember it or know my boots."

"Well, you do clean up well. Enjoying Daniel's money."

Jemina blew him a kiss. "Everything, everything he has to offer."

Lavinia frowned and swished past the table. Jemina hit her with the door when she opened it too quickly. "Sorry. Guess I'm the clumsy sort."

The shrew adjusted the brim of her crushed bonnet. "Another time then."

She left as Mr. Mosey entered, but Jemina still slammed the door.

"Good. Lord Ashbrook, Mr. Willingham. You are both here," little man said.

"Mr. Mosey," she said, her voice low and trembling, "we're here to settle the matter of my assets. I'm formerly Jemina St. Maur, recently wed to Lord Ashbrook."

Again, the worm's five-finger forehead looked up. There was probably no admiration for Daniel's Pomona green waistcoat with gold threading about the buttonholes or his indigo jacket cut with deep revers.

The plain Mosey probably only saw the barrister, the proud man who bested him in front of the Lord Mayor. Yes. And that was sufficient.

"Lord Ashbrook," he said, "No hard feelings, I trust?"

"Spare me the pleasantries. Get on with this, sir."

"I have been appealing to you for a while when I learned you found Mrs. St. Maur. The nature of Cecil St. Maur's will has it that his holdings are in trust for her and nothing can be done without her agreement."

"Nothing. Nothing can be sold?" Daniel sat on the long table within punching distance of Willingham. "That's unusual."

"Yes, the family had finally arranged for Mr. Willingham to buy the outstanding interests, but that was when Mrs. St. Maur was of diminished capacity."

Jemina flexed her swatting hand. "You mean as long as I was held as a lunatic, the St. Maur family could sell my interests?"

"Quite simply, yes, but as your husband can attest, you are quite sane."

Daniel hesitated for dramatic effect, but after a cough and Jemina's glower, he decided to speak up. "Lady Ashbrook is quite sane. I suspect that she was placed in Bedlam to defraud her of her due. She suffered there for two years. Don't you think that's wrong, Mr. Mosey?"

The man looked down, pushed papers about, then nodded. "I see why you help these women. I am truly sorry."

"She's a lunatic. I was there." Willingham said. "She raved like a lunatic about the *Minerva*'s sinking. She didn't know her own name."

After seating his wife at the end of the table opposite Mosey, Daniel went to the right closer to Willingham. "You admit to having her committed?"

Willingham slipped away and dropped into a chair in the middle of the table.

"No need to answer. Dr. Scottson of the Royal Hospital Haslar remembered you and your horrid tailor."

"So I committed her. She was a loon, a danger to herself. So what?"

"Ol' Jancros, the thief who tried to steal my life isn't sorry." Jemina's whisper was loud.

Daniel kept his hands to his papers and not fisting. "Sir, you worked with the St. Maurs since living in Jamaica. You served as Cecil St. Maur's witness on his marriage contract to the former Jemina St. Maur."

Willingham nodded. "Yes. And Cecil St. Maur and I were good friends."

Daniel cast a document from his coat. "You knew of his will and the provisions. I recently procured a copy at my wife's insistence to keep looking for the truth. Quite unusual provisions for patriarchal fools."

Willingham grunted. "It's all that woman's fault. Cecil St. Maur was supposed to sell off everything as a condition to marry her. The viper doesn't even remember my poor friend."

Daniel chuckled. "Principled even in Jamaica, Lady Ashbrook."

Then he leaned over and took another document out of his leather pouch. Leafing through Jemina's marriage contract to St. Maur, he fingered a section for Mosey to look at. "Lady Ashbrook is owed four thousand pounds as her dower."

Willingham shook his head. "She received twenty thousand. She's owed no more."

"The twenty thousand pounds is not from the St. Maur estate. That was from a mysterious, swarthy benefactor."

Mr. Mosey looked at the paperwork. "I'll have funds drawn

from the St. Maurs' London accounts to pay this. Sorry for the oversight."

Willingham pounded the table. "We're not here to enrich her. She needs to sell her interests in the shipping business."

Daniel raised his hand. "In due time. We must make sure everything has been accounted for."

"Agreed," Jemina said as she scooted her chair closer to Daniel.

Mr. Mosey didn't look up but furiously nodded as he made notes. "I agree too. Mr. Willingham, being a witness and a friend to Cecil St. Maur, why didn't you see to this?"

"She wasn't asking for it and had said she wanted none of the St. Maur's dealings."

Daniel played with the bone buttons of his waistcoat. "Cecil St. Maur's will has so many complicated provisions meant to protect his widow. Amazing. He must've loved you dearly."

Jemina's face went blank. The poor dear had no memory of him.

"It's too much paperwork, gentlemen. It must be why I hate solicitors." She clasped her finger together. "Hate them."

Mr. Mosey looked up, his frown seemed to tighten, but Jemina was mostly harmless. Mostly.

Before she became distracted and did something that might reopen the sanity question, it was time to get the toughest answers to the questions she most wanted to know. He'd press to liberate the secrets about Hope and prayed that his skill wouldn't put their greatest miracle at risk.

CHAPTER 60

JEMINA—TRUTH OR DARE

Daniel stayed within striking distance of the fool Willingham, and all I could think of was my love laying battered in Lady Shrewsbury's hall. This brute did it.

I wanted to protect my husband. " 'Proceed, great chief, with virtue on thy side,' " I said in a voice that wasn't so loud but wasn't a whisper.

He smiled at me, his shiny eyes sparkling with the recognition of Miss Wheatley's words. "You have been studying, Lady Ashbrook." He turned away. "Mr. Willingham, I believe you had a hand in cheating my wife, like in snatching away an engraved fob."

"The man is a thief. Ol' Jancros probably sold off my ring from Cecil."

Willingham smiled but didn't answer.

"If it is proved that you, Ol' Jancros," Daniel said with an island accent and his courtroom flare, "aided in fraud with this contract, you shall pay damages."

"What are you talking about?"

Daniel flung the paper at Willingham, "I don't see a provision for minor children. We've located him. The St. Maur assets you want are his."

"Now I know this is a ruse, Ashbrook. There was no boy, but a girl from her previous marriage to Philip Monroe, a free half-breed very much like yourself. Though Cecil tolerated the sprat, he did so only to get Jemina Monroe to marry him. So, no money. The boy, whoever you found, isn't a St. Maur and isn't to inherit a thing."

My gaze soared to Daniel, maybe through him, his beautiful silken waistcoat straight to his heart. I touched my stomach, swaddling the wool of my carriage gown. Hope was born of me and she was born free.

With a hand to the buttons of his tailcoat, Daniel preened like there was more. "You are claiming that there was no son or provision for any children between you and your . . ." He counted his fingers. "Monroe; St. Maur, your second husband. Good God, Countess, I'm your third?"

Daniel wasn't smiling anymore. But I didn't know what to say to him of the men I didn't remember. *You're my favorite.*

I sat on my hands wanting to shrug, but Daniel's glance said he loved me and we shared a secret, our Hope.

Mr. Mosey's fist fell to the table. "According to the documents you've given me, Lord Ashbrook, this list of passengers, quitting the colony of Jamaica, indicates that only Mrs. Cecil St. Maur and Phoebe Monroe Dunn survived the sinking. You're some kind of lucky, Lady Ashbrook."

"Yes, we are," Daniel said, "but it appears Mrs. Dunn—your sister-in-law, Jemina, Mr. Monroe's sister—was never accounted for. The confusion at the docks and the Royal Hospital Haslar was incredible."

Willingham's eyes widened, then he reared back, crossing his arms in another ill-fitting baggy coat. "I was there on the docks, hoping Mr. St. Maur survived. He didn't. Then they found Mrs. St. Maur, a raving loon. She still is. She should be in Bedlam."

Mr. Mosey's face drained of the red, his ruddy complexion. He waggled his finger. "No. No. The Lord Mayor has threatened . . . warned me not to mention that again. That last gambit you swore was true almost landed me in Newgate. Stop this. Lord Ashbrook, you can see I'm not a party to that talk, not anymore."

"Yes, Mr. Mosey. My husband took up a dismissive tone. "Duly noted."

Sputtering and losing, Willingham pounded the table and pointed. "She was mad, a lunatic. The St. Maur family didn't want her back. She was trouble from day one. The only reason she turned Cecil's head was to come to London with her sister-in-law and make sure she was settled."

Daniel moved back to Willingham, towering over him. "It's your testimony that you thought Jemina St. Maur was a loon, and that was why you ordered for her to be committed to Bedlam."

"This woman never liked our business. Always talking abolition and freedom. You were a troublemaker. Your nonsense got to Cecil. Then he died trying to please you."

Daniel walked behind me and put his hands on my shoulders, pinning me in place. He knew me, knew the words that would stir me and trigger a horrific response.

My slapping hand itched.

"Then why did you try to court this woman, Mr. Willingham? Why ingratiate yourself and try to bore her into marriage?"

The fool laughed. "Twenty thousand reasons, and she's not so bad to look at. Any man can take a little trouble for twenty thousand pounds and control of Cecil's assets." He sneered and looked at me. "Your sister-in-law wasn't so bad either, as far as those people go."

My husband's finger tightened, and I put my palm on his tensed knuckles. "Finish him, my love."

"Yes, Lady Ashbrook. This is my virtuous wife, so caring and protective. Her St. Maur assets are under my control. Sell your half of the business or buy me out for seventy thousand pounds."

Willingham's eyes went wide and stormy. "It's not worth that, and I haven't got that type of money."

"I suggest you figure it out, or St. Maur's assets will be divested, sold off piece by piece."

He bounced up, knocking his chair, making the legs screech. "You can't do that. It's a thriving business."

Holding tight, weaving my pinkie with Daniel's, I turned to the solicitor. "Tell him, Mr. Mosey, tell this belligerent fool what my husband can or can't do."

"They're quite right, Mr. Willingham. They can sell off each ship, even pieces of the hull if they want."

"Ol' Jancros, you've lost." Daniel hovered about me, his stance strong and ready to fight. "Mosey can tell you how I sold off all my uncle's holdings, bit by bit. I've learned twenty thousand ways to do it, and I'll do it again for the St. Maurs. Come along, my dear."

Willingham flustered; the veins of his neck blued and bulged. He lunged.

Daniel caught his arm and spun him back, wrenching his arm surely out of the socket by the way the pig howled.

That wasn't good enough. I stepped forward and slapped the man *hard*. "That was for the Widow's Ball." I slapped him again. "That's for anything I forgot. Don't even think of coming after my husband again, or I'll have each boat sunk."

Daniel tossed Willingham to the floor. "She'll do it. You have no idea what she's capable of. Me either, and I love it."

Rubbing his elbow, his face, Willingham scrambled to rise. "They're both crazy, Mr. Mosey. Stop them."

The solicitor bowed and held the door. "There's nothing to do. I drew up the original contract. It's ironclad."

"Like ironwood with sweet lignum vitae. Don't get any ideas, Mr. Willingham, you have a number of personal debts amassed. You'd hate a swarthy benefactor to call them and have you locked away in debtor's prison. I hear rat-infested King's Bench on Borough High Street has room for new inmates. You wouldn't mind being locked away until you could pay?"

Now Willingham paled, whiter than snow. Knowing that my husband could have him imprisoned on a whim—maybe he'd have nightmares fearing for the moment when he no longer had control.

With his half smile showing, Daniel took my arm. "Good day, Mr. Mosey."

Soldiers in tow, he escorted me to our carriage. Soon, we were on our way, and I took the opportunity to jump into his arms. "Thank you," I said with kisses. "Hope is confirmed to be mine."

"Technically, she was all along, but confirmation that she's born free may give you comfort."

"Hope was birthed of my flesh, and Phoebe Dunn and I were sisters-in-law. We had to be good friends."

He nodded, but a cloud seemed to swallow his face, dulling his pretty eyes. "Number three? Three, Jemina."

"At least you know I love you, Daniel. I don't remember Philip at all. Still don't know if I loved Cecil. I'm done looking. No one, no family has been looking for me. I don't need to search anymore. Who or what I was is done. I'm Hope's mother again and your wife. That's enough."

"Are you sure, Jemina?"

"Yes, we are enough."

His arms tightened about me as he nuzzled my neck. "It's because opposites attract. Me, a handsome reserved barrister, you, my lovely, volatile lady. Well, not quite opposites, but so right."

"And so good together." I turned my face to his. "Should've asked Willingham my baby's name."

"The less the St. Maurs or any naysayers know about how we live, the better. Our daughter is named Hope. She's wonderful. So is her mother, my wife."

"I don't remember Phoebe. I wish I did. I'd like to honor her and Philip Monroe."

"We shall, by raising Hope to be extraordinary."

I buried myself in his chest, my sobs drizzling his cravat. "I'm sorry, Daniel."

"Phoebe led me to you, I suppose." He put his chin atop my

brow. His beard felt so good. "With the sinking of the *Minerva*, I was lost, then I was found in Hope's glances, then yours. Her birthday is the day I claimed her. That's the day our family was born. You were just a little late in joining our party."

Kissing Daniel, slow and easy, I tasted my tears. They were happy ones, mostly happy ones. And I was content with the secrets shared between me and my beloved barrister.

EPILOGUE

October 18, 1814
Finchely Hall

I held Patience's head over the basin. She'd come to Finchely for Hope's celebration but spent the morning in Daniel's study on all fours.

Max hopped about running to the hall and back, but he had no use for people with nausea.

Patience took four long breaths. "I'm sorry, Jemina. I can't believe this. And this is your daughter's special day."

I brushed at her falling chignon. "You can't believe that you are with child?"

"No, that Busick has surveilled everything like a military campaign. My own lady's maid is apparently a batman or is it ball girl? I don't know, but she is some woman who followed the soldiers along their battlefield campaigns. She gives him notices of my health and monthly courses. When I can stomach more than dry biscuits, there will be changes."

My laughter was loud and long. "The man loves you. You know he does."

"I know, and I love Busick dearly. I'll have to comply with his overprotection and rules until this bonbon is born. Then I will have civilians in my household." She smiled, and then heaved again.

When she stopped, I offered her another napkin and rubbed her back. "Lionel will be so blessed to have a sister or a brother."

"Yes." She gulped air. "This is true. Love that crazy man. He is so happy for this child to come."

"You and this little soldier to be, Patience, are blessed to have a house of love and cannons."

My friend sat back and lifted her head to the ceiling. "We are going back to Hamlin Hall at month's end. I'll miss you terribly."

"Daniel and I are looking at property, too. Very near Hamlin. We will keep Finchely, but he's thinking of retiring from London."

"How do you feel about it.?"

"Honestly, it's great. I'll be near you, not letting go of my family. And I may finally tackle more watercolors. Maybe I can match this one."

Patience's eyes grew wide. "I hadn't noticed it before. Jemina, where did Lord Ashbrook get that painting? I have to have it."

"I'm not sure. I think he said from the marketplace at Covent Garden this spring."

She wiped at her mouth. "Find out for me."

"Patience, you've paled. You look scared."

"That picture. I have to have it. I think I know the artist."

The look on her face was more than awe. It was a burst of pride and relief. I took the painting down expecting a secret door. Nothing.

I heard footsteps coming from the hall and then arguing. Well, more so Lady Shrewsbury's voice probably harping on my husband.

Helping Patience sit with her feet up on Daniel's ottoman, I tucked a blanket about her. "You rest."

"Look at me getting all flustered. This is your first birthday reunited with your daughter."

If she knew how special those words were she'd burst. "Let me go see what's happening in the hall. Then, I will find Mrs. Gallick and send hot tea. I suppose no cake with bliss frosting for you?"

She had her hand on the gold frame. "The painting. That's all. Lord Gantry will be here any minute to take me back to Sandlin Court. Please ask Ashbrook if this can be mine."

"Yes, for you anything."

When I crossed into the hall, I saw Daniel and his aunt, fussing.

"No, my dear, Lord Ashbrook." She patted her fluffy Angora kitty. "I'm not ready to retire."

"Technically, Aunt, you could and find someone else to run the Widow's Grace. But I know it should not end, not yet. When your ladies hoisted me by my own petard out of your ball and threw me safely into a carriage, it made me more appreciative of your gang of women."

Smirking, she folded her arms. "Gossip has it that you expressed your unvarnished opinion to the Lord Mayor."

"Yes, and now he wants the Court of Chancery to be more sensitive to women whose custody and interests might be threatened by relatives who use Bedlam for coercion."

"Excellent, Daniel. Maybe something you said made him think."

"Perhaps," my husband said, "or maybe he's hoping I won't tell the Prince Regent about his poor attitude."

I moved and stood at Daniel's side. "The horrible Lord Mayor should listen to his top barrister while he has you."

Mrs. Gallick passed me with a pile of freshly starched napkins. "How's the duchess, ma'am?"

"Miserable, Mrs. Gallick. Can you bring her a large pot of tea?"

She nodded with that knowing smile. "I'll do so, and you should take note, ma'am. Little Thackerys could bless Finchely someday."

I peered again at Daniel chatting legal precedents with Lady Shrewsbury and smiled. I was more interested in now. "Thank you, Mrs. Gallick."

"Lady Ashbrook," he said, "why don't you go get our birthday princess?"

His voice held so much pride, my crazy beating heart swelled.

"Yes, and the duchess is very interested in your painting. She's desperate for it, like she recognizes the . . . artist." Patience recognized the artist. My heart pounded.

"Lady Ashbrook. You've gone silent. Does that mean you've given it away already?"

"Troth, benefactor . . . please, my lord. Her Grace must have it."

Over Lady Shrewsbury's laughter, he nodded. "If it will make you happy. Of course, my dear."

Happy for Patience, happy for me for having such an understanding husband, I floated up the stairs to the nursery. My friend would tell me later whom she suspected the artist was so I'd know who to find. Daniel left me in control of my twenty-now twenty-four-thousand-pound dower. That could help a lot of women.

Hope sat at her table. Bliss icing from her special cake was on her yellow and pink pinafore. A glob of the sweet frosting sat on her smile.

I loved this little girl so much. I didn't need the rest of my memories. Hope and Daniel were everything—now and forever.

I sat at her table. "What do we have here?"

Hope played with her horses. Patience had sewn a doll with a dress of silk and taffeta with tan breeches hidden beneath her lilac pink dress. "She has a secret, Mama. She can stay up better on a horse, like you and me."

I hugged my baby, my precious little girl.

Clasping her hand, I led her down the stairs. Her little legs wobbled less. Chasing me about the grounds with Max in tow had surely helped. She leaped from the last tread and ran to her father.

He leaned down, and she grabbed Daniel's neck. He swung her around. My daughter, our daughter was his pride and joy. Couldn't have dreamed up a better man.

Lady Shrewsbury took Hope in her arms. "Ready for our treat?"

"Yes, Auntie." My daughter squealed.

"What treat? Lady Shrewsbury did you bring something for *us?*" Daniel's eyes loomed large. His hands were out, twiddling his fingers.

I hated disappointing him. "My dear, once Her Grace is on her way back to Sandlin Court, Hope and I and Lady Shrewsbury will head to Gunter's for a pink treat."

Daniel's lips pushed out like Hope's in a pout. "Pomegranate pink, without me?"

"My Lord, your vingt-et-un game is to start promptly in the dining room. It's returned to its proper place. No more hiding away in your tiny study. That room is far too small to promote singing."

He arched his brow and surely knew I'd betrayed Mr. Anthon. Our man-of-all-work had told me of their songs to Hope, and I had to hear it.

Daniel clicked his tongue, his hand catching mine and keeping it close to his silver buttons. "I'll accompany you, my love."

The way he said *my love* was no secret. It was *his truth*, our truth.

"*Mi luv yuh.*" My patois was light and easy, and my husband offered his special smile just for me.

Jingling coins in his pocket, Mr. Anthon stepped forward. "Lord Ashbrook, do you require the carriage for the family, now?"

Daniel wound his arms around us all. "Yes. An outing with my family takes precedent. Mrs. Gallick will feed the gentlemen, keeping them well stocked until we return."

Loving my husband's hand about my waist, I couldn't agree more.

ACKNOWLEDGMENTS

Thank you to my Heavenly Father, everything I possess or accomplish is by Your grace.

Esi Sogah, thank you for expanding my lens and giving me the push to tell Daniel and Jemina's story better than I knew I could. Thank you for keeping my feet to the fire.

To my sister agent, Sarah Younger, I am grateful we are doing this thing together.

To those who inspire my pen: Beverly, Brenda, Farrah, Sarah, Julia, Kristan, Alyssa, Maya, Lenora, Sophia, Joanna, Grace, Laurie Alice, Julie, Cathy, Katharine, Carrie, Christina, Georgette, Jane, Linda, Margie, Liz, Lasheera, Alexis, Denny, Rhonda, Kenyatta, Angela, Vanessa, Pat and Kerry, and Ann—thank you.

To those who inspire my soul: Bishop Dale and Dr. Nina, Reverend Courtney, Piper, Eileen, Rhonda, and Pat—thank you.

And to my family: Frank, Ellen, Sandra, Kala, and Emma: love you all so much.

Hey, Mama. I think you'd like this one.
Love you always.

RECIPE

Daniel loved his shortbread biscuits (cookies for the Yanks). It is a blend of cultures, Irish and Trinidadian, to produce a buttery, sweet and savory treat.

Currant and Carraway Shortbread

Ingredients
½ cup dried currants
4 ounces (1 stick) cold unsalted butter, cut into 8 pieces
¼ cup sugar
1 cup plus 2 tablespoons all-purpose flour, more for flouring
   paper
⅛ teaspoon or pinch of fine sea salt
½ finely diced crystallized ginger
1 tablespoon whole caraway seeds

Directions
   1. Steep currants in hot water or warmed brandy for 7–10 minutes. Drain on paper towel. Set aside to cool to room temperature.
   2. In your mixer, cream butter and sugar together at medium speed until light and smooth. This should be about 2–3 minutes.
   3. Add all dry ingredients along with currants, ginger, and caraway seeds. Mix well until blended. This should take about 3 minutes.
   Gather the dough into a ball.
   4. On a lightly floured piece of parchment (or floured fancy nonstick baking mat), place the dough and roll out to ¼ to ½ inch thick. Make it even.
   5. Refrigerate for an hour.
   6. Preheat oven to 350 degrees F.

7. With a pizza cutter or sharp knife or large biscuit die, cut out shapes. I usually do triangles or circles.

8. Lay these on a parchment-covered baking sheet and bake 12–15 minutes or until edges are lightly golden.

9. Cool on the baking sheet for 5 minutes, then transfer shortbread to a cooling rack to cool completely.

10. You can store these in airtight containers up to 1 week or freeze for year-round goodness.

Author's Note

I hope you enjoyed Jemina's and Daniel's love story and the continued antics of the Widow's Grace. Racial harmony is something that has been a struggle since the beginning of time. The Regency time period was no exception, but there was more fluidity than one may think. In battles for hearts and minds, the character of the soul and the strength of convictions win over differences. Or at least it should (Galatians 3:27). I write of a world where good people are of one mind and the walls between us crumble because of love (Ephesians 2:13–22).

This tale covers many themes, showcasing a sliver of the diversity of the Regency, the treatment of the Black men, Black women, the disabled, and the power structure afforded women of all races. I do a lot of research to build these inclusive narratives, and I've added some of my notes for you.

Want to learn more? Visit my website, VanessaRiley.com to gain more insight. Join my newsletter to be in the know.

Mulattoes and Blackamoors During the Regency

The term *mulatto* was a social construct used to describe a person birthed from one parent who was Caucasian and the other of African or Caribbean descent. Mulattoes during the Regency period often had more access to social movement than other racial minorities, particularly if their families had means.

The term *Blackamoors* refers to racial minorities with darker complexions, which included mulattoes, Africans, and West and East Indians living in England during the eighteenth and nineteenth centuries.

Mulattoes and Blackamoors numbered between ten thousand and twenty thousand in London and throughout England during the time of Jane Austen. Wealthy British with children born to native West Indies women brought them to London for schooling. In her novel *Sanditon*, Jane Austen, a contemporary writer of her times, wrote of Miss Lambe, a mulatto, the wealthiest woman. Her wealth made her desirable to the *ton*.

Mulatto and Blackamoor children were often told to pass to achieve elevated positions within society. Wealthy plantation owners with mixed-race children, or wealthy mulattoes like Dorothea Thomas from the island of Demerara, often sent their children abroad for education and for them to marry in England.

Swarthy

Swarthy is a term used to describe a person with dark or black complexion. Originally it was not intended as a compliment and offered in a context of suspicion, such as in Heathcliff's description in *Wuthering Heights*.

The *Minerva*

The *Minerva* was one of many ships that journeyed from Jamaica to London during the 1800s. The *Minerva* was wrecked by a hurricane on August 28, 1812, and everyone on board was killed. This same hurricane also endangered the *Jamaica Planter* on August 27, 1812. It was last seen passing Bermuda on its way to London.

The HMS *Belvidera*

The HMS *Belvidera* was a war frigate for the British navy. It was a thirty-six-gun ship. It was built in Deptford in 1809, patrolled the West Indies and Atlantic Ocean, and saw action in the Napoleonic Wars and the War of 1812.

George Bridgetower

George Augustus Polgreen Bridgetower was a Blackamoor master violinist whom the Prince Regent (King George IV) took an interest in. He used his influence to oversee and encourage Bridgetower's musical education. The prince (Prinny) made sure that Bridgetower studied under the leader of the Royal Opera, François-Hippolyte Barthélémon and professors at the Royal Academy of Music such as Thomas Attwood. Bridgetower performed more than fifty concerts in London at the famed Covent Garden, Drury Lane, and the Haymarket theater. During a concert at Abbaye de Panthemont in Paris, he performed for Thomas Jefferson.

Jack Beef

Jack Beef was the illustrious man-of-all work who worked for Magistrate John Baker. Beef was a Blackamoor who had free reign over Baker's household, even his children. Through Baker's day we gain pieces of Beef's life, including socializing with other men of color, attending balls, and wearing expensive clothes.

Bill Richmond

American born, enslaved Bill Richmond won his freedom and entered the British service under nobleman Hugh Percy. When he married Mary Dunwick, people slandered Mary for marrying outside of her race. Richmond fought for her honor and bested everyone, he even beat five men in one day. After becoming employed by Thomas Pitt, 2nd Baron Camelford, Richmond and Pitt became fast friends and often attended pugilist events together. Richmond's fame as a pugilist builds and he trained men to fight. For the king's coronation, a lavish banquet was thrown,

and eighteen men, leading boxers and sports figures, came to be celebrated among the *ton*. Richmond was one of these men, the only man of color. Some say he taught Lord Byron to box.

Phillis Wheatley

Phillis Wheatley was the first African American author of a published book of poetry, *Poems on Various Subjects, Religious and Moral*. It was published in London on September 1, 1773. Enslaved at the age of seven, she was purchased by the Wheatley family of Boston. They taught her to read and write and freed her. She wrote poems for the Revolution, about George Washington, African sun worship, Christianity, and inspiration.

The Royal Hospital Haslar

The Royal Hospital Haslar was built in Portsmouth in 1745 and was the largest brick building in Europe. Dr. James Lind pioneered his research in discovering a cure for scurvy at this hospital. The Royal Hospital included an insane asylum for sailors experiencing psychiatric illness. Early phrenology, the study of lumps on the head and trauma also occurred here.

Lincoln's Inn

The Lincoln's Inn is a historic building set in the London borough of Camden. It represents one of the four Inns of Court to which barristers belonged when they are called to the bar as a practicing attorney who can argue a case on behalf of another individual.

Mr. Weston

Mr. Weston of 10 Clifford Street was one of the premier tailors of the day for men's fashions.

The Case of Samuel Towl

The case presented in *An Earl, the Girl, and a Toddler*, the Towl cloth affair is modeled after the indictment of John Tow. Mr. Tow was indicted for feloniously stealing sixteen and a half yards of linen from the property of James Gray. Tow was convicted at the Old Bailey, confined in Newgate for three months, and whipped.

Regency Colors

Many colors popular during the Regency are mentioned, such as Saxon blue, which is a grayish-lavender, and Pomona green, which is an apple green. Dead salmon is a dull, flat pink color.

Lignum Vitae and Ironwood

Ironwood trees (British name) are called lignum vitae in Jamaica. The lignum vitae is the official flower of Jamaica. The wood of the tree is one of the hardest woods in the world.

Court of Chancery

The Court of Chancery was a court in England that had jurisdiction in matters of equity involving trusts and land laws. It was also the deciding factor to the administration of the estates of lunatics and the guardianship of infants and minor children. This is where one would appeal to change guardians and custody arrangements.

The Blackamoor Barrister

Francis Williams was the son of wealthy free blacks in Jamaica. He was sent to England for an education and to study some aspects of the law. He used what he learned to become a naturalized citizen of England, taking the oath in 1723. Upon his return to Jamaica to set up schools for black children, he was assaulted by a white planter, and Williams defended himself. The planter took him to court for his injuries. Williams defended himself in the proceedings, arguing to the court on his own behalf and won the case with ease.

Pott's Artificial Limb

With England being in so many wars, the number of wounded veterans increased. Medical technology advanced to create artificial limbs. In 1816, James Potts crafted an artificial limb for the Marquess of Anglesey, whose leg needed to be amputated as he fought alongside Lord Wellesley during the Battle of Waterloo (June 1815).

Invalid Chair

Self-propelled chairs for disabled people date back to the seventeenth century. The most noted one is from 1655. Johann Hautsch made a three-wheeled chair that was powered by a rotary handle on the front wheel. The chairs were often armchairs with large wheels in the front and casters in the rear.

The War of 1812

The War of 1812 (June 18, 1812–February 17, 1815) was fought between the United States and Great Britain over violations of maritime rights and the continued impressment of sailors by each side, more so the British Royal Navy impressing Americans. The British enacted a blockade in November 1812, which limited travel across the sea and affected many British colonies in the West Indies interrupting trade with America.

The Peninsula War

The Peninsula War (May 2, 1808–April 17, 1814) was a series of military campaigns between Napoleon's empire, Spain, Britain, Ireland, and Portugal for control of the Iberian *Peninsula* during the Napoleonic *Wars*. Napoleon was not fully contained until Waterloo in 1815.